# ETERNAL ON THE WATER

# ETERNAL ON THE WATER

A NOVEL

*Joseph Monninger*

G

GALLERY BOOKS

*New York London Toronto Sydney*

Gallery Books
A Division of Simon & Schuster, Inc.
1230 Avenue of the Americas
New York, NY 10020

This book is a work of fiction. Names, characters, places, and incidents either are products of the author's imagination or are used fictitiously. Any resemblance to actual events or locales or persons, living or dead, is entirely coincidental.



First Gallery Books trade paperback edition February 2010
GALLERY and colophon are registered trademarks of Simon & Schuster, Inc.

For information about special discounts for bulk purchases,
please contact Simon & Schuster Special Sales at 1-866-506-1949 or
business@simonandschuster.com.

The Simon & Schuster Speakers Bureau can bring authors to your live event. For more information or to book an event contact the Simon & Schuster Speakers Bureau at 1-866-248-3049 or visit our website at www.simonspeakers.com.

Designed by Jamie Lynn Kerner

Manufactured in the United States of America

10 9 8 7 6 5 4

Library of Congress Cataloging-in-Publication Data

Monninger, Joseph.
Tender River / Joseph Monninger.—1st Gallery Books trade paperback ed.
p. cm.
1. Married people—Fiction. 2. Spouses—Death—Fiction. 3. Domestic Fiction.
I. Title.
PS3563.O526T46 2010
813'.54—dc22

2009025680

ISBN 978-1-4391-6833-2
ISBN 978-1-4391-6962-9 (ebook)

*One for sadness, two for mirth,*

*Three for marriage, four for birth*

*Five for laughing, six for crying*

*Seven for sickness, eight for dying.*

*Nine for silver, ten for gold*

*Eleven for a secret that will never be told . . .*

—Scottish folk saying about seeing crows

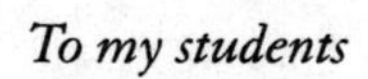
To my students

*They found Mary's body in Round Pond. It had been washed downstream, the authorities assumed, from the last set of rapids, a Class III set of quick water that bent slightly to the northeast. The Allagash River had claimed a number of lives over the years, so no one imagined it as anything but an accident. Two fishermen in a canoe found her just before sunset on the tenth of October and reported her to the ranger station. Her down jacket collected an egg of air between the shoulders, sufficient buoyancy to bring her to the surface. Her face peered down into the water as if she might spot something she needed passing beneath her. Leaves collected in her long hair; her Mad Bomber hat had fallen free and drifted away. One Teva sandal had also come undone, but the Velcro binding strap had somehow found her black wool sweater and had attached itself near her belly, a remora fish, or barnacle, the current stirring it no longer.*

*She did not wear a life jacket.*

*They brought her body to the Round Pond Ranger Station—across the lake—and temporarily set it out on two picnic tables in front of the cabins that served as the rangers' bunk room. The chill air, the full moon, the scent of woodsmoke: she would have liked that, I knew. She would have liked the men circling, their fingers around cups of coffee and whiskey, the radios crackling, the hubbub of officials trying to act decorously.*

*They asked the usual questions. Name, date of birth, and so forth. A few people made sounds of acknowledgment when they heard her name. She hadn't been to the Allagash in some time, but they remembered her. Had heard something about her. They recalled someone saying something about a Mary who loved the Allagash.*

*Your wife? A conservation officer named Barnes asked after the details of the body had been arranged. He was a tall man with a broom-brush mustache and a dozen Maine Fish & Game patches on his mackinaw. He put his foot up on the bench of the picnic table where I sat. Something Henry, a young guy, short and stout and bullet-headed, stood next to him. Something Henry liked being in on the action. You could tell that by a glance.*

*Yes, my wife, I said. We were both doing research.*

*That was our story. I had rehearsed it many times.*

*Were you two together? Barnes asked.*

*Yes, I said.*

*Were you with her when her kayak tipped?*

*No, I said. She was alone for that.*

*Did you two fight?*

*No, I said.*

*Then why weren't you with her when she ran the rapids upstream of here? Barnes asked.*

*She wanted to run them herself, I said. She was leaving to get back home ahead of me.*

*Leaving you?*

*I nodded.*

*So, was this a big domestic fight? I mean, I'm trying to understand. . . . Something Henry said.*

*That's when they pulled me off him. That's when they told me if I tried anything like that again, they'd stick me in cuffs; they didn't care where we were or what they had to do to get us out of there. Just chill out, they said. They were sorry, Something Henry had been a bit indelicate, sorry, let it go, sorry, everyone is tired. Barnes made us shake hands. He said you can't have enemies in a logging camp, an old Maine saying about the need to put trouble behind you when you are in the woods.*

*I stayed that night beside Mary's body. They planned to airlift it the next morning by helicopter to Bangor or Millinocket. Whatever the downstaters wanted, they said. Officer Barnes had covered Mary's body with a green blanket and they had tied it—like a roast—with brown twine to keep the wind from blowing the blanket off her. Mary would have had a good laugh out of that, too. Death as a rib roast. A young officer, Sarah, sat up with me. She was tall and angular and calm. She came from Wyoming and had a prairie quiet about her. We made a fire in the Allagash fireplace—a horseshoe of deep, heavy stones that had been made famous on the Allagash from Thoreau's travels there—and fed it through the night, burning pine mostly. Sarah explained she had been on duty by the dam when she heard about the accident. A woman victim usually required a woman warden. Silly, probably, she said, but probably better, too. She didn't mind staying up, she said. A good moon always made her restless. And, besides, how many soft, quiet nights did you get in Maine? Indian summer, these rare days and nights, she said.*

*The fireplace gave a sweet, gentle light. The moon banked slowly and threw a white path across the water. A few fish, chubs, mostly, ran and jumped in the black beyond the shore. I did not turn and watch Mary. She was not there. She promised me she would not remain in her body. Instead I watched Sarah make coffee in an old, tin pot. She boiled the grounds in the water. When she finished, she grabbed the handle of the pot and swung it in a circle like a softball pitcher winding up, forcing the grounds to the bottom. Then she poured us two cups.*

*"Careful," she said. "That's what we call hobo coffee out West. It's been known to bite."*

*"Smells good."*

*She turned and looked at Mary. Then she raised her cup.*

*"To your wife," she said.*

*I touched my cup to hers.*

*We sat and sipped our coffee awhile. I could not keep my eyes from the place where the dark trees met the pale light of the fire. The bears' changing room, Mary called that particular ring of shadow. Bears who wanted to come to a campfire to warm up, or sometimes to dance, changed themselves into humans in that half-light.*

*"You know," I said to Sarah, half-thinking aloud, "Mary thought bears sometimes came into town to dance. She thought she had danced with one once at her cousin Maurice's wedding."*

*"Seems possible," Sarah said and I liked her for that.*

*"She said the man smelled overpoweringly of honey," I said, "but could dance very well."*

*"I have heard they are gentlemen, too," Sarah said and smiled at me.*

*"Absolutely," I said.*

*"I like this Mary," she said and turned to look at the picnic tables.*

*"I've never met anyone like her," I said. "I don't expect to again."*

*"You loved her, didn't you?"*

*I nodded. A deep, solid plug caught in my throat.*

*"The real deal?" Sarah said.*

*I sipped the coffee. Then I toed a piece of pine that had slid out of the fire. I pushed it back into the flames.*

*"It's difficult to talk about without sounding like a cliché," I said. "You know. True love, true soul to soul stuff. Silly, right?"*

*Sarah shrugged.*

*"No, not necessarily silly. I believe it exists," she said. "But it's rarer than people might guess."*

*"Have you ever experienced it?" I asked.*

*Sarah smiled and sipped her coffee.*

*"No," she said, shaking her head. "I don't think I have."*

*"In a universe, on a continent, in a country, in a state, in a county, on a river, in a small yellow boat," I said. "That's what Mary used to say to explain the odds of us meeting. And you have to be born in roughly the same period. Those are the odds. And probably you need to speak the same language."*

*Sarah nodded. We sat for a while listening to the fire and to the wind. Then Sarah said in a soft voice, "This wasn't an accident," she said. "Her drowning. She wasn't wearing a life jacket."*

*She moved her chin slightly toward Mary.*

*"No," I said. "Not an accident."*

*"You think she turned the boat over herself?"*

*I shrugged.*

*"Unofficially," Sarah said.*

*"She didn't have long to live," I said. "She would have preferred that her body hadn't been found. She made a choice. I went along with it because I loved her."*

*"You let her go," Sarah said. "I respect that."*

*"Nobody let Mary do anything."*

*"I meant," Sarah said, "that you acceded to her wish."*

*"She wanted the crows to make use of her body. To have her after her death. Mary loved crows and ravens. Corvids. She brought earrings into the woods to end a crow situation."*

*Sarah studied me. She reached over and poked the fire with a branch. Then she poured us each a bit more coffee.*

*She said, "We're here together and we have a good fire. I'd like to hear about Mary. Whatever you want to tell."*

*And in this universe, on this planet, in this country, in this state, in this county, beside this river, I told her.*

# Maine

# 1

I first saw Mary on the highway well before we reached the Allagash. I saw her near Millinocket, the old logging town on Maine Route 11. I noticed her truck first, a red Toyota, and I noticed the yellow kayak strapped on the bed. We both had New Hampshire plates. I also had a Toyota truck, green, and a yellow kayak strapped on top of a truck cap.

Toyota love.

She pulled into an Exxon station. I passed slowly and watched to see her get out. But she fumbled with something on the seat next to her and I couldn't see her face.

Her hair was the color of cord wood. She wore a red bandanna that sometimes waved with the wind.

The Allagash Waterway runs ninety-two miles northward from Chamberlain Lake to the St. John River on the border of Canada. It is surrounded by public and private lands, thousands and thousands of acres of pine and tamarack and hardwoods. To get to the starting point on Chamberlain Lake, you must pass Baxter State Park and Mount Katahdin. Mount Katahdin is the beginning or end—depending on the direction you hike—of the Appalachian Trail.

The indigenous people did not climb Mount Katahdin until late in the nineteenth century. The world, they said, had been built by "a man from the clouds," and he lived at the summit in snow.

I stopped for gasoline at the last service station before entering the Allagash preserve. The station catered to rafters and kayakers who ran the Penobscot, a wild, dangerous river that churned white water in spectacular rapids through steep cataracts. Three blue buses—with enormous white rafts tied to the tops—idled in the parking lot. A bunch of kids loitered around the door to the service station, all of them wet and soggy. It was a warm day for September in Maine, although the cold held just a little way off, somehow up in the branches of the trees, waiting to fall. The kids went barefoot mostly. A few ate ice cream cones.

I filled my tank. I felt good and unscheduled, but also a tiny bit nervous. Ninety-two miles through a wilderness by kayak. As Dean Hallowen said when I proposed my plan for a sabbatical from my teaching post at St. Paul's School, a secondary prep school outside of Concord, New Hampshire, "That sounds like an undertaking."

And it did.

But he had approved the plan, even contributing funds for a trip to Concord and Walden Pond to research Thoreau's activities there. Now I planned to follow Thoreau's path into the Allagash, a trip he had undertaken in 1857. Thoreau went no farther north in Maine than Eagle Lake, a still-water camp I hoped to reach my second night. I did not know what I hoped to gain by standing on the same land as Thoreau, but it seemed necessary for the paper I hoped to write about his adventures in Maine. I also thought—and Dean Hallowen concurred—that it would be a useful footnote in any future class I gave on transcendentalism.

Leaning against the flank of my truck, though, the entire project seemed hopelessly academic. Why bother researching a writer who had been researched to death? Did the world really need another appraisal of Thoreau? It seemed hideously theoretical. The river, by contrast, had become more real with each passing mile. Ninety-two miles, solo. Three enormous lakes, two portages, one Class IV rapids, cool nights, warm days. Not easy. Any time you went solo in the wilderness you risked a simple injury or mishap developing into something much larger. Dump my kayak, wet my matches, turn turtle, and what I had drawn up as a seven- or eight-day trip would turn into something more frightening and real. I had promised myself to be brave but cautious, intrepid but level-headed. Prudent and sober. Smart.

"Hurry gradually" was my motto. It had become a little buzz phrase I used with everyone when I described the parameters of my proposed trip.

*Ninety-two miles alone on a river*! marveled various people—men, women, fellow faculty members, family, friends—when they asked what I intended to do on my sabbatical. *I can't imagine,* they said.

*Hurry gradually,* I answered.

That's what I was thinking about when Mary's truck cruised by. I saw it more clearly now. Red. Beaten. A yellow kayak with duct-tape patches. Obviously one of us did more camping and kayaking than the other. And it wasn't me.

I nodded a little with my chin. Then I ducked as though I had to adjust the gas nozzle, trying to see into her cab. She drove past without braking, and I gained only a quick glimpse of her hair again.

A bumper sticker on her tailgate caught my eye.

A HEN IS ONLY AN EGG'S WAY OF MAKING ANOTHER EGG.
SAMUEL BUTLER

I BOUGHT THREE LOTTERY tickets for luck, a Diet Coke, two bags of Fritos, and stuffed as many packs of paper matches in my pocket as the checkout girl—a dark, Gothy-looking girl with a large stud in her right eyebrow—allowed. When I finished, I nodded to her. She had no interest in me. She watched a pair of boys her age who sat in the doorway, flicked their hair repeatedly, and talked in quiet voices. Dreamy boys, I'm sure she thought.

"Heading down the Allagash," I said in one of those lame moments where we feel compelled to explain ourselves.

Or maybe I simply wanted human contact.

"Hmmmm," she said, her eyes on the boys.

I left before I could embarrass myself further. I checked the kayak straps to make sure nothing had jiggled loose along the dirt roads, then climbed into the cab.

As I started the engine, I wondered if this hadn't been a mistake. I also wondered what it would cost, psychically, to back out. I wasn't afraid, exactly, but uneasy, a little out of my element. I turned on the radio and found an oldies' station. I wanted someone to go with me, but it was a strange time of year. Most of the people I knew—teachers, primarily—had already returned to school. If they weren't already in school, they had to prepare classes, get a new academic year under way. I had stepped out of cadence by having a sabbatical. Everything in my training pointed me toward school, the bells, the new classes, the fresh notebooks, the whistling radiators, but instead I was heading down a river I didn't know. I kayaked confidently on flat water, but going down a river, through rapids, setting up camp—it made me edgy to think about it. What I needed at that moment was a buddy, a companion, someone to kick a foot up on the dash and pump his fist that we were heading into the wilderness.

Instead I listened to Marvin Gaye sing, "Let's Get It On."

But that didn't make me feel better.

A MOOSE BROUGHT ME out of it. Driving along, eating the orange curls of corn chips from the bag I held between my legs, a moose appeared from the right side of the road. A black, dark mass. At first

I thought I had somehow seen a stump walking freely through the scatter woods at the roadside. Then the moose turned and angled as if looking down the road the way I had to travel. A male. Enormous palmate antlers. A string of grass and mud dangled from his left antler. His shoulder came well above the top of the Toyota.

I slowed.

He didn't move. He didn't respond to me at all. He stood with his nostrils streaming two tubes of white air into the first evening chill, and his body blended into the woods behind him. If I had looked away at that moment, perhaps I could have let my eyes lose him in the forest. It seemed fantastical that a creature carrying a TV antenna on its head could maneuver through the puckerbrush of Northern Maine. I turned down the radio and braked. Then I slipped the truck into neutral and climbed out.

The bull moose could not have posed more perfectly. I had a moment when I thought, *Oh, come on.* The whole thing seemed a bit too much: crisp air, black moose, yellow maples, bright white breath. I felt no fear, despite knowing the rut had begun. The moose had no interest in me. As if to prove it, a female suddenly broke out of the woods perhaps a quarter mile away and crossed the road. She did not stop or look back, but the male, becoming vivid, suddenly trotted down the road. He ran with the classically awkward moosey gait, his bottom shanks throwing out with each step. He disappeared into the woods approximately where the female had disappeared. I heard him for a second clatter through the slag piles of brush at the roadside, then nothing.

*Okay,* I said as I climbed back in the truck. I turned on the heat a little higher. I looked for the moose when I passed their point of disappearance, but the woods had covered them.

You require a permit to run the Allagash.

I pulled over at four thirty to a small government building with a sign that said: *Permits Here.*

Mary's truck took up the best spot. I parked behind it and a little off to the side.

I checked myself in the mirror. Quick smile, quick hair brush, quick glance at my jeans. I climbed out. The office appeared closed. I also realized that the temperature had dropped way off. What had been a warm day had changed in the course of an hour. I made a mental note to remember how fast the temperature sank once the sun went behind the pines. *Travel early, camp early.* Everything I had read about the Allagash had stated that as a basic survival law. If you left late in the morning, you risked facing the wind as it inevitably rose throughout the day. If you didn't find a place to camp sufficiently early, then you risked missing a convenient spot and having to set up a tent and campsite at night. *Learn to pace yourself,* the books said. *Think ahead.*

I would also need a fire going, I realized. Every night.

I climbed the stairs to the office and pushed open the door. I looked for Mary, but instead a large, raspy woman with a bright yellow shirt stepped out of a back room at my appearance. I understood that the woman lived in the quarters beyond the front desk. Her daily commute averaged around ten feet. She wore a name tag identifying her as *Ranger Joan.* She wore a baseball hat, army green. The patch on the forehead crest said *State of Maine.*

"What movie did you want to see?" Ranger Joan asked.

She paused for effect. Then she laughed—a large, smoky laugh. A pinochle laugh.

I supposed I looked as dazed as I felt.

"Don't worry," she said. "It's just my way. A little joke. People show up here a little high-strung. I loosen them up."

"Good to know," I said, trying to recover.

"'Course we're not showing movies here," she said. "We're holding a square dance!"

She laughed again, but this time she pushed some papers toward me.

"Okay, you'll be wanting a permit, I guess," she said. "Standard stuff we ask. We like to know when you go in, when you come out. Be sure to sign the logbook at each end so we can track you. You going all the way?"

"Yes," I said. "I guess so."

"Ninety-two miles," she said. "Best time of year to do it. No bugs, no no-see-ums. Good crisp air and the water is still reasonably warm. You can still take a quick dip after a day of paddling. You picked the right time of year, I promise."

"Thank you," I said, as if I deserved congratulations.

"I suppose you know already that the moose are mating?" she asked. "We like people to know what's ahead of them."

"I'd read about it."

"Just give them room, especially the males. They can get a little funny this time of year. Spring is worse with the mothers and babies. You don't want a mother moose thinking you're going to bother her little one."

I looked up. Slowly she realized I couldn't fill out the forms and have a conversation at the same time. She smiled. I smiled, too. Then she went up on her toes to see my truck. She nodded.

"From New Hampshire?" she said, happy to talk even if it did distract me.

"Yes."

"Well, you might want to think about camping here for the night. Once you enter the waterway, you have to camp by boat. In other words, you'd have to start tonight, even if it's dark."

"I thought I'd camp by my truck," I said. "Once I arrive at the Chamberlain Lake landing."

"Can't," Ranger Joan said. "Ranger in there is a man named Coop and he is a bug about the rules. He'll push you right into the water to get you going. Rules are rules to Coop."

"But if I camp here?" I asked, trying to move my pen on the form at the same time.

"No problem. You get a fresh, early start tomorrow. That'd be my advice. Sun will be down shortly."

I looked out the window. Under a small group of pines, I saw a woman setting up a tent. She had backed the Toyota into position so she could unload it without difficulty. She had slipped into a red-checked mackinaw; she wore a Mad Bomber hat, the kind with fake rabbit fur earpieces that buckle under your chin.

"I'll stay," I said. "Is there a charge?"

"Ten dollars," Ranger Joan said.

I paid for the permit and for the ten dollar camping fee. Ranger Joan stamped a few things, tore a piece of perforated paper off a long form, then folded it all and handed it to me.

"You should keep this with you," she said, nodding at the forms. "If a ranger along the way asks to see your permit, that's what you give him. This time of year, though, you won't find many people on the waterway. The rangers are out patrolling deer season. The Chungamunga girls are out there somewhere, but that's the only group that came through this way in the last day or so."

"Chungamunga girls?" I asked, fitting the paper into my rear pocket.

"Oldest girls' camping school in America. They run it every year, sometimes twice a year. They do it for school credit. Just girls, no boys. You don't want boys and girls in the woods together if you're a supervisor."

"I guess not."

"They take their time," Ranger Joan said, pulling the pad of permits back to her. "Learn crafts as they go. Read history, natural science, mythology books, a little of everything. We schedule a few talks with naturalists and the like. Some of the girls have never been out of their backyards before. They get a little homesick and a little crazy before they finish, but it's a great experience for them. They say it's good luck for a lifetime if you run into the Chungamunga girls on the Allagash."

"Well, then, I hope I run into them," I said.

"You'd be surprised who's been a Chungamunga girl. Presidents' daughters, captains of industry. And so forth."

I couldn't help wondering if anyone used the term "captains of industry" anymore, but I nodded in any case. Ranger Joan walked around the counter and pointed to a camping spot near where the woman had set up camp.

"You can camp right by her," Ranger Joan said. "Just pull your truck beside her. Johnny cut up some scrap pine and you're welcome to burn some for a fire. It's going to get downright nippy tonight."

"Thank you," I said.

"She's a pretty little thing," Ranger Joan said, jutting her chin at the campsite. "Her name is Mary Fury. Everyone around here loves Mary Fury."

# 2

SATURN HAD CLIMBED FREE OF THE pines by the time I maneuvered my truck into position. The planet dangled on the eastern horizon, a bright white flicker that seemed to draw the final light of day into its center. To the north, Ranger Joan had flicked on a lighted sign, but it shined away from us, toward the road. Stepping out of my truck, I had the sudden realization that now, this moment, I needed to know how to set up my tent, get a fire started, arrange a bedroll. I had practiced plenty of times in my living room, going quietly over a checklist in front of my fireplace, some of the students—young men taking a study break, or a few of the outdoor club guys clucking around my gear—but I had never actually set up camp in near darkness. Not with my new acquisitions bought specially for the trip. Not with the temperature dropping in quick bumps that registered in my spine.

And not with a stunning woman in the campsite beside mine.

At least I *though*t she was stunning. I couldn't tell for certain. Backing the truck in, stepping out, slipping into my mackinaw, I couldn't quite get a full look. Instead I gave what a friend of mine, Bobby G, called the horse look. You employ a horse look when you are sitting at a bar and someone attractive—you suspect—moves in beside you, and you can't turn and look, and you can't catch her eye in the bar mirror, but you *can* slip your ears back and let your eye move as far to one side in the socket as possible. Then you open your nostrils a little, because that pushes your eye farther to one side, and you look. You glance. You look as a horse looks at a man approaching with a rope, and you don't look for particulars, or for any details, but take her in as an impression.

That's a horse look.

Carrying my tent to a flat spot beside the picnic table and clunking it down, I wondered if she had given me a horse look. *A pretty little thing,* Ranger Joan had said.

I put the permit and the Allagash map on the picnic table. A short breeze pushed it off immediately, and I had to retrieve it before it rolled toward Mary's campfire. The second time around, I weighted the map down with a rock. On the spot where I placed the rock, the State of Maine had included a caution:

CAUTION

THE ALLAGASH WILDERNESS WATERWAY IS NOT THE PLACE FOR AN INEXPERIENCED PERSON TO LEARN CANOEING OR CANOE CAMPING.
LACK OF EXPERIENCE AND ERRORS IN JUDGMENT IN THIS REMOTE REGION CAN CAUSE CONSIDERABLE PERSONAL DISCOMFORT AND ENDANGER ONESELF AND OTHERS.
IMMERSION IN COLD WATER, FOR EXAMPLE, CAN BE FATAL IN A MATTER OF MINUTES.

"There you have it," I said under my breath. "Couldn't be clearer."

"No reason to make two fires," Mary called to me from her camp, a pot in her hand. "You're welcome to cook on mine."

"Thanks," I said.

Then I added: "I'm all set."

As soon as the words cleared my lips, I wanted to bite them back. All set? An attractive woman in the Maine woods invites you to join her campfire, and you say no? I could rationalize that it had been a refusal out of politeness, but the voice, honestly, felt as if some larger, dumber self had squeezed through my ribs and answered for me. Why in this world would I say no?

Instantly I felt stupid and embarrassed. With a well-timed horse look, I watched Mary peer in my direction, her face not quite clear in the soft firelight. *Beautiful,* I realized. *She looked like Saturday morning,* as my dad used to say.

"Okay," she said, "but if you change your mind, you're welcome."

"I'm all set," I said again. "Thanks, though."

I raised my hand. Waved a little.

I grinned, but my face slowly swiveled toward the ground—where I had nearly finished pounding in tent stakes—and grimaced at the dirt. The second time, I understood, I spoke to cover the stupidity of the first refusal. If I *had been* all set the first time around, wasn't it incumbent on me to *still* be all set? Simple logic dictated as much. But she had gracefully extended the invitation twice and I had refused both times.

"One for sadness," Mary called, bending back to her fire, "two for mirth."

I looked up.

"What's that?"

"A folk saying," she said. "About crows."

I gathered my courage.

"Why am I saying no thanks to an invitation I want to accept?" I asked.

"Because you're being shy?" she asked, her voice rising at the end a little. "And because you're all set."

WOODSMOKE. PINES. DARK EARTH. Sparks scattering into the night. A wind rising in the south, the trees sipping the air, the pine needles flinging themselves into space. A gray picnic table.

I walked over to Mary's fire. She stood in front of the large horseshoe-shaped fire pit, her front side bronzed with light and heat. The fire cast her shadow backward, up into the lower branches of the pines, and she appeared, for an instant, as a mythical creature, something bright and inviting and skilled with flames.

I carried a camp fry pan and a Tupperware container of black beans and rice. I put them on her picnic table.

"You're not a bear, are you?" she asked, turning her head from the fire to regard me.

"A bear?"

"You wouldn't admit it if you were, would you?"

"If I were a bear?" I asked, trying to understand.

"Oh, you're playing it cute. You are cute, as a matter of fact. Come closer."

I stepped around the picnic table until she could see me. She stood up straight from the fire.

I looked at her. She looked at me. Our eyes didn't move.

"Animal behaviorists," she said, her eyes still on me, her mouth forming the words slowly, "call this a copulatory gaze. Don't flatter yourself. We're sizing each other up. The gaze helps continue the species, that's all. It is a million years old, so don't flatter yourself too much. It's just Darwinism paying a visit."

"It's still nice," I said, hardly able to move. My mouth felt dry. Neither one of us had looked away.

"But it wouldn't be honest if you are a bear."

"I'm not a bear," I said.

"I smelled honey when you stepped into the light."

"How do I know you're not a bear?" I asked. "Maybe it's a trick you're pulling on me."

"I only have raven tricks," she said. "Bears are too needy."

"I've always thought so."

"You're not bad," she said. "So far so good."

"Good to meet your approval."

"I didn't say that. I said so far so good."

"And you said I wasn't bad."

She looked away. Then she looked back. Our eyes did the same thing. I had the feeling they would always find each other that way.

"If you help me pull the picnic table closer," she said, "we could have it next to the fire."

"Okay."

She circled to the far end of the table and put her hands on either side of the top. I mirrored her at the other side.

"Ready?" she asked.

"Yes."

We turned the table and moved it so one of the benches rested a few feet from the fire. It wasn't easy to move. Someone had made it to last with broad metal legs. We rocked it a little between us to get it level.

"Mary Fury," she said, when we finished, holding out her hand to shake.

"Jonathan Cobb. People call me Cobb."

"Like Ty Cobb, the baseball player?" she asked, her hand still in mine.

"Exactly."

"How tall are you?"

"Six feet two. Why?"

"I couldn't tell for sure. Your hat is puffed up."

She motioned to the bench and raised her eyebrows. I nodded. But something about the position of the fire pit and the nearness of the bench to the heat caused us both to move awkwardly to sit down. Absurdly, our foreheads hit. It wasn't a light hit, either. We bonked. Mary stumbled a little backward, and I put a hand out to steady myself. A bright white star clicked for a second in my vision, then disappeared, only to be replaced by a quick, throbbing pain.

"Holy mackerel," Mary said, rubbing her head. "Are you okay?"

"I'm not sure," I said.

Then we looked at each other. And we began to laugh.

It had been a long, long time, I realized, since I had laughed so hard.

The absurdity of our situation, the incredible awkwardness of hitting heads with a person you have met two minutes before, the evident nerves I felt about soloing down the Allagash fueled it for me. Mary, for her part, sat slowly down and bent over, rubbing her head and laughing at the same time. She had a great laugh, full and hearty, without any self-consciousness. Each time we looked at each other, we began again. Sometimes it started to fade, then resumed again without warning.

"How's that for a first impression?" she asked when we had slowed enough to breathe.

"Perfect."

"It kind of is, isn't it?" she said.

"Hard to take things too seriously afterward, I guess."

She took a deep breath. Then she looked at my container of rice and beans.

"What do you have to eat?" she asked.

"Rice and beans."

"Can I have some? I'm a lousy cook. I usually eat peanut butter and jelly when I camp. And instant oatmeal. And hot chocolate, and that's about it."

"We could probably do better than that."

"Are you a good cook?"

"Yes, as a matter of fact," I said, "I'm pretty good."

"Cobb?" she said. "I've never known anyone named Cobb before."

"Well, now you do."

"Do people make jokes? You know, corn on the cob? That kind of thing?"

"Sometimes."

"Are you going to start cooking soon?"

We looked at each other. I nodded. She smiled. Her smile was irresistible.

"Sometimes I don't filter the things I say," she said. "Some people find it charming, but others find it annoying. How are you feeling about it?"

"On the charming side, I think."

"Okay," she said.

"Do you like beans and rice?"

"Yes. Especially if I don't have to cook them."

I opened the beans and rice. I realized I needed cooking oil.

"Do you have cooking oil?" I asked.

Mary looked at me. I understood she wasn't going to have cooking oil anytime soon.

"You're very beautiful," I said, "but you probably know that."

"Thank you," she said.

"For a bear," I said.

She stared at me.

"Okay," she said.

"I'll get the oil," I told her.

She ate three platefuls of black beans and rice and would have eaten more if I had served it. She hardly spoke as she ate.

"Good," she said finally, pushing away her camp cup.

"You were hungry," I said.

"I forget to eat sometimes," she said. "Strange but true."

"That doesn't happen to me," I said.

"Were you saving it for down the trail?"

"No," I said, not sure if I told the truth. "It's fine."

"The Chungamunga girls will have plenty of food," she said. "They always do. We can mooch some meals off them. They're always way overstocked. And the rangers make a couple deliveries to them."

"Do you know the Chungamunga girls?" I asked.

She smiled.

"It's good luck," she said, her face toward the fire, "to run into the Chungamunga girls on the Allagash."

"So I've heard."

"I'm giving a couple talks. On corvids—crows and ravens. That's my specialty. I do it whenever our schedules match. I have this semester free. And you know, it's good to get girls interested in science."

"How do they take it?"

She turned back to me. She smiled and began stacking the dishes.

"They hate it at first. Then they warm up to it. I throw in a bunch of mythology. You know, the blessed triangle. Wolf, man, crow. Sacred hunting and scavenging. Every culture has a relationship with the crow. I get them hooked with that, then I sneak in the science. I convert them."

"And you have raven tricks?"

She regarded me. Not many people look attractive in a Mad Bomber hat, but she did.

"Now would be a good time for our first kiss," she said. "I mean, if we are going to kiss anyway, sometime, tonight or some other time, right now seems like a good moment. It is for me, anyway. How do you feel about it? Or maybe you don't want to kiss me and I've overstepped. I do that sometimes in other areas of my life. I guess what I mean is, I want to kiss you and so there you go."

I kissed her. My body wanted to go toward hers, but I held back.

Wind tucked the fire back into itself. A few shadows climbed our lower legs. Her lips opened the smallest bit, then closed again. She smelled like woodsmoke and pine and peppermint.

"Was that okay?" she asked when we stopped, her face not far from mine.

"Yes," I said.

"I haven't kissed anyone in 374 days."

"You keep track?" I asked. "But you forget to eat sometimes?"

"I count days," she whispered. "I like to keep track."

"Okay," I said.

"I've been alive for 12,680 days. I like to know things like that."

I nodded. She moved away.

She picked up the dishes and disappeared from the fire.

"Once all the birds in the world met to decide how the food should be apportioned," Mary said, her voice sleepy and warm. We were in our sleeping bags on a blue tarp she had spread near the fire. She still wore her Mad Bomber hat. We lay side by side, looking up at the stars. The fire had quieted and now only burned brighter when the wind touched it.

"This is a tale from Somalia, East Africa," she said. "Are you awake?"

"Yes, I'm awake."

"Well, when the birds convened, the crow recommended that any bird larger than a crow should eat meat. Smaller birds should eat plants. The rest of the birds saw that as a fair division, because a crow is a medium-sized bird. What they didn't know, of course, is that a crow's brain is 2.3 percent of its body mass. A human's brain is only 1.5 percent. So crows actually have more brains than they strictly need for survival. That's why they make up games to play and argue at the drop of a hat. Do you know the story of Abel and Betty?"

"Not yet," I said.

She bumped my shoulder with her shoulder.

"Abel and Betty were two New Caledonian crows in an Oxford laboratory run by Alex Kacelnik. They were given a tube of food and two wires, one hooked, the other straight. You needed a tool to get to the food, so it was a little puzzle. Abel flew off with the hooked wire almost immediately. But Betty bent a new hook to get at the food. Not only that, but she improvised, sometimes bending the wire with her feet or beak, sometimes applying pressure until it bent on a second object. When they tested chimps and monkeys on the same puzzle, the primates failed."

"Made those chimps eat crow," I said.

She slowly rose from her sleeping bag and put her head on her hand. She looked at me.

"You're a wise guy, aren't you?" she said.

"Sometimes," I said. "But I like your crow story."

*"Corvus moneduloides,"* she said. "Latin name for the New Caledonian crow. I'm not being pretentious. I repeat the Latin names so that I don't forget them. It's a little dementia test I administer to myself."

"And so?" I asked.

"What?" she asked.

"Do you think we should kiss again?" I asked.

"Not yet," she said.

She slid back down onto her back.

"So the crow suggested that the birds divide the food," I said, reminding her. "East Africa."

"Right," she said. "So at the meeting the crow put that proposal forward. The other birds looked at their relative sizes, then figured it seemed fair. So they agreed. Then they all flew off. A few weeks later, they saw the crow eating plants. The smaller birds complained that the crow should be eating meat. The crow reminded them that birds smaller than a crow were allowed to eat plants. The same thing occurred when the bigger birds saw the crow eating meat. That's why the crow eats both meat and plants. That's a classic crow tale."

"I like your crows," I said.

"Stop me if I go on too long. I get carried away by things. My father called me an enthusiast. I am enthusiastic about things. A lot of things."

The night had turned as dark as it would be. I guessed the temperature had dipped into the forties. We had been talking for hours. We had kissed only once. It had been her recommendation to sleep outside on the blue tarp. It wasn't going to rain, she said, and the insects had already been killed by frost. She said it made no sense to sleep indoors until you had to, and even then she planned some day to have a sleeping porch where she could sleep outside every night. She had investigated Gore-Tex coverlets, a kind of all-purpose duvet that would shed water and permit one to sleep in a full bed outside.

"I don't want to sleep yet," she said, although she sounded sleepy. "We'll never meet for the first time again. If we fall asleep, then it's no longer the first time."

"I'm trying," I said.

"Tell me about Thoreau."

"What do you want to know about him?"

"I want to know why you admire him."

"I guess," I said, "because he talks about living simply. 'A man is rich in proportion to the number of things which he can afford to let alone.' And he got the environmental thing as early as anyone else did in America. And he climbed into canoes and traveled to Maine, which probably struck him as a true wilderness. But I think mostly because he sought something important. He probably failed at it, but it never deterred him."

"I've never read *Walden Pond.* I'm pretty sure I've read parts, but not the whole thing."

"It's a great book. It's easy to look at it now and see its flaws, but it was revolutionary for its time. I'd like to live simply. I try to."

"And you'll write about him?"

"Yes," I said. "I'll try. Just some papers."

"Do you like teaching?"

"Yes," I said. "I do."

"Me, too," she said. "When I think of other things to do, other kinds of jobs, I can't imagine them. Schools live with the seasons. That's what I like, I think. Other jobs never end. Teaching ends in the spring and begins again in the fall. I can't imagine a job that never ended."

"And you like the research?" I asked. "On corvids?"

"I like crows," she said. "When I was little, I read a story in the paper about a man who had a crow for a pet. He claimed that if you slit a crow's tongue, it could speak. I thought that was the cruelest thing I had ever heard, so I wrote the man a letter. I got his address from the phone book and I wrote him and told him I thought it was terrible to do such a thing to an animal. He wrote back. His name was Floyd Jebins. Great name. Floyd wrote back and said he would never hurt a crow, he loved crows, and he included a small book about crows. He could tell I was a whacky kid. But that book, holy mackerel, it got to me. That's the whole thing about teaching, isn't it? You never know when you nudge someone's boat if it won't change them in an important way. You can't predict the outcome. Floyd Jebins got me started studying crows by something that probably took him ten minutes to do. And crows were everywhere, so they became a perfect subject for a kind of kid field research. But I think of Floyd often."

"Did you write to tell him?"

"I did. Years later. But the letter came back as undeliverable. He had died, I guess. I don't know. End of story."

I began to drift off. But it was sleep mixed with the trees over us, and the cold wind coming across Chamberlain Lake. I pulled the sleeping bag as high as I could under my chin and listened to the sounds around our campsite. We did not have the hum of the river yet, but the trees sieved the air and made a sound like early snow falling against glass. Later, a barred owl began to call.

*Who cooks for you, who cooks for you, alllll?*

I had nearly fallen off for good when Mary's voice came to me.

"Thoreau slept under these same stars," she said quietly. "That's why you're here. That's reason enough."

# 3

Coop wore his ranger hat with the earflaps down. He wore a green jacket with a dozen patches on it, and underneath it, peeking out, bright red suspenders formed a goalpost on his chest. A brown mustache lived under his nose, and his eyes, a bit rheumy, had the red tint that distinguished long drinking.

He bustled out of the ranger station as soon as he saw our trucks pull next to the unloading dock. We were his only customers.

"I've got big news for you, Mary," Coop said, hurrying down the dirt path that connected the station to the lake, his walk slightly bowlegged and round. "Joan called down to say you had arrived. No sooner did I get that news than Glen called from over on Eagle Island to report a moose carcass. Fresh, too. Not sure what happened to it, but it's only been dead a day or two. So you're in luck."

"That's terrific, Coop," Mary said, her pleasure in the news genuine. "This is Cobb. He's here to research a little about Thoreau."

Coop studied me, apparently decided he didn't need to bother with me much, nodded, and then went back to Mary.

"You know that raven colony will be on that moose like gravy on corn bread," Coop said. "I mean. "

"It's perfect," she said. "I can bring the girls to study it."

"You read my mind," Coop said. "They're over on Eagle Lake, last I heard. 'Course, they take their time, but maybe they moved on. Like a small, crazy army, they are."

"I've always heard," I said, unable to resist, "that it's good luck to run into the Chungamunga girls on the Allagash."

Coop studied me.

"That's what they say, all right," Coop said. "'Course, like most things, it depends on your point of view."

Coop and Mary spent a few minutes talking about the precise location of the carcass while I unloaded my kayak from the truck. I had a strange sense of déjà vu, but I imagined it came from planning a trip so often in my mind, then finally arriving at the water. My hands moved automatically, but I found I kept looking at Mary. She wore the earflaps of her Mad Bomber hat up, and her hair rolled out in beautiful waves along her flannel shirt. She wore L.L. Bean boots and a pair of old jeans, and she could not have been more exquisite. I felt a giddy lump in my stomach. How in the world had this happened? We had kissed only once, but when I woke I found my arm over her, her body pushed back into mine to spoon. I felt like a man who has lived in a house all his life who, opening a door he expects to lead him into a closet, finds the house possesses other, more gorgeous rooms. Rooms he had not dreamed of, rooms he had not imagined.

I caught her eye. I pointed to her kayak, asking if she wanted me to unload it. She nodded. Her kayak had a dozen decals depicting ravens.

"This is Chamberlain Lake. It's the biggest lake," Mary said, her boat beside mine. "It's deep, too. People come here to troll for togue."

"It's beautiful."

"Don't trust this lake," Mary said. "Two men drowned in it the spring before last. Their motor quit when they were trying to cross to

Lock Dam and the wind pushed the waves over their stern and the boat went down. Two of them clung to the boat as long as they could. A third made it to shore but he nearly froze to death before people found him."

"It's deceiving. It's calm now."

"The wind blows up here. The strongest wind ever recorded on earth occurred over on Mount Washington in New Hampshire. It's the same wind here."

"Duly warned," I said. "I'll keep an eye to the weather."

Mary paddled a dozen strokes. She had a strong, confident style. Her top hand pushed. Most people kayaked incorrectly by using the paddle in a canoe stroke, yanking on the bottom half and trying to drag the blade through the water. Mary exhibited perfect style: she employed her bottom hand as the center of a fulcrum, then pushed the top hand over it. It was a technique I had been lucky enough to learn from the first person who showed me how to kayak, an old timer named McGee who taught water sports at St. Paul's.

"I'm not staying with you tonight," Mary said, her kayak gliding next to mine.

"Bad first kiss?" I asked after a moment.

She looked at me.

"Amazing first kiss," she said. "But you came here to do something solo. I don't want to insert myself into your plans."

"I like you in my plans," I said. "You have more or less become my plan."

"I was going to leapfrog up a little ahead of you. I'll go and meet with the Chungamunga girls. You want to investigate Eagle Lake and spend some time on the Thoreau site. Maybe you want a night alone. Maybe a couple nights."

"You're a mind reader on top of everything else?"

"I'm being serious, Cobb," she said. "You're being polite now, but you came to feel something about Thoreau and his experience here. I'd get in the way of that."

"I'm pretty sure you will starve to death without me."

Our kayaks had drifted close enough so that she could reach a hand to the gunwale of my boat. She pulled our boats together, then put her hand over mine. She lifted my hand and kissed it.

"I haven't liked someone so instantly and so strongly ever in my life," she said. "I don't know why it's happening. It shouldn't happen, really. But it is."

"I know," I said. "I know. I feel the same way."

"All morning I thought how strange our meeting was. I mean, we have to be in a universe, on a continent, in a country, in a state, in a county, on a river, in a small yellow boat," she said. "Long odds. And we had to leave our homes at the right time, drive at such and such a pace, stop for lunch, or not, get gas, or not. A thousand coincidences that arranged themselves so that we would meet. And then, of course, we have to be attracted to each other. When I was little, my girlfriends and I called it Yeti love. You never expect to see it, but you've heard it's out there and it might just be a legend. But you keep looking for it anyway."

I turned her hand over and kissed it.

"I have to go away from you for a night or two," she said. "That's the truthful thing. I'm feeling too much too fast and I don't want to be confusing a fantasy with this extraordinary man who came into my life."

"Okay," I said.

"We don't know each other well. I understand that. But I think you may be my Yeti and I didn't expect to see you. I need a little time to collect myself."

I held her hand. We had stopped moving forward or going in any direction at all.

AT NUGENT'S CAMP, MARY made me a peanut butter and jelly sandwich. Nugent's catered to fishermen and birders, but now, this deep into September, the management had boarded it up. We sat at a picnic table a dozen yards from the lake. The sun had strengthened throughout the morning. I glanced at the tiny thermometer attached to the zipper of my fleece. Fifty-two degrees. Mary sat in the sun. She had removed her Mad Bomber hat and had spent a few minutes combing her hair. I had washed my face in the lake and cleaned my hands. The water had been cold and green.

"There," she said, handing me a peanut butter and jelly sandwich. "Blackberry jam. I hope you like it."

"I like blackberry jam," I said.

"After lunch we should swim."

She took a bite of her sandwich. She turned it around as she ate it, spiraling in toward the center. I watched her. I had never seen anyone eat a sandwich that way before.

"If you eat it in a circle," she said, seeing my perplexed expression, "then you are traveling ever so slightly on each bite toward the heart. If you eat it across, as you're doing, you have to finish with the corner. Everyone knows the corner is the least talented part of a peanut butter and jelly sandwich."

"What if you prefer the crust?"

"Oh, you can pretend to like the crust, but no one will take you seriously. Spiral is the way to go. At least it is for peanut butter and jelly sandwiches."

"Did you discover this yourself?" I asked.

"Years of study."

"Any other tips?"

"For improved living?" she asked, still turning the sandwich. "Too numerous to mention."

"You're a righty kisser," I said. "Did you know?"

"How?"

"You tilt your head to the right to kiss. Most people do. We have a dominant kissing side. If you meet a lefty kisser, you probably would have a problem."

"Are you a righty kisser?"

"No," I said. "Actually, I am a spiral kisser."

She looked at me. She slipped her feet out of her sandals and propped her heels on my legs.

"Knock knock."

"Who's there?"

"Owl."

"Owl who?"

"Owl you know unless you open the door? Knock knock."

"Who's there?"

"Otto."

"Otto who?"

"Otto know, I can't remember. Knock knock."

"Who's there?"

"Dishes."

"Dishes who?"

"Dishes the FBI, open up."

Mary laughing, delighted at her own jokes. The sun, the lake, the trees turning.

"So listen," Mary said, "we'll be naked in the water in a few minutes and it doesn't have to be a big deal. I mean, we don't have to kiss and go all shivery and make it into this momentous moment. We can just swim and clean off. I have biodegradable soap."

"You're a buzzkill," I said.

"I'm going to take my clothes off in front of you, Cobb. So just give a girl a break."

"And if we do kiss, it has to be righty."

"We've kissed only once, you know."

"Why is that?" I asked.

"It's the Thanksgiving rule. That's another life tip."

"Explain," I said.

"Oh, Thanksgiving is this massive meal that usually takes someone about three days to prepare, and then everyone sits down and eats it in about fifteen minutes. The trick is to learn to take your time with Thanksgiving. You have to get everyone to promise that they won't get up for anything for at least an hour. Maybe two."

"So don't rush things is the moral of this story?"

"I prefer to think of it as taking pleasure slowly."

"You have a lot of notions," I said.

"I am the anthropologist of my own life," she said. "Are you ready to see me naked?"

"Yes," I said.

"I'm just a girl with the regular girl parts."

"I gathered that."

"Now?" she asked.

"Pretty much now," I said.

Mary put her legs around my waist. The water held her weight and I kissed her, righty, again, righty, our mouths open and willing. I held her tight against me and she pulled herself closer with her legs, kissing me, her lips always on mine, her body pushing to be inside me, to be through me. She kissed my neck, my cheeks, my shoulder. We kissed again and again, over and over, and the water stayed chilled around us, and the wind passed by and pushed at the trees, and I felt something wild and primitive in my heart. Something good, and full, and it climbed me and had nowhere to go except toward Mary, and we kissed hard, subsided, kissed again in a rush and anguish of yearning. Her skin perfect, her eyes closed, her hair damp, her body, rib, hip, shoulder, spine, all mine, all given over and taken back and given again.

WE DID NOT MAKE love. But we lay for a long time on the blue tarp, our clothes back on, the sleeping bags spread out under us, the late afternoon sunshine slowly moving toward the west. We kissed a thousand times. The edge of the breeze held a chill, but the sun pushed it back.

"I'll leave tomorrow," Mary said at one point. "I can't leave you today."

"Okay," I said. "Tomorrow it is."

"It is the sensible thing to do. We're not teenagers."

"Okay."

"I mean it," she said. "According to Coop, the Chungamunga girls are on Priestly Point. That's one of the first stops on Eagle Lake. I can make it there tomorrow. And you can stay at the Thoreau site, which is just before it. You know, we have only come about three miles today. We are complete slackers."

"I don't want you to go."

"I don't want to go either, but I need to clear my head."

"Am I supposed to try to talk you into staying? Because I will."

"No," she said. "I need to catch my breath, that's all. But don't stay more than two nights on the Thoreau site. Do you promise?"

"I do."

We kissed again. We kissed deeper and deeper until our bodies strained against each other. When we stopped, she rolled on top of me and made herself comfortable. She supported her chin between her two hands.

"Where did you come from?" she said.

"I was waiting around for you," I said.

"Were you ever married?" Mary asked, her eyebrows drawing

together for an instant. "I want to know a little of your past, you know, with women, but not too much."

"I've been married four times," I said.

She bit my ear.

"Tell me. Tell me you're not living in your parents' basement and trying to write comedy skits. Tell me you don't have a girlfriend waiting for you."

"I've never been married," I said. "Not even very close. I dated a woman named Carol for about a year. I suppose she was my major deal."

"How long ago?"

"Maybe a couple years ago. A year and a half ago. She was a visiting teacher on exchange from a school out West. It was one of those sort of inevitable things. Same age, same school, same kids goading us on. Sometimes it felt like we were playing out something for the benefit of the people around us."

"And what happened?"

"She wasn't my Yeti," I said. "I wasn't hers."

"Was she the only one you almost married?"

"And Mary-Jo Simmons in sixth grade," I said. "And there is no girlfriend waiting. It concerns my father, probably, that there is no girlfriend waiting, but that's the way it is. I spend a little too much time on my classes and working with the students. My father is worried I'll become an Irish bachelor. You know, married to my work and a little too tidy."

"You say your father. Is your mom . . . ?"

"She died. A long time ago, so you don't have to be sensitive about it. I'm not. Car accident. My dad has played the mom part right along. He's a good man. No brothers and sisters."

She nodded.

"Now your turn," I said. "Spill."

"No one," she said softly.

"Come on," I said.

"No one," she said again.

I pushed her a little to one side and tucked my chin down so I could see her expression. She met my eyes.

"No one?" I asked.

"Crushes," she said. "And that one guy I kissed. And I went to the prom with Gil Rollins. We slow danced and his hands got incredibly sweaty. A couple other boys. But I've never come close to being married or even asked. I don't think I've ever been in love. I'm an old maid."

"That's hard to imagine," I said. "Do you have cats?"

She shrugged and put her body closer to mine.

"Lots of things are hard to imagine," she said, reaching around my neck to fix my collar. "But to answer your question, no cats. No pets, really, although I've always wanted to raise a raven. I knit. That's my guilty old lady thing. And I've been known to play bingo. Every time I play bingo, I mean every single time, I expect to win. Isn't that lame?"

"Very lame," I said. "But I guess everyone does, right?"

"Yes, but I get this horrible sinking feeling that I should win and that something is wrong when I don't. It's pitiful, I know."

"Okay," I said. "Is that enough of the past? Or do you want to know more?"

"I want to know everything. But not about the girls in your life. We already know they are dopes for letting you go."

"I'm not sure they would see it that way," I said.

We kissed again. We kissed and over her head a few birds banked and moved across the sky. Her hair, damp and thick, dangled against my cheek. A few crickets started to rub their legs, but they were autumn crickets and did not last long.

"We should set up camp," Mary said between kisses. Our lips moved together when she talked. "It will get dark fast."

"Okay," I said.

"Do you like crows?" she asked.

"More and more."

"You haven't seen my tattoos, have you?"

"No," I said. "Of crows?"

She pushed off me and stood above, her legs on either side of my waist.

"You'll find them," she said. "You have my permission to search for them."

"When?"

"You'll know," she said. "I promise."

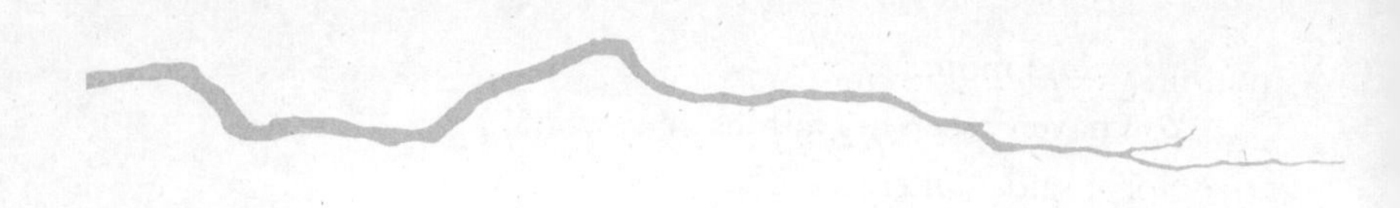

# 4

BANKS OF BLACK MACKEREL CLOUDS PILED on the western horizon at sunset. Mary saw them first. She called them to my attention, pointing and warning me to pull the boats higher on the bank. I ran down and dragged the boats up, secured them by rope to a gnarled little hemlock and headed back. Before I reached camp, a wind bucked straight from the darkest portion of the clouds and cut down and across Chamberlain Lake. It turned the gray water speckled for a moment, then flicked tiny wavelets everywhere. The air became charged with the sweet summer odor of rainfall, and the pines leaned away from the wind and began to thrash.

"Do you think it will pass?" I asked when I returned to the fire.

Mary had already begun putting things under the picnic table.

"In about a week," she said.

I couldn't tell if she was kidding or not. I hustled around the site and put things under cover or shoved them into our two-person tent. The wind raced us, though, and soon the storm had progressed from the horizon to our small inlet. A thick bolt of lightning ran sideways on the western edge of the lake and cracked down viciously at the forest. A bright, vivid explosion followed, and it took me a second look to realize the lightning had struck a tree. Before I could take that in, another lightning pattern webbed across the lake. The lightning doubled in its own reflection off the water.

"She's a corker," Mary said of the storm as she straightened from stashing things under the picnic table. "I didn't hear anything about a front coming in, did you?"

"I thought they called for perfect weather. That's one of the reasons I came right now."

"Me, too," Mary said. "Looks like we're going to have a cold camp. No fire tonight."

"How hungry are you?"

"Hungry enough," she said. "You must be starved."

The wind knocked some ashes from the fire and tossed them into the air. Rain began to fall, softly at first, then with more force. We stood beneath the blue tarp that we had strung above the picnic table. For a few minutes we did nothing at all. I suspected we both thought the same thing: *it can rain for days on the Allagash.* I had read plenty of stories about voyagers getting socked in for a week at a time. And although the idea of being marooned with Mary had definite appeal, I knew enough about camping to understand how dismal it could quickly become. Everything would be wet, we would be confined to the tent, and gradually we would become cold and damp. Even with Mary beside me, it was difficult to see the rain as anything but an annoyance.

The tarp dipped in the wind and a stream of water poured off the lowest end.

That was when we heard a woman calling us.

"JOHN SAID HE SAW someone out here!" the woman said as she entered our campsite. "You're going to get drenched!"

She had appeared through the woods in a red rain parka, her hands up to hold the collar tight around her neck. She looked to be in her early thirties, our age, and she moved easily through the woods.

She wore shin-high muck boots, a pair of old jeans, and a green flannel shirt. She had a kind, slender face, slightly goatish, and a voice deeper than one expected for such a small person.

"We just got back from hunting and we saw your tent!" she said, her voice pushing through the rain. "I'm Annie. We're caretaking the cabins up here and we're just about to make a fire in the lodge. Would you like to join us?"

I raised my eyebrows in question to Mary.

She nodded.

"We'd love to," I said.

We followed Annie. The rain came harder and the trees popped and creaked around us. The wind pulled leaves from the branches and scattered them. Someone inside the lodge flicked on a few table lamps. I saw John—it had to be John—pass by a window with an armful of wood. Annie said, *There's John,* or *that's him,* or something, but the wind and sound of the rain drowned out her words.

"It's a great old place," Annie said when we finally reached a small roofed porch near the back door. "Please come in."

"Does she smell like honey?" I whispered to Mary.

Mary shook her head. She squeezed my hand.

We ducked into a wonderfully preserved 1950s version of a kitchen, complete with linoleum floors and red Formica countertops. It had once been someone's dream kitchen, but now it existed as a reminder of a quieter life, lower expectations. We stood for a moment taking it in while the wind and noise of the rain subsided. I smelled woodsmoke and something cooking. Ella Fitzgerald sang "They Can't Take That Away from Me," but her voice came from somewhere deeper in the house, away from the kitchen.

"Throw your coats over there," Annie said. "They have hooks for the guests. Please make yourself at home. What a miserable turn of weather. Nobody expected this. We heard on the radio that it was supposed to be fine weather for a week or more. But this is New England, after all."

We hung up our coats. Then we went back into the kitchen and introduced ourselves properly.

"So are you two married?" Annie asked when we finished.

"Not yet," I said. "She hasn't asked me."

"Well, if we had come back a half hour later, we would have missed you. John spotted your tent. We didn't know anyone had come out this way. We've been out scouting deer ruts."

"Any luck?" I asked.

"Oh, John always gets a deer. He loves venison, grew up on it, really. But right now he's just surveying the herd to see what's available. It's just good to be outdoors in these last warm days, so I go along with him. We'll be bottled up here pretty soon."

She adjusted something quickly on the stove. Stirred a pot. Then she turned on the oven dial. "Just one second," she said, holding up a finger. When she satisfied herself that the cooking progressed properly, she threw a hand towel over her shoulder. Her cheeks had taken on color from coming indoors after a long day in the woods.

"Come and follow me," Annie said finally, leading us gradually toward the interior of the lodge. "If we're in luck, John's opening some wine. Or maybe you would prefer a whiskey? To chase the cold out? We have tons to eat and drink. It's all provided by the company, so don't worry on that count. The owners are very generous and they know the winters are long up here. We're tickled to have visitors. You're our first ones."

She had shed her own coat. My first impression seemed accurate enough. She had a lean, delicate face and brown hair cut at shoulder length. She appeared compact and balanced and she walked as a dancer walks, slightly open-toed with her torso settled quietly on her hips. She had a white turtleneck under her flannel shirt and she had slipped out of the muck boots and into house moccasins while we had hung up our coats.

We entered the guest lodge, and John, who had been busy laying a fire and getting the lamps lit, turned and smiled at us. He might have been Annie's brother, so much did they resemble each other. He wore a cranberry corduroy shirt; water had dampened the neck while they were out hunting, I assumed, and he had not had time to change it. His hair, cut short along the sides and allowed to grow on top, recalled prize fighters of the 1930s, Jack Dempsey, maybe. He smiled easily and stood to shake our hands. I felt none of the awkwardness that can sometimes attend first meetings. Perhaps the rain had made us all more grateful to have company, or perhaps the drumming of the downpour, the lovely scent of the fireplace, the pure, graceful voice of Ella telling us nothing essential could be taken away, gave us all a warm, nostalgic feeling. It was a good moment—a lucky, unexpected combination of people of about the same age and interests—and we all knew it, somehow.

"Scotch?" John asked.

He poured us all two fingers' worth of Scotch, no ice. The fire, meanwhile, had begun to throw heat, and the lamplight illuminated the knotty walls of the lodge. It was not a grand place. It was not designed for modern comfort—no Jacuzzis or marble bath counters—but the windows, I saw, could be pushed up like safari tent flaps, and the screens, old and venerable, had red glazes of rust in places. It was a Maine lodge, an authentic Maine fishing lodge, and its dark wood and age made it ideally suited to its setting. The late gloominess pushed through into the windows, but it was held off by the calm lamplight and the sizzling logs. Carpenters had situated the lodge perfectly to collect the sunset, and a bank of Adirondack chairs, their arms sufficiently wide to hold an evening cocktail, pooled around the largest window so that guests could watch the final show of the day. The lodge and the lake had been together longer than any of us had been alive.

I put my arm around Mary's waist. She leaned the slightest bit into me and sipped her drink. She listened to something Annie said, but I knew, as she did, that we were a couple. As simple as that. She lifted her arm and used her elbow to hold my arm tight around her. She listened to John from politeness, but our senses, our bodies, talked quietly one to the other.

"Our dream is to move to a fishing camp up in Labrador. We want to own our own camp, fly in customers, you know, make our living that way. I've been talking to a few owners who might be willing to sell out and retire. From what people are saying, all the attention that went to Alaska these past decades—you know, the glamour of Alaska as the last great place—well, that's fading as more people move up there and the countryside gets more crowded. Labrador, on the other hand, is more accessible to the major Eastern cities: Boston, New York, Montreal, even Portland. And the brook trout fishing in Labrador is the finest on earth, really. Spectacular. Annie will do the cooking; she's a trained chef, and I'll do the guiding and general maintenance. Labrador has been overlooked, we're betting, and we like living this way no matter what. It appeals to us."

John said all this as we moved a sturdy, four-person table in front of the fire. We had been left to arrange the furniture and set the table while Annie and Mary had disappeared into the kitchen. Annie had onion soup and corn bread ready for dinner. Simple but hearty, she had promised. John, meanwhile, had taken me through the lodge, pointing out features he admired. He looked at the lodge as a business apparatus, mentioning features he thought worthwhile—a fly-tying bench, complete with thousands of feathers and rooster necks, deer hair, and dubbing wax—and others he felt were unnecessary. At the same time he clearly loved the lodge and knew its history, its characters and ghosts, and could name in many instances the hunter who had brought down this or that trophy deer head. He could not have been more suited to his profession.

The brief tour concluded next to the turntable and four enormous shelves of vintage records. Someone had put together an impressive collection of old crooners and swing bands, with an emphasis on Louis Armstrong and Dinah Washington. He flipped the Ella Fitzgerald record as we went by. The needle made a crackling sound, then sank into the warm voice of Fitzgerald singing "I Get a Kick Out of You." The music, combined with the old-fashioned flavor of the building, its wide porch, its sloped roof, its smoky walls, lent the atmosphere a 1940s feeling. Planes overhead, Germans to fight, and the lake and summer sun eternal and soft.

We set the table with plates, cloth napkins, and candles. As we finished, Mary and Annie returned. Annie carried a tray and Mary balanced the pan of corn bread between two oven-mitted hands.

"John," Annie said, sliding the tray onto the table, "do you realize these two people just met a day ago? This is their one-day anniversary. Mary told me out in the kitchen."

"Well, congratulations. I'm glad you could share the first one with us," John said, raising his glass. "Here's to many more days."

"So far so good," Mary said. "We both have a pretty fresh coat of paint."

"We should open a nice bottle of wine," John said. "I'm trying to learn about them. You know, for customers. The lodge here has a solid collection. It's one of the reasons they want to keep portions of the place heated all winter. That and the plumbing, of course. Any preferences?"

Mary shrugged and said, "I'm no expert."

"Hurry, though, John," Annie said. "Dinner is served."

She placed four bowls on the plates John and I had set. She added a piece of corn bread to each plate and grated a sprinkle of Gruyere cheese on top of the soup. The bowls were wide and oxblood red. Steam rose from the table. Wind hit the lakeside of the building, then made a hollow drone in the chimney. A black-cat night, but we were safe inside.

"How's this?" John asked, returning a minute or two later with a bottle hoisted in front of him. "It should be excellent with the onion soup. Just an average merlot, I think, Californian. Fox Farm."

John opened the bottle quickly and grabbed four glasses from a table near the records.

"Now," he said as he moved around the table, "I refuse to be fussy about wines. No rolling the cork around and all that nonsense. Either we like it or we don't. I haven't met many wines I didn't like in some way."

When he finished, we stood quietly by the table. Beautiful food, a fire, fine music. I looked at Mary. Her beauty still surprised me. I thought, *This is how I want to live, with this woman, with friends, with food, with fires.*

"Please," Annie said. "Let's sit."

I held Mary's chair.

"How DID YOU LEARN to cook?" I asked Annie. "The soup is delicious, by the way."

"It's wonderful," Mary said.

"I learned to cook from my mother," Annie said. "She was French Canadian and she ran a little commissary in our town. Not a restaurant, really, just a place where one or two things appeared each night. She made soups and stews, mostly. And loggers would swing by, most of them with a bottle of whiskey in their coats, and they would eat and talk and flirt with her. My father died in a logging accident before I could remember him. My mom ran the commissary out of our kitchen in a little hall built on to the back of the house. Like a garage, really. It wasn't a fancy place, but she made enough to keep it going. The house had been in my father's family for years, so she had no mortgage. We didn't want for anything, but we didn't have extra, either."

"She makes the best *poutine* in the world," John said around sips of wine. "Have you had *poutine*? French fries with gravy. And cheese, lots of cheese. It's guaranteed to push you one step closer to a coronary, but it is a French Canadian delicacy. You see it all over Canada."

"My mom used the best ingredients she could find, the freshest," Annie said, "but she didn't overproduce her food. That's what she called it. When she visited restaurants, which wasn't often, she found the meals overproduced. The cooks had to do something to warrant the costs, and in her opinion that ended up spoiling the meal. She liked to ask how many times you ate an ear of corn in a restaurant. What could be better than an ear of corn? But in a restaurant you couldn't really get fresh corn, because then people would see through the illusion of restaurant food. She considered that unconquerable proof."

"Sounds like a sensible woman," Mary said. "I lost my taste for cooking when my mother told me she was making shepherd's pie and I heard shepherds' eyes. Ick."

"The only restaurant Mom ever enjoyed was a crab restaurant in Maryland," Annie said, holding out her glass for another spot of wine. "We had gone down to visit relatives and they took us out to a place where the crabs were served with fresh corn. The management covered the tables with newspaper and they served the crabs in big bowls. You ate and you picked at the crabs and you ate corn and drank Bohemian beer. She loved that place."

"That's the best kind of place," John said. "That's the kind of place you look for."

They asked about our trip and what we did for a living. I listened closely as Mary talked about her research, her teaching at the University of New Hampshire. She had told me the outline of her career, of course, but hearing her describe it to two relative strangers gave me a more complete understanding.

"I did my dissertation on bird parasites," she said as the meal wound down and one bottle of wine was replaced by a second. "Biologists are asking questions about how parasites evolve. A friend down at the University of Connecticut is looking at shark parasites. We know sharks have barely changed in their evolutionary patterns, so that begs the question: If sharks do not evolve, do their parasites evolve? And if so, what does that say about natural selection? If an organism is satisfied and prospering, why does it need to evolve?"

"And does it?" Annie asked.

"Inconclusive. But it appears not. Anyway," Mary said, slowly spinning a spoon between the tabletop and her right index finger, "I changed my research focus over time. Now I'm more interested in bird behavior. Crows, as Cobb knows. I am interested in measuring animal intelligence and observing social interaction. What makes a crow a crow and not, say, a robin? That probably sounds crazy, but if you look at it closely enough, it's a fairly complicated question."

"Could you ask it of any animal?" John asked. "Why isn't a dog a cat?"

"It seems to me you can ask anything of anything," Mary said. "But corvids, for my money, are more interesting than most birds. They have definable social interactions and hierarchies, teenagers, and message boards. For instance, we have all seen that crows make a loud noise when they see something of interest. The classic *caw, caw,* sound. But what makes no sense, at least as far as we know, is why a biological entity signals to another competing biological entity over the appearance of a food reward. It would make more sense, when you think about it, to not say a word. But crows alert one another, and other animals, and partially, we think, it's to have larger animals open up the corpses so that they can get at the juicier parts. The organ meats, which are extremely rich and nutritious. And part of it seems to be about the crows' desire to have the entire flock survive. Anyway, that's what I'm interested in these days. No more guts and parasites for me. And I hope I wasn't lecturing. It's an occupational hazard."

It was my turn next and as Annie served brownies she had baked the day before, I told them what I knew about Thoreau, and about his travels in Maine. But I told them more about teaching and living beside students. They found the prep school experience entertaining, asking if it was like Harry Potter, and they were astonished when I told them it resembled it more than a little. They wanted details—St. Paul's School was notoriously well-endowed, with influential American families drifting in and out over the years—and I did my best to recall interesting details. Then, when I didn't even expect it myself, I found myself telling a story I had told no one before.

"I had a boy show up at my door around midnight one winter. His name was Francis. A black kid, on scholarship. It matters that he was a black kid and that he was from inner city Philadelphia. It was late and he was out past curfew, but one look at him and I knew something had gone wrong. So I asked him inside, and you know, if you teach, you have a million things going through your mind at that moment. What are your responsibilities to the young man, but also, are you correct to allow the kid to be out? Those kinds of administrative questions that plague teachers."

"What did he want?" Annie asked, slipping two plates together quietly.

"Well, I had him in an American studies class, so I knew he had been gone for a few days. The dean had sent over a note saying his friend had killed himself. A friend from Philadelphia, a real street kid. The boy who committed suicide, he lived in an apartment house with part of the roof missing. No parents around. You can imagine."

John poured us each a little more wine.

"So," I said, "Francis had gone down to the funeral and he had returned. He came back to class and everyone was happy to see him. The reason he had come out that night was a letter he had received from his friend. The boy from Philadelphia, right before he shot himself, mailed letters to his best friends, reminding them that they had signed a pact to die together. Francis hadn't picked up his mail for more than a week, so he didn't even know the letter existed until right before curfew on the night I am describing. That's why he came to see me. He wanted to know, and it kills me to think about it still, if he was obliged morally to live up to his promise to his friend."

"He thought he needed to kill himself to keep his friend company?" Mary asked.

"Something like that," I said.

"What a burden for him to live with," John said. "You, too."

"I wasn't much help, I don't think," I said. "You can't prepare for something like that. So we sat for a long time and I made him hot chocolate. We talked. I called his dorm father so he would know Francis was with me. I told Francis that I had to tell the dean, too, and he protested at first, but then saw the necessity of it. It was a long night. And now I'm forgetting why I told you all this story."

"We're just sharing things," Annie said. "That's a poignant story. Do you know what happened to Francis?"

"He went home in the spring. He made it through the summer and was scheduled to come back. I don't know if he did. I'm here and I haven't heard news. Teaching just has a lot of stories like that."

No one said anything for a moment.

"Okay," I said, "it was not my intention to kill a wonderful evening. I'm not sure what got into me."

"The rain," Annie said. "It makes us moody."

"It's a beautiful story," Mary said. "It makes me want to date you for another day at least."

Afterward Mary and I did dishes; we insisted. It took no time to clean up. Annie poured the remainder of her soup in a plastic container and set it out on the back porch to keep it cold. Mary dried while I washed. Annie told us to put everything in the dish drainer and not to worry about finding where it went. She had time, she said. Lots of time all winter.

The rain slowed. I realized it had diminished first by the absence of sound—the droning, steady hum of the drops against the roof—now dissipated. It felt, almost, as if the rain had decided against continuing. What followed was a sense of quiet and calm and the music became sweet and tender, like something heard across time.

"Come here," I said to Mary and I took her in my arms.

We danced. She leaned into me and we moved slowly around the kitchen, her head tucked into my shoulder and neck, her body against me, her feet following. She felt familiar and warm and I held her hand tucked against my chest, the length of her with me one instant, then removed and brought back again. Once I turned her face gently up to mine and kissed her, but it was not about kissing, not at that moment, and we kept dancing until the song stopped and a new song started.

"This is our song," she said against my chest. "Whatever comes on, we have to remember it forever."

"What is it?" I asked when it started.

"I have no idea," she said.

I laughed and said, "I've missed you. Even with these lovely people, I've missed you."

"I want them to have the best fishing camp in North America," she whispered. "We'll go there every year and catch enormous fish and all of our children will work for them. Freckle-faced kids on long docks in a massive lake."

"And we will force the kids to get poison ivy even if they don't go near the woods. And we'll make them collect fireflies in a bottle even if they hate bugs," I added.

"They will be Uncle John and Aunt Annie and they will spend every Christmas with us for the next thirty years. And we'll only have fishing lures for ornaments on our trees."

She kissed me. We danced. The roof dripped and a drainpipe made a gurgling sound. We heard John say something about more wood on the fire; then Annie's voice answered but we couldn't hear what she said. The music skipped a little, then sorted itself out.

"You know, I half-mean it all," I said. "As crazy as that is after knowing you for only one day. We probably shouldn't be talking about kids, should we?"

"Shhhhh," Mary said.

"I do. I half-meant it. Maybe more than half."

"Don't spit into heaven," Mary said. "Don't tell the gods your plans; they'll only laugh."

INSIDE THE TENT, OUR sleeping bags a soft bed, she lay with her head on my chest. The rain had not penetrated the tent, though we heard the trees slowly dripping. The air had turned heavy and cold. It was midnight. Now and then the wet, heavy odor of the fireplace drifted to us, its burned logs souring in the rain. Winter did not seem far away.

"Tell me a story," I whispered. "I don't want to fall asleep yet."

"It's late. I only know crow stories."

She sounded tired. She moved a little against me. We were warm and safe.

"I love your crow stories. A short one, if you can."

She did not speak for a while. I thought she might be sleeping. But then quietly she whispered a story.

"Once upon a time Muhammed hid from his armed enemies in a cave. Crows were white then. When the men searching for Muhammed passed by, the birds called treacherously, *cave, cave, cave*. In Arabic, it sounds more like *ghar, ghar*. The crows called over and over, getting louder and louder, because it's a characteristic of the crow to be a mischief maker. They didn't care about Muhammed one way or the other, but they have a sense of humor that is dark and tragic and they like to see people in difficult straits. Well, despite their calling, the enemies passed by without noticing, and when Muhammed came out of the cave, he cursed the crows for their betrayal and turned them black. He condemned them to circle the earth calling, *cave, cave, cave,* wherever they went."

She whispered *cave, cave, cave* as though it were echoing away.

"You have corny sound effects," I said.

"I know."

"Are you asleep now?"

"No."

"How many days have you been alive now?"

"You count," she said, "I'm too sleepy."

"I think I need another story."

"You're greedy."

"I've never heard crow stories before."

"I have one about lovers," she said. "Do you want to hear it?"

"Yes," I said.

"This will take great effort," she said. "Are you sure you are worthy?"

"I'll try to be."

"You can't try to be worthy. Either you are or you aren't. Ain't. You are or you ain't."

"Am I?"

"It's still being decided."

"Will you let me know the verdict when you know?"

"How much do you know about magpies?"

"I know they are really good in stories."

She made a phony snoring sound. I shook her.

"The price of sleep is one more story," I said.

"If we sleep beside each other," she said, "do you think we can dream each others' dreams?"

"No," I said, "definitely not."

"I like those films of people sleeping," she said. "You know, like in labs, with wires on them. And the people roll around and don't even know it. But when they film couples together, they realize the couples have learned to move in the same way in the night. I like that."

"Is that true?"

"Maybe," she said. "But it should be, no matter what."

"You're stalling. Crow story, please."

"I'm all out. And I am sleepy."

"This is the time when I make a high-pitched, whining sound until you relent."

"You wouldn't dare."

"You don't believe that," I said. "I will start telling you knock-knock jokes and that will wake you up. You can't resist a knock-knock joke. It's like playing shave and a hair cut, two . . . but leaving off the end."

"Two bits," she said. "You're very cruel."

"If the sun blew up and you had ten minutes to live, what would you do?"

"I would do push-ups, because time passes really slow when you do push-ups."

"Do you think John or Annie might have been a bear?"

"John has some ursine qualities. Annie is definitely not a bear. A bear can't cook without eating everything."

"But could a bear open wines?" I asked.

"Yes, and they probably would. Wine is grape, after all, and bears love grapes."

We didn't talk for a long time after that. I thought she was asleep. But then, quietly, she whispered a last story.

"Do you know what magpies look like?" she asked.

"Sort of. They have white feathers."

"And long tails. They can mimic human voices better than crows," she said, just on the edge of sleep. "The magpie is a cousin to the crow and is the patron of lovers. They also weave beautiful nests, so they are associated with weavers and cloth makers throughout the east. In one of the legends a weaver girl, who is a granddaughter of the emperor of heaven, fell in love with an ox herder. In her happiness after her marriage, the girl weaver forgot about her job of weaving the celestial cloth, which is the source of clouds. After repeated warnings from the emperor of heaven, the newly married couple was banished to different parts of the sky. The weaver girl in the east and the ox herder in the west. The couple cried so much at being separated that the earth was overrun with water. No one could console them. On the seventh day of the seventh month of the Chinese calendar, the magpies flew to heaven and formed a bridge with their bodies. The star Vega is the weaving maiden, and the herder is Altair. They are apart all year except for the moment that the magpies go into the sky and reunite them."

"When is the seventh day of the seventh month in the Chinese calendar?"

That was all. She slept. Her breathing became quiet and calm.

For a long time I lay beside her without sleeping. I did not feel restless but content and warm instead, my mind stirred from meeting John and Annie, from the events of the past twenty-four hours. I thought of Francis, his return to school, the quiet gentleness he exhibited when he had come to my door. For a while I recollected work that required finishing back at school. Papers, recommendations, books to read, truck tires to change, checks to write. I pictured the map of the Allagash, and how we had not reached Lock Dam, and how the weather could turn cold, truly cold, at any moment. I did not want to be on the river in snow if I could help it, although I imagined it would be beautiful to drift in the dying flakes, the snow mounting on the banks as the river remained liquid and moving in a world increasingly rigid.

To chase the everyday cares from my mind after a while, I tried to imagine the wild animals going to sleep. It was a means of meditation I had practiced for years, taught to me, oddly enough, by a car-salesman uncle known for his loud laugh and horrible suits. In bits and pieces I gradually pictured deer dozing in a pine copse; a red tailed squirrel curled in a hollow in a dead tamarack; the painted turtle, humblest of creatures, nestled down in the leafy mud of a pond bottom, its blood quieting to a single drip of oxygen every now and then, its body indistinguishable from the lake water, a whirling molecule of antifreeze keeping it barely alive, the carapace shining under the blue ice and the distant turning stars.

A moment longer and I would have fallen asleep, but then Mary suddenly sat up. She did not say a word, and in the darkness I could barely see her. But her body flexed against me, and in the dimness I saw her move quickly and harshly, as if shedding a sweater. Her hands continued to peel at the sweater, and her head, moving rapidly, rocked back and forth.

I did not know what to do. Absurdly, I could only recall a sort of inexact warning that you should never wake someone having a nightmare. Why one should not do that, I could not imagine. Nor could I see any advantage to allowing someone near you to struggle so violently. People died, I remembered childhood friends recounting, if you woke them from a falling dream before they hit the earth.

It didn't matter in the end. Before I could think of anything to do, Mary suddenly snapped down at me, her head striking me remarkably hard on the shoulder. If she had been trying to butt me, she could not have done so more effectively. I heard the clack of her jaw and felt the impact throughout my body. Whatever passing thought I might have had about it being some kind of joke disappeared instantly at the loud clipping sound of her teeth snapping shut. It sounded like a skull cracking against a frozen lake, or a castanet falling on a hard floor. Her arm shot out and raked the length of the tent.

In a count of three, it passed. I felt whatever storm the dream had swept over her pass away as silently as it had come. Her body relaxed. Her breathing slowed once more. The strong, discordant tension in her body disappeared. She became Mary again, and I the person suddenly closest to her.

# 5

"DO YOU OFTEN HAVE NIGHTMARES?" I asked.

Morning had come quietly across the lake, pushing us out of the tent and into the crisp air. I checked the thermometer on my jacket and found that it read twenty-seven degrees. In the sun, perhaps, the temperature rose above freezing. Mist coiled from the lake, and a pair of mergansers cut southward above the water, their wings flapping in desperate beats that explained summer had ended. *Late, late, late,* the wings said. We had watched them disappear above the line of forest. Mary wore her Mad Bomber hat.

It had been a quiet, peaceful morning, so I was not prepared for the tone of Mary's response to my question. She had been rolling up her sleeping bag on top of the picnic table while I cooked. Her voice, when it responded, came sharp and vibrant, entirely out of sync with the gentleness of the morning.

"What do you mean?" she said.

I turned and regarded her. She had stopped rolling the sleeping bag.

"It's okay," I said.

"It's not okay," she said sharply. "What kind of nightmare did you see me having?"

I moved the fry pan to the side of the fire where the scrambled eggs would slowly warm. I squatted next to the fire and looked up at her.

"What's going on?" I asked. "Are you upset?"

"You said I had a nightmare. I want to know what you mean."

Her tone, the style of conversation, seemed completely out of character. I studied her. Then I began slowly scraping the eggs back and forth so they would harden. I tried to understand what I had said or how I had stepped on her toe. But she gave me no time to speculate.

"Cobb," she said, her voice flat and serious. "I mean it. What about my nightmares?"

Before I could answer, we heard Annie calling to us. She shouted, "Hello to camp!" then came into the sunlight carrying a pan full of coffee cake. It smelled of cinnamon. Annie wore the same red poncho and gum boots from the night before. She wore a gray watch cap over her hair. She looked cute and happy.

"Thought you guys might be hungry," she said. "John's off in the woods tracking that deer herd. He has the sleep habits of an old man already. Early to bed and up before the birds."

"Morning," I said. "Would you care for some eggs, too?"

"No, thanks," she said, sliding the coffee cake on the table. "I ate with John at first light. I also wanted to tell you two that the weather should be clear for at least a week. I listened to the radio this morning to get an update for you. I'm not sure what that storm last night was about. Did you sleep okay?"

Mary said yes, but seemed deliberately to avoid looking at me. Then she tossed her sleeping bag into the open tent.

"We had a nice time last night," I said. "You're good hosts."

"We try to be good hosts, but it's easy with nice folks like you two."

I brought the eggs to the table and served Mary. Annie cut into the coffee cake. She gave us each a piece. I observed Mary. I had no inkling why she should care so much about a nightmare. I went through a list of possibilities, but nothing made sense. But a few moments later her cheerful nature gradually reasserted herself. When I sat down next to her, she rubbed her hand over my back and smiled at me. Done.

Sunlight broke the morning cold as we sat and ate our eggs. The coffee cake was delicious and we said so.

"It's not bad," Annie agreed. "It's kind of nerdy of me, but I keep a list of things that work and things that don't. I collect cookbooks. I've got the regular ones, you know, *Joy of Cooking,* and all that, but the ones I like are from PTA sales, and historic camp cookbooks. I'm always looking for them in yard sales."

"It's not nerdy," Mary said. "It's smart."

"Where do you get your food during the winter?" I asked.

"Oh, they run things out for us on snowmobile. Once the lake freezes, it's pretty simple to get around. It's this time of year, just before freeze up, and early spring, that are a bit tricky. We can use a launch once the lake breaks up again in April."

"I envy you," Mary said. "All that quiet. People dream of having peace and quiet and then they are afraid of it when it is available."

"Maybe so," Annie said. "But I am looking forward to it. I always think about the fact that one day at the start of winter, things don't move anymore. You know, you use a rake, and you forget to put it away, and that's where it will remain until the spring. Lockdown, I guess. It's like a photograph of your last autumn day, somehow. It's kind of haunting, really."

"And I always feel as though we always resume exactly where we left off," Mary said. "Like we put things down, go inside, and come back out five months later to start our spring work."

"You know you're both already going a little nutty," I said. "And we haven't even had snow yet."

"Snow on the mountain," Annie said. "Winter is already there."

After breakfast Annie copied out their address and told us if we sent a letter they could get it eventually, although she couldn't say how long it would take. She promised, too, to let us know their plans next summer and to send a knitting pattern for a sweater that she had discussed with Mary.

When the kayaks stood ready and as filled as they could be, Mary gave Annie a hug. Mary did not lean in chest first, hips back, but grabbed Annie and hugged solidly. Annie responded in kind. When it was my turn, I hugged her, too.

"Be good to each other," Annie said. "John and I think you two are just perfect for each other, and John never says anything like that."

Annie shoved us off backward and we turned north and east, bending toward Lock Dam. The water felt smooth and full on my paddle. A late dragonfly landed on the rope handle on my bow and stayed there for several strokes, eventually lifting into the morning light. In minutes we each rounded the point and looked back to see Annie. She had already gone.

A SMALL RED MOTORBOAT with a two-stroke engine trolling for lake trout. A beaver swimming west, his head out of the water like a retriever, the V of his wake spreading until it became flat water again. Sunlight through pines, sunlight in sparks and cracks off the surface of the water. The smell of granite and musky reeds and mud.

Knock knock.

Who's there?

Sam and Janet.

Sam and Janet who?

Sam and Janet evening . . .

Mary laughing hard at her own jokes. Singing, *Some enchanted evening* . . . Her kayak beside mine. Her eyes looking into mine. Her boat gliding over to touch mine, the gunwales nudging, the lean across close enough to kiss.

"TELL ME, THOUGH, COBB. Tell me about the nightmare."

"Tell me why you're so curious," I said. "It's not like you. At least not like what I know of you so far."

We drifted a quarter mile from the Lock Dam portage, a dent in an embankment that severed Chamberlain Lake from Eagle Lake. In former days loggers used the lock dam to reverse the direction of water from north-running to south. Instead of running logs north to Canada, they could float logs from Eagle Pond to Chamberlain, and then on to the Penobscot and downriver to market in Bangor. Mary knew exactly where to find it, although Thoreau had said of the Lock Dam that "There is no triumphal arch over the modest inlet or outlet, but . . . it trickles in or out through the uninterrupted forest, as through a sponge." It was 9:12 a.m. and we had made good distance. The sun had warmed the air and now we both felt comfortable in light fleeces.

"My mother used to tell me I had nightmares and I walked around," Mary said. "She said I'd get up and travel in my sleep. So I've always found the accounts a little alarming."

"Where did you go?"

"In my sleep?"

I nodded.

"I slept under a hedge once. A forsythia bank, to be more exact. And I once put my head through the spokes of a staircase and I couldn't get out. I had gone down the block and up the stairs onto another porch, and for some reason I put my head into the railings of the porch and my head wouldn't move."

"And you woke there?"

"Terrified," she said. "Alone and trapped. I hate thinking about it even now."

"But that was a long time ago."

"I saw a purple lady once. That's the one that still gets to me. It was late at night, long after everyone else was in bed. I guess I made it outside and I found a spot under a streetlamp on a road near our house. Birch Avenue; I could take you there. I was up on a small hill, and when I looked down, I saw a woman approach. She wore a long gown, a gown straight out of a Dickens novel, and the woman walked slowly and with difficulty. Her gown was a deep, deep purple. That's what I remember most. It was like the color inside a closet, if you know what I mean. A darkness so complete that it is purple, somehow blacker than black."

"And what happened?"

"The lady had her chin tucked into her chest, and she wore a hat with a veil, so I couldn't see her face. But I knew she had come looking for me. When she reached the end of the pavement—it was on a sort of cul de sac, she began to float upward toward me. I can remember that much. And then her hem touched me; her gown sort of became this crazy curtain of cloth, and I heard her laughing, and the cloth kept tangling around me, and I felt I couldn't move, that if I did anything, the woman would look down at me and then I would see her face. I never wanted to see her face."

"That's a frightening story."

"Tell me," she said softly. "I need to know."

I looked at her.

"I couldn't see much," I said finally. "You acted as though you were climbing out of your sweater, but it was mostly just arm movement. Then you snapped down and your forehead hit me on the shoulder. End of story."

"How hard did I hit you?"

"Hard," I said.

"And how did my arms move?"

"As I said. Like you were trying to get out of a sweater or something. A lot of elbow thrashing, I think. Then maybe you just turned around and tried to lie down, except you had forgotten I was there or something. And your head hit my shoulder. It was no big deal, honestly."

She nodded. I watched her. It was like seeing one cloud on a perfect day and I couldn't understand how such a simple thing affected her so keenly.

"I'm sorry," I said. "I didn't mean to turn it into a joke or anything."

"No," she said. "I've been silly, that's all."

"It was dark and it was a strange place. You were probably just a little disoriented."

"I always wonder," she said, "if one day I won't wander off a cliff or into traffic while I'm asleep."

"I won't let you," I said.

"No," she said. "You wouldn't, would you?"

WE PULLED OUR KAYAKS up on the embankment separating the two lakes. Chamberlain Lake fed into Eagle Lake through a large water pipe beneath the embankment. The water made a loud gushing sound as it descended into the lower watershed. Then it spread and formed a brook running northward into Eagle Lake.

"It's not a really tricky run, but sometimes trees and brush get knocked down here and they block things," Mary said, her hand raised to keep the sun out of her eyes. "You can get in a pickle because it's so narrow."

"How long is it?"

"Not long at all. Maybe a quarter mile, total. Not even. Nothing like what we will run later."

"And this leads out to Pillsbury Island?"

"Yes, where Thoreau slept. Does it feel strange to be doing what he did?"

"Yes and no. He didn't have an expert on crows with him."

"True. He was at a disadvantage."

"Are you good in white water?"

"I'm okay."

"You're being falsely modest, but I appreciate it."

"No, seriously," she said. "I'm only okay. I've been around people who are good and that's how I know. How about you?"

"Lousy," I said.

She looked at me. "Seriously?"

I nodded.

"What fun," she said.

"KEEP THE BOW POINTED straight downstream. You can paddle, but mostly you want to use the paddle blade as a rudder. You know how to do that, right?"

I nodded. I squatted next to her kayak. Three quarters of her boat already bobbed in the water. She sat in the cockpit and gave me final instructions. She wanted to run first in case we had to dodge a tree or a downed stump. We could wade the last part if necessary, but the first section was quick water and had several good drops over rocks.

"This is no biggie," Mary said. "What's the worst that can happen?"

"I could get dragged under and die."

"Always possible," Mary said, smiling. "And cheerful of you to point it out. Not on this run, though. Pretty easy going, honestly."

"Am I sounding wimpy?" I asked.

"Borderline." She nodded at me. "Let's go. Push me off."

I did. She paddled twice and the current took her.

She disappeared before I could count to ten.

I felt the current trying to grab the boat as I climbed into the cockpit. Because the stern still rested on the bank, the boat wobbled back and forth. I used my paddle as a brace to climb in, then took a deep breath.

"In days of old," I said aloud, "when knights were bold."

It was something I had always said before taking my turn at something mildly perilous.

Then I pushed off.

The water grabbed me immediately. Suddenly the sense of paddling, of being in charge, drained away. I saw at once what Mary meant: this was not a river, but a connecting brook instead, a short, bony water path that connected two bodies of larger water. Its narrowness made it tricky, because no sooner had I left the bank than it tucked in and became a fast-moving freshet.

*Stroke, stroke, attack, stroke,* I told myself.

Then things came quickly. A tree on my left, a birch, then another, a third with half its top bent over and wobbling in the current. Stump. Second stump, then down quickly, up and over, and the first dump of water over a shelf of rocks. For an instant the kayak hung, teetered, then shot down, the bow catching the water and dragging it forward, and I felt a giddy exaltation, go, go, go, and I paddled twice before the stream bent to the left, the north, and I paddled hard, then shoved back, using the paddle blade as a rudder on my port side, the bow jumping quickly to avoid a boulder.

Faster.

A tug of water shipped over the bow and flooded the cockpit for a second, then the bow dipped down seriously, nodded, and the water shoved me forward, released me, and I passed through a second stone stairway, one, two, rock on the left, rock on the right, duck at a branch that hung low over the right-hand side, paddle.

Go. I felt myself understanding this, getting it, and I said again, "In days of old, when knights were bold," but then the bottom left side of the kayak raised. It seemed improbable, like a whale surfacing beneath a boat; it took me a moment to realize the kayak had run up on a partially submerged boulder. I tilted hard to my right and would have gone in if somehow I hadn't paddled once quickly to keep the momentum going, to keep going forward, and the kayak slid free, and up, up, more paddle. My hips started moving with the boat better, side to side, forward, and the light came through the trees, beautiful light, and a phoebe called somewhere, *pheeeebee pheeebeee pheeebeeee,* and I felt happy, profoundly happy, excited and moving forward, faster, faster, the water tucking me into its center and carrying me. I passed a blue heron, its body still, its legs holding knee deep in a backwater, a frog pond, and I had passed it before I could be certain it was a bird, perhaps it had been a bush, a tree trunk, but then the water shot me out and over a second shelf of rock. I scraped my paddle blade on the rocks and I suddenly realized, that the water was absurdly shallow, the draft no more than inches, and paddling no longer made sense. I used the blades as rudders, shifting back and forth, guiding the boat smoothly now, with confidence, and then, imperceptibly at first, the water broadened. Its urgency departed and what had been compressed now diffused and the water flowed through cattails and reeds, and two red-winged blackbirds made a chittering call, like a piece of paper caught into a fan blade, like grass speaking if it could speak.

MARY WATCHED ME COME out of the funnel of water. She smiled and nodded.

"How was it?" she called.

I liked her smile. And I knew that I had fallen in love. I knew that I wanted to run rivers with her, and camp, and go out to dinner and dance, and meet people with her at my side, and establish routines, and hear every knock-knock joke in her repertoire. I knew that. The knowledge came as simply as clean linen.

I didn't say anything. I felt too full and happy.

"That's Pillsbury Island," Mary said, pointing directly north. "That's where Thoreau camped."

"He came in from Mud Pond," I said when I could speak, "and he was glad to get in fresh water. The bottom of Mud Pond has the consistency and color of peanut butter."

"That doesn't sound good."

"And leeches."

"Most of these Maine lakes have leeches. Good food for the trout and chubs."

The sun stood nearly at noon. Pillsbury Island rested in the center of the lake, perhaps a mile distant. I waited for a transcendent moment, some great, sweeping emotion now that I spotted Thoreau's landing, but it didn't come. I felt too comfortable in the day, too warm and calm and fulfilled. I paddled closer to Mary's kayak.

"Are you sure you have to go?" I asked.

She looked at me.

"A day," she said.

"And a night."

"You know we're both a little nuts right now," she said.

"Do you feel nuts?"

"No," she said. "I've never felt saner."

"I think this is Yeti."

"I wasn't looking for Yeti."

"Yeti just appear," I said. "You take a picture of Aunt Lucy at the waterfall, and when you examine the photo later you realize a Yeti had been watching from behind a bush. Yeti show up when you least expect them."

"This is all happening too fast, Cobb. I didn't come expecting anything like this."

I nodded.

"You understand," she said, "that I could not be crazier about you than I am right now. I couldn't be."

"But . . . ?"

She looked at me.

"No but," she said.

"There's a but in there somewhere," I said.

She smiled.

"You liked running the stream?"

I nodded.

"We're going to run some beautiful water on this trip. You know that, right?"

I nodded again.

"I'm going to go spend a day with the Chungamunga girls," she said. "You'll come later, okay? Tomorrow or the next day."

"Okay," I said.

"Just show up when you want to. Just come and find me."

"Okay."

"Let's get your camp set up. Then I'll push on."

"Where's Priestly Point?"

"Up past your island. You'll see the boats. You can't miss the Chungamunga girls. You'll hear them before you see them."

# 6

I PITCHED MY TENT WHERE HENRY DAVID Thoreau, on July 28, 1857, pitched his.

I felt teary doing it. It was ridiculous to get caught up in such emotion, but I felt it anyway. If I had a hero, if life provided any model, they existed together in his writings. He had been an environmentalist; he had been a staunch abolitionist; he had been the author of *Civil Disobedience*. He had predicted the future toll of rampant industrialism. He had called on us to live simply. An admirer of Darwin's writings about the Galapagos Islands, he had observed and charted the flora and fauna around Concord, Massachusetts, undertaken journeys with Native Americans into the wilderness, had traveled to the Great Lakes and Cape Cod, always searching and watching. His writings had influenced the Russian novelist Count Leo Tolstoy, Mahatma Gandhi, John F. Kennedy, B. F. Skinner, E. O. Wilson, Willa Cather, Sinclair Lewis, Ernest Hemingway, Marcel Proust, William Butler Yeats, and Martin Luther King Jr. The son of a pencil maker, and a pencil maker himself, he had nudged the world in a different direction.

At age forty he had spent a night where I intended to spend a night. Four years later, at age forty-four, he had died of tuberculosis.

MARY WAS GONE. AT my insistence, she had paddled off shortly after we arrived. I did not want her to cross the open stretch of Eagle Lake at sunset. She had sufficient time, but not if she stayed and helped me erect my tent and make a fire.

We kissed quickly. She did not linger.

"'Welcome the coming, speed the parting,'" she said, quoting an old Irish saying. She hated people who could not say good-bye, she said. She jumped in her kayak and left.

I missed her. I decided, though, not to think of her for the time being. Later, at night, in my sleeping bag, I would think of her. For the moment I concentrated on Henry David Thoreau.

When I finished setting up my camp, I scouted to the north, circling the island. It felt good to be out of the kayak and walking. The sun had already begun to lower in the west, but the temperature remained in the fifties. Straight north of the island, Eagle Lake ran in pewter gray as far as I could see. To the west, just off true north, I saw smoke rising. A glance at my map informed me it was Priestly Point. The Chungamunga girls. Hard to miss. *You will hear them before you see them,* Mary had said.

I continued around the island until I came to the western edge. The sun had already found the tops of the pines along the shoreline of Eagle Lake. I sat on a boulder that extended over the water and watched the sunset. The sun fell beautifully, drawing light back along the water until it had collected everything and pulled it, like a blanket, behind it. Light became diffuse and gray, and the boles of the pines suddenly became clear and definite. Fish puckered the surface of the lake. A late blackbird—maybe a crow—flew high above the woods across the lake. It drifted slowly downward in a spiral, then lighted in a tree. Its landing disturbed other birds who began crying and yawping. Seconds later the birds quieted and the sun was gone.

DINNER: RAMEN NOODLES, BREAD, tea, a raspberry energy bar, a 3 Musketeers, and a long drink of filtered water laced with orange drink mix. When I finished, I washed everything in the lake, scrubbing with sand on the tin plates and turning them upside down to dry on a few rocks. I turned off my stove and checked the valves. I looped a rope through my backpack, tied the other end to a rock, then stood back and tossed the rock over a likely branch on a nearby beech. Tried to toss it over. It took three attempts before the rope followed the rock over the horizontal branch of the beech. I grabbed the rope and tugged it. The backpack lifted off the ground. I pulled harder and it swung up and bounced against the tree trunk. On my next good tug, the rope slipped and I stumbled backward. The pack shot down the spine of the tree, twanged on a short, stubby branch, and rolled down the remainder of the tree to arrive nearly at my feet.

I looked around in embarrassment.

Henry David Thoreau did not speak a word.

I retied the pack and hoisted it again. This time it bounced leisurely up the tree trunk, high enough, finally, to dissuade any marauding bears. I tied off the rope on the picnic table and then realized, naturally, that I had left my night's reading in the backpack.

I smiled, again glad no one happened to be nearby. My smile had grown a little tighter.

Welcome to camping.

I brought the pack down, removed the book—*Walden Pond*—and then went through the process of hanging the pack again. This time, on my third try, I managed to swing the pack pretty well into thin air, making it a sort of backpack piñata for any black bears wandering through camp. I stood on my toes and tried to reach the pack. Couldn't do it. I felt a touch of silly pride at my camping skills.

Afterward I took off my clothes and went swimming.

It was not even a conscious thought. The night had grown very still and quiet and the effort of hanging the pack had made me warm. I stripped out of my clothes and waded in, wandering deeper and deeper until I could simply push forward into the lake. No mumbo-jumbo spiritualism, I warned myself. No forced connection to Henry David. It was a swim, that was all, and I commanded myself to take a dozen strokes out of the small cove. The distance I covered cleared my vision from the tree line, and I realized, without at first fully understanding it, that the moon had already risen behind me. I hadn't seen it because I had been busy with the pack, but now, rolling onto my back, I saw the moon, nearly full, and the gray clouds moving past it like dog shadows running behind summer sheets hung to dry on a clothesline.

The water felt cool and clean on me and my nakedness felt wonderful and free. I lolled in the water, ducking my head back until the sound of the world shrank to the sound of blood moving through my body. *This,* I told myself, *is a good moment.* It was a moment to remember, and as filled as I felt with meeting Mary, I promised myself to store this instant, this time near Henry David Thoreau's camp, with the moon above me and the water quiet and flat. It was my moment alone.

I stayed in the water until I started to shiver. Then I stroked slowly back to shore, climbed the rocky slope, and stood for a long time naked in the dark night. The wind dried me. The fire flickered and pulled shadows out of the forest.

FIRST YOU THINK: BEAR.

Then, even more chilling, you think: person.

It was possible, I thought from the quiet of my tent, that someone had entered my camp looking for food or whatever paltry valuables I would have on a camping trip. Some young local kids, maybe, bent on giving the flatlander visitor a scare. I stayed completely silent and held my breath, sending my hearing out like a small dog to scout the immediate area.

Because I heard footsteps. And because it was three thirty in the morning, give or take a quarter hour plus or minus, and I was on an island far, far away from anyone else.

*Be rational,* I told myself. *Think it through.*

Regardless of how I slowed it down and turned it around to the light, the possibilities seemed fairly limited. Bear, man, ghost. Maybe Henry David Thoreau had appeared, dragging his muddy canoe behind him, his wiry neck-beard brushing against his shirt, his body odorous and foul, his breath tinged with scallions. Or maybe it was one of Mary's bears slowly transforming itself into a human, its step oddly delicate, its teetering near the campsite a mark of indecision. Bear or man, he had no dancing partner, no music to draw him closer.

*A bear, probably,* I thought more seriously. But then I realized that the sound I heard had a sharper quality than a bear's would have. It sounded like heels, not moccasins, and for the tiniest instant my heart rose.

Maybe it was Mary.

Then I heard steps again. They came from behind me. *To the west,* I told myself as if that mattered.

I cleared my throat.

The steps stopped. A little while later the steps moved again.

"Take what you want and leave," I said aloud.

I didn't expect a response. I didn't expect *anything.* I felt a little like the rattled boy who creeps toward the door of his closet some stormy night, telling himself the closet contained no monsters, none at all, but that he must, to acknowledge a sort of psychic passage into adolescence, open the door and look for himself. Deep down, of course, the boy understands he wouldn't bother looking if some small, infinitesimal chance didn't buzz in his brain to remind him that perhaps, maybe, *could be,* a monster lived in his closet. Hadn't he spent a million nights peering at the crack in the closet door frame, wondering, from moment to moment, if the door hadn't opened a little more? Was the opening door an invitation to come inside and join, or a slight push outward so that the monster would slide more quietly into the bedroom the minute the boy finally closed his eyes?

The last thing such a boy *expects* is a great, drooling monster tucked back behind the sleeves of Grandma's old sealskin coat. If he really expected a monster, what kind of dope would he be to venture near the closet?

I didn't expect a reply.

Fortunately, none came, so I said, "If you are a bear, go away."

*Raccoon,* I thought. I heard a half dozen more steps.

Then I experienced a moment of impatience. *Stop it,* I told myself. I squirmed around in my sleeping bag until I could reach the zipper of the tent. I zipped it open and stuck my head out. Nothing. The lake had turned to pearl and the temperature had become brittle and sharp. The moon cast a bright white light. The steps came from my left, close to the shore, and I reached behind me for my headlamp. I pushed the on button and flashed the beam around for a second until the light picked up the glowing eyes of a creature standing not more than twenty feet away.

A deer. A buck. I took a deep breath.

The beam of the flashlight lifted the buck's head from where it had been nibbling something. It turned to look at me, its eyes becoming two crepuscular jewels. I flicked off the light and let my eyes adjust. For a few seconds I listened to the deer move quietly around the shoreline, its sharp hooves clear and distinct now that I comprehended what caused the sound. It appeared to want something in the bushy grass near the shoreline. Dimly, I watched its mouth chewing sideways on grass. It settled its head down, then lifted. Its body remained tense and alert, a string waiting for a vibration to make it sound.

I watched until a stripe of moonlight fell across its hindquarters. The moon had lifted free of a tree or a cloud, I couldn't know, but a beam suddenly shook free and landed on the haunch of the buck. Half in light, half in darkness, I saw the deer lift and chew, its nostrils emitting two cones of vapor, autumn caught somewhere in the velvet antlers atop its thin skull.

NEAR DAWN I HEARD a drumbeat.

But it was not precisely a drumbeat. It was sharper, more violent, and I wondered what kind of woodpecker made such a rapping. It was still too early to care, so I turned in my sleeping bag, finding a comfortable position for my hip on the sleeping pad, and tried to go back to sleep.

But then I heard more drumming.

I started to grin at the foolishness of this night. Bucks, creeping bears, raccoons, moonlight—it had all combined to make me feel a bit of a neophyte. It would get better, easier, I told myself. *Hurry gradually.*

The drumbeat came again. This time it became insistent. It rattled quickly, almost in a military tattoo, and then it was joined by a second drumming. It took a moment longer for me to realize that the drumming had a purpose. If nature is swirling and cornerless, this sound, by contrast, had a rhythm and pattern that called attention to itself. *This is not nature,* the drumbeat said. *This is a human manifestation.*

I pushed out of my sleeping bag and unzipped the tent.

The temperature hit me. It rolled in off the lake and explored the interior of the tent. I grabbed my fleece and a wool hat and climbed outside. I could see nothing to indicate the origin of the drumming. It had stopped now, and the lake was quiet. The sun had made the morning pink.

Then someone made a one-two-three sound with a drumstick against a solid object.

An instant later a bagpipe began to play.

It was morning, and cold and foggy, and the bagpipe began tentatively, limning an air, and then, gradually, another bagpipe joined. I heard it, but it made no sense. I could see no one, although I now understood the bag-piping rose from the flat lake. A third bagpipe joined, then another and another. One by one the tune emerged without drumbeat, without anything but the sound of the lake and the breeze and the morning birds.

Then slowly the fog lifted enough to let me see the canoes partially. I counted five canoes, with three girls in each. Fifteen girls, and they played not the bagpipes, but their noses and mouths. It should have been absurd—it was absurd!—but the music they created, the great weeping skirl of the pipes, the troubled ascension of emotion, replicated with uncanny accuracy the pain of a lament. In any instant, if they had laughed or called attention to the insanity of their enterprise, they would have turned themselves into a parody, a Monty Python skit. But they had perfect seriousness in what they performed. Clearly they had risen in darkness and had paddled across Eagle Lake in fog and quiet, their paddles deliberately kept free of the canoe gunwales. They had positioned themselves so that their voices, their bagpipes, would echo and resonate across the open water to me. And they were sufficiently strong in numbers to carry the thing off.

The music meant more to me than any single song I had ever heard. I felt tears build in my eyes.

Although I only learned the name later, the air came from the Isle of Skye. It was called "Tog Orm Mo Phiob" *Lament for Rory Mor*.

How many hours had gone into perfecting it, to harmonizing, I couldn't imagine. They performed it effortlessly, each sound and movement lifted and made more solemn by the opening light. The sound built into a tug and then receded. I had a sense of a storm passing.

When it ended, a single girl's voice carried over the water.

"We are the Chungamunga girls, eternal on this water."

Then they turned and left. They paddled in formation, peeling away one by one. The drumbeat resumed. The middle passengers, I realized, provided the rhythm.

When they had entered the fog, again one single voice called out. "Mary says to come to breakfast!"

And all the girls laughed.

"I'm a Chungamunga girl," Mary said. "I couldn't tell you, in case you were a bear."

She had waded into the lake and pulled my kayak forward. She wore a fleece and a pair of shorts and Teva sandals. She kissed me. It was not a small kiss. We kissed for a few minutes and then she broke it off slowly.

"There are children about," she whispered. "The Chungamunga girls are strictly PG-13."

"You are a Chungamunga girl?" I asked.

She nodded.

"And you are eternal on this water?" I asked.

"I am," she said with surprising earnestness. "We are eternal on this water, we Chungamunga girls. Generation to generation, we will be here always. As long as there is time, there will be a Chungamunga girl on these waters."

"Did you send the bagpipers?" I asked, climbing out of my kayak.

"That depends if you liked it."

"I loved it."

"You should be honored," she said. "Few people ever hear an air by the Chungamunga girls on their river. It's a privilege they don't often grant. It is more than luck, Jonathan Cobb."

"Thank you for sending them."

"They took it on themselves to go and greet you. They are mad to meet you. I just sent them off gathering so that they wouldn't swarm all over you. They think our meeting is the most romantic thing they have ever heard."

"I was promised breakfast," I said.

"Come and meet Wally," she said. "Wally is the cook. You should be able to get something or other. There's almost always something to eat."

"The Chungamunga cook is a man?" I asked, surprised.

"Not a man," Mary said. "But we suspect she is a bear and has been for years. She simply refuses to go back to the woods."

I could see why Wally could be mistaken for a bear. Without question, she was the largest woman I had ever encountered. She was round and soft and tall, a pudding of a woman, maybe six feet four, and she wore a cat-eyed pair of glasses on a beaded necklace around her neck. I tried not to show my astonishment; I wondered if she were a man in drag, wearing an outfit—a crimson caftan with a white yoke that narrowed into an arrow aiming at her shins—more suited for a suburban beach party than a camp out in the Maine woods. A leather-topped pair of Bean gum boots stuck out from below the hem. Her gray hair stood on top of her head in a pancake, and remained there by a piece of birch wood jabbed through it.

*Like Little John,* I thought, *from the Robin Hood story. Only female.*

She stood in the middle of her camp kitchen, an impressive mess of pans, Coleman cookstoves, teakettles, Dutch ovens, and dirty dishes surrounding her. She held a large cup of steaming something in her left hand and a tiny cigar in her right. It was easy to see breakfast had only recently concluded. Two long picnic tables stood under a screened tent and the dishes had not been cleared away.

"Are you hungry?" Wally asked, flicking her cigar ash.

She did not bother with introductions. She knew who I was.

"Yes," I said, not sure how to proceed.

"How will you pay?"

I glanced at Mary, who had taken up a position beside me.

"Do you mean cash?" I asked, confused.

"Money means nothing on the Allagash," Wally said. "Do you have any skills?"

I looked at Mary.

"I pay with knock-knock jokes," she explained. "Wally accepts all compensation. The girls all have to pay with a skill of some sort. Not every time, but now and then to settle a bill. Nothing is free, but nothing costs, you see."

I thought about it. Wally smoked. I liked Wally.

"I can put a dollar bill on the ground, stand on one end, put you on the other, and you can't touch me," I said, remembering a corny old routine my father had taught me. When I was ten, it had fascinated me.

Wally smoked.

"Intriguing," she said, her voice deep and quiet. "A riddle, eh?"

"A game."

"Let's make sure I understand," she said. "I put my foot on one side of the dollar and you put your foot on the other side, right?"

"Right."

"A typical dollar?"

I nodded.

"American currency?"

"Yes," I said.

"And you're betting I can't touch you?"

I nodded again.

Wally looked at Mary.

"I like him," she said. "He has skills."

A breeze pushed her cigar smoke behind her.

"Is your breakfast any good?" I asked while she considered. "I should know before I show you my skill."

Wally took a long sip of coffee. Then she reached forward, set the cup down, and shot a spatula under a cinnamon bun. She held it out.

I broke off a piece and took a bite. It was in the top ten of best things I had ever eaten.

"Not bad," I said.

She smiled.

"Let's see your dollar," Wally said.

I reached behind me and took a dollar from my wallet. Then I walked to the screen house, and placed the dollar on the ground so that it was half in, half out. Wally could not stand on her end and touch me. She did not bother walking over to try it out. She put her cigar down and dished out a curl of scrambled eggs, home fries, three pieces of bacon, and the remainder of the cinnamon bun.

She handed me the plate.

"Not bad," she said.

"Have you eaten?" I asked Mary.

"Long ago," she said. "Now come and eat before you're swarmed. They'll be back any minute."

"Thank you," I said to Wally after I'd finished eating. "The cinnamon bun was delicious."

"I know," she said. "The bears have told me so."

"You're not a bear, are you?" I asked.

Wally took a drag on her cigar.

"Impertinent, isn't he?" Wally asked Mary.

"Spirited," Mary said.

"Am I a bear?" Wally asked, looking back at me.

"That was the question."

Before she answered, the forest suddenly filled with shouting and laughter. Mary whispered that she had warned me. A moment later, what seemed like a thousand girls came running through the camp toward me. Most carried a plant or a branch of some sort, evidently the spoils of their gathering. They all wore khaki shorts and green T-shirts or sweatshirts. Across the front white letters spelled out *Chungamunga*.

Before they quite reached me, Wally shouted, "Greeting line to meet Jonathan Cobb, our guest. We are not wild animals."

The girls instantly stopped and grouped themselves in a straight line extending across the camp and into the start of the forest. What had begun as a swarm now tucked back in a tidy line. Mary stepped forward. In a line, the girls did not appear quite so numerous. No more than twenty total.

"Chungamunga girls," Wally said in a loud voice, "I present to you Jonathan Cobb, who attests that he is not a bear."

The girls moved forward. Mary took my plate. Each girl stepped in front of me, paused, extended her hand, declared her name, and continued on. Each one met my eyes to the point where I knew this must be the fruit of some instruction. As soon as the girls passed by me, they ran off to whisper and stare back at us. A city of green, two-person tents stretched down to the water.

Three counselors—Jill, Tiger, and Doris—brought up the rear of the line. They wore the same clothes as the campers. All three, Mary whispered, attended Dartmouth but had taken the semester off to usher the Chungamunga girls down the river. Jill and Doris resembled each other enough to be sisters. They each had black hair, pulled back in a ponytail, and a slender build. Tiger, on the other hand, stood out. She had deep red hair the color of a Mexican roof, and her hair frizzed out in a halo of light. She had a redhead's white skin that had already peeled and tanned by this time on the trip.

"They left school to come and do this?" I asked quickly.

"They are Chungamunga girls," Mary said.

"And they are eternal on this river?"

She nodded and whispered, "There are a lot of us."

"Would anybody like last servings?" Wally called to the group when they had finished.

That released them. They ran to her and began pushing plates in her direction. Mary took my arm and led me to the dining tent.

"WHAT DID YOU THINK when Mary said you could join her fire?" asked one girl.

"I thought I should."

"But she said you didn't," another girl said. "Not at first."

"I was a fool," I said, eating a little of my eggs.

"Boys are so weird," another girl said.

"No weirder than girls," I said.

"Oh, come on," the first girl said. "Boys think punching each other is fun."

"You mean it's not?" I said.

And so on.

The girls sat in a bunch around Mary and me, their bodies pouring over the picnic tables, each one leaning in to hear something or to lob a question at us. They were preteens, eleven and twelve, and they ate food as they waited to hear our answers. They had been in the woods, they said, for two weeks. They had another week to go if the weather cooperated. They said Mud Pond was gross in the extreme, and the water had leeches, and the trees made banjo sounds when they rubbed together, and they had eaten frogs' legs one night when Wally cooked them, and acorn flour, and one day, one warm day, they had all had to wear bare feet all day and not shower, and then another day, it was a Tuesday, they had all written letters home and sent them in bottles down the river, and they weren't positive, but they had heard that some people's letters had actually been scooped up by Mrs. Gravy, an old Chungamunga girl, and the thing about the letters was that you could ask for wishes in the bottles, and sometimes, they had heard, the wishes came true. Big wishes, too. Like trips to Disneyland or Paris, or a bike or a pickup truck for your father, weird crazy stuff, and the bottles sometimes didn't make it, they just disappeared and floated away, but the wish, according to Tiger, the counselor, still counted. According to Tiger, if Mrs. Gravy caught the wish bottle, that was great, but if she didn't, the wish still counted for something you had asked for, something from your heart, and that was half the game. The point was, they repeated, to keep wishing.

And another day they had all had to switch sleeping partners, no tentmates could stay together more than a night or two, because everyone had to get to know everyone, that was the Chungamunga way, and they *had* seen a bear, a black bear, it had come into their camp one night during their first week, and it had stood on its back legs and reached up for a sack of food, and they were frightened until someone pointed out that it looked like a dancing bear, no, it looked like Wally, and they searched for Wally but couldn't find her, so you couldn't say for sure, maybe Wally was a bear, or someone else, and now they were going to study ravens and crows because the eternal triangle of man, wolf, crow—no *woman,* wolf, crow, one of them amended—was the triangle of hunt, kill, scavenge.

And didn't I think Mary was pretty?

"Yes," I said. "I think she's beautiful."

The girls hooted. Mary blushed.

AFTER BREAKFAST WE CLEANED. The Chungamunga girls belonged to work parties, all named after former Chungamunga girls, and so I worked with the Lucy group to set things straight. Wally supervised. Mary excused herself to get ready for the excursion she intended to lead to the moose carcass. I was invited.

When the camp was cleaned to Wally's satisfaction, she came and sat with me in the dining tent. The girls had been sent to get ready. Wally sat with a final cup of coffee and lit another small cigar. She appeared tired and happy. Now and then we heard a shriek from the tents.

"The girls are lovely," I said.

"Yes, they are," Wally agreed. "They're good girls. They come from all over and we try to give them an experience to remember."

"Are you the head of it?"

She pursed her lips.

"Field operations," she said. "I take the girls down the river. I'm an emergency medical technician in my free time. And in case you're wondering, I don't always dress in a caftan with cat glasses. This is a persona I adopted to give the girls something a bit marvelous and strange. I worked for fifteen years as a cultural anthropologist. West Africa: Burkina Faso, Benin, Ghana. I play the priestess."

"Are you affiliated with a university?"

"Brown, for many years. Then the University of Chicago. I was hired by the Chungamunga board to establish tribal rituals here on the river."

I looked at her. She must have seen my puzzlement.

"The bears, our enemies, but also our friends," she said. "The rituals. The rules and songs and special inside information. Even the bag-piping. Cultures function on belonging and secret information. Fraternities and sororities have known that for years. Most of the rituals had already been established when the original Chungamunga girls had a camp up here. That was in the nineteen twenties. Then the paper company reclaimed the land and sold it to a Korean concern and the camp was abandoned, and so it became a floating operation, just a name and a memory of a camp. The name stuck and the board members fought like hell to keep some identity. When I first heard about it, I thought the camp lingered on out of simple nostalgia. And maybe at first it was. But then the first donors re-envisioned the camp experience. They came up with this idea."

"And it is eternal on the river, and can never be taken away from them?"

"Exactly."

"How is it funded?"

"All scholarship," Wally said. "Funding is not an issue. It doesn't cost too much to run a river trip. Canoes, food, some transportation. I'm the only year-round employee, although we hire some people for mailings and such on a part-time basis. The Chungamunga

Foundation is extremely well-funded. Influential, you might even say."

"And the girls remember the experience and can contribute to it in later years."

"Many do. Some, like Mary, come to lecture or help out. Our counselors this year are all volunteers who have taken time out of college to pay back a responsibility they feel. Terrific young women. And the Maine rangers dote on us. We make contributions to different funds dear to the rangers' hearts. They make sure we are provisioned twice during our time on the river, and they assist us with any girl who can't continue the trip. "

"How did you happen on the bear mythology?"

"Well, I could bore you with an entire dissertation on the bear-human relationship, but that's for another day. I didn't actually come up with it. It's been part of the Chungamunga story since its inception. From an anthropologist's point of view, it's an inspired choice. It's as ancient as these things go. If you've seen a bear track in the woods, you know it resembles a man's footprint. It seemed like a natural fit to include the bear mythology. There are stories about humans surviving the winter by denning with bears. And of course the girls only partially believe it, which is the beauty of a myth. They can engage with it while not being terrified. There are bears around, of course, and we turn them into something interesting and potentially friendly. It makes it easier on the girls who might be a bit timid and worried at night."

"It seems like a wonderful program."

"More than a program, really," Wally said, sipping the last of her coffee. "We are deliberately inculcating them with a sense of magic. Brainwashing them. We only let them go down the river once. That way there won't be know-it-alls to spoil things for newcomers. We believe the world has become tired because it cannot sleep. I know that sounds a little hippie-dippie or terribly new age, but the world has become a place filled with electricity and games and noise and music. We don't allow any electronics here. Nothing. We don't even let them play cards or Monopoly or anything like that. They have to devise their own entertainment, and of course enjoy the natural beauty around them. For a month we try to turn them back into themselves."

"Do some girls resist?"

"Almost all of them do at first. They are trapped with the whole American mess of malls and movies and beauty products. It's shameful, really, what we do to our girls in this culture. We sexualize them, vamp them up, then scorn them if they actually misbehave sexually. You know all that line of thinking, I'm sure. Sometimes our motto is that we reclaim their girlhood. They put on plays and skits, they make up songs and invent rituals to add to the existing rituals. They skip rope and do hand-clapping games. They tell stories, but not about boys and kissing and all of that. They make their own culture, where the girls are strong and heroic."

"How come I've never heard of this before?"

Wally put out her cigar and finished her drink. We both heard the girls beginning to gather. I looked up and saw Mary at the front of one group, a clipboard and a pair of binoculars in her hands.

"It's passed on quietly," Wally said. "Former Chungamunga girls nominate candidates who need to go backward, who may need a little magical thinking in their lives. Most of the girls face serious illnesses. Most will be bombarded with modern medical applications before all is said and done. With all those tubes and tests and needles, we hope they can remember their time on the Allagash and the bears who sometimes come to a campfire to dance. No one speaks of any illness or test or anything medically related to their conditions while on the trip. They leave that behind when they step into a canoe. That's the one inviolate rule."

I looked at her and nodded, but it was a dull movement, one carried out without fully understanding what I intended by it. Wally stood. Mary had a hive of girls around her now. As I stood and got ready to join her, a single thought started deep down in my core and slowly gathered force as it rose. Absurdly, it reminded me of those strongman tests at the carnival, where you are persuaded to swing a hammer and strike a lever and a piece of metal rises and clangs a bell. If you do it well, you win a doll and the applause of the small crowd gathered round to watch the showoffs. But this time I did not want to ring the bell. I did not want the final understanding that came with the memory of Mary announcing as I arrived:

*I am a Chungamunga girl,* she had said. *As long as there is time.*

She had gone down the river as a girl. She was eternal on this water.

Tubes and needles, Wally said. Girls who faced medical procedures.

GIRLS YELLING AND SCREAMING and laughing, sitting on the ground in the tribal camp manner, small Buddhas, knees out, feet pinned together. Sunlight on pines. A brook spilling across white rocks. Mary, a pair of binoculars around her neck, holding her hand up for silence. Slowly the girls stilled and gave her their attention.

"This is the story," Mary said in her storyteller voice, "of how the crow saved the world."

A few girls laughed. A few more tittered.

Mary faced them. She did not give them a schoolteacher's frown. It was a theatrical gesture, calculated to make the girls buy into the performance. And it worked.

"This is the story," she began again, "of how the crow saved the world."

No one spoke. Mary waited. She was irresistible.

"The crow," Mary whispered loud enough for us to hear but soft enough to make us lean forward, "brought fire to humans. In those days the crow had been rainbow colored and perhaps the most beautiful bird in the universe. But one day a great wind passed over the world and all the cooking fires sputtered and went out. Even the smoky mountains of Wyoming and the bubbling pots of Yellowstone were extinguished. For many days smoke covered the world. Then more wind came and the earth stood for the first time without fire."

Mary paused. She looked around. The girls, by now, had bought it. They leaned forward as if their leaning could bring the story faster. But Mary worked them perfectly, delaying each plot point until the girls demanded it by their postures.

"At first, the animals welcomed the loss of fire, because what is fire to an animal except one more thing to threaten them? On their daily chores, they commented about how wonderful it was not to be concerned with fire. That is how shortsighted they were. That is what happens when the world is not in balance! No Chungamunga girl would be so stupid!"

The girls laughed. The laugh quickly subsided in order to make way for the story to resume.

"Little by little, though, the world turned colder and colder. Each day the wind blew and the land grew more rigid. Animals who had delighted in the absence of fire slowly realized the creatures of the earth faced extinction if someone did not relight the fires. A meeting of all the animals occurred, and no one could summon a solution. But the crow, wisest of all animals, understood what had to be done. At night he flew to the eastern horizon and waited. When the first tip of the sun lifted to begin the day, the crow flew next to it and from that one light ignited a taper he carried in his beak. He flew around the continents and the seven seas, relighting cooking fires and boiling volcanoes. But by carrying the flame of life, the bird's feathers blackened. That is the price the crow paid for such unselfish heroism! Forever after the crow was a black bird. Many animals—ignorant ones who did not know of the crow's sacrifice—mocked the crow for its drabness.

"'Black is the color of night,' some said to the crow. You are a bat, surely.

"Others said the crow had a message from the devil and could never accomplish its delivery.

"Hearing the laughter, the great god of the plains—this is a Native American tale—took pity on the crow.

"The bird had been burned too severely to restore its rainbow color, but the great god thought of a thing to do.

"'Come here, bird,' the god said.

"Then he breathed onto the crow. At first the other animals barely suppressed their laughter, because nothing had changed in the crow's appearance. The crow remained black and some of the animals even went so far as to mock the great god.

"'The crow is the blackest animal in the world,' they said. Even the skunk, who is black and smells like dead fish, is not entirely black.

"But on the next day, when the sun rose to its full height, the crow landed on a tall pine tree where many animals happened to be collected. The sunlight struck the crow from the side, and suddenly the animals held their breath . . . for there were the colors of the rainbow still present in the crow's blackness. The blackness, containing all color, is the most beautiful of any color.

"Look closely at a crow today," Mary said. "The colors are there, more beautiful than ever."

No applause. Nothing but wind and the quiet lap of the lake.

# 7

"THE GIRLS LOVED YOU," MARY SAID, pulling on her fleece. "And Wally gives full approval."

"They're all wonderful."

We camped at Pump Handle as the sun slowly moved to the western edge of the sky. We had kayaked to the next stop. The Chungamunga girls permitted no men in their camp after dark. No exceptions. Mary had kayaked with me to the next tent site. In the morning she planned to return for talks about what we had witnessed at the moose carcass. Corvid science, she said, behind the stories. What we had witnessed—the crows and ravens hopping on the body of the moose—had been incredibly impressive. Now, she said, was the time to give the girls the necessary background.

I watched her moving around the camp. She lit our candle lantern and took out our cooking gear. She appeared more beautiful than ever, her hair back in a bandanna, her face browned from the sun. The memory of her with the girls, especially a short, rather awkward girl named Myrtle, still warmed me.

"You know," I said, "the girls adore you."

"Well, they like the stories anyway."

"They like you. And they like your area of study. If you hadn't been with us to explain what we observed today, the girls would have been grossed out. But it seemed natural watching the ravens devour the meat. The whole cycle of life thing. You're a wonderful teacher, Mary."

"I want to see you teach," she said, closing the glass base of the candle lantern.

"I'm a good teacher," I said. "But you're better. You have a gift."

"Well, it's not a contest, is it?"

"No," I said, "it's not."

She looked at me. Then she came around and sat next to me on the picnic table bench.

"You've been a little reserved all day," she said. "Is something wrong?"

"We should build a fire," I said.

"We will," she said. "But in a second. Tell me what's wrong."

I looked at her.

"It's way too early to be so dramatic about things," I said. "I'm sorry."

"What things?"

"Wally told me the background of the Chungamunga girls. Their mission. And you said you are a Chungamunga girl. So I am trying to add it up in my head but I'm not sure I know what to calculate."

Mary took a deep breath.

"Let's make a fire," she said. "It's a long story."

"I AM A CHUNGAMUNGA girl," Mary said when we had settled with hot soup in front of a solid fire. "When I was eleven, I was contacted by Wally's predecessor, Daphne Miller. You understand, the Chungamunga invitation comes without any warning. You don't apply. You are selected. In my case, a single bagpiper stood on my lawn at sunrise and played the most exquisite air. You have no idea how special it makes a girl feel to wake in the morning and discover this poignant, beautiful melody is for her and her alone."

"Do they always deliver the invitation that way?"

"Usually," Mary said. "Sometimes by horseback, if a girl loves horses. They try to be inventive and match the girl's interest. Of course there are practical concerns. But the invitation itself . . . oh my. It's pink and beautiful and handwritten. I've never talked to a single Chungamunga alumna who did not keep it as one of her great treasures. Imagine the knock on the door to tell Harry Potter he is a wizard! This is a girl's version of that, but it is older and it is real. It's not fiction. Suddenly a girl who feels trapped or bored by her everyday life . . . well, suddenly, magic enters."

"You must have been bowled over."

"I was. I think my mother knew vaguely that I might be extended an invitation, but the actual day was a surprise even to her. Who had ever heard of the Chungamunga girls? And what a crazy name! And now they wanted me to join them on a trip down the Allagash River! It meant so much, Cobb, I can't tell you. I was absolutely wild for it. I couldn't sleep for days. I tried to find out more about it, but of course you can't. That's the joy of it. It begins in your head as a fantasy and slowly builds."

I threw a branch of pine in the fire and the light built for an instant. Mary sipped her soup. Her leg pressed mine.

"How's the soup?" I asked.

"You're a good cook."

"Do you have enough?"

She nodded. She stared into the fire. I understood she had let her mind drift backward to her days as a Chungamunga girl.

"Every Chungamunga girl is brought to the opening ceremony by a former Chungamunga girl. Can you imagine that in this day and age? My sponsor was named Mrs. Prouty. She was the most beautiful woman I had ever seen. She had beautiful silver hair and she arrived at my door in a limousine. She wasn't rich . . . don't think that. The limousine is just part of the experience. When we assemble at a certain place at a certain time—I'm sorry, I can't tell you those particulars—we are led to an enormous bonfire. Everyone stands around, jumping out of her skin, wondering what in the world this is all about. But everyone is intensely excited, too. Then far off on the horizon we see something appear. At first it's difficult to know what it is. Little by little you realize it is a hot air balloon. Will you get on it? Will you be asked to fly away? I don't know if little boys fantasize in the way little girls do, but to see a balloon flying toward you and to know that it has something to do with you . . . that your life isn't just dripping by, but suddenly has emotion and romance involved in it, it's the most compelling thing most of us will ever experience."

"I think I understand," I said.

"The balloon arrived with Daphne. Nowadays it would be Wally. The operator of the balloon is a bear. You can laugh, but that's what he looked like to me. Maybe he wore a suit. Maybe he is a bear. He only stayed a moment. Then the balloon departed. At the same time former Chungamunga girls paddle the canoes that had been stashed away and bring them toward the beach. It's all orchestrated, Cobb, and maybe now, seeing it now, it wouldn't be so extraordinary. But for a group of girls who may have given up a hope they didn't even know they had, well, it was by far the most marvelous thing to ever happen to any of us."

"And many of the girls are sick?" I asked.

Mary looked at me.

"All of the girls are sick," she said.

"I'm sorry," I said.

"I'll get to that," she said. "Don't be sorry about anything."

The sun no longer filled our campsite. A cool breeze began pushing the water higher on our beach. She took another deep breath.

After a moment she said, "Like any good fantasy, the participants sustain it. So we had a number of rituals. You turn over your watch and cell phones—not many people had cell phones then—and all your makeup and lipstick. Strip away the old world. They give you a new identity, in other words, just like the military. That's how basic training goes, right?"

"Right," I said.

"Well, that's all, really. For an eleven-year-old girl it's big. Each trip is a story of sorts and it takes eleven months to plan. Imagine the most wonderful fantasy in the world, and each girl sharing it. And the girls are involved and the counselors play along and guide them. Mostly it's about autonomy. The girls run the show, in a way. Anyway, you know all that, probably. You want to know about the sickness?"

"Yes," I said. "But I want to know everything. Don't leave anything out."

"I'm afraid to tell you everything. It's a little involved. Not every girl is sick right there and then. Most aren't, in fact. But they have a cloud on the horizon, a bad diagnosis. In my case it is Huntington's disease. Do you know about it?"

"Not really."

"It's a genetic trait carried in the alleles. Right down in the DNA, in other words. I tell people my father died of a heart attack in a Chinese restaurant, but that's not true. He died of Huntington's when he was forty-one. The life expectancy for people with Huntington's is short. And the disease itself is a horror. Shakes, dementia, involuntary spasms. You name it."

"So that's why you wanted to know about your nightmare?"

She nodded.

"That's also why I test myself on the Latin names of things. It's a memory check," she said. "I'm not showing off when I do it."

"You don't have to tell me all this," I said. "I had no right to ask."

"Yes, you did," she said. "You do. I want you to know."

We sat and sipped our soup. She was extremely soft-spoken when she began again.

"I'm a scientist, Cobb, so I know this stuff cold. I don't have the capacity to delude myself. Not about this kind of thing. Nancy Wexler is the leading researcher on it. Long story, but she had worked in Venezuela for many years in one small village where the incidence of Huntington's is astonishingly high. The kicker, of course, is that she has the genetic profile herself. I read about her years ago and I am her number-one fan. Partially due to her work, they have a test for it now. Go in, give some blood, and you know the future. The irony is, Nancy Wexler has steadfastly refused to take it."

"Why not?"

"She doesn't want to know. It's the old question: if you could know the day of your death, would you want to know it? One day she will either manifest or she won't. Until then, she will not give the disease a place in her life. Those are her words."

"But if she took the test and found out she didn't carry it . . ."

"She carries it. I carry it. I have already arranged things so I can't have children. That's something you should know, even though I understand it is way too early to talk about any of this. And I'm sorry I got caught in a fantasy the other night talking about children and Annie and John. Sending them up to Maine to fish, I mean. I forget sometimes or I get swept up in things."

"When you say you carry it, though, that doesn't mean it is manifesting?"

"No, not yet. Maybe never."

"And you don't want the test?"

She shook her head. She turned so she could look directly into my eyes.

"If I have it, if I begin to manifest, then my life will be significantly shortened. The end will not be pretty. One thing Darwin taught us is that adult-onset diseases are of no consequence to human DNA. Once we finish our biological breeding period, nature is pretty much done with us. Our bodies fight like hell to get to sexual maturity, but our DNA code has little interest in adult disease. At that point we are less than biologically viable. Nature doesn't much care for old-age homes."

"A chicken is an egg's way of making another egg," I said. "I saw it on your bumper."

"Is the chicken evolving, or is our DNA? We like to think it is the chicken, but evidence actually supports the DNA. This isn't supposed to be all about the science. But that's my intellectual bent."

"I still don't know why you can't take the test."

"I don't want to lead my life waiting for another shoe to drop. That's something I learned way back as a Chungamunga girl."

"But if you took the test and found out you were free of it? Wouldn't that be liberating?"

"The downside is too huge. What if the test comes out and I learn I won't make it to forty? Or even thirty-five? How do you go on after that? I try to live my life fully right this instant, every instant. I sleep under the stars because the stars might not be there for me for as long as the next person. In some ways, Cobb, it is a gift. A strange, powerful gift, but a gift nonetheless. I can't kid myself about having enough time, or about, well, I'll get around to it one of these days. I live with urgency. I count the days I have been alive. The only area I have found any conflict is with relationships. I am picky anyway, but most men don't want to book on a ship that might be the Titanic. There are more stable ships by far than I am."

"That isn't quite fair," I said.

"No, of course it isn't. Sometimes some bitterness slips out. But I saw my father at the end, Cobb. And, as I said, I'm a scientist. So the price I've paid for not taking the test is a reluctance to get overly involved with a man. But then you came along."

I took her hand.

"I already know I'm falling in love with you, Cobb. There, it's out in the open. I am. You are pie and I am ice cream or some other cornball thing, but it's true. John and Annie knew it. Wally saw it right away and so did the counselors. Because I may not have as much time on earth as I would like, I can say things right out. I have never felt this way before. I am mad about you. I want us to be the whole thing. Sunsets and long walks . . . all that absurd stuff. And you don't need to say a word, because I wouldn't do that to you. I wouldn't ask you to take the bet with me. Believe me, I talked this over with Wally. So let's have a gentle fling, Cobb, and then when we finish the river trip, we go our separate ways. No drama. That's just the situation."

"What if I want to take the bet with you?"

"You're sweet to say so. You almost have to say so, because you're honorable. You are. I know that already. I know you care about me. But we are away from the world. I am a Chungamunga girl here and you may be a bear after all. Do you understand me, Cobb?"

"Any of us could die tomorrow, Mary. I could turn over in the kayak."

"Of course. No guarantees for anyone. I understand that. But we both know this is a little different. If one of us had a more common disease—I don't know, pick one—and we met, that would be a factor neither of us could ignore. Sometimes I feel I have a big clock ticking in my belly, a clock like the one in the crocodile from Peter Pan."

We sat without speaking for a while. The sun disappeared and night took its place. The wind died and the fish began chasing the late insects.

"You're wrong about one thing," I said after a time. "You said you live your life fully. You said you refused the test because you didn't want to go through life with a sort of halfway approach. But isn't that exactly what you're doing? You won't fall in love because you *may* manifest this disease. Doesn't that mean you've already accommodated the disease? Given it a place in your life?"

"Maybe," she said. "I've thought of that. I said, though, that I live my life fully. I don't know morally if it is fair to ask that of anyone. I don't think it's fair to ask for a companion to assume that kind of risk."

"What if someone is willing to take the chance with you? How come you're the only one allowed to make that gamble?"

She kissed me. She held my head in her hands.

"Wally said you would say that," she said. "Now we need to forget all that. Can we, for the time being? And we need to go for a swim, and then will you make love to me? Out here, under the stars. Please."

Skin, and darkness, and the sleeping bags high over our shoulders, so that we might have been trappers from years ago, or Native Americans, our bodies joined under buffalo robes, bright cold air falling on us, the wind soft and pleasant, no bugs, no noise, just the heat of two bodies moving together over and over, each movement met by another movement, entertained, then dropped, begun again. It was not awkward. To my amazement, it felt as though we had always been together, that our bodies had learned of each other long ago, and she gave herself to me, took from me, and we kissed through everything, our mouths breaking apart only to whisper. We said we loved each other, and we amended it, said it was crazy to say that, but we said it again anyway, kissing, our bodies joined at the waist, her body yielding to mine.

The world was somewhere else. The only world that mattered existed under the sleeping bags, but then, after a time, we pushed them down and we lay in the dark night with nothing but air around us. Stars above us, a loon calling. Then it grew and became something bolder, older, two animals, and we lost each other for a second, concentrated on our own pleasure, only to reunite and discover each other again. Her wet hair dripped from time to time on my chest.

"There?" she whispered sometimes. Or "like that?"

And to her, "Yes? Better? More?"

Always kissing. Then a wind pushed the leaves of the trees back and summer ended on that one wind, and fall was irrevocably here, and she climbed on me, the most beautiful woman I had ever seen, the most sensuous, and she bent to kiss me, then she raised up, and it became primitive and sweet, and she leaned down and whispered to me that now, now, and I did, and she kissed me until I could not bear it any longer. She kissed me until she lowered her body against mine and we hung together, man and woman, betrothed in a way we could not say even to ourselves.

GEESE FLEW OVER NOT long afterward. We could not see them, but they called with longing, moving south, their bodies sensing the earth's magnetic fields, the stars guiding them.

"IT SMELLS LIKE SNOW," Mary whispered.

It was late. Her head rested on my chest.

"Do you like snow?" I asked.

She nodded.

"I have a fireplace," I said. "At the school. The insurance companies complain about it, but the school argued for quality of life. The maintenance people bring wood from the grounds and I have a fire at the least provocation. I make up reasons to have fires."

"Yes," she said. "You should."

"Are you okay?"

She kissed my chest.

"I'm suddenly hungrier than I have ever been in my life."

"Do you know what you want?"

"Crackers and peanut butter," she said. "I can find them. I know right where they are."

She disappeared and started rummaging around in her pack, which she had to lower from the tree where it hung. I jumped up and made a container of cherry water. We met back in our burrow at about the same instant.

"Perfect," she said.

She unscrewed the cap of the peanut butter. Then she held up her knife.

"Do you know what this is?" she asked.

"A knife," I said.

"You disappoint me, Cobb," she said, fun in her voice. "This is an everything-knife. Look at it and realize that your own feeble knife is ruled by this knife."

"Let me see it."

It was a Boy Scout knife with a bone-faced handle, the body as wide as a hot dog bun. I hadn't seen a knife like it in years. It contained two or three dozen blades of various kinds—screwdriver, knife, fork, spoon, awl, corkscrew, magnifying glass, and so forth.

"My theory is," she said, taking the knife back and smearing peanut butter on a bunch of crackers, "that everything-knives live lives of their own. You cannot own an everything-knife. It will eventually leave your possession somehow."

"Someone will steal it?"

"Sometimes," she said, doctoring the crackers. "Or borrow it and forget to give it back. Now, is that the person or the knife living its fate?"

"You tell me," I said.

She stuffed a peanut butter cracker in each of our mouths.

It was delicious.

"I'm pretty sure," she said when she stopped chewing, "that a limited number exist in the world. I look for them at yard sales and pawnshops. That's another old-lady thing I do, by the way. Yard sales."

She put another cracker in each of our mouths.

"Why don't you eat your crackers in a spiral?" I asked when I could.

"No," she said. "Don't try to hang me up on eating techniques. We both know crackers have to be eaten pretty much in one bite or they will crumble all over."

"How many everything-knives have you come across?" I asked, handing her the cherry drink.

"Seven so far. I give them as gifts. I gave one to Wally, as a matter of fact."

"And you think they rule over other knives?"

"Other penknives," she said. "They are the kings and queens of penknives."

"I see what you're saying."

After we had eaten two more, she asked, "Do you want more crackers?"

"I think I'm good."

She twirled the top back on the peanut butter. Then she darted down to the water, cleaned the knife, darted back to her backpack, stored everything, yanked it back up the tree, and jumped back into our bundle of sleeping bags.

"Holy mackerel," she said, shivering a little. "It's chilly."

"You're beautiful," I said. "Just now, running around like a nut, you were beautiful."

"I'm happy," she said.

"So am I."

Then we began kissing again, at first laughing about the peanut butter taste. Then we kissed more. We became a long, joined thing, a braided rope, a garden hose twirled on a fresh flower bed. From deep down we rose to each other, linked. It became strong, then quiet, then strong once more. We pushed the sleeping bags off us again. For a while we used each other, then returned and kissed, and then we finished like a pot being slowly lifted off a burner.

"THEY WANT US TO marry," she said just on the edge of sleep, her body spooned into mine, her face toward the lake.

"Who does?"

"The girls. They are putting on a sort of play but mostly they want to put on a marriage. A fairy wedding, they say. They want us to be the bride and groom."

"Count me in," I said.

"It would just be a game, sort of. Just a fantasy. You don't have to agree to it if you think it's too weird."

"No," I said. "Not weird."

"It gives them a special focus. That's all. They get to plan a wedding."

"Girls have such cooties," I said.

"We do, actually," she said.

We fell asleep. It was warm under the sleeping bag but cold outside. Mary pulled on her Mad Bomber hat sometime in the night. I tucked closer to her and lifted a portion of the sleeping bag over my head. I couldn't know for certain, but the temperature seemed to have gone well below freezing.

"Do you pray?" she whispered when we woke in the middle of the night.

"No," I said. "Do you?"

"No," she said. "Except sometimes I pray that one day I could pray."

"To have magic words?"

She nodded.

At sunrise she slipped away and rejoined the Chungamunga girls.

My calculation went like this:

My breakfast: *powdered eggs, ramen noodles, a 3 Musketeers bar, oatmeal.*

Wally's breakfast?

*Cinnamon buns, eggs, home fries, coffee, juice.*

I did a quick camp cleanup, left the main articles where they were, stored the sleeping bags in the tent, and climbed in my kayak.

The morning sun had just cleared the pine; mist ran along the first rays as the light cleaved into the water's surface. I paddled quietly. To my right, my west, a solitary moose stood in a small cove, its head and neck dripping from where it had ducked its mouth to feed. It looked like an adolescent, gangly and unable to manage its body, but it ate with big slurping gobbles that produced the only sound in the area.

I lifted my paddle and drifted. I sat for a while and watched it eat. A long time ago a biology professor told me when witnessing an animal for identification one should take note of the creature from the head to foot, remarking anything that seemed distinctive, but that seemed a terribly dry way to go about things, an approach that missed whatever was essential about a moose. What I would have preferred was to climb out of my kayak and stand beside the moose, to bend down with it and try a mouthful of water celery, to lift my shaggy head up into the morning sunlight and chew contentedly. That was moose.

I paddled slowly away. The moose continued to eat.

When I rounded the next arm of the lake I heard the girls. Their voices carried everywhere. It was a bright, cheerful sound on a wonderful September morning. As I paddled closer I saw Wally standing knee deep in the water. She was in the middle of washing her face and hands.

"Survived the night, I see," Wally said when I landed the kayak and climbed out.

"Appears I did."

"So did your friend," she said. "Positively glowing, as they say in novels."

I felt a blush pass quickly over my cheeks. Wally laughed.

"Well, looks like you'll be working for your breakfast," Wally said. "Today is picture day in addition to being about twenty other things. By popular vote, you have become the camp photographer."

"You took no vote, Wally," I said. "I know your tricks."

"You're right. You were sacrificed. That might be the better word."

"I refuse to work without coffee," I said. "Union rules."

"We could probably manage coffee," she said. "And Mary should be somewhere around preparing another crow outing."

"Then I came to the right place," I said.

Wally looked at me.

"Yes you did," she said. "More than you know."

A half hour later, with coffee in hand, I watched the girls assemble on the beach. They dressed uniformly, either with a green sweatshirt or T-shirt depending on their tolerance for a morning chill. Khaki shorts or jeans. Most wore flip-flops. The three counselors, Tiger dominant among them, rounded the girls into a classic camp photo shoot. I expected a dozen girls to hand me cameras for their own shots, but then I remembered the injunction against electronic devices. Wally handed me a beautiful Canon digital camera and explained its workings briefly.

"You any good with these?" Wally asked when we finished the tutorial.

"No, I'm horrible."

"Well, just remember this: the difference between a professional photographer and an amateur is about a thousand exposures."

"Meaning, take plenty."

"As long as we can hold them."

"Where's Mary?" I asked.

"She went off to the crow site to prepare. I didn't know when I talked to you earlier. We'll catch up with her after the photos."

I didn't lie; I am horrible with mechanical things like cameras. But I don't have a horrible eye. While they continued to arrange the flanks of girls, I began snapping shots to become comfortable with the camera. After about ten or twenty shots, I gained a feeling for it. I also found a small tree with a branch about chest height and I steadied the camera on the branch when I shot. That worked and gave the shots better clarity. By the time Wally yelled that they were ready, that everyone had checked for a buddy to make sure we hadn't left anyone out, I felt prepared.

"Say cheese," I said.

Then a wag said, "Say Mary . . ." and she made her voice rise up in the classic taunt of the playground.

The entire group laughed and said, "Marrrrrryyyyyyy."

I smiled and snapped a dozen photos. One, I found out later, caught them all just right. Girls on the verge of adolescence, gangly moose girls, beautiful in their green shirts, young, alive, filled with joy.

"In 1937," Mary said from a position of height on a granite outcropping, "a couple from Detroit named Blanding, a society couple, crashed in a plane not far from here."

The girls, sitting in a ring around her position, looked up at her. So did I. She wore a crow headdress. Under different circumstances, it would have been over the top, but in the late morning sun we could not help but notice the rainbow colors hidden in the black of the neck feathers. The headdress followed a kind of Cleopatra look—severe and black and all business. Underneath, she wore her Chungamunga T-shirt.

"In those days loggers and logging camps filled the Maine woods, so once the Blandings realized they had survived the crash—Jeanette, the woman, had a sprained ankle and a cracked rib, and the husband, Robert, who had sustained a concussion and a broken shin bone . . . they decided they would have to wait for help. It was about this time of year and getting cold and both of them understood the danger of shock. Robert decided the best thing to do was to get a fire going, so he scouted around for wood and a proper clearing and pretty soon they had a good, warm fire not far from the beach.

"Now, you need to understand that these were society people. By that I mean they wore formal wear and they had been on their way to a costume ball at the governor's house in upstate Maine. It wasn't like today, where everyone wears a funny Halloween costume. In those days people often wore beautiful clothing and simply added a mask. The rescuers—they get rescued, so don't worry—took a photo of them when they eventually got them back to a logging camp. You can see it in an old Maine newspaper. Jeanette wore a blond gown, nearly gold, and Robert a smoking jacket with a white shirt and a black bow tie."

Mary stopped speaking for a moment. She slowly moved her eyes until she made contact with each member of the audience. Then she went on. She knew she had us.

"The Blandings could not have known it, but they had crashed in the kingdom of Madrid. There have been several raven lords in history, but for the state of Maine, Madrid was unquestionably the most clever and dominant bird ever to live in these woods. At least, that's what biologists have concluded after comparing notes. He presided over one hundred acres of forest and scrub, and his colony had grown to nearly two hundred birds. When the colony flew together, as it sometimes did, they could cause a sunny day to become dark if they passed overhead. And Madrid—who was large, with a great black beak and yellow seeking eyes—flew near the front of the pack, never in the lead. He was too smart for that.

"As soon as the sound of the crash subsided, the first scouts from Madrid's colony lighted in the trees around the plane and watched the Blandings struggle to land and safety. Instantly they reported back to Madrid. Madrid came to look for himself. You could say he came in search of food, and you would be correct, but ravens have an appetite for news, and Madrid soon took up a spot well up in a pine tree and watched the Blandings gather wood and start a fire. He stayed in the tree until nightfall, watching and studying the pair as they attempted to make themselves comfortable through the night.

"Right at sunset, Madrid saw Jeanette's diamond earrings. They were large, drop earrings, by the way, and insurance documents submitted by the Blandings later claimed that they were worth one hundred thousand dollars, which was a fortune back then and is still a great deal of money today.

"Have pity, if you can, on Madrid. We never know what will enter our heart and take up residence, but for Madrid, that moment had come. He lusted for the earrings. No, he more than lusted for them. He did not believe he would be able to survive if he did not have them in his possession. An old saying warns us about want: *want, want, want, and want will be your master,* the saying predicts. To want too much is to put yourself in danger."

Mary stopped. She gazed out at the lake. It was good theater. The morning had grown long and thin. It was the hottest part of the day.

A girl back in the crowd waited as long as she could, then shouted out, "What happened then?"

Mary shook her head as if remembering reluctantly.

"I think that's as far as the story should go," she said. "The rest is too sad."

"Tell us!" another girl said.

Mary looked at us. I realized, watching her, that I was totally head over heels for her.

She sighed. Then she continued.

"Madrid got what he wanted," Mary said after a pregnant pause. "That's the irony. We all think if we could only have this or that, get this next thing, then we will be happy. Madrid was no less foolish than we might be. For three days he waited in the tree, his eyes fixated on the earrings. The Blandings, by the way, did not fare very well. They were injured and they were hungry, and it required all of their energy to keep a fire going. It rained twice while they waited for rescue and they stood under the wing of the plane like cattle sheltering under an oak tree. Jeanette Blanding wrote about the ordeal in a chapter of a memoir called *Outside My Garden.* That's how the story became known.

"The day before a work crew of loggers found them, the Blandings decided to bathe, hoping it would lift their spirits. They stripped out of their clothes gingerly, careful not to touch their injuries. Jeanette Blanding removed her left earring. Yes, they were worth a fortune, but they were in the middle of the woods, so why should she worry? Also, their near-death experience had made material objects seem less important. A diamond is just a hard piece of carbon, after all, so why worry about it?

"Under normal circumstances, Madrid would have been shrewder. He would have waited until Jeanette's back was turned, or she had gone in swimming, but the accumulation of time and longing, the sight of the earring left exposed on the log the Blandings had dragged near the fire for a seat, was more than he could bear. Silently, he sprang from the pine branch and swooped down. A few other birds—crows mostly—had also seen the earring, and they too had begun for it. Crows and jackdaws, ravens and corvids in general . . . well, they love shiny objects more than food.

"No bird flying could match Madrid and he beat them to the earring. Jeanette Blanding described the theft as the most extraordinary thing she had experienced. She heard a whisper of wings and for a moment, just an instant, she thought an angel approached. It sounds funny now, looking back on it, but she had injuries, she was tired and filthy, and she thought perhaps death had finally found her. But no! Madrid did not even land. He swooped by, ducking low at the last second, and in one quick movement snatched the diamond earring from where it sat and carried it away.

"What joy for Madrid! Jeanette shouted at him, and Robert Blanding hurriedly threw a stone, but they were in no condition to contend with a healthy raven. Madrid flew between the pine branches, heading back to the core of his territory, but other birds continued to hector him. The smaller crows flew close to him, trying to get him to drop the earring, but he was an athletic bird and carried the earring with little difficulty.

"He landed near a deer carcass, a juicy find the colony had discovered the day before. Remember, he had not eaten or left his vigil for three days. Now he was hungry and wanted to eat, but it wasn't long before he realized his problem. If he put down the earring, someone else would have it! It was a kind of Midas bargain—he had the earring, but he could not open his mouth or put the earring down while he ate. You might think he could hide it, but you cannot hide things from crows and ravens. They watch everything and they are everywhere.

"You have figured out what happened, haven't you? Madrid could not put the earring down, and in that way the thing he loved most cost him his life. There's a lesson in that, I guess. He carried it with him for the next ten days or so, the weight of the earring getting increasingly burdensome. Naturally, he thought of various schemes to possess both the earring and eat to fill his belly, but he could not bear to risk letting the exquisite earring leave his sight for even an instant. In fact, he used whatever strength remained in him in order to fly to certain vantage points where he knew the sun would catch the diamond and cast rainbows. He was lost in the beauty of the earring. Sad, but true.

"On the last day of his life, his body weak, his throat parched from dehydration, a thousand crows and ravens gathered around him. He understood what they were after and he couldn't blame them. With his last strength, he tried to put the earring down. But by this time the small hook that attached the earring to a human's ear had dug its way into Madrid's bottom beak. He couldn't have released the earring even if he wanted to do so. The weight of the earring finally bent his head against his chest.

"When he died, he fell from the highest tree in the woods. The earring led the descent, pulling him through space and time. If you know about biology, eyes do not require energy. Even at the moment of death, they receive images, because the energy to create the images comes from outside the organism. Some scientists believe that is the meaning of the white light at the end of the tunnel people claim to see in death. The eyes are the last thing to go and light is the last thing of meaning."

Mary stopped. Tears filled her eyes.

"Would you die for beauty?" she asked us, her eyes finally settling on mine. "Was Madrid mistaken in the end to give himself entirely to one perfect thing? Or was his death a death we should all hope for? You see, when he fell, by a trick of light his feathers turned rainbow colored and he died resplendent, a great arching blur of light and blackness and color. And as soon as he landed on the ground, a dozen birds swooped down and wrestled the earring free. In my research, I have observed three ravens with earrings dangling from their beaks. It is the same earring each time—I've watched them through binoculars and taken pains to see the details of it. So I know. Jeanette Blanding's earring is still here, still in these woods. Today, at last, we are going to do something to end this phenomenon. Will you help me? Will you honor Madrid by helping his descendants?"

The girls nodded.

"Come with me, then," Mary said in a soft, quiet voice.

And she lifted a backpack onto her back and began walking into the woods.

WE FOLLOWED. THE GIRLS barely made a sound. I caught Wally's eye as we trooped by. She had already said she intended to stay back with two counselors to prepare lunch and dinner. The rangers, too, promised a visit. They had provisions and letters from home.

"If you find Mrs. Blanding's earring," she whispered, "I got dibs."

We followed a path that led to the moose carcass. The trees bent and shaded the trail, and in places the rocks and roots remained slippery despite the sunny day. Now and then I caught a glimpse of Mary, but she walked at the head of the procession while I brought up the rear. Tiger walked in the middle. The girls remained quiet. The smell of pine and fresh water pushed everywhere around us.

The crows and ravens alerted us to our proximity to the dead moose. We heard them before we saw them. Twice they made a loud ruckus, the sound twining in a narrow rope through the trees. When we were almost at the site, Mary stepped up on a boulder and put her fingers to her lips. Then she swung her backpack off her shoulder. She held up a hand and twice flexed her fingers. The girls apparently understood the signal. They sank down onto one knee and waited for instructions.

Mary pulled out a brown paper box from her backpack. Then she took out her everything-knife, slit the top, and stepped down off the boulder. She whispered something to the first girl, who, in turn, spun around and whispered it to the next girl. And the next. Each girl nodded on receiving the message. When it came to me, I understood.

Mary had about a hundred diamond earrings.

They were chandelier prisms, of course, but they resembled Mrs. Blanding's fabled earrings.

I smiled. I couldn't help it.

At another sign, the girls stood and began passing by. Mary stopped each girl, handed her four or five chandelier prisms, and whispered something. Then the next girl received her allotment, and so on. They took the prisms and disappeared around the bend. When I reached Mary, she kissed me. I put my arms around her.

"You're absolutely wonderful," I said.

"I look like Cher in this headdress."

"The girls love the story. Is it a true story?"

"All stories are true, Cobb; you should know that."

"But," I said, "aren't we going to cause more raven deaths by giving out more earrings?"

"You might think so," she said, "but ravens are very practical. This is called flooding the market. When everyone has an earring, the mystique of Mrs. Blanding's earring is reduced. No more glorious deaths by beauty."

"Ah, I see. Poor Madrid."

"Now come on. The girls need us. We have quite a little project ahead of us."

She had already been busy, because when we rounded the bend, we found a perfect maple tree, its leaves dry and yellow, decorated with white bows. The idea, as it became clear, was to achieve our own beauty. The ravens might or might not take notice, but twenty girls had a tree to decorate, and they had already started.

I don't know if Mary had given thought to the timing of the sun and the movement of the clouds, but light reached the maple tree and shot strong bolts through the prisms. Here a girl lifted a sparkling, flashing crystal to a low branch; above her another girl climbed a branch and inched her way out, a bright, glinting prism in her fingers; more girls stood back and commented, calling to each other where the crystals should go. If the crows and ravens at the moose carcass took any notice, they did not bother to fly closer to investigate.

Mary was everywhere. Touching this girl on the arm, another on the back, each exchange calm and peaceful and reassuring. After getting instructions from five or six girls at once, I hung my chandelier pieces on a branch twenty feet up. When I climbed down, Myrtle, the smallest girl in the group, stood next to the trunk. She smiled at me. She could not do much with her crystals. I realized now, standing beside her, that her body lacked proportion. Her arms and shoulders appeared too large for the rest of her. Her head, too, seemed heavy on her neck.

"Want a lift?" I asked.

She nodded.

I ducked down and let her climb onto my shoulders. When I straightened, her lightness surprised me. She couldn't have weighed more than sixty pounds. She felt lighter than a backpack.

We moved around the tree trunk until, listening to the other girls, she hung the chandelier pieces on a series of thin branches. She moved a white bow so that it would reflect onto the prisms and the prisms, in turn, would reflect on it. She asked several times if she was too heavy. I told her no. I told her to take her time.

"I don't believe Mrs. Blanding lost an earring here," she said when I put her down.

Her voice, froggy and breathy, seemed to require her concentration, as if each word, like a Scrabble tile, needed connection to the ones in front and behind it.

"Well, you never know," I said. "It's certainly a good story."

"Mary wants us to see beauty and wonder in the world. I understand."

"That's probably part of it," I said.

Myrtle watched the girls arranging the prisms.

"Mary is a pure soul," Myrtle said. "My mother is a Unitarian minister, so we talk about that stuff. We don't believe in the devil and all that sort of religious punishment, but we believe in good souls. Everyone who meets Mary senses they have come into contact with one. You know, the way animals can detect earthquakes before humans? People know they have met someone when they meet Mary."

"I agree."

"You would be lucky," she said, "to join your life with hers."

I nodded.

"Sorry," she said, "if I am speaking out of turn. I know you two just met."

"How did you get so wise at such a young age?"

She shrugged.

"My mother says everything in this world receives compensation. No one is without a gift. For every hole dug, there is earth to fill it, she says."

"That's a good philosophy."

"My compensation, for the rest of me," she said, her chin ducking down to indicate she meant her physical proportions, "is some of this understanding. That's what I am good at, I guess."

"Would you want to be a minister?"

She looked at me.

"I won't live long enough to be anything," she said matter-of-factly. "Today I am whatever I will be. My mother helped me with that, too."

"I think you're someone," I said. "I think that's why you understand Mary so well."

Myrtle smiled. She looked up at the tree. The prisms glinted everywhere, stars in a sunny day, light in autumn's quiet morning.

THE TENT. HEAT. MARY'S body under mine. The sound of water shifting in its bed, a lake moving quietly to a small tidal range. Sunset. The tent sides billowing softly, occasionally puffing with the day's last breeze.

"I LOVE MYRTLE," I said, handing Mary a glass of wine. Wally, to our surprise and delight, had passed on two bottles of red wine that the rangers had brought with them. A present, she told us. The wine had a great deal of work to do in order to complement the ready-to-eat spaghetti we had in our bowls for dinner.

We toasted. We sipped. The wine was delicious.

"Is it just that I'm hungry, or is this the best wine ever created?" Mary asked.

"It's great. A 2009 vin de Allagash."

"I love Myrtle, too," Mary said, putting down her wine and beginning on the spaghetti. "Isn't she amazing?"

"Can you talk about her condition?"

"Not on the river. Not about a Chungamunga girl."

"Got it," I said.

I ate some spaghetti. It tasted like canned spaghetti.

Mary looked at me. Her head tilted a fraction. She seemed to weigh a few considerations, then she spoke quietly.

"She'll die in her twenties," Mary said. "At least as averages go."

"Okay," I said and felt something hard and bitter in my stomach.

Mary moved her hand across the table and took mine. She met my eyes.

"Sorry," she said. "That's why we don't talk about it. Not much anyone can do."

"Except give her a magical trip down a river."

"If that's a help," she said.

"It is."

"Okay, now we're gloomy. And we shouldn't be gloomy with this lovely wine."

"Eat your spaghetti," I said to lighten the mood. "It's okay."

"It's delicious," she said, twirling more onto her fork.

"Is it?"

She laughed. She took a sip of wine.

"The wine is," she said. "Your spaghetti is appropriately filling for a kayak trip."

"I'll take that as a compliment."

We ate. The night had already settled in. We had a good fire going, its flames waist high and bright yellow. We sat at the picnic table. I felt sleepy and happy and content. I did not let my mind move to consider Myrtle's circumstances. That was for a different time.

We cleaned dishes at the edge of the lake. Then I pushed her against a large oak and we made out. We kissed a long time. Every time it became stronger, we teetered away, then returned. Her body moved with mine. We shared one tide or one current or one something.

"Will you walk me home?" she said after a while.

"I'd love to."

We piled the clean dishes on the picnic table. Then we pulled out our sleeping bags and pads from the tent and slid them onto the blue tarp. We went to the lake and brushed our teeth, washed our faces, then hurried back. Away from the fire, the night had become too cold to be comfortable.

We stood on either side of the bedding and took off our clothes. Enough light reached her so that I could see how perfect she was. I told her so. She shook her head and said I had been in the Maine woods too long. I told her she better hurry into bed, because Madrid was probably up in a tree watching.

"Warm me up," she said, sliding next to me.

"That's dangerous," I said, turning to take her in my arms. "That's a very thin line."

"I live for danger."

"I want to ask you something," I said. "You in the mood for a talk?"

"What kind of talk?"

"You, me, talk."

"It's very hard to talk when I have no clothes on next to you."

"It's just a hypothetical conversation," I said. "A bunch of what-ifs."

"Okay."

I pulled her closer. Our bodies connected down to our feet. I kissed her for a little while.

"I've been thinking. If a boy met a girl," I said, "and he really liked her, he would be a fool to let her go, right?" I asked.

"Maybe."

"And if they went on a crazy river trip, and they escaped dancing with bears, and they fell in love, then maybe they should stay together, right?"

She kissed me.

"And if a boy decided that he wanted to be with her no matter what might come, wouldn't that be enough?"

She kissed me again. Then she rolled on top of me.

"We've just met, Cobb," she said. "It's too early."

"I don't think it's too early. Neither do you."

"Love is my psychosis reaching out for your psychosis. Isn't that what the psychologists tell us?"

"You are a cynical thing."

"Okay," she said, kissing my neck, "I'm probably falling in love with you. I'm probably in love with you. I've already said so. But I am a Chungamunga girl in the end. That's just the fact. It's a fact as much as Myrtle's fact."

"I'm going to be with you," I said. "I don't care if you are a Chungamunga girl."

We kissed a little while. Then she pushed back the sleeping bags and let the air get to us. She rolled off me and put her head on her hand, her free hand tracing lines on my chest. She waited a while before she spoke.

"Okay," she said, "I've been doing some thinking, too. Here's a proposition for you. But first you have to know something."

"Okay."

"My ending, if you want to call it that, will not be pretty. I know I've mentioned that before, but it's true. If the Huntington symptoms present, as they might, then it will be grim. I'll lose my balance. I'll make strange movements and my face will make odd grimaces that I won't detect myself. You'll see it before I do. The Greeks called it *chorea,* which means dance. Not a pretty dance, I promise. And no beautiful love affair on a canoe trip will make the whole thing less grim. Do you understand me? I don't want you to see me that way. I don't want to be that way. Call it vanity, or aesthetics, but I intend to keep open the possibility of ending my life if I present symptoms."

I nodded.

"You're saying okay now, with us both here in bed, and everything just starting. But I can't have children. I can't have a natural life. It's very sweet and brave of you to say what you've just said, and

I love you for it, I do, but it's complicated. And not all of it has to do with your capacity for living with me. I may not want you to be beside me. Do you see? I may need to give up on life. I may need to end things. I may not want you near when I have to make those kinds of decisions, because it's possible I will want one more day with you, or one more week, and I will fool myself into believing it will be okay. But it won't. When I face those kinds of decisions, I don't want to be constrained by my love of you . . . or of anyone, really. In this one great thing, I intend to be entirely selfish."

"Okay," I said.

"That's too easy," she said.

"It's what I feel."

"Here's my proposition," she said, speaking carefully. "I am just putting this out there and I may revoke it, okay? Whenever I like."

"Agreed," I said. "Your rules."

"Just on this, Cobb. It has to be."

"Okay."

"When we leave this trip, I will go to Dartmouth-Hitchcock Medical Center in Hanover. I need to see my mom anyway. Then I am going to Indonesia to see my brother. That's been set up for a long time and I'll be on a tight schedule to get going. My mother can arrange to have a test taken. It's not complicated. I've always resisted it, Cobb, but this time, for you, I won't. That's my deal with you. Now you have to agree to my terms."

"Go ahead."

"I'll leave the results with my mom. I won't look at them. You can know, or not, but I don't want to know. That's your end of the bargain. Eventually, if things go against me, we'll both know. But I don't want to live with that knowledge right now. But you need it. And you need to factor it in when you consider being with me. You need all the information for that. Okay?"

I nodded.

"Do you promise?" she asked. "Because I want you to have

everything for your decision. I have no choice, but you do. Your eyes need to be wide open."

"Okay," I said. "I get it."

"If you decide to come, we can stay with my brother. He says it's beautiful there. Blue water and coral."

"Okay," I said. "Count me in."

She looked at me and studied my face.

"I don't know if you can understand completely until it happens to you," she said. "It's why I like being with these girls on this river. Maybe, given a little time, a little breathing space, you'll decide this was a great love affair but that we should leave it that way. That would be okay. I mean it. I don't put too many expectations on things. Independent of the test, so to speak. You can call this off at any time. I'm saying, no hard feelings."

"I'm going to see you in Indonesia," I said.

"I hope you do. More than anything. But it's your decision. I won't know one way or the other when you walk onto the beach there. That's your burden. And if the test says I'm clean, I don't want to know that, either. Do you understand? It may sound odd, but that's how I feel. I can't leave any space in my life for the disease. Give it even a fraction of an inch, and it will seep in and change things. I don't want to look back at my life and say, gee, I should have taken that test years ago. I lived without knowing and it would have changed everything if I knew. This way, living fully no matter what, is ingrained in me."

"Fair enough."

"I'm trying to read you," she said, her eyes intently on mine.

"What else is in Indonesia? Because I plan on visiting it, in case you haven't heard."

"Turtles," she said after studying my face once more. "My brother loves sea turtles as I love crows."

"Okay," I said. "It's decided. We both have to be back in late January, right? When school starts up again?"

She nodded. I nodded in return and tucked her closer. She reached down and pulled the covers over us. It was cold and the lake hardly made a sound.

AT DAWN FOUR GIRLS in two canoes came and paddled us back to their site. It was our wedding day. The girls did not speak. Before we boarded, Mary whispered we should play along. We sat in the middle of the two canoes like Polynesian royalty riding the surf to shore.

The entire group met us at the water's edge and I noticed immediately that the girls operated on their own—no Wally, no counselors. The girls had fashioned earrings from acorns; others wore necklaces made of maple helicopter seeds. Two girls I recognized as natural leaders stepped forward and put pine wreaths on our heads. They kissed us on both cheeks. Then they helped us out of the canoes and bound our hands—my left, her right—together with twine. The sun began to climb free of the lake.

They walked us to an arch decorated with wildflowers—black-eyed Susans, asters, late grasses. Sticks bent and twined together made up the arch. We stood beneath it when they directed us to do so. Girls pulled Mary's hair back. An older girl stepped forward. She handed us each rings made of hollowed wood. We waited until she nodded. Then I slipped the ring on Mary's finger; Mary slipped the other ring on mine. To my surprise, Mary's eyes began to tear.

The girls circled us. They pressed close. The acorns and maple helicopter necklace–accents on their cheeks and foreheads gave the moment a fairy-tale feeling. The lead girl—the one who had handed us rings—took the hands of the girls on either side of her. One by one the girls linked hands and pressed closer. They ringed the arch and walked slowly clockwise. In one voice, perfectly matched, they began to chant:

*To the wedding one, to the twoing-two*
*To the side by side, and the who loves who*
*To the family around you, and all in the room*
*To love and memory, to the bride and groom.*

*Remember us, remembering you*
*Remember time, remember new*
*Remember now, remember then*
*Remember how, remember when.*

When they finished, they led us back to the canoes. A half hour had passed, not more. The girl who served as a priestess dipped her hand in the lake and dripped a thin stream on both of our heads. She said we were married by this water and we were eternal on this river. Then they cut the twine that bound us and returned us to our campsite.

# 8

A COLD FRONT MOVED IN LATER THAT day, and we truly pushed for the first time through Eagle Lake, Round Pond, Churchill Lake, Heron Lake. I knew what waited. All the water, all moving north, drew to a tight waist at the Chase Rapids, a nine mile stretch of Class IV white water and rips. The cold weather prodded us and the water drew us, and at midmorning the day after we left the Chungamunga girls, we handed our camping gear to a ranger named Dave, who promised to ferry it to a spot beneath the rapids where we could repack our boats and continue. Dave was a large, heavy fellow, with a melon head and wonderful smile. He stowed everything in the back of his pickup and tipped his fingers in a salute as he drove away. We were alone. The water below Chase Dam churned like smoke going through a narrow opening.

"Nine miles of rapids," I said to Mary as Dave pulled away.

I couldn't take my eyes off the water.

"This is the juice," she said, bent over and fiddling with her kayak. "You can do it. All those Chungamunga girls will do it."

"But they're eternal on the river. I'm just a schoolteacher."

"Did I tell you about the dinosaur they had around here?"

"Not yet," I said.

"It was called a whimp-o-saurus."

"Are you calling me a whimp-o-saurus?"

"Would I do a thing like that?"

I kissed her. Then I checked the temperature on my small thermometer. Thirty-nine degrees. The water, I imagined, was warmer than the air.

It took us a few minutes to prepare. We climbed into our spray skirts, then tightened our life jackets. Mary dragged her kayak to the water's edge first. I took a quick inventory of my nervousness. I didn't expect to die, I realized, but if I went over, if either of us went over, it would be a problem. The boats would float away, the paddles would disappear, and we would end up wet and afoot, with sixty miles to go. Hypothermia was a genuine concern. You could not be wet and cold in thirty-nine-degree weather and expect to survive for long. One way or the other, we needed to make it nine miles to our gear. Otherwise, we would be in a mess.

At the same time, I watched Mary. She could not have been happier. She had already climbed in her kayak, ready to go. The water lathered a few feet from the bow of her kayak. One shove and she would be in it and paddling to survive. She turned and looked at me, and I realized that I loved her, that she was the woman for me, that I could stay beside her without conscious effort, without any effort whatsoever, that we were a cliché, a pair of geese mating for life, and we would stay together through everything; there was no turning back, not an inch, and she made me happy by her joy.

"In days of old, when knights were bold," I said.

"See you at the other end," she said.

"I'll be right behind you."

"Remember," she said, repeating what Dave had told us about the initial wild section directly below the put-in. "Right, right, left, right, then two lefts."

"Got it."

"Big rocks," she said.

"We'll make it."

I kissed her. Then she shoved her hips forward and the water took her. She made a crazy whoop as she instantly took on speed. She disappeared an instant later, the white water waves sealing her from me.

I scrambled into my kayak. I told myself not to think. *Just be,* I said to myself. *Just paddle.* I fitted my spray skirt around the gasket of my Walden kayak, then shoved forward. The water snapped against my bow, then it dragged me into the current and the water became everything.

MY FIRST FEELING WAS the sensation one gets at the top of the roller coaster when the car begins to click softly past the apex and starts downward. I *knew* something big was about to happen, could feel it in the little survival nerves at the base of my neck, but I also felt a giddy anticipation. What next? What would happen? In an instant the knowledge came to me, the settled, almost contented sensation in my gut that I was meeting something over which I had no control, no power, except to paddle like crazy, to lean on my paddle like a rudder, and to keep my eyes forward.

*Go,* I said to myself.

And suddenly it was okay.

I was no longer afraid, or nervous, and I leaned forward in my boat and, of all things, a sort of Native-American war chant arranged itself inside my skull. During my undergraduate years I had spent a summer on the Crow Reservation in southeast Montana, a land of rolling hills, rattlesnakes, golden trout, and clouds. Twice I had spent days beside a drumming party, listening to their rhythms, and now the rhythm came back to me. It goosed me. I began attacking the river, challenging it, and the first rock passed on my right, another on my right, then the kayak dipped down and shot its bow into something dark green. A wave broke over me, sloshed around my waist, then the kayak pulled back up, and I let the chant grow louder in my head. Another rock, this time on my left, and now the waves frothed around me and I could see next to nothing, water water everywhere, and I dug at the surface with my paddle, but my speed made paddling absurd.

I switched the paddle back to a rudder, tucked it against the gunwale of the boat, went right, left, then left again. The river shot me forward and I felt a rock click under my bottom, then another, and for a second, an instant, the boat hung on the rock, friction temporarily more powerful than the white surge all around me, and I dangled. I started to spin slowly, the rock forming a pivot point underneath me, and I knew if I turned broadside I would go over. I reached down and shot my left hand onto the rock, jumped with my body like a man pulling a chair closer to table, and the kayak caught more water and yanked me free. Free. Then a wave hit me straight up, sluicing around my body, and I felt good, alive, happy.

*Go, go, go,* I said to myself, and I paddled, then shifted the paddle to a rudder again, and suddenly the water calmed. Just a little. But I had a second to look around, the river now running through a ravine, and everything was in order. I had made the roughest run, one mile down, eight to go, and let my heart lift a little. Then the water turned white again and I dashed into a wall of waves and rocks, and a boulder scraped me on the port side, another slid under my decking, and then, up ahead, I saw Mary.

She had capsized. Her kayak was gone. Her paddle was gone. She stood in the center of the river, clinging to a rock, obviously trying to figure her next move. She could not walk in the force of the waves. Before I could reach her she came to the same realization, and so she let herself go, feet downstream, and put her weight back in her life jacket. A second later she disappeared. The water took her ahead and I followed, more to her right than behind her, and I told myself to think quickly. But the river prevented any realistic plan.

This wasn't an action-adventure movie. I could not paddle down and swing her onto my kayak. She was on her own.

After another hundred yards, the water calmed. I spotted her near the left bank. She had managed to cut across, scrambling and kicking. I leaned hard on my paddle and sliced across the current as much as I could. I couldn't stop.

"Are you okay?" I yelled.

She nodded. She looked miserable.

"Keep going," she shouted. "Look for my kayak."

"Meet me," I said, but I wasn't sure how or where she should meet me.

At the equipment, I supposed. Somewhere down the river.

Then I was back in the current and the water took me. But the fury of the water had lessened. The great tumbling waves now rose only a little from the surface. The strength and force generated directly below Chase Dam had dissipated. Class IV had gone to Class II. I had run rivers of this calibration before.

I found her paddle first. It swirled in an eddy near the left shore. To my surprise, it was a simple matter to retrieve. I paddled close to it, bent over my left gunwale, and scooped it up. I secured it to the paddle fastener near my cockpit. One thing down. I didn't dare let myself dwell on Mary's circumstances. Nothing I could do would help or hinder her. She had made it to shore. Now she had to bushwhack downstream to catch up to me.

I went two more miles, I estimated, before I saw her kayak. It had flipped and now stood bowed around a rock. I could not tell if it had sustained any damage. It clung nearly in the middle of the stream, and I realized I had one crack at it. Its bottom faced upriver; its cockpit probably held it pinned to the rock. I made a quick calculation. The bottom gave me nothing to use as a handhold. I could risk passing by and trying to grab the handle on the bow, but that was like hoping to grab the brass ring on a tilting, powerful merry-go-round. I decided the only chance I had was to ram the boat, somehow knocking it less horizontal to the stream and releasing it from its precarious position on the rocks. I hoped, too, that I could do it while still remaining upright in my own boat. I didn't have time to come up with a second or third plan. I aimed my kayak toward the right-hand third of Mary's boat, and rammed it as hard as I could.

The shock knocked me backward and nearly scuttled me. But I felt Mary's kayak shudder and move, and before I slid by, her kayak tumbled free. It rode on its side, its core filled with water, but it remained sufficiently buoyant to move downriver.

I paddled hard to get ahead of it, and at the next slack water I jammed my kayak onto the shore and waded back to midstream. A few seconds later Mary's kayak came slowly toward me. It hit me square in the chest, and I felt as if I had entered one of those old circus acts where a man catches a cannonball in his gut. But I stayed on my feet and managed to grab the stern handle. Water filled the boat and made it as heavy as a dead body.

I pulled it back to shore, each step a little tightrope walk, with the force of the river on me and the boat tugging at my arm. When I finally secured footing a few feet from shore, I rolled the kayak onto its stomach and let the water drain. Then I muscled the kayak onto the low shore. It sat next to mine, apparently still intact.

I climbed onto the shore and took a seat against a pine. I tried to catch my breath. I had almost managed it when I began to shiver.

IT'S IN ALL THE books on outdoor recreation.

Hypothermia. The lowering of the core body temperature. Chills. Then an odd desire to remove one's clothes. Then a hot flash. Then trembling like Saint Vitus' dance. Then stupor and lethargy and death.

I shivered against the tree trunk. It wasn't a small shiver. It came from down in my center, a nervous, tingling shiver that was so powerful it was nearly enjoyable. Or not enjoyable exactly, but profound, and interesting, a biological fact about one's self that you did not have to consider often. I let my mind roll it around so that I could understand the phenomenon. The fire in the stove, I realized, had gone down to embers.

And Mary?

She had no options. She had to bushwhack along the shoreline as best she could. Eventually, if we were lucky, we would reunite. If we both thought alike. If we both stuck to a plan. But we had no plan, I reminded myself. Then I thought of Mike Tyson's famous line: *"Everyone has a plan until they get punched in the mouth."*

I stood and began doing jumping jacks.

*Move,* I told myself. Water had saturated everything I wore. I tried to remember if survival guides suggested you take off wet clothes, wring them out, then put them back on. Or was it better to keep them on, no matter how wet, in order to keep every calorie of body temperature in place?

Ten jumping jacks. Twenty. My legs felt heavy and wooden.

Somewhere after my twentieth jumping jack I thought of matches. A fire. But before the thought formed fully in my mind, I realized the matches waited with the other gear where Dave the ranger had deposited it. A miscalculation, for sure. Always have matches. Have a magnesium bar and flint. Have a source of fire-making.

When I finished the jumping jacks, I felt somewhat warmer. I glanced at the thermometer on my jacket. Thirty-four. The river, I thought, would turn to a blade of ice if the temperature dropped two more degrees. In time, I reminded myself. Not for a long time yet.

I busied myself arranging the kayaks. That I could do. My mind worked in simple, blocky thoughts. Do kayaks. Empty water.

Arrange and have ready. The longer thoughts—about what I would do if Mary did not show up soon, if she were lost, or injured, or too exhausted to continue—proved too complicated to tackle. One thing at a time, I told myself.

When I finished with the kayaks, I did another twenty jumping jacks.

"Cobb?" someone said.

I turned. It was Mary, of course, but the slowness of my brain had not connected the sound of her voice to her appearance. *Mary,* I thought dumbly. *Oh, yes.*

She limped toward me. She had been crying.

"Are you okay?" I asked.

"Fine," she said.

"Are you sure? How bad is your leg?"

"It's my hip," she said. "I either hit it on a rock or I wrenched it. I'm not sure."

I took her in my arms. She shivered violently.

"Mrs. Blanding," I said, "it's good to see you."

She didn't say anything for a moment. She put her cheek against my chest.

"I'm freezing," she said eventually.

"We have to go," I said. "We have to run the last of it."

"I can't," she said.

"You have to, Mary."

"I'm afraid I'll tip again."

"No you won't. It's easier now," I said. "The river is half of what it was."

"I want to walk," she said and moved away from me.

"It's five miles at least," I said. "We can be there in minutes by kayak."

She looked at the kayaks. Then she looked at the river.

"My balance," she said. "I've never tipped over before."

Through my cold brain, I understood her fear. Huntington's.

Loss of balance. Though we had not known each other long, I had never seen her show a moment's lack of confidence.

"We'll make it, I promise," I said.

She looked at me. Then she nodded.

THE RIVER DID NOT let us go easily. For the first mile the water churned in a regular, predictable manner. But near what I guessed to be the halfway point of the entire rapids, the riverbed dropped from under us and we found ourselves in rough water. Big rocks. Mary followed me. I navigated the best line I could, but I could only guess how she fared behind me. The rule was that if either of us tipped, we would not stop until we reached the gear. Whoever made it first had to get a fire going no matter what. Without fire, both of us would die.

After the patch of deep water, the river slowed. In fact it became shallow enough so that we scraped bottom several times. Finally Mary paddled up to me and yelled that the gear drop was around the next bend. We both angled to the left-hand bank. A small bridge had once spanned the river there. Our gear sat on the left-hand abutment, stacked there neatly by Dave.

I let out a whoop.

Mary didn't say anything.

We scrambled onto shore and yanked our boats up behind us. It felt good to be out of the water. The paddling had warmed me a little, and I felt more confident by the minute. Mary, on the other hand, seemed quiet and slightly lethargic. I told her to start gathering wood. I told her we needed a fire.

She followed my lead, but she moved slowly. I found a bunch of dry pine twigs on a dead tree and bundled them together. I ripped part of the Allagash map into small pieces and put a match to it. In no time, with the dry pine fueling it, we had a small, sturdy flame. Mary dragged back a couple pieces of birch. We peeled the bark and added it to the fire. The fire dipped down, then grabbed the wood and became more aggressive. We fed it slowly, careful not to overload it.

When I was certain the fire would not die, I grabbed Mary and hugged her.

"It's okay," I said. "We made it. We're okay."

She nodded against my chest.

"We need to make some tea and get something warm in our systems," I said. "You can see our breath. And we need a big, strong fire. You sit here next to this and keep it fed. I'll get more wood."

She nodded again.

"Come on," I said. "We have to rally."

I put her next to the fire. Then I scouted the area for wood. It was not a regular campsite, so no one had picked over the immediate forest surrounding us. In no time I had a decent pile of tinder. I told Mary to add as much as she liked. I didn't wait for an answer. I bustled around until I found two dry logs to serve as firedogs on either side of the flames. I topped the firedogs with four or five stout legs of maple. The fire began to throw heat.

"Better?" I asked, squatting beside her.

She didn't answer.

I spread the tarp, slipped the sleeping pads and bags from the pile of gear, and set up a bed. Then I grabbed Mary by the hands, hoisted her onto her feet, and began to strip her. She moved dully. Lifting her hands to let me pull her shirt over her head seemed difficult for her. Little by little, I undressed her. I made her climb into the sleeping bag while I added as much wood as I could find. Then I hurried back, stripped out of my own clothes, and climbed into the sleeping bag with her.

I held her face-to-face. I held her as tightly as I could. She shivered in enormous bolts of energy. I could not determine if her lethargy came from the cold or depression over losing her balance. But it didn't matter. She had to warm up and I spent a half hour rubbing her body, keeping her close to me. I kissed her neck and lips to force her body to respond with heat. Eventually she pushed farther into me, the frozen marrow of her body melting slowly into mine.

She fell asleep. Or I did. When I woke, she had turned over so that I spooned her. Her face pointed toward the fire. It was dark. The fire gave the only light in the entire forest.

"What I won't know," she said quietly when she felt me come awake, "what I will never know is if any little stumble is just an accident or the beginning of the disease making itself known."

"Shhhh," I said.

"I've run these rapids twenty times," she said. "Never went over."

"Law of averages."

"Maybe," she said. "Or maybe the first knock."

"You're not usually so gloomy," I said.

She shrugged. She might have been crying.

I pulled her closer to me. I kissed her ear.

"You have to get up and put on more wood," I said.

She elbowed me a little.

"You," she said.

"Rocks paper scissors?"

"This is not gallant on your part."

"Warm here," I said. "Cold there."

But then she turned to me and began kissing me. It was a wild, crazy kiss. She had been crying, I understood, but that was passing. She kissed me again and again, and eventually she took me and I responded, and we made love violently, quickly, so that the world resolved into this small cocoon beneath our sleeping bags.

When she finished, she kissed me long and gently. The stars had come out and the river chased their reflections northward.

WAKING BESIDE HER. THE call of a robin mixed with the *birdie, birdie, birdie* of a cardinal. The river running and sipping at the banks. Frost on the tarp beside me. Frost on the sleeping bags and underneath it Mary, all Mary, the shape of her body a bracket to fit mine. A kingfisher diving and missing, diving again, diving a third time and coming up with a chub held crosswise in its bill, a silver strand of protein and sustenance for another day. Then Mary turning, still asleep, her hand finding mine under the bedclothes, her fingers twining in mine. A late mosquito, nearly impossible in the frost, buzzing lazily through a band of sunlight. For one shimmering moment a ruby-throated hummingbird hovering near the bed, inspecting us, moving onward. The light finally finding Mary's hair and combing it slowly, light and shadow, leaves dancing on her skin.

We heard the falls an hour before sunset. The sound of cascading water bounced off the trees and spilled upriver to us. It sounded like wind, or trucks running down a distant highway on a summer night. The river gradually pinched and two signs, both dangling on chains across the current, warned us that the Allagash Falls, forty feet high, should be portaged on the right. *Warning,* it said. *Last Warning,* the second one said.

"This is the rally point for the Chungamunga girls," Mary said loudly so that I could hear her over the river. "We take up all three campsites and we do our final nights here. Sometimes alumnae join us."

I nodded and followed her to the right-hand side of the river. The water sounds grew louder. She beached her kayak on a small turnout and jumped out. I climbed out after her, aware of the water beginning to pull and speed toward the funnel of the falls. We dragged our kayaks out of the water. Our spray skirts dangled from our waists.

"This is where Bunny lives," she said, her face excited. "There has been a rabbit here for twenty years or more. Bunny has greeted every Chungamunga trip since I don't know when."

"And it talks to you?"

She gave me a look. I was beginning to know that look.

"You're a wisenheimer," she said.

"Does Bunny serve cocktails?"

"Bunny doesn't, but I might if you're good. We have another bottle of wine, you know? I was saving it for snakebite."

"Good precaution. And Bunny could turn rabid."

"You'll see," she said. "It really is uncanny."

"Everything about you is uncanny," I said.

I kissed her hard. Her lips tasted of salt and the sun still made her skin warm. She stayed in my arms.

"We should get camp set up," she said after a little.

But we didn't. We kept kissing. I pushed her back against a tree and kissed her more. It felt cloddish and stupid to wear our spray skirts, but I didn't care. I wanted her, wanted every inch of her. I felt her push into me and hold me. When we finally broke apart, she took one step back, then nearly dove at me and began kissing me again.

"Always like this, always like this," she whispered, kissing me like a crazy woman.

I lifted her and carried her, and on the picnic table at the first campsite we took each other. We made love with the trees gathering darkness and the sound of pounding water crushing rocks for a million years. We were soft and then violent, then somewhere in between, somewhere deeper, and we did not quit kissing for more than a second. Kissing was everything, was much more than the rest of our bodies, and I felt myself joining her, our bodies no longer separate, our mouths tasting and pulling the other, who was no longer an other, into our throats and souls and mouths.

And then for a long time we stayed together, our bodies connected as men and women have connected for as long as the water went against rocks, and we kissed until I could not stop telling her I loved her. We kissed and the stars came out and the darkness filled in all the space between the trees and nothing in the world mattered, nothing but us. Softly, gently, we kissed until each kiss became a surprise, became an old thing brought out and discovered to be more valuable than one could have dreamed possible, and I told her I loved her, that I had never known love like this, that I wanted her body and her laughter and her heart. And she said words back to me, all the words one wants to hear, dreams of hearing, and we kissed until whatever force in me could no longer remain my own. She kissed my ear and whispered that she loved me, always this, always this, always this.

BUNNY VISITED AFTER DINNER.

She was a long, rangy cottontail, gray as wedding trousers, and much less timid than one would expect a magical rabbit to be. Mary saw her first. The rabbit came out of the woods from the upriver side, and for a time she did not move closer. We had a fire going, the tent erected, our kayaks pulled up to the foot of our site. Mary had been on the lookout. Bunny, from the way she explained it, meant nearly as much as a symbol to the Chungamunga girls as a bear.

"Why's that?" I asked, my voice low once she pointed out Bunny's shape in the near darkness.

"You ask too many questions," she whispered, fishing out a piece of bread from our mess kit. "A rabbit is fertility and a rabbit lives on its wit and speed."

"And on handouts, apparently."

"We always feed Bunny."

"'All the thoughts of turtle are turtles, and of a rabbit, rabbits.'"

"Who said it?"

"It's my one Emerson quote. Mentor to Thoreau."

"Pretty good," she said and waved the bread at Bunny.

She broke up pieces and put them halfway between us and Bunny.

"It's possible a Chungamunga girl once turned herself into a rabbit," she whispered again. "To escape her destiny. She was given a choice to remain human and live through her illness, or she could eat a few magical berries and turn herself into a rabbit."

"Tough choice," I said. "What kind of berries, exactly?"

"Blueberries."

"High bush or low bush?"

"You can have no more wine," she said, moving my glass to the center of the table.

"Did the girl have a name?" I asked, retrieving the glass.

"Bunny, of course."

"So Bunny is both a bunny, and a Bunny?"

She nodded.

"Clear as glass," I said.

Bunny hopped forward. It seemed evident to me that Bunny had been trained over the course of the summer to come to the campsite for handouts. It moved in the cautious way of rabbits—front legs pushing forward in a sort of prayerful shrug, then the meaty back legs following. Bunny's haunches rolled full and muscled under her fur. Her nose twitched and her ears rotated to pick up sound. She ate a piece of bread, then hopped back to the forest line.

"The girls will love this," Mary said.

"Can the spell be reversed? Can Bunny become a girl again?"

Mary thought about it for a moment. Then she answered quietly.

"Yes, if she goes over the falls," she said. "She has to believe she will be a girl again and surrender herself to the falls. That's why she remains here."

"Eternal on the water," I said.

She nodded.

"Can anything harm her?" I asked.

"Yes," she said. "She's a rabbit. Everything wants to kill a rabbit. Owls and snakes and foxes and cats. To be a rabbit is to be food. That's why we are sworn to be kind to Bunny. She will not be harmed when the Chungamunga girls assemble. No other animal would risk it."

"So she can rest."

"And listen. And remember what it is to be a girl once more."

I nodded.

We watched Bunny until she blended back into the forest. Then Mary took my hand and walked me down the portage trail toward the falls. The sound increased and tucked itself everywhere. It was difficult to imagine not hearing the water on rocks, the graveled churning that made all other sound secondary. At a small turnout, Mary led me onto a slab of granite where we could survey the falls above and below us. The water passed like black rope, then exploded in a knot of white, then became rope again. Air pushed forward with the water and made the night colder.

"The end of the waterway is just a few more miles," Mary said. "The Allagash joins the Saint John River."

"Have you ever run the Saint John?"

"No, I'm an Allagash girl, I'm afraid. I like its wildness."

"A one-river girl."

"Be careful," she said, taking my hand and moving me a little. "There's usually poison ivy around here."

"Now you tell me."

She stared out at the river. It was big and hungry there. Paw prints of swirls rolled down the river beneath the rapids. I looked to see if there was any possibility of running the falls, but I couldn't see clearly enough. It wasn't anything I wanted to attempt, in any case.

Mary spoke quietly: "You don't think that we might finish the river and then look at this whole thing and think it was crazy, do you?"

I turned her and took her in my arms.

"It is crazy," I said.

"I mean, you know, like love at summer camp. But when we get back to regular life, this will all seem like a pretty dream."

"I've been dreaming about you for a long time," I said.

"I mean it," she said.

"I don't know, sweetheart."

"You just called me sweetheart," she said and bumped me with her hip.

"How does anyone meet? At a bar? Through friends? I mean, you have to admit we have a lot in common. We're teachers, we like kayaking, we like the outdoors. You're a lousy cook and I'm pretty good. We have the same color kayaks and we both drive Toyota Tacomas. You like crows; I like Thoreau. We both live in New Hampshire. Should I keep going?"

"Yes, keep going."

"We make love like something—"

"Like snails," she said, kissing me, smiling as she did it. "Snails hang together by a transparent thread suspended from a flower on a summer night. They are the world's homeliest animal and they have the world's most beautiful mating ritual."

"Okay, like snails," I agreed. "And you're the perfect height for me, and your body fits mine, and we are standing beside a waterfall in the middle of Maine and we're in love. So that's that."

"You left out knock-knock jokes."

"Purposely."

"Let's go to bed."

"Are you asking as Mary or as a snail?"

"Both."

"Now that I have poison ivy."

"The Indians used to eat poison ivy a little at a time so they would become immune to it," she said and took my hand to lead me back.

"Bunny can eat poison ivy, I bet."

"Come to bed," she said.

We walked back quietly. We had almost reached the campsite when a black bear crossed the path. It crossed perpendicular to us, its body entirely relaxed, its face turned to us in a casual glance. Its withers came to waist height. We stopped. The bear disappeared. A second later we heard it running and crashing up through the woods.

One final branch gave a loud snap; then the woods became silent again. Mary grabbed me and kissed me hard, her body clinging to mine. When a mosquito buzzed my ear, we both reached to brush it away, our hands touching, then locking. I pushed her arm behind her back and pulled her into me. "A bear," I whispered.

THE CHUNGAMUNGA GIRLS DROWNED out the sound of the falls. It hardly seemed possible. But Mary and I heard them in the late morning three days after we had arrived. They poured down the river, a dozen or more green canoes, a few female rangers with them. The rangers helped through the rapids, I knew, and they made sure the girls hit the portage correctly. But the girls had run the Chase Rapids on their own, and they yelled and screamed and shouted from boat to boat as they came. One of them splashed water at another canoe, and the second canoe answered back, and far behind them Wally lifted her paddle like a referee signaling a touchdown. The three counselors—Tiger, Jill, and Doris—rode in the middle of the flotilla. They wore bandannas over their hair, and a bunch of the girls had copied them and wore bandannas also. I spotted Myrtle in a canoe with Tiger. Myrtle sat in the middle without a paddle. A girl I didn't recognize paddled the bow.

"I don't even have your phone number," Mary said sideways, both of us watching the girls flutter down the last hundred yards. A ranger—a tall, thin woman in khaki—had pulled her canoe sideways and blocked off any approach to the falls. She pointed the boats to the right bank.

I had my kayak packed. With the girls'arrival, I would have to move to the next campsite anyway, but I had decided to push for the town of Allagash, where my truck waited. Mary wanted to spend the last few nights with the Chungamunga girls.

"I wrote it down. I left you a note. I left all my information."

"Where?"

"In your kayak. It was supposed to be a surprise."

"It is," she said and took my hand.

But then, chaos. The first girls hit the shore and climbed out of their canoes, their voices rising and yelling, everything pandemonium. Then some of the girls discovered they could not get to shore while the first canoes blocked everything. They sent up a howl.

"It's time for me to go," I said.

"Coward."

"Walk me down and push me off."

She agreed. I caught Wally's eye and waved. She waved back. She had her hands full steering a group of girls into the bank. One of the rangers hopped out and began ordering the girls to lift the first canoes higher onto the bank. The girls did as they were asked, but noisily. Bunny, I figured, had headed for the hills.

We followed the portage path down to the water on the other side. The falls blocked most of the sounds from the girls. I slipped into my spray skirt and grabbed my paddle.

"I won't see you until Indonesia," Mary said, checking a bungee cord on the front of the kayak. "That doesn't seem possible."

"You're leaving in days. There isn't time."

"You'll call me to tell me you can get a flight?"

"Yes. I'll call you every day."

"Twice."

"Three times. Breakfast, lunch, and dinner."

Mary stood. She grabbed me and pulled me close.

"This was real, right?" she asked. "This really happened between us?"

"Yes," I said.

"And we won't change our minds when we get away from the river?"

I kissed her and pulled her tighter against me.

"I won't."

I kissed her then. And kissed her more. And the kiss flashed inside us and tried to become more, and it might have, even under the circumstances, except that two girls, exploring the campground ahead of everyone else, suddenly made a *wooooowwoooooo* sound of discovery. They turned to each other and laughed and Mary began to smile under the kiss and I raised my hand to wave at the girls as I climbed into the kayak. Mary pushed the stern of the boat forward and the fast-moving water from the falls began to grab me. I paddled a few strokes to keep the bow pointed downstream. The hills on either side of the river climbed away from the water and lifted every color imaginable toward the sky. When the speed of the water slackened, I turned the kayak around and drifted backward. I watched Mary waving. The two girls had joined her and they waved, too. *Always this*, I thought. *Always Mary.* And then the river carried me away.

# INDONESIA

# 9

INDONESIA IS AN ARCHIPELAGO OF APPROXIMATELY seventeen thousand islands. Its capital, Jakarta, is one of the busiest cities in the world. Merapi, one of the world's most active volcanoes, rests 250 miles to the east of the capital, not far from Jogjakarta, the culture and university center of the nation. Only three countries are more populous than Indonesia: China, India, and the United States. It is the location of Komodo Island and therefore also the Komodo dragon. It is almost exactly on the other side of the globe from New Hampshire, approximately sixteen thousand miles away; when it is noon in Boston it is eleven p.m. in Jakarta. Cathay Pacific, when I booked my flight, listed the flight from New York to Hong Kong as 15.5 hours. Over the North Pole. From Hong Kong another five to six hours to Jakarta. Then two hours to Bali. Then a three-hour speedboat ride to the Gili Islands.

The week before I left for Indonesia, four British divers, trying on vacation to spot a pygmy seahorse—a rarity that exists only in Indonesian waters—were swept away by currents. They surfaced miles from the dive boat and drifted, clipped together by carabiners to stay in a group and lessen the risk of shark attack, for nine hours until they put in on a splinter off Rinca Island. Grateful to be alive, they soon discovered that Komodo dragons shared the island, and throughout their three day marooning, a dragon circled and tried to bite them. A bite from a Komodo dragon is toxic; its saliva contains virulent bacteria. The divers kept the dragon at bay by throwing stones at it.

Fishing boats eventually spotted the divers and picked them up. I left a few days after the rescue.

We traveled over the North Pole during the daylight hours. Beneath us lay miles of sea and ice and fog. When the sun went down, I watched two episodes of *MASH,* a Sylvester Stallone movie, a Larry David *Curb Your Enthusiasm* show I had seen before, another movie about wedding dresses and bridesmaids, a documentary on a tribe in Africa near the Somalia border, and a clip on the reef-running, nomadic peoples of Indonesia. Afterward I played a bastardized version of *Who Wants to Be a Millionaire* and got to 34,000 points, which made me about the third highest scorer on the plane at the time. I played twenty games. I read thirty pages of an A. J. Liebling book called *The Road Back to Paris,* then about ten chapters of a John D. MacDonald novel called *The Girl in the Plain Brown Wrapper.* I had always had old taste in literature and music.

Even after all that, I was still seven hours away from Hong Kong, still a day and a little more from Mary.

On the plane to Bali I thought, *"Bali Ha'i," "Bali Ha'i,"* the old song from *South Pacific,* the Broadway show and famous movie. The song got stuck in my head and I tried to recall if *that* Bali was the same as *this* Bali. Was James Michener writing about the Indonesian island of Bali, or someplace else? Before I could settle that in my mind, the theme of "Some Enchanted Evening" shoved "Bali Ha'i" out of my head. *South Pacific,* I knew, was in revival in New York and was the most popular ticket on Broadway. People cried at the overture, I read. A more innocent America, they liked to think, one reviewer said.

When I saw Merapi smoking through the clouds, I had the melody of "I'm Gonna Wash That Man Right Outa My Hair" lodged into my exhausted cortex. The volcano smoldered and the smoke leaked into the clouds, appearing almost as if it had a cartoon thought bubble above its stern head.

As we landed on Bali, I watched the breakers sweep in from the sea and curl perfectly over themselves until they fell. A bar of butter being scraped by a sharp knife. I had reservations for a night at Kuta Beach, a famous surf destination. In the morning I was scheduled to climb on a fast boat to Gili Trawangan, where Mary and her brother waited.

JET LAG IS SAND in your eyes. It is a flutter in your muscles.

I ate dinner at a small restaurant called Un's and had the best frozen margarita of my life, served by a husky waiter named Boodie. He wore a red headdress that flattered him and a white chef's coat that seemed out of place in the tropics. He told me he had never been to Gili but he heard it was beautiful and that he hoped to go there some day. He told me there were three Gilis and that Trawangan, where Mary and her brother lived, was the largest. "Most party," he said. Two smaller islands, Menos and Air, lay farther to sea, all of them paradises without cars or police.

After dinner I walked to the beach and watched the waves file in, their noise like sand poured on a plastic kiddie pool. The moon rolled out of the sea and sent its light onto the waves, shoving them forward. I counted fifty waves. At the end of fifty, I glanced at my watch. It was nearly ten p.m. in Bali, which meant, halfway across the world in New Hampshire, it was eleven in the morning.

It meant Mary's mother waited for my call.

I went back to my room at Kuta Puri—a lovely hotel with a bright pool in the center of a large courtyard—and sat on the side of the bed. I pulled Mary's mother's phone number out of my wallet. She had given me a card and she had promised to be in her office from eleven a.m. until noon on my second day of travel. She would have the results of Mary's test.

I dialed twice. The first time the call didn't go through. The second time it did.

"DARTMOUTH HITCHCOCK," SHE ANSWERED. "Joan Fury speaking."

The connection was clear.

"Hi, Joan," I said. "This is Jonathan Cobb."

"I thought it might be you," she said in her firm, deep voice. "Hold on a second, would you? I just want to close my door."

I heard her chair squeak. A door closed. Then another squeak.

"How was the flight?" she asked, her breath slightly shorter from the movement.

"Long."

"I bet."

We didn't say anything for a second. I pictured her sitting at her desk, where we had had a short meeting a week before. She was a solid, cheerful woman, maybe in her late fifties, director of pediatric nursing. She had naturally gray hair, cut short, and wore a navy cardigan over her street clothes. The cardigan served two purposes. First, it kept her warm in the sometimes chilly air-conditioning. Second, it gave children a chance to pin notes or brooches or small stickers on her. She wore the cardigan without any twinge of self-consciousness. *This is what children need,* she seemed to say, *and therefore this is what I will provide.* I had liked her immediately. I think she liked me. She had agreed to Mary's request to give the test results to me.

"Did you get the results?" I asked, a stone rolling in my stomach.

"I didn't, Cobb," she said.

"What happened?"

"I didn't need to, sweetheart. That's what I mean."

It took me a second to understand her.

"They didn't come in?" I asked, not actually believing my question.

Joan took a long breath. She was accustomed to giving people bad news.

"Mary was a spunky, active child, Cobb. She had a number of injuries over the years, as any child does. I'm a nurse. I needed to know; that's my nature. When she was about ten we—my husband and I—we asked the hospital to run the tests. We had to move heaven and earth to get it done. If I remember, she had gouged herself on an old iron cemetery fence. Her calf. They used part of the blood for a test."

"And does Mary know?"

"Does she know?" Joan asked. "That's a question I've asked myself a thousand times, sweetie. That's a very good question. Up until this point, she made a decision not to know conclusively, not to have the tests. That doesn't mean she doesn't know, if you follow me. I work with plenty of cancer patients, Cobb, and some of them pretend not to know how severe their illness is. Others ignore it completely. And some, like Mary, maybe, know in their gut what the diagnosis is, but they surround it with other notions."

"So she is positive for Huntington's?"

"Yes," Joan said without pausing. "Yes, she is."

I didn't say anything. I looked at the wall, then at the air conditioner. It buzzed quietly.

"You're the only man she's ever loved, Cobb. You're the one. I believe you love her. You have a decision to make. She will grow ill, Cobb. That's certain. And your boat, heaven forbid, may sink under the sea tomorrow. You have five good years, at least. Maybe ten. Maybe even more, who knows? Mary is the finest person I've ever known, and I am not saying that as her mother. I'm saying it as a fifty-something woman who has seen her share of people and her share of human suffering. I don't take any credit for her goodness or her light. I marvel at it. She has always been something exceptional, something too good for the world. That's a cliché, I know, but it's true."

"I don't know what to say."

"You don't have to join her, sweetheart. And if you do, you don't have to stay forever. No one would hold it against you. You're a handsome, charming man. Mary is wild about you. You two match. But maybe it's all too much, and that's okay. I hope you don't feel I led you on. She's my daughter and I don't see any reason she can't have the man she loves with her on a beautiful island in the South Pacific. The hell with everything else, Cobb. All of us are dying, honey. Mary just has a shorter expiration date."

I couldn't say anything.

"That last," Joan said, "about an expiration date. That was a joke."

"Ha ha," I said.

"I'm sorry. I'm older than you two, so I'll just say this: you're in love and you can be together on an island in one of the most beautiful places in the world. Say yes. Say yes to good things in life. Grab them. Don't hesitate. Maybe there will be pain at the end, but there usually is anyway. Say yes. Not for me, not for Mary, but for yourself if you love her as I believe you do. You don't value a fire any less because some day it will go out."

"But you think Mary knows?" I asked. "I don't want to lie to her. I don't want to mislead her in any way."

She sighed.

"I appreciate that. Mary wants not to know, so maybe she doesn't. The human heart is a sticky, tricky thing. Consciously, does she know? I don't think so. But somewhere inside she does, I suspect.

She once told me that the disease was like the first turn of the leaves before a summer storm. You know that feeling? She said she could sense it a long ways away, that the day still felt wonderful, but she was aware of clouds moving overhead and the barometer dipping."

"So you're saying she simply doesn't look too closely?"

"I don't know," she said. "Mary has her own way of dealing with the world, as you know. But you get my meaning?"

"Yes," I said. "I do."

"I have to run in a second, sweetheart. You need to follow your heart. And I apologize if you feel I set you up. I thought about that a lot these last few days. I didn't mean to mislead you. Fate threw you two together. You do what you need to do. Mary is a big, strong soul, and she can weather anything. She loves you, but she doesn't need you. You understand the difference?"

"Yes. But I'm going. I was always going no matter what."

"It's what I always thought. From the minute I met you."

"For as long as we have."

"Okay, sweetheart," she said, her voice brightening. "If you see my kids, give both a kiss. You'll like my son, by the way. He's a crazy boy, but he's full of life. I never understood where they came from. Their dad and I were hopeless squares. Weird, huh?"

"Weird," I agreed.

"All things end, Cobb," she said. "In my job, I know it and see it. I wish I could say Mary would live to a ripe old age, but that just isn't the fact. Go to her, Cobb, and love her as much as you can. Concentrate on what is, not what can't be."

"Are you sure I won't be lying to her?"

"No. It's a bill at the end of a fine meal. You'll both have to pay, but not for a while. If you love her, Cobb, then go to her. Nothing else matters. Or you can have a nice time in Bali, forget about Mary, and head home at the end of your stay. It's up to you and no one will judge you. Mary won't judge you, I promise. If you go over, tell her Mom said it was all okay. Then you won't be lying."

"Okay," I said.

"I've got to run."

"Do I have to laugh at her knock-knock jokes?"

"No," she said, "there are limits, after all."

THE BOAT, NAMED DULLY enough, *The Gili Transport,* was thirty-two feet long and had three four hundred–horse power Honda outboard motors on its tail. It made good time. I sat next to an Australian man named Mark who stood two years away from retirement from the Sydney Police Force. He intended to move to Gili, lock, stock, and barrel when that day arrived, and he and his wife had purchased four hectares on Gili Meno, not beachfront, where he intended to build when his pension kicked in. He invited me to stand at the back of the boat while he named the local landmarks. Lombok. The volcanoes of Bali. He explained the positions of the three Gili Islands: Meno, Air, and Trawangan. His wife, he said, waited for him on Gili Trawangan, arranging contracts with builders and importers. Everything, he explained, had to be brought in, but if you built with bamboo and used natural, local materials, you could cut the cost down to almost nothing.

"It's a paradise," he said in his thick Australian accent. "This is the place you meant to go when you went to all those others places, but they weren't this place, so you got sidetracked. It's like being shipwrecked in the nicest way. No cars, no police."

"Do you happen to know Freddy Fury?"

"The turtle guy?" Mark laughed. "Of course. Everyone knows Freddy."

"Where does he live?"

Mark pointed at a misty speck on the horizon. "On Gili Trawangan. When we land, you can go left or right. Left is where the bars are located and some of the dive schools, and that's for the younger, party crowd. You want to go right. Better beaches, quieter. Freddy is set up down there. He's got quite a place. You tell Freddy we met on the boat over."

"I will."

"You know Freddy nearly single-handedly saved the coral reefs around here? The native Indonesians used a technique called fishing bombing. They dropped huge weights down onto the coral to displace the fish. Freddy made them see their long-term interest was in tourism. He taught them to fish a different way and he helped set up some local businesses. He did all that to save the turtles. People call him Turtle Freddy. Quite a guy."

"Is it working?"

"Saving the turtles? Actually, I believe so. The census count is up. Bring back the coral and you bring back the turtles. And then you bring back the bumphead parrotfish and the pipefish and so it goes. Freddy worked out a scheme so the divers who come here are hit with a surcharge for reef restoration that goes to the local fishermen. A kind of public relief. He's improved this place. Now he's working on garbage removal and recycling. Have you ever met him?"

"No," I said.

"Impressive man," Mark said. "Big beard, big voice, big go-to-hell attitude. Wears a polished baby turtle shell dangling from his beard, but only when he dresses up. Kind of a pirate, really, but an ecological one. He's a bit of a local Robin Hood. He makes sure the natives get a piece of the action."

I nodded. I kept an eye out for the island. It came quietly through the fog and mist, white sand, blue water, narrow boats with outriggers.

MARK HELPED ME HIRE a *janur,* a pony cart, to drive me to Turtle Freddy's. Mark arranged the matter in Bahasa Indonesian, the national language, but as soon as we left—vowing to catch up in one of the bars today or the next day—the driver tried out his English on me.

"Don't worry, be happy," he said.

"Absolutely," I agreed.

"Every little thing," he said, quoting Bob Marley, "is gonna be all right."

"What's your name?" I asked, trying to distract him from the song lyrics.

"JJ," he said.

"Nice to meet you, JJ," I said, choosing not to pursue the conversation.

I didn't want to appear unfriendly, but I couldn't concentrate on his English at that moment. Instead, my eyes gobbled the details of the beachfront. No cars. No noise. No TV. Just the sound of the Bali Sea pushing up onto the beach. Beyond the shoreline, fifteen feet out, the blue-green water gave hints of the ripe coral heads. If I had an image of paradise, I supposed it was something fairly close to this. Palm trees. Slender boats holding wide outriggers into the patient ocean. A pony cart with a friendly driver. A pod of naked children—incredibly beautiful in the warm sun—swimming in the sea. When they saw me pass, they waved and smiled.

We followed a small cobblestone path that JJ promised went all the way around the island. "Seven kilometers around," he told me. He said sharks lived on the other side of the island, but here, in the strait between Gili Trawangan and Gili Meno, no sharks. Turtles, though. And lots of fish. We passed *warungs,* outdoor eating places under thatched roofs, where you could get *nasi goreng,* the national dish of rice and Chinese greens, sometimes served with chicken or beef. And Bintang beer. JJ waved and talked to the different shopkeepers. He turned frequently to ask if I wanted to stop and eat. The *janur* drivers, Mark had said, got kickbacks from the hotel and restaurant owners for any tourists they could bring to them.

We went a mile, maybe more, and then came to a wooden arch stretching across a wide dirt driveway. The arch had two turtles carved into the posts. JJ didn't slow the *janur.* He flicked his reins at the pony and drove me into a gorgeous, fragrant courtyard. Plants pushed in every direction, and I recognized orchids and ferns and a few climbing roses. The dirt road turned gently in a U, bringing us to a complex of bamboo huts. The huts, handsome and set up on posts, were connected by walkways. Robinson Crusoe, I thought. To the north—the right from where JJ parked the *janur*—the boardwalks merged together and expanded into a spectacular deck overlooking the Bali Sea. Palms surrounded the porch and provided shade in the late morning light.

I paid. JJ said he would see me tonight, that a good party usually happened at the Sama-Sama Club, no worries, be happy—it went till dawn, and he clicked his tongue and trotted off. I lifted my backpack and threw it over my right shoulder, feeling for the moment like every movie I had ever seen: guy arrives, feels dislocated, stumbles into a strange situation with a butler, or mother-in-law, or the wiseass little sister. I looked for a bell or anything to announce myself, but eventually I settled on going to the wide front veranda. "Hello," I called, but I knew instinctively no one was around.

I dropped my backpack on the veranda and took a moment to absorb the spectacular scenery. It was a dreamscape, bright water, mountains, dense jungle forests. A sand beach climbed up to the edge of the veranda, and maybe forty feet away the ocean began. A second island, Meno, I guessed, rested across a blue strait maybe a mile away. I breathed deeply. The air smelled fresh and filtered by the sea and the deep greens behind me. The fatigue of travel, the stale, canned-air feeling of airplanes, slowly slid away.

It took me a few moments to notice the aquariums.

For a second they didn't make sense. Glass pools on a white beach, shaded by trees. But then I realized the aquariums contained turtles, hundreds and hundreds of turtles. The first few contained small turtles; the next few slightly larger turtles. And so it went. Maybe twenty aquariums. I stepped down off the veranda and remembered I still wore a pair of sneakers. I untied them, kicked them off, and then visited the turtles. They swam against the side of the tank, fresh and active, their round bodies colliding and drifting in a foot of water. A solar charged bubbler made certain the water stayed oxygenated. I didn't dare pick one up for fear of transferring bacteria, but I bent down and put my eyes directly on the turtles' level. They swam slowly past, one then another, their front lips like a kid with an overbite, their skin alligator-ed with wide scales, their legs as stumpy as a baby potato.

"ARE YOU A BEAR?" a quiet voice asked from behind me.

"I am not a bear," I said softly, still squatting to inspect the turtles. "Do I smell like honey?"

"Not that I can detect."

"I know a woman who danced with a bear once."

"Really?"

"So she claims."

"Come here," she said.

I stood. My Mary. She moved into my arms. She wore a man's white shirt, a bikini bottom, and bare feet. Her hair had been tied up in a pink bandanna. I kissed her. She kissed me.

IN THE HEAT, IN our bed, we made love. She had a bamboo cabin to herself and we moved into bed still kissing. A fan moved the air quietly. I kissed her until I could not separate before or after, the river in Maine or this moment in Indonesia. She did not ask any questions. She held my head between her hands so that she could kiss me more, whispering, "shhhh, shhhh, it's okay." She said she loved me. She said whatever happened was okay. She said whatever I had found out was okay, that she had thought of never seeing me again and couldn't bear it. She said she had me in her life, that it would stay that way, *shhhh, it doesn't matter,* that I was here, nothing else counted.

I moved into her and we turned quiet, then fierce, and we kept kissing, our mouths together, the chirp of strange birds outside, the sound of the sea just beyond our full hearing, a whisper, and we kissed more, opened our mouths, kissed until we had our ribs locked, our hips hinged, our hands together. I kissed her neck, her shoulders, her ears. And we stayed together, the sun pushing slowly away from us, the day becoming quieter, afternoon, and the feeling of her body mixed with the memory of the turtles, their curious green heads, and the ocean where larger fish shot in off the reefs and cut prey from their coral hiding places. Mary. I told her I loved her, that I wanted to marry her, that we could face anything. I told her she was my Chungamunga girl, that I had waited all my years to find her, and that I would risk whatever came. We kissed more, kissed until it all finished, quietly, serenely, both of us understanding that this place was ours alone, that we could return to it, that it existed only when we wanted it to, but that it waited and lived beside us.

We dozed.

When we woke it was early evening.

"Where's your brother?" I asked, my voice constricted with sleep.

"He thought we might need some time together. He's with his girlfriend. He'll be back for dinner. In fact, he's bringing dinner."

"I met a man on the boat who knows him. Turtle Freddy, they call him, right?"

She nodded against me. We remained in bed. Her body fit against mine. The light outside had changed and the air had become fresher. She kissed the side of my neck from time to time. I kissed her hair. Occasionally we heard the purr of an outboard passing by, but mostly we listened to birds and wind.

"He's done good work here," she said. "And he has built a life for himself."

"It looks like it. It's a great home."

"It's a sweet home and so entirely Freddy in so many ways. You know, he's becoming a little famous. People from some of the wildlife foundations are sending him money and funding to keep the turtle projects going."

"That's wonderful."

"And people show up. Donors. Different people who love turtles. He is exactly what they hope he will be. A madman, but with dignity and passion."

"I want to meet him," I said.

"You will."

"Who is his girlfriend?"

"Her name is Lamb. That's what everyone calls her. Tiny little thing, and she bosses him around. It's wonderful to watch. Everyone defers to Freddy except her. He met her when he first came out here. She's a little older than he is, and she took him in and helped him. She's a Hindu from Bali. She keeps her own house and her own life separate from Freddy. But they are tender with each other."

"And you?"

"Freddy is at his most tender with me."

We shifted positions. She kissed me. Then she sat up against the wicker headboard and grabbed my hand.

"You're here," she said. "I almost can't believe it."

"I'm here," I agreed.

"And you met my mother. Did you like her?"

"I liked her very much."

"Isn't she the sweetest thing? That's my mom. Aren't you curious to know what she thought of you?"

I nodded. She pinched my ear and looked me in the eye.

"She thought you were handsome," she said, "and a true gentleman."

"Does she have an everything-knife?"

"She does. We are both on the lookout for yours. She's my

companion at junk shops. Now come on. You must be starving and exhausted. I'm being selfish, keeping you awake. Are you hungry?"

"Hungry and thirsty," I said.

"First a swim," she said. "Then Freddy should be here. He's terribly prompt despite his pirate reputation."

Before we climbed out of bed, we kissed a little more. And it grew again, threatened to delay us. Mary finally slipped away.

"No need to dress," she said, when she saw me pulling on a pair of shorts. "This isn't *Gilligan's Island.* Naked coed swimming. Freddy's whole life is comprised of T-shirt slogans."

"Nice," I said.

"Come on," she said and led me back to the veranda.

A SMILE SPREAD ACROSS my face as I slipped into the ocean water without the slightest shiver or moment's hesitation. Bathwater warm. Mary dove ahead and came up ten feet farther out. It was evening. The sun had begun to sink. I realized, watching it, that Indonesia lay almost precisely on the equator. The day split like a melon on the equator, twelve hours of darkness, twelve of light.

"That's Lombok," Mary said, pointing to the south at a bulky landmass. "Those are volcanoes."

"And across the strait?"

"Gili Meno."

She swam over to me.

"Not like Chamberlain Lake in Maine," she said. "A little warmer."

"I think your brother may be on to something here."

"Paradise, some people call it."

"It's beautiful."

"Jump in," she said, "and I'll show you the turtle pens."

I dove forward. Mary swam beside me. We breaststroked twenty feet out until we came to a netted enclosure. Inside the netting, from what I could see through the water, a couple hundred turtles swam in lazy circles. They were larger than any turtles in the aquarium tanks back on shore. This, I figured, was the final stage.

"These are the twos," Mary said, treading water. "The two-year-olds. They are about to be released. We waited for you. Turtle rodeo tomorrow."

"What kind are they?"

"*Chelonia mydas.* Green sea turtles. They are on the endangered list. They get tangled up in shrimp-boat nets. People eat them in turtle soup. Tiger sharks eat them, too. Freddy improves their odds of survival by getting them older before they have to go out on their own. He stacks the deck as much as he can in their favor."

"I want to get a mask and take a closer look."

"We'll help Freddy tomorrow. You'll get plenty of turtle lore from Freddy. More than you can stand, probably."

"Crows are cooler, though, right?"

"I knew you were smart."

Then for a while we kissed in the water. The sun moved closer to the sea. Down the shoreline, lights began coming on. I tucked her body close to mine. We were still kissing when we heard a man's voice calling from the veranda.

"Dinner," he called. "Come on, you lovebirds."

We didn't break apart right away. For a while we kept kissing.

I LIKED FREDDY FURY instantly.

He was tall, nearly six feet five, and broad in the shoulders. His belly stuck out, but he had the kind of posture that made it seem substantial and powerful rather than heavy. He wore a ratty T-shirt, ratty shorts, flip-flops, and a straw hat that might have served a horse in Central Park. His beard, though, was his most startling feature. It stretched down to his chest and he had braided it near his chin and curled it out like two pigtails. His eyes—blue, like Mary's—snapped and moved quickly over me, the room, anything they fell on. The sun had turned him permanently brown and sleek. He reminded me of a stout otter, raised on his feet and slick as a ribbon. He possessed an obvious playfulness and seemed happy to meet anything, or anyone, who swam into view.

We shook hands. He had been busy unloading food from a cloth carry bag. He stopped and studied me for a moment.

"So you're the famous Cobb," he said. "Happy to meet you."

"And you," I said.

"Give the man a beer," Freddy said to Mary. "Are you trying to kill him?"

She brought three beers. We put them on the table where Freddy busily spooned out rice mixed with marinated pieces of chicken, and a few beef kabobs. He also had a full fish tucked in a foil wrapper. "Coral trout," he announced as he slid it on a plate. His hands moved quickly. In no time he had the meal plated and asked each of us to carry things out to the veranda.

We spread everything on a wide, wicker table. Then we pulled up three chairs. Mary remembered napkins and hopped up to retrieve them. From where we sat, the water splashed gently thirty feet away. A palm tree above us stirred a little in the breezes. The sun had disappeared, leaving behind a gray quiet that wrenched last calls from the birds in the jungle behind us.

"Your home is beautiful," I said. "Thank you for inviting me."

"You're entirely welcome," Freddy said. "Mary has talked about you nonstop since she arrived, and if you know Mary, you'd know she never does that."

"Glad to hear that," I said.

"Do you like the ocean?" he asked, portioning some of the fish on the plates.

"I do," I said.

"Some people don't, you know? Some people find the whole concept of an ocean too foreign. It's a little frightening to them. Me, I feel most at home near the sea. Did Mary tell you when we were kids we tried to grow gills?"

"No," I said.

"Not that story," Mary said, returning. "This is not Mary's childhood in review night."

She placed the napkins next to the plates and took her place.

"We got it in our minds that we might evolve into fish," Freddy said, cutting the fish and slowly loading our plates. "So we began going to a local stream up in New Hampshire near the Baker River and we stayed underwater for as long as we could. You know how kids are. We'd tell ourselves that we seemed to be getting more comfortable without air and that we seemed to be evolving. We drew gills behind our ears with red paint, and Mom made us cover up the marks with Band-Aids when we went to school. Of course, that only proved to us that we had hit on something and Mom knew she had given birth to strange creatures."

"And we put duct tape between our fingers and toes to web them," Mary said, passing plates as Freddy finished filling them. "We painted the duct tape flesh colored and we caused a sensation when we went to anyone's pool for a swim party."

"I really believed I was evolving," Freddy said. "It thrilled me."

"How did you finally leave it?" I asked.

Freddy looked at Mary. Then Mary shrugged.

"I'm not sure we did," Freddy said and laughed.

He had a loud, full laugh. He raised his glass of beer and clinked ours.

"At Smutty Pete's and Dirty Dicks," he said by way of a toast, "we drank our whiskey straight. Some went upstairs with Leonor, and some, alas, with Kate."

We drank. In the quiet, I heard the turtles moving against the glass of the aquariums.

"VERNAL POOLS," FREDDY SAID.

We had eaten and cleared the table and now sat outside with our brandy. Freddy smoked a cigar. Cuban, he said proudly. Now and then Mary took it from his mouth and puffed. She waved the smoke away as quickly as she exhaled. She had her feet in my lap.

"Dr. Hager," she said.

He nodded.

"This madman lived in our neighborhood. Small, little guy, nearsighted, always in Converse sneakers and white socks. He studied biology, but ended up working for the state agriculture department. Hated his job, or was bored by it. This was before the big ruckus, by the way, with the Boy Scouts. I don't know if today Dr. Hager could have functioned as he did."

"He took kids on field trips." Mary said. "Called us the Explorer Club."

"Wonderful man," Freddy said. "No kids of his own and a mousy wife. He loved, loved, loved nature. His wife wouldn't camp with him to save her life. So he created a sort of informal Explorer Club. Made it really exciting. He had bird lists we had to fill out, dissections we had to perform. He taught us to use a compass. That kind of stuff. The camp headquarters was on a Ping-Pong table in his garage. High tech, believe me. Pickle bottles for specimens. Mary and I were nuts about it. Most of it just took place in the farmlands around us. One spring we went to a vernal pool he knew about up on Carr Mountain. Spring pools. They are temporary, just a holding tank right after the first thaw, and they are absolutely key for salamanders and frogs and turtles, of course. That's where I met turtles for the first time. Little box turtles and painted turtles. I liked them right away."

"The Hagers moved away eventually," Mary said.

"They did," Freddy said. "Not sure where they went. We had grown out of it a little by then and I remember waving to Dr. Hager as he drove away. I happened to be out in the yard, maybe mowing it.

You know how it is. You wanted to say thanks, that it meant something, but time just wore it away. It would have required an entire conversation and I was a pretty tongue-tied boy."

"How did you find out about this place?"

"Surfers," he said and smiled. "Believe it or not, I used to go surfing at Hampton Beach, New Hampshire. In the winter the sets get pretty big, and people up and down the coast come by if they get a chance. I was sitting on my board one day and these guys started talking about surfing Kuta Beach, Bali. I didn't have much direction for my life, but that sounded good, so I decided to try it. I saved up money and came over. In Bali I heard about this paradise place called Gili, so I scraped together some money and bought a one-way ticket over. That was it. I saw green turtles on my first snorkel around the place. I decided to stay a couple weeks, and weeks turned into months, then years."

"How long have you been here now?" I asked.

"I was nineteen when I got here. I'm thirty-six now. Mary, do the math."

"Seventeen years, I guess," she said. "You left after dad died."

"Nothing Freudian there," Freddy said and laughed.

"That's a long time to be on an island," I said.

"Well, sure," Freddy said. "When I arrived here I was stony broke. Lamb gave me rice and a place to sleep. She liked me. She had two kids. One had been in a bad accident. The kid jumped off the pier here to go swimming and landed on a piece of metal rebar. Impaled himself. Terrible thing. He survived, believe it or not, but it was a horrible scene. Luckily it didn't hit an organ."

"And you worked as a diving instructor," Mary said.

"At first, yes," Freddy said, blowing a good cloud of cigar smoke into the air. "I worked for food, mostly. Then I started seeing the reefs were in a bad state. Divers were flocking here, and they arrived with this gold rush mentality. See it now before it is all used up! It was crazy. So I started thinking and figuring how we could go at it a little differently. Some of the fishermen didn't like it at first. But the town elders saw the wisdom of it. They helped me. Eventually the turtles attracted some wildlife folks. And the pygmy seahorse. You can find it in these waters and nowhere else. So that was a big attraction, believe it or not. I started to see where this could go."

"He's being modest," Mary said. "*National Geographic* came to do a piece on the dwindling coral reefs and he was profiled as an activist working to preserve them. That caught peoples' interest. He built on that."

"A woman named Cartwright came out to visit. She was an avid diver based in California. We talked. Turns out she had some money behind her and knew where to get even more. We set up the Indonesian Turtle Restoration Project. Put us on a solid financial platform. I file a biannual report. Every now and then someone flies in to spend a week. I take them diving or just show them the turtles. That's it."

"Did you know," Mary asked, leaning forward and grabbing his cigar, "that green turtles cry? They do. It has something to do with maintaining the proper salinity in their system. They have to get rid of salt, so they cry it away. Once Freddy starts talking about the crying green sea turtles, the donors nearly break their arms reaching for their wallets."

Freddy laughed.

"We'll let some go tomorrow," Freddy said. "We're going to make a video and post it for the donors. I've got a whiz-kid photographer helping. Indonesian kid genius. His name is Lloyd. Raised by Christian nuts over on Gili Meno. They tried to save his soul, but he wiggled free, thank goodness. He's the tech ace for the whole island."

"What time?" Mary asked, stretching and yawning.

"Oh, midmorning. Lloyd needs the right light. Lamb is coming by to help. It should be a good day. But you should sleep in a little."

Mary took my hand.

"Time to get this guy to bed."

I nodded. I felt exhausted. But it was hard to let the evening go.

Freddy stood and to my surprise hugged me. It wasn't a typical guys' hug. He hugged me and meant it. Then he hugged Mary. He said he was going to finish his cigar, then turn in. We left him on the veranda. Halfway around the world in New Hampshire, my school was rising from breakfast.

IT WAS VERY LATE and I couldn't sleep. Jet lag had tricked me. I had fallen asleep almost immediately when we had left Freddy, but after an hour or so I woke completely. Mary had been reading beside me. When she saw I was awake, she put down her book and slid close to me. Breezes moved the shades.

"Awake?" she asked.

"No, I'm asleep."

She elbowed me softly.

"Tell me about school," she whispered. "What was it like to go back?"

"It was fine. I think the head of school is going to ask me to be dean of students."

"That's wonderful," Mary said. "Would you like that?"

"It would take me out of the classroom a little bit, but it would also give me more say in the school's direction. I'd have a hand on school policy, the discipline code, and all of those goodies."

"Dean of Students Jonathan Cobb. Will the students automatically hate you?"

"Probably."

"No they won't. They won't hate you. They couldn't. You'll be good and fair and you will wear tweed. It's a shame pipes aren't good for you, because you would be perfect smoking a pipe."

"Some deans of students become hated. I guess it depends. When I went to school, we had a fellow by the name of Edward Peen. You can only imagine what we did with his name."

"When do you have to go back?"

"New Year's. The second semester starts in February. You too, right?"

"Right. I'll go with you."

"February in New Hampshire, or winter in Indonesia? Gee, that's a solid decision."

"Wither thou goest, I will go; and where thou lodgest, I will lodge; thy people shall be my people, and thy God, my God."

"My people are a bunch of teenagers who knock on the door late at night or try to slip out to meet girls. I live among them, you know?"

"I know. I also want to meet your dad."

I nodded. She slid closer.

"And Francis," she said. "How is he?"

"He's playing indoor soccer and doing pretty well in his classes. I saw him and said hello. He looks solid."

"Because of you," she said.

"Francis is strong, that's all. I just listened."

She pushed up and kissed the side of my neck, then sunk back.

"I've been thinking about all this," she said. "I'm going to keep teaching at the university. You're going to be dean of students at St. Paul's. We could find a place between us. Only about sixty miles separate us."

"Yes. That's what we'll do."

"Our place," she said. "I wouldn't care what kind of place. Remember, we're married. We got married on the Allagash."

"I remember. But a place where we can sleep outside and watch the stars?"

"Yes," she said. "That's a must."

"I need to write while I'm here. I need to do work on that Thoreau essay."

"Of course."

"Why does it feel so natural to be with you?" I asked.

She shrugged. I could tell sleep had started to take her.

"Did I tell you the Chungamunga girls made it home okay?" she asked, barely hanging on to consciousness. "They had a seven-moose trip. No bears. And one of the girl's wishes was granted. The wish in the bottle? Her family needed a convalescent ramp for her father. The local Rotary Club built it and it was financed by the Chungamunga Foundation. They gave him a new wheelchair, too. And one girl's family received a used pickup truck. A Ford, I think."

"You're asleep," I said.

"No, I'm not," she said.

Her words mumbled together. Then her body made a quick, sharp jolt and she dozed off.

"Turtles tomorrow," I whispered.

"WHAT WE WANT," FREDDY said, "is a sense of turtle freedom."

"Oh, good grief," Mary said.

"Turtle rapture," Freddy said.

Freddy stood in his ratty green bathing suit, a snorkel and mask propped on top of his head. Mary wore a one-piece suit, and she also had a mask and snorkel on her head. Lloyd, I knew, waited out near the turtle pens. He wore a diving tank and had spent the early morning checking his equipment. Lamb also waited with Lloyd. She was his gofer, a role she accepted readily from Lloyd, but refused to perform for Freddy to a remarkable degree.

"Turtle ecstasy," Mary said.

"Knock it off, Mary," Freddy said. "This is funding porn. It's got to be right."

"I get it," Mary said. "What do you want us to do?"

Freddy looked out at the surface bubbles brewing from Lamb and Lloyd's tanks.

"Lloyd and I talked it over," he said. "I need to be in the tank with the turtles. I'll dive down, hold a couple, you know. Do the Turtle Freddy thing. Then when Lloyd gives the sign, you two can lower the seaside edge of the net. Not the shore side, the sea side. Got it?"

"Which side?" Mary asked and Freddy tried to kick her rump.

"The idea is to capture the net coming down, the turtles sensing their freedom, and then into the wild blue yonder," Freddy said.

"With them streaming past your hands as you give them birth, so to speak?"

"Exactly," Freddy said and laughed.

"Do you see, Cobb, why crows are so much cooler?"

Freddy chased her into the water. I followed. The sun sat at forty-five degrees from the horizon. Midmorning. It was hot everywhere except in the shade or in the ocean. I adjusted my mask and snorkel and lowered myself into the water. I experienced that strange, but welcome, feeling of leaving land and submerging. Freddy convened us in a small group out by Lloyd and Lamb. He and Lloyd did a bunch of okay signs that obviously held meaning for them. Lamb hardly bothered with us. She had arranged a bunch of equipment on the sea floor and floated a few feet above it, trying to keep it in place.

Thumbs up from Freddy.

Mary rolled her eyes behind her mask, then pretended to vomit into the water.

I swam to the northern edge of the net while Mary took the southern edge. Freddy climbed over the top of the net and suddenly appeared in the midst of hundreds of turtles, his bulk remarkably vivid beside the army green of the sea turtles. The turtles did not panic or flee, nor did they pay much attention to him. They continued swimming in their leisurely way, flippers slowly pushing water backward, bodies cast like old metal between lime limbs.

Freddy swiveled to look at Lloyd. Lloyd again gave a series of hand motions.

After another minute or two, Freddy pointed at Mary and me

and nodded. He swam to the place where the net would fall. I looked at Mary. She nodded.

I unfastened my side of the netting. Mary nodded again. I let my side fall. The net sagged slowly downward and the turtles, little by little, began to sense they were free. Given the buildup, the joking with Freddy, it should have been funny. But I felt my throat close and tears come into my eyes. Freddy raised his hands and the turtles he had cared for during two long years gradually began to swim past him. He touched them as they moved, not to stop them, but to say good-bye. It wasn't faked. Freddy dangled in the water among the twos; I felt my heart going with the turtles, these ancient reptiles. You could not watch without wishing them safe seas and coral blooms beyond counting. Some of them, I knew, would live a half century or more. Others would die before the sun set on the water. Freddy had done this, had given them a chance, and his body curved in tenderness as they passed. How many turtles, I wondered, had he observed swimming free in the sea, knowing that many of them he had placed there? It seemed like an enormously worthwhile thing to do.

Ten minutes later, it finished. Freddy swam out after the last cluster of turtles. He swam well out into the current, watching them. I knew he worried about sharks. Tiger sharks, in particular, possessed jaws so powerful they could crush the sea turtle's carapace. Off the Hawaiian coast, he had told me, tiger sharks regularly prey on green turtles, but here, in the South Pacific, the sharks did not represent such a large hazard.

Mary swam over to me. We talked while treading water and clinging to one of the buoys that marked the nets. Together we dived down and secured the edge of the net to a cement block placed on the bottom for that purpose. Then, after surfacing, we repeated the process on the southern end. By the time we finished, Lamb and Lloyd had lugged most of the equipment to the shallow water. We helped them with the gear. Freddy swam in a few seconds later.

"All right so far," he said, spitting out the snorkel mouthpiece.

"They headed straight south, toward Lombok. Followed the current."

"That was amazing, Freddy," I said. "Thanks for letting me help."

He nodded. Mary hugged him.

"It's a beautiful thing to see," she said. "Kidding aside. I'm very proud of you."

Meanwhile, Lamb and Lloyd had stripped out of some of their diving gear. Lloyd, maybe eighteen or nineteen, had a thin, almost bony body, with dark straight hair and clear skin. He moved rapidly, as if all of life had dials and he had to keep things tuned. Beside him Lamb grumped along, kicking out of her fins and dragging more equipment up on the beach. Twice she told Freddy to quit goofing around and to lend a hand. Her voice came out of her short body in quick, explosive pants that reminded me of an inward breath on a harmonica. Something slightly uneven, out of key, hung in her voice, but it made it unique and interesting to hear. Despite her quick ways with Freddy, she was a kind, gentle person, and once the equipment was safely back on the beach, she demanded a round of Bintang beers for us all.

We drank them on Freddy's veranda. He toasted us.

"To a good day's work," he said. "Especially a day of work that finished before noon."

"To the turtles," Mary said.

We drank. The beer slid down my throat. I reached over and held Mary's hand. The sun came through the palm fronds above us. I realized, as I sat holding the cold beer in my hand, that I was happy. I was happy in the best of ways: with sun and friends and worthwhile work to do. Mary made it all count somehow. I understood that living without her would be like looking at vacation pictures by oneself. It's mildly interesting, and maybe you had a good time, but who ultimately cared if you went to an unusual market or saw a beautiful sunset unless they experienced it beside you? Mary was my witness as I was hers. That was new to me and I liked the sensation and squeezed her hand to let her know I wanted her beside me. She squeezed back.

NAPPING. DOZING. THE BAMBOO shutters tapping slightly in the breeze. A fly hitting itself endlessly against a lamp shade. Ocean sound. Mary on my shoulder, whispering softly. Her hand moving slowly over my chest.

"Once," she said, "King Arthur played against the great Welsh hero Owain ap Urien in a game similar to chess. There is a rook in chess, remember? Some people call the endpiece a castle, but its earlier name is rook. Anyway, Owain maintained three hundred ravens as messengers and spies. They were a gift from Cenferchyn, another Welsh hero. The ravens could speak to Owain and they supplied him with secrets and information from around the British Isles.

"King Arthur, who was an ambitious man, instructed his men to kill the ravens during the game, because he knew Owain would be distracted. Arthur's men did as they were told, and they slaughtered the ravens and left their bodies lying throughout the kingdom. When Owain learned of the treachery, he went to Cenferchyn and asked for more ravens. The next day the ravens attacked King Arthur's men wherever they went. Eventually the men lost their ears to the ravens and could no longer hear Arthur's commands. Whenever the men assembled and tried to come up with a plan of counterattack, the crows clustered together and cawed more loudly than ever, making it impossible for the men to arrive at any workable plan. Why they needed to do this after the men had lost their ears isn't entirely clear. But that is why ravens make loud noises today whenever they see men together.

"Later on, Don Quixote tells us that Arthur did not die as legend claims, nor is he buried in a hillside awaiting England's summons for help, but he was turned into a raven by his enemies. He could not be killed, although he could be injured, and he flew through time with many arrows sticking from his body. He still flies over the English countryside, his body indistinguishable from other ravens. Only a spot of blood marks his passage. His wounds cannot heal for his treachery. He has been known as the Crow King for centuries and he rules over birds where he cannot rule over men."

Then sleep. Waking and kissing her. Kissing more. Her body naked beside mine, and our flesh pulling us together, hair, neck, arms. I kissed her body, roaming, then made love to her, the world somewhere distant, just her, just Mary, and then in each other's arms again, sweaty, warm, the chill of the air-conditioning pushing us back down to sleep, to languor, while a single gecko climbed the wall, its wide toes spread to find crevices and holds in what looked to the rest of the world like a smooth surface.

IT WAS CLOSE TO sunset when a pony cart pulled into Freddy's compound and the driver jumped out, yelling for the doctor. It didn't make sense at first, then it sank in: they wanted Mary. Someone on the island had heard she was a doctor and they did not make the distinction between a physician and a Ph.D.

Freddy, inside and bent over a computer console with Lloyd, stepped out and asked the driver what he wanted.

The man spoke rapidly and pointed south toward Lombok. Freddy nodded.

"He says a boy has been bitten by a banded sea snake," Freddy said. "They think so, anyway. The boy is unconscious but his friends report they were snorkeling and suddenly found themselves in a nesting area. One of them was bitten."

"I'll go," Mary said.

She had been reading on the veranda. I had been in our room trying to find something interesting to say about Thoreau. It wasn't fruitful.

"I'll go with you," Freddy said, "but they need to know you're not a physician."

Freddy spoke quickly to the driver. The driver nodded, but didn't seem to care about the distinction for the time being.

I jumped up and went with them. We squeezed into the back of the *janur.* The driver—a solid looking man of about fifty, with graying hair and a few strands of beard extending from his chin—whipped the pony to get it moving. The pony trotted faster. The driver squeezed a small horn to make a squawk that scattered the people as we moved past. A number of people motioned for him to slow down, but the driver didn't hesitate. He kept the pony moving at a good clip. The *janur* bounced along and knocked Freddy and me against the roof a dozen times.

"What do you know about sea snakes?" Freddy asked.

"I actually know a little bit," Mary said. "They dry strike about seventy percent of the time. They have a lousy delivery system. If they do break the skin, they are about ten times more lethal than a rattlesnake. Nerve toxin. It will shut down the boy's breathing. They're related to cobras."

"Do you know the boy?" I asked Freddy.

He shook his head and said, "I know the family. The driver is an uncle, I think."

"Do they have antivenom in the infirmary?" Mary asked.

Freddy shook his head.

"It's the same compound as tiger snakes in Australia, so it should be pretty common," Mary said. "If you can call someone, it's not that rare."

"There's no one really to call," Freddy said.

"Well, we'll do our best," Mary said.

We arrived at a small thatched hut set back from the main road. A number of Indonesians clustered around the door. Two white chicks pecked at the ground in the middle of the road. A tabby cat watched them from the top of an earthen wall, its eyes lazy and predatory at the same time. A woman who sold chicken *satay* had set up a table on the other side of the street and did business with one hand while keeping her eye on the hut with the injured boy.

Freddy climbed out. We followed. A woman—not the mother, but an aunt, Freddy quickly informed us—explained the situation. The boys had been swimming at the south end of the channel; they had disturbed a nest of snakes, or had come into a feeding trough. Long round objects like fins or air hoses always attracted snakes, she said. Everyone knew that. The boys tried to reverse out of the spot but it was too late. One of the snakes had become tangled in the fishing net dangling from the victim's belt. The other boys had seen it, but the victim hadn't. He had kicked out of the area, but the agitation stirred the snake into striking. The boy almost immediately began to swell.

They had not contacted anyone. By the time help came from Lombok or Bali, it would be too late. She did not doubt the snake had bitten the boy. His breath had become a tight string.

"Does she understand I am not a physician?" Mary asked Freddy.

He nodded, his eyes still on the boy's aunt.

"If we can keep him breathing, the effects of the venom will lessen in about ten hours."

"Mouth to mouth?" I asked.

She shrugged.

Then the aunt cleared a passageway for us through the people collected at the door. Freddy ducked low and disappeared inside. Mary went after him. I went after them both.

The boy lay on a wooden cot, a light sheet over him. His left leg rested on top of the sheet. It was twice, maybe three times its normal proportion. The boy did not open his eyes or acknowledge our entrance. He was a handsome child, delicately built and brown.

Someone had tied a white cloth across his head to keep his hair off his brow. His breath came in shuddery gasps, as if air passed like a bucket into a well, then was drawn out again.

The boy's mother sat next to him. She looked up at us, her eyes watery and tired. She appeared to be about forty. Freddy stepped forward and introduced us. She seemed to know Freddy. When he finished speaking to her, he turned to us.

"She understands you're not a doctor," Freddy said to Mary. "She wondered if you could recommend anything."

"I've got nothing," Mary said, her eyes looking up and down at the boy. "His leg is swollen, obviously. It might help to ice the leg, but I don't even know if that's useful. What have they done so far?"

Freddy translated from a half dozen people around the bed. Put him in bed. Gave him liquid when he could drink. Made the boys repeat the story several times to ensure that this was in fact a snakebite and not some other boyish foolishness. It had been a long time, the people conveyed, since a person had been bitten by a snake. Rare. The local medicine men did not have a cure or were unwilling to come forward. The boy's breathing had been unsteady for the past two hours. Air had become more difficult for the boy to find.

Mary listened. Then she stepped forward and moved the sheet gently from the boy's leg. His testicles had also swollen. She put her hand on the boy's head, feeling his temperature. Then she squatted next to the bed and tried to find the bite mark. She asked if anyone had seen the puncture wounds. An old man with eyes tinged yellow with jaundice stepped forward and pointed to two puncture marks near the boy's ankle. Mary bent very close to the wounds.

"Freddy?" Mary asked, still looking at the wound, "do they have oxygen on the island?"

"I don't think so, but I'll ask."

"We're going to have to breathe for this boy. Probably all night. Do they have any other plan?"

Freddy spoke rapidly to the room. A variety of voices answered. Freddy shook his head.

"They went to the infirmary but the woman who runs it is gone for a couple weeks. She went to Bali. There isn't much equipment in any case. And no, no oxygen."

"We need a breathing mask," Mary said. "Short of that, we'll tape his mouth shut and put a snorkel mouthpiece inside it. The lungs will stop working soon. If someone knows how to perform a tracheotomy, you better alert them. I'm not doing it."

Freddy spoke to a couple of young men who ran off in search of a breathing mask. Freddy asked the man with jaundiced eyes for the boy's snorkel. A little confusion ensued, but then the snorkel appeared inside the hut, carried forward from hand to hand.

"Okay, translate this to the mother," Mary said to Freddy. "Tell her again I am not a doctor. I am happy to leave right this moment if she says so."

Freddy translated.

"She doesn't want you to leave," Freddy said when the woman stopped speaking.

"Okay, tell her that sea snakes produce a neurotoxin. Tell her that the lungs will no longer receive messages from the brain to keep pumping. When that happens, the boy will die. If we can keep his lungs moving and his air passages free, he stands a chance. Tell her in a hospital they would have an oxygen ventilator and the boy would likely survive. Tell her his survival in this situation is not at all certain."

Freddy looked at Mary. Then he translated.

The mother took it stoically. She nodded.

"Tell her that normal air has about twenty-one percent oxygen. After we breathe, the exhalation contains about seventeen percent. That's why we can breathe for him. If the lungs work, we'll get enough oxygen to the boy's system. If he makes it through until the morning, he may be able to breathe on his own again. Or he may die. I am not a doctor. Make sure you tell her that again."

Freddy translated. A few people in the room nodded. I watched Mary.

A LONG NIGHT. MARY taped the boy's mouth securely to hold the snorkel mouthpiece after she cut off the top portion of plastic. Absurdly, a long discussion passed about a bicycle pump. Would it provide air? Mary said she didn't know and wasn't willing to depend on it. She entrusted me with dividing the people into three teams. Each team took a turn. Mary stayed beside the bed to supervise everything. Freddy served as translator.

Breathing. The snorkel projecting from the boy's mouth like a dull tongue. Each person breathed five minutes for the boy. In, out. A rotation of people. Neighbors brought in more lights and so the room shimmered in whiteness. Far away, we heard the bars begin playing music. The boy's mother sat at the head of the bed, her hands loosely settled on his shoulders. Freddy roamed in and out of the room frequently, bringing information and translating whenever requested.

The boy's lungs moved up and down. Our entire world centered on his lungs. Each breath held hope and potential disaster at the same time. His leg did not diminish in size.

In the early morning someone brought food. I made Mary step away and take a break. Outside, she stretched her back and leaned against me for a moment. I put my arms around her.

"I don't know his name," she whispered. "I don't even know that."

"It's okay."

"They've said it to me a dozen times, but it keeps slipping away. It's horrible to not know his name."

"Eat something."

She shook her head.

"I'm not hungry," she said. "Not now."

"Okay," I said. "When you're ready."

"He may not make it no matter what we do."

"We do the thing we can. The thing in front of us. We do our best."

She nodded. We stayed quietly together for a moment. It was warm.

"Weren't the turtles wonderful this morning?" she asked, her voice sleepy. "I keep remembering them."

"Yes."

"And Freddy with his arms outstretched to say good-bye," she said. "I want to remember that."

I squeezed her tighter. She didn't say anything for a little while.

"Okay, back at it," she said. "He's still alive."

"You're doing great."

"He's so small. The venom may take longer to dissipate than we thought."

"Then we keep breathing for him a little longer. No one will quit."

"He's a beautiful child."

"Yes, he is."

She squeezed me. She squeezed with all her might.

"Knock knock," she whispered.

"Who's there?"

"Little Old Lady."

"Little Old Lady who?"

"I didn't know you could yodel."

She pushed away. I stayed outside and ate some rice. Freddy joined me. We ate standing, our bowls held in front of us. The pounding music from the bar had stopped. Now it was merely a night on an island with stars above. The palm trees beside the road bent a little in the wind. But it was a quiet night.

"Your sister is incredible," I said to Freddy.

"Always has been."

"Think the boy will make it?"

"I'd never bet against her. She'll get him through it. She used to nurse animals back to health. She had a little infirmary behind the garage at home. She became a pretty accomplished veterinarian."

"The boy got a lot of poison."

"Looks like it," Freddy nodded. "But the Indonesian people are strong. They're resilient."

It was my turn to nod.

"You mind if I ask you something personal?" Freddy asked, brushing rice from his beard. "I think this might be the time to talk about it. With everything going on, I mean, and I'm not sure when we'll have another moment alone."

"Go ahead," I said.

"If it ever becomes time for her to go, you won't hesitate, will you?" Freddy asked. "You know what I mean. Sorry. She's my sister, so I have to ask. You don't seem like the kind of guy to blink when the time comes, but I wanted to ask anyway."

"Are we talking about what I think we're talking about?"

Freddy nodded.

"I'll do what I need to do when the time comes," I said. "I promised her."

"You're going to have to help her do what she has to do," Freddy said. "There's a difference."

"That's down the road. If it ever arrives at all."

Freddy smiled. He ate two quick forkfuls of rice. We both knew what had to arrive, but we didn't say it openly.

"Let's hope it's a long way down the road. Let's hope it never has to come to it. But if you ever have any doubts, you contact me and I'll be on the next plane. You remember those turtles. You let them go because you never owned them to begin with."

"What's your mother say?"

"Mom works in a hospital. She sees people linger too long every day. I'm not getting mystic on you, Cobb, but death is a part of it.

Mary knows that. I will mourn her from that day forward, but I won't equivocate about her dignity or her right to leave."

I nodded.

"Let's hope it all remains theoretical," I said.

"I'm glad you two met," Freddy said, changing the topic. "She's never been happier."

"I'm glad, too."

"A friend asked me once after a drunken night if I could know how or when I would die, would I want to know the answer to either question? And if so, which one? You couldn't know both, you see. Not in this game."

"What did you pick?"

"I figured it this way. Knowing how would be too gruesome. I mean, you might die by being crushed under a steamroller, right? Horrible death and you'd spend the rest of your days worrying about it. On the other hand, if you knew when, would you change the way you live? The thing with Mary is, she knows the whole equation. Not exactly. Not precisely. But she has a better idea than most. And she doesn't change anything because she is so entirely Mary. I love her for not wanting to know without any surety."

"It's a bar game," I said. "Your test, I mean."

"I know it is," he said. "But imagine how happy it would make you to know that someone who loved you, someone who would stay beside you, would make sure the how and when were as graceful and gentle as possible. In that small way, Mary is luckier than we are."

"Thoreau said, 'Live your life, do your work, then take your hat.' I understand."

He hugged me again. Freddy the Turtle Guy.

AT DAWN THE BOY reached a crisis. I was inside, waiting my turn to breathe for him, when his lungs suddenly gave up. An Indonesian woman had been breathing for him. Suddenly the boy arched and then stopped. A terrible quiet came into the room, and Mary, just to one side, shot past the woman and checked the mouthpiece.

"No, no, no, no," Mary said, her hands moving over the boy.

She nudged the Indonesian woman to one side and the woman gladly departed. The boy's mom stood as tall as the room allowed and spoke rapidly in Bahasa. Mary put her lips to the mouthpiece and breathed evenly into the boy's lungs. The boy did not respond. "Jesus," Mary whispered between breaths.

"You have more air, Cobb," she said. "More volume. Come here, please, and take over."

I did. I pushed hard into the snorkel tube. Mary told me to blow harder. The boy did not resist, but he did not breathe, either. His lungs refused to function. His good leg began to dance slightly on the table.

"We're going to have to administer a tracheotomy," Mary said. "Freddy!"

He didn't come right away. When he did, he had obviously been asleep.

"I need a sharp knife, fast," she said. "Sterilize it as best you can. Fast!" she yelled. "Keep breathing, Cobb. Keep air going in even if his lungs don't move. Cobb, nice and steady. Freddy? Freddy, come on."

Mary took the mother's hands and led her outside. The mother did not protest. When Mary returned, she had a bunch of white cloths and a small filleting knife in her hand. Freddy came in behind her.

"Christmas cookies, I don't want to do this," Mary said, her hands moving to lay out the knife and cloths. "This is your island, Freddy, you do it."

"Do you want me to?" he asked.

I breathed hard into the snorkel tube. The boy's lungs rose and fell. They rose less dramatically than before, but they rose.

"Oh, thank God," Mary said. "Keep it going."

I looked at her. Counted. Then breathed again into the tube. The boy's lungs inflated more solidly. When he let out his air, it came out smoothly. I nodded. Earlier in the night, he had breathed just this way.

"Maybe that means we're over the hump," Mary said.

"Why did you wake me up, then?" Freddy asked, smiling.

"Oh, Freddy, only visiting you would I end up doing something like this."

"You love it."

"No," she said, "I don't."

"Lamb is coming by in a few minutes. She said she figured everyone would be willing to help in the beginning, but later on, now, in other words, you would need reinforcements."

"Smart woman," Mary said.

"She loves me, so you knew she was smart already."

Mary shook her head.

"We'll keep the knife in case," Mary said. "Go back to sleep. Tell the mom she can come back in if she likes."

"Yes, Captain," Freddy said. "Cobb, did you know she was so bossy?"

I nodded. Counted. Breathed.

Freddy left. For a minute or two we worked alone on the boy. Mary wiped his forehead with a damp cloth. The boy's eyes opened.

"Hello," Mary said to him.

The boy shut his eyes again. Mary looked at me. A fever breaking.

# 10

On our last day in Indonesia, Freddy rented three horses and went with us around Gili. We left at six o'clock, an hour before sunset. The horses were bays, all from the same bloodlines. We rode in shorts and flip-flops, not ideal for horseback riding, but Freddy pushed us into a gallop as soon as we reached the northern end of the island anyway. The road that led past bars and hotels on the eastern side of the island gave way to open beaches and wilder seas. A few bamboo huts stood on poles deeper in the forest, their views worth a million dollars anywhere else in the world.

Freddy pulled us up once we had rounded the point. The sun had begun to fall into the ocean. Freddy waved out to a group of coral heads.

"When I first came here, a fisherman told me that reef was loaded with sharks. I didn't believe him, of course. So one day I came out here and went diving. A friend went with me. As soon as we got in the water, I'm telling you, it was like a house where your parents are fighting downstairs. Weird, creepy vibe that I'd never experienced anywhere else. But we didn't care. We swam out and dove down and it was like swimming through a gang fight. Sharks cruising everywhere, and not just little black tips, I promise. We turned around and headed back. That water gives me the heebie-jeebies."

"How long are you going to stay here, Freddy?" Mary asked quietly.

He shrugged. He kept his eyes out on the ocean.

"Maybe always," he said. "I have days where I get itchy, but mostly I love it here. Sometimes I wonder if I'm hiding out. You know, the real world is somewhere else, I tell myself. But the real world is always somewhere else, isn't it? I remember that feeling in the States all the time."

"Do you own the house and land?" I asked.

"With Lamb. You need an Indonesian partner to own land here. Lamb's my Indo-par. That's what they call Indonesian partners."

"The world seems to be right here," Mary said.

"As much as any place," Freddy said, looking around. "And you know, I couldn't wear a suit and tie and punch a clock. I couldn't. Not after living here. So this island is shaping us all the time. Island people are different from mainland people. It's hard to put your finger on it, but it's true. I plan to come back to the States one of these days. It probably wouldn't be a bad idea to make the rounds and talk to donors. We'll see how it goes."

"Do you miss New England?" I asked.

"Sometimes I miss those cold winter nights. You know, when you happen to be outside and the temperature is just brutal but the air is as clear as—what? Someone give me a metaphor."

"As pain," Mary said.

"As dice," I said.

"I'll go with dice," Freddy said. "You know what I mean. And the wind stops and the woods are quiet and you feel peace and serenity. I miss that. I don't think Indonesia has the equivalent, but it has different pleasures. But, yes, I miss New England."

"You miss New Hampshire," Mary said, "not Massachusetts."

"Goes without saying," Freddy said.

We rode on. The horses were jealous of the lead, so they kept surging to get in front. If one of us broke into a trot, the others followed. It became a little game. None of us knew much about riding horses, so a trot served as a serial spanking by the horse's back on our backsides.

When we turned the last end of the island, we trotted three across, with Mary in the water kicking up a splash. It was a cliché moment—horses on a wild beach—but it was also lovely. The sun rolled into the ocean the way it sometimes can. A set of waves broke on a tide ridge far out into the sea. Lombok, tall and dark, seemed to duck slowly downward until it washed its face in the waves.

We were halfway down the beach when Lamb met us. She sat in the back of a *janur* and chatted with a young driver. The boy smoked a cigarette.

"The Carters are here," Lamb said when we came into range. "They arrived early."

"Oh, Jesus Christ," Freddy said.

"Who are the Carters?" Mary asked.

"Our biggest donors," Freddy said. "They've never been out here, but they've sent their friends. Did they say where they'd put up?"

Lamb said, "The Irish place. They're waiting to have dinner with you."

"I knew they were coming, but I figured you two would be gone by the time they arrived," Freddy said. "I don't want to spend my last night with my sister and her boyfriend being polite to the Carters."

"It's a command performance," Lamb said. "They want to meet the great Turtle Freddy."

"I stink of horses," Freddy said.

"Message delivered," Lamb said.

She spoke quickly to the driver. He laughed and they spun back toward town. Freddy asked where she was going.

"Anyplace but the Irish bar," Lamb called over her shoulder.

"You rat," Freddy called after her, then turned to us. "That means you two have to come. I won't take no for an answer. Have mercy."

"Grovel," Mary said.

But Freddy kicked his horse forward instead. Our horses cantered after him.

THE RESTAURANT WHERE WE went to meet the Carters was named Tír na nÓg, but the waiter—a young man Freddy knew and called Sinbad for reasons he didn't explain—said the Carters had stepped out for a moment and they would return soon. They had asked us to have a drink and wait. Freddy ordered Bintang beers for us all. Mary looked at the menu, and after she had studied it for a while she read the legend of the name off the back cover.

"Once, a long time ago," she read, "the Celtic hero Oisin fell in love with a ban-sidhe named Niamh. A ban-sidhe is a fairy woman, but more than fairy, she is a woman. Winning her love, Niamh carried him to Tír na nÓg, a blustery island off the west coast of Ireland, and there she kept him three hundred years. They lived side by side in bliss and no mortal, before or since, has lived such a life of pleasure and joy. The island—known also as the Land Over Sea and the Land Under Wave—could be reached only by the fairy horses, who ran on the sea as on ice.

"In time, though, being a man, and given a man's vision of life, Oisin longed to set eyes on his native land. When he told his love that he wished to go, Niamh cried for a year, then called her favorite horse to her. She told Oisin that the horse would carry him back to his land, but that he must be mindful of two things. First, years had passed, and Oisin must be prepared to visit the many deaths of his loved ones and over that she could not protect him. Second, he must not dismount the horse, because to do so would be to add his years in one instant to his living frame, and he would grow old in a moment.

"Kissing Niamh farewell, Oisin rode a white fairy horse across the sea. When he arrived, he found his comrades dead, his family dispersed, his land under rule by foreigners. It brought him great discontent to see the state of the world, and he turned his horse back to Tír na nÓg. On his return, however, he came across a group of men struggling to load a stone onto a wagon, and in his attempt to help, he slipped from the saddle and his feet struck the earth. In the time it takes to blow out a candle, he became a blind, helpless old man. The horse ran into the sea and became salt.

"Oisin wandered the western Irish coast for many years until Saint Patrick took pity on him. Saint Patrick allowed Oisin to live in his house and attempted to convert him to Christianity. But Oisin—despite the kindnesses shown him by Saint Patrick—continued to haunt the western coastline, the scent of salt water calling him to turn his head in the direction where his love waited. For her part, Niamh caused the island to appear in the mists from time to time, hoping against reason that her love might return.

"Over the years a few people have claimed to have seen the island where the fairies continue to live, but whether their reports are true or not, no living person can judge with accuracy. One claim made by people who follow such legends is that the island may only be seen by those who have lost their true love. The island, they say, appears in the heart, not before the eyes, and there the ice imprisons the sea, which beats against the underside of the cold north wasteland, where many loves sing in silence to the seals."

"Oh, my," she said when she finished.

"Mawkish Irish," Freddy said.

"Sing in silence to the seals," I repeated, taking a drink of beer. "That's a mouthful."

"It's meant to be this island," Freddy said. "We'll never grow old here. That's the idea, anyway."

The Carters arrived at that moment. They looked like donors. Ken Carter, as he introduced himself, was in his early seventies, fit, and tan the way wealthy people often seem to be. He wore a blue blazer over a blue shirt and khakis. His wife, Millicent, not Milly, wore her hair swept back. She wore capri khakis and espadrilles.

"You must be Freddy," Ken said when the rest of the introductions were finished. "How nice to meet you finally."

"And you," Freddy said.

"Do you know," Ken said to us, catching the bartender's eye, "we have known Freddy and his work for more than a decade and this is the first time we've met. I was beginning to think you were a myth."

"Except for all the fine reports we received from friends over the years," Millicent said. "The Van Deusens haven't stopped talking about you and this island. They have actually talked about retiring here for part of the year."

"They could do worse," Freddy said.

Ken ordered two vodka gimlets. Freddy ordered another round of Bintang beers.

"Well, we were just out riding," Mary said, "so please excuse our appearances."

"No, it's our fault, no need for apologies," Millicent said. "Our travel connections worked out better than we anticipated. And Ken wanted to see the south shore of Lombok. The United Arab Emirates have purchased a hundred miles of coastline there with plans to develop it. Money is no object, as you can guess, with their oil dividends. They are planning three first-rate golf courses, a resort, the whole thing. Ken has some friends who are looking into it. We're hoping they can be persuaded to go about it as gently as possible from an environmental standpoint."

"Actually," Ken said, gathering the two gimlets from the bartender and passing one to Millicent, "we hoped you would consider doing some consulting there, Freddy. You know, to help preserve the coral and the sea life."

"I'd heard rumors," Freddy said. "So they're going forward with it?"

Ken and Millicent raised their glasses. We nodded our beer necks toward their glasses.

"It's a short flight from Australia," Ken said after taking a sip.

"And the Chinese and Asian countries will use it as a resort. From a business point of view, it's a perfect fit."

"And no chance they will simply halt work on it?" Freddy asked. He meant it as a joke, but I wasn't sure they caught it.

Ken shrugged. Millicent drank some of her gimlet.

"It will go forward," Ken said. "That's the reality. That's why we want to get you on board as a consultant. They are smart businessmen. They know the ocean is the selling point, so it makes sense to keep the ocean attractive. I know that sounds horribly pragmatic, but pragmatism is a virtue when it comes to projects like this."

"Sounds as though we could be launched on a political discussion. Should we get a table?" Millicent asked. "I confess, I'm starving."

At dinner they asked about our plans, and when they learned we were heading home the next morning, they apologized for intruding. We assured them it was not a problem. Out of politeness, they asked where we lived in the States, and when I mentioned I taught at St. Paul's, Ken's eyes lit up.

"Now you've done it," Millicent said. "Ken went to St. Paul's a hundred years ago."

"Finest school I've ever known," Ken said. "Best in the country—university or otherwise."

"It's a great place," I said.

"You teach history?" Ken asked.

"He's stuck in about 1947," Mary said. "Music and literature."

We went through the name game, recalling past professors, buildings, maintenance workers. He recalled the campus with uncanny accuracy. He had read about the recent floods, when the Turkey River overflowed; he had contributed to, but had not yet seen, the new library; he had followed with interest some of the controversy surrounding the past headmaster.

"Do they still dig the foxholes?" he asked as our conversation about the school slowed.

"Yes, they do," I said.

"It's a tradition at St. Paul's for the students to creep out in the woods and dig these earthen shelters," Ken explained to the table. "They do it first thing in the fall. In some cases, they pass down the dugouts from one class to the next. Then they cover the holes with boards and twigs and everything else they can drag out there, and finally they have a first class little clubhouse. Keeps them away from the prying eyes of the instructors. Most of the clubs have a way to vent smoke, so they can have a fire and stay pretty warm, insulated as they are by earth. Some of my fondest memories are of that silly mud hole in the ground out by the Pillsbury fields. We'd make tea, and sometimes someone would come up with a little whiskey. Oh, we thought we were quite something."

"It still goes on," I said. "But now that everything is coed, it gets more complicated."

"I bet it does. I heard of an alumnus who wanted to be buried in his group's foxhole, but the headmaster wouldn't hear of it. He feared it would start a trend."

We finished our meal two hours later. We walked the Carters to the hotel portion of the restaurant, then said good-bye. Freddy spent a few minutes going over plans to show them the turtles and to take them out on a glass-bottomed boat. They listened politely, but then promised they could pick all that up tomorrow. For now, they insisted, we should go have a final visit together. They shook hands with us and turned to leave.

"I owe you all a drink," Freddy said as we began our walk back north toward his compound.

He bought us ten.

The Sama-Sama Club ran a special on half-price frozen margaritas, and a reggae band covered a selection of Bob Marley. Halfway through her first drink, Mary pulled Freddy and me onto the dance floor. We danced and slid around, while Mary, enjoying herself, tried to invent a turtle dance for Freddy. She performed various turtle pantomimes, but conveying turtle-ness was more difficult than she anticipated. She settled finally on something a little more generic.

We danced until one, when the band stopped playing, then we took the beach back, walking through the water. Not far from Freddy's compound, Mary put her arms around both of our necks and made us swing her.

"Someone likes her margaritas," Freddy said, helping me hoist her.

"You guys are too tall," she said.

When we reached Freddy's deck, he took us to inspect the turtle aquariums. In the darkness, the turtles swam in quiet disarray, bumping into one another, circling. Freddy reached in and picked one up and held it skyward. He demonstrated how you could imagine a turtle flying if you closed one eye and imagined it going from star to star. The turtle rowed his small flippers, looking for water. Freddy placed him gently back in the tank.

"The only word that rhymes with turtle is girdle," Freddy said, his voice drunk. "That doesn't seem fair."

"And Myrtle," I said.

"Yes, but that's a name," Freddy said.

"I'm going to bed," Mary said. "Suddenly it's time to go to bed."

She put her arms around Freddy.

"I love you," she said to him. "I always will."

Then she hugged me.

"I love you, too. You are my two men. I would make you both pancakes every day of your lives."

"But you're a lousy cook," Freddy said, "so that's not saying much."

"Pancakes every day," Mary said. "There is no greater love."

"Knock knock," I said.

"Who's there?" Mary asked, her voice rising in pleasure and curiosity.

"Lionel."

"I know this one," Mary said.

"You know them all," Freddy added.

"I know this one, but I can't think of it. Too many margaritas."

"Lionel," I reminded her.

"Lionel who?"

"Lionel eat you if you don't feed him."

"Knock knock," she said.

"No," Freddy said, "absolutely not. I am going to bed. No knock-knock fest for me."

Mary looked at me. She had had a few drinks.

"Barry," she said. "Barry the treasure where no one will find it."

Freddy groaned and went to bed. He called over his shoulder that he would be up with us in the morning and that the *janur* driver had promised to pick us up at nine. Freddy shouted that he expected pancakes in the morning.

"He's been alive 13,703 days," she said, watching him leave. "My brother."

"I'm putting you to bed."

"Okay, good idea. 'And flights of angels sing thee to thy rest.' My father used to say that to us."

"Now cracks a noble heart," I said.

"I swoon," she said and did.

BEFORE WE BOARDED THE jet boat for our return trip to Bali, we watched five Indonesian men loading cattle onto a long boat. Most of the island's population turned out for the entertainment. The men had a strategy, but so did the cattle. Without cranes or ramps, the men jammed the stern of the boat onto the beach. Then they secured a lead rope from either end of the cow's muzzle, keeping the cow centered like the leather patch on a slingshot. When the boat dipped, and all other portents seemed right, they poked a needle into the animal's behind and made him leap on board.

Sometimes it worked. Mostly it didn't. But it was entertainment either way.

"Where are they taking them anyway?" Mary asked Lamb.

Lamb had come along to say good-bye. Freddy had gone to breakfast with the Carters, but he promised to see us off. The sun had begun to throw its heat. Some schoolchildren stood close to the boat and laughed when the cows jumped out.

"To Lombok," Lamb said. "They'll take them by truck around the island."

"Aren't they worried they could jump out in the middle of the sea?" I asked.

Lamb sucked her teeth. I took the sound to mean that cattle are not as stupid as that.

Meanwhile, the *janurs* lined up along the beach, arranging themselves for the new wave of Europeans and Westerners who would arrive on the incoming jet boat. The drivers joked and smoked. A teenage boy played some music on a small stereo system and pretended to dance. Another boy brought a monkey along the path. The monkey wore a harness over its lower quarters, which left its hands free to do tricks and to beg. The monkey handler rehearsed his pet a little while, killing time.

"Where's Freddy?" Mary asked me. "Do you think he's tied up?"

"He'll be back, I bet."

"I'd hate to leave without saying good-bye."

I put my arm over her shoulders.

"How you feeling this morning?" I asked.

"Margarita-riffic," she said.

The jet boat appeared on the horizon, flying northward from Lombok. It was easily identifiable by its speed and by the brilliant white wake it left behind it. "Oh, Freddy," she sighed. Before we could give the jet boat much thought, or look again for Freddy, we saw the crowd parting. It had been an unusually large crowd because of the cattle loading, but it began to move apart, making room for something approaching.

Because I was taller, I saw it before Mary. The boy Mary had saved approached with his mother walking behind him. Both wore traditional Indonesian clothes, bright and clean. The boy limped a little. The mother kept her eye on him. They both wore a single kernel of rice in the center of their foreheads. If I had to make a guess, I suspected the mother had borrowed the clothes. Neither outfit conformed to their builds, but they wore them proudly and moved comfortably in them.

"They have come to pay their respects to Mary," Lamb said. "It's our way."

"They don't have to," Mary said, but she understood it was beyond that.

"You have saved a life here," Lamb said. "They will not forget that."

The boy looked beautiful. He stopped a few feet away from Mary. His brown eyes focused on Mary's. Then he bent forward and took her hand. He pressed the back of her hand to his forehead. He did not do this quickly or with any of the impatience of a child. When he stood, he spoke a long, quiet monologue.

"What is he doing, Lamb?" Mary asked in a whisper.

"He is pledging himself to you and your children. His life, in this time or next, will be overjoyed to see you. You two are bound. Your soul is not alone and it has been met."

"Please thank him," Mary said.

"They're not quite finished," Lamb said.

The mother moved forward and handed the boy a plate. The boy, in turn, handed the plate to Mary.

"That is *baten tegeh,*" Lamb said, pronouncing it carefully so we would remember. "It is a great gift. The woman has saved for it, believe me. A baker has sculpted rice cakes with the scene of you saving her son. If you were not leaving, she would add fruit to it. But the cakes are your story and the record of your being here."

Mary nodded.

"How should I respond, Lamb?" Mary asked.

"It's not for you to respond. It's for you to receive," she said.

"Please tell them thank you and that I am honored."

Lamb translated. The woman nodded. Then the boy and the woman turned and left. The monkey made a loud chattering sound that made everyone laugh. When we turned back to the sea, the form of the boat had cleared the horizon and now came down on us swiftly and too soon.

THE JET BOAT TURNED backward and let the passengers climb down into ankle-deep water. One of the mates, a young fellow with a baseball cap, told us to wait a moment while they cleaned the boat. We stood and watched the Westerners become absorbed by the *janur* drivers. Like water going into a sponge, Lamb said, and she was right. We hugged her and said good-bye. Mary asked her to take care of Freddy. Lamb nodded. She held her hands in front of her and bowed slightly. We bowed back.

Freddy arrived just as we stepped on board. He jammed a small dive boat onto the beach next to the jet boat and hopped out. The Carters sat midship, and they stood when the boat became steady. We waved. They waved back. Freddy jumped out of his boat, then over the railing into ours.

"Didn't think I'd make it, did you?" Freddy boomed.

The mates knew him. Everyone seemed to know him and smiled at his size and happiness.

"We're off, Freddy," Mary said. "To infinity and beyond."

He hugged me. He looked me in the eye, then patted my shoulder. Then he turned to Mary.

"The only tragedy in my life is that you live too far away from me," he said.

"I feel the same."

"Give Mom my love. Tell her to come out here. Tell her she has to."

"She will one of these days, Freddy."

He scooped her up and held her close.

"Pedal down," he said. "Live it all."

"I will."

He set her back on the deck. Then he hopped over the side into the water. It was only up to his knees. He lifted his hands free of the gunwale when the mates pushed the boat into deeper water. He waved. Mary waved back.

# Wolves

# 11

MARY'S FAVORITE MOVIE WAS *All That Heaven Allows,* a 1955 film starring Jane Wyman and Rock Hudson. Rock Hudson plays a down-to-earth nurseryman who comes to prune Jane Wyman's apple trees. Jane Wyman is a widow, but also a member of a stuffy country club society that looks down on Rock Hudson as "not their sort." Jane Wyman's adult children are repulsed by Rock Hudson's blue collar roots, his love of agriculture, his ability to work with his hands. Nevertheless, Jane Wyman is charmed by Hudson's arty, bohemian friends—who drink red wine, eat large potluck meals while listening to jazz music—and she can't help seeing the inherent beauty in his life's work.

But it was a window and an old mill in the film that Mary loved more than anything.

When Rock Hudson shows Jane Wyman the grounds of his nursery, they enter an old grist mill that has been abandoned. Hudson is apologetic about the mess, but Jane Wyman sees the potential in the building and says she would renovate it and bring it back to life. It is as different from her suburban house as a building could be, but it possesses an enormous round window overlooking a brook. The window is taller than a man, and easily as wide, and they share their first embrace in front of it.

We watched the movie on a snowy Saturday afternoon when the sun refused to come out at all and Indonesia seemed a million miles away. We built a fire in my fireplace. She lay on her side with her head on my chest, her left leg over my legs, and now and then we pulled closer to each other. We didn't turn on any lights, but watched the movie on my laptop.

"Didn't they say he was gay?" I asked at one point, my chin on the top of her head.

"Who?"

"Rock Hudson."

"Still," she said.

"A gay nurseryman and Ronald Reagan's first wife? That's your favorite movie."

"Shush," she said.

"You have strange tastes."

"It's Romeo and Juliet, only they're separated by social class. Don't you get it?"

I nodded. I didn't care. I liked having her near.

When they entered the mill, she sat up.

"Watch now," she said.

The mill had a mill wheel and gigantic beams suspended over granite floors. Jane Wyman, dressed warmly against the cold, slowly lets her eyes travel over the interior. It's beautiful. She sees it all—what the house could be, what their life could be like, what beauty they could share. It's different from her country-club life, but more genuine and substantial, and all she needs to do in order to embrace it is to stop caring what other people think.

"All my life I've been looking for that window," Mary said.

She climbed over me, waited next to the computer, then hit the pause button when the camera rested squarely on the window.

"That's our house," she said to me.

"What's our house?"

"Right there. Like that. We have to find it."

"You're cracking up."

"I'll find it."

"How will you go about finding it?"

"I'll look. Don't worry; I'm good at things like this. I'll find it."

A month later, she did.

ON THE COLDEST AFTERNOON of the winter, with the truck heater going full blast, we drove to Newmarket, a former mill town on the Lamprey River. It was not far from the University of New Hampshire campus and under forty miles from the St. Paul's campus. We stopped at a bakery shop and got two teas and two old-fashioned doughnuts, and balanced everything as I drove carefully through the frozen streets. Even with a warm cup of tea and the truck heater going at the top of its power, cold penetrated the cab. It had been minus twenty at eight o'clock in the morning, and the sun had not warmed us all day.

"This, my friend," Mary said, her voice excited, "is what positive thinking can do."

"Teach me, master."

"The universe has heard my call and is now responding."

"But you've not actually been in this place, have you?"

"Details, that's all."

"I think that's a yes-or-no question."

She looked at me. She picked up the Realtor's prospectus sheet.

"Incorporated in 1727," she said, "Newmarket was one of six towns granted by the Massachusetts Bay Colony in the last year of the reign of King George the First. It was named for Newmarket in Suffolk, England. The Lamprey River, running through town, was named for John Lamprey, whose name was Saxon for 'a woodland enclosure where peace is to be found.'"

"Can't get better than that," I said. "Quite a boy, John Lamprey."

"A cotton textile mill, built in 1823, dominated the town's

waterfront, with seven textile mills harnessing water power at the falls. Newmarket was a center of the New England shipping trade with the West Indies."

"Is this from Wikipedia?"

"Yes," she said.

"And your friend said this is an old carriage house?"

"Yes. Beaten down a little, but with good bones."

"Bones are good."

"It's brick and stone. It can't be in horrible shape."

I looked at her. She fished an old-fashioned doughnut out of the bakery bag and bit it, her eyes on me.

"It can't hurt to look, can it?" she asked when she stopped chewing.

"Am I Rock Hudson in this scenario?"

"More or less."

We took Woodlawn Avenue. Then Birch. Then Onquiquisit Trail. Mary studied the map on her lap and looked back and forth from the directions to the landscape. The afternoon light fell on the hillsides. An apple orchard appeared on our left, the branches white and cold.

We saw it almost at the same instant. An enormous house—an estate, really—took up the entire right side of the road. The estate obviously kept horses, because white fences ran everywhere, dividing the sweeping hill that ran down from the house. A gravel drive went up the center of the land, bisecting the paddocks, and led the eye to the magnificent home at the top of a knoll. The estate had no name that we could see. Instead it had the quiet calm of real money, of buildings that had lived side by side for centuries.

And to the left, beside a small stream, stood a brick and stone building.

Mary reached over and grabbed my hand.

"That's it, Rock," she said.

"It looks sweet."

"It looks perfect."

"What's the Realtor's name again?" I asked, noticing a car with a Century 21 sign on its side, parked beside the building.

"Danny Sullivan."

I pulled in beside the Century 21 car. Before I could turn off the engine, Mary climbed out. No one had plowed the driveway or shoveled the walk to the house. I saw Danny Sullivan's tracks leading to the front door. An enormous oak took up the right-hand section of the yard. Casement windows—leaded and old—looked out from the stone façade. The building's proportions were simple and balanced.

I caught up with Mary at the door. Danny Sullivan opened it.

"I apologize for not shoveling," Danny said, his face red and round, his blue suit coat straining to hold its buttons, "but I've got a balky ticker. We should have gotten someone out here, but this just came on the market, so we don't have things set up as we'd like. But come in, come in. Mighty cold out."

I knew we wanted the house on our first step inside. Mary knew it, too, and she glanced at me and nodded.

I shook Danny's hand. He was short, maybe five feet seven, and his wispy red hair covered his balding scalp only reluctantly. He closed the door behind us. It shut with a solid, quiet authority.

"You've got the listing sheet, I see," he said. "So you know this was a carriage house for the manor up on the hill. It was actually a stable, and then was converted years ago. Solid. We've had a building inspector go through it—and of course you would want to go through it on your own if you're interested—but the foundation and roof are excellent. The walls are stone and brick, so naturally they're solid. The brick needs repointing, the stone, too. Upkeep. No one's lived in her for twenty years or more."

"Why are they selling?"

Danny Sullivan shrugged. Mary listened, but I knew she was impatient to look around.

"Time, I guess," he said. "You know, you think you'll have a use for something, but the house on the hill is so big, and has so many bedrooms, that they really don't need a guesthouse or anything of the kind. The carriage house is not in view from the main house, so they're interested in having quiet neighbors. That's more important than the price, believe me. If you're a dirt biker, or have ATV's or snow machines, forget it. They won't sell."

"Who are they?" I asked.

"Dudleys. They made their money in shoes right here. Boot manufacturers. They built this is 1801. The compound, I mean. They are involved with the Appalachian Mountain Club. Charter members. You know the conditions of this sale?"

"Not exactly."

"Well, it's modeled on the forest lands up in Maine. You will own the house, but they will retain the rights to the land beneath the house. Not everyone feels comfortable with that setup, but there are thousands of camps in Maine that work under the same provisions. Your lease will be for ninety-nine years, with options for renewal. The price of the house is lowered accordingly. This is quite a good deal if you can live with the notion of someone else owning the land under you. The Dudleys reserve the right to be first buyers if you decide to sell."

"I'm dying to look at the house," Mary asked. "Can we talk as we go?"

"Of course, of course," Danny said, holding out his arm to guide us to the right. "I'm sorry to get carried away. It's just such an interesting property."

Then Danny had the good sense to be quiet.

We took two steps down into the living room. The building, I decided, was a cottage more than anything else, but it had a remarkable resemblance to the mill building in *All That Heaven Allows.* It had the same feeling. Wide pine floors. A Count Rumford fireplace. Casement windows, lead lined, and bookshelves everywhere. I imagined the room on a fall day, with a fire working in the hearth, the chatter of leaves hitting against the building in the heaviest winds.

"We'll take it," Mary said, quietly turning to see everything.

"I'll wrap it up this minute," Danny said, joking. "Just let me get my briefcase."

"I'm serious," Mary said. "We're both serious, aren't we, Cobb?"

I nodded.

Danny Sullivan didn't know what to say.

"Did bears ever live in this house?" Mary asked, still moving around the room to study its features. "Because I have a feeling maybe they did."

We did not buy the house that day, but by March, on a blustery, cold day, we signed papers in Danny Sullivan's Century 21 office and took possession of the house. Danny presented us with a broom, a traditional gift, he said, when people purchased homes. A new broom sweeps clean, he said, but an old broom gets in the corners. The bank had sent a lawyer, a dour, gray man named Mr. Sommers. Danny Sullivan represented the Dudleys' interest. Mary and I had worked out a fair financial arrangement between us. The mortgage was well within our means.

My father came to the signing.

He arrived after we did, stamping his boots on the welcome mat, his olive Windbreaker puffed around his body. The Windbreaker whistled when he moved. On the back, in white letters, it read: *Post 73, Wentworth.* He had been my American Legion baseball coach and he still owned the jacket. Beneath the jacket he wore a red plaid L.L. Bean flannel shirt, a pair of insulated khakis, and Chippewa work boots. Without checking, I knew he carried a Leatherman knife on his left hip, his belt rubbed white from years of carrying the tool.

We were already seated near Danny Sullivan's conference table. I stepped into the vestibule and brought my father inside. I introduced him around the table.

Mary stood and hugged him. Mr. Sommers and Danny Sullivan shook his hand.

"Have a seat, Mr. Cobb," Danny said. "We're just beginning. Your son tells me you're a contractor."

"A house carpenter, really. I was a mortgage broker in my last life."

"Well, you'll like this house. Solid as a tick," Danny said, passing out papers.

My father kept the Windbreaker on during the signing. I knew he felt uncomfortable when he met new people. He placed both hands on the table and watched. I also knew he had dealt with men like Danny Sullivan and Mr. Sommers every day of his working life. They did not dazzle or confuse him. He watched them quietly, listening attentively, understanding the rhythms of a closing as well, if not better, than they did. I looked at him and smiled. He smiled back. It was good to have my father at the signing.

Danny Sullivan went through the papers quickly. No toxins left on the property. Bank assessment. Waterlands access as a result of the brook running past the house. Loan agreements. A paper giving us forty-eight hours to reconsider. Standard paperwork. Mary signed each paper first, then slid it to me. I signed beneath or beside her name. We were on the fourth document when I realized her name had become nothing more than an erratic line.

My stomach dropped. I had the sense that the room had become smaller and smaller, shrinking until nothing existed except the white landscape of the documents. To stall, I pretended my pen had gone dry. Danny Sullivan laughed when I passed him my pen and asked for a new one.

"We have no shortage of pens around here," he said and laughed.

Mr. Sommers smiled. My dad nodded.

I looked down again at Mary's last signature. Not only did it fail to cohere in any meaningful way, it also ran at an odd angle, covering more than the slot allotted for her signature. I tried for an instant to attribute it to her excitement over the closing, but I knew better. I took a breath. I had difficulty seeing. I listened to Mr. Sommers and Danny Sullivan discussing something related to other closings, a new aspect of such deals, but I couldn't concentrate.

I looked at Mary and sneaked my hand under the table. We held hands for a moment. Then more papers arrived and she bent over them, her hand driving the pen in a jerky motion across the page. She did not seem to notice or sense anything out of the ordinary. No one else remarked on the signature. The papers flowed around the table and returned to Danny Sullivan, who collected them and danced them together on end. He clipped them into appropriate packets.

"Congratulations," he said when the last paper had made its way around to him. "You own a beautiful carriage house."

Mary leaned over and kissed me. A burst of wind hit the side of the office hard enough to make the venetian blind covering the window lift for an instant, then swing quietly back against the glass.

MARY CLIMBED INTO MY father's Dodge Dakota for the ride to the house. She waved and held up a bottle of champagne Danny Sullivan had given us. I smiled and waved back. I followed my dad's truck as it moved slowly through the winter streets. As I drove, I tried to collect myself.

My mind went back and forth over the meaning of the signature, the importance of a single line of writing. As quickly as I dismissed its significance, the force of its meaning reasserted itself. I consoled myself that I didn't honestly have a solid notion of what her typical signature might be, but I doubted it looked anything like a straight line going up at a curious angle. I had memorized the possible symptons—involuntary, jerky motions; trouble swallowing; the need to move the entire head when shifting one's gaze; problems with balance; dementia; hesitant, slurred speech—but nowhere in the literature did it say anything about hand coordination. It was possible, I supposed, that she had forgotten how to sign her name, but that seemed like reaching for an explanation. Something had gone wrong. The only thing I couldn't know for sure was whether she knew it or not.

My dad pulled into the driveway and I parked beside him. He had already seen the house. I wouldn't have bought it without his approval, and he had spent a day checking everything about it. I had told Danny Sullivan our house inspector needed the keys. On a moderate day in February, when both Mary and I were busy teaching, my father had worked his way through the house, top to bottom, and had given his report.

"A pretty house," he had said. "Satisfactory in all ways. For the price and style, you couldn't do better."

I grabbed a cooler full of sandwiches and followed them to the door.

"Hey," I said before Mary could get the door open.

She turned. I handed the cooler to my dad and scooped her up.

"I have to carry you across the threshold," I said.

"We're not married," she said.

"We are eternal on the river, married by the Chungamunga girls. Dad, if you'll open the door," I said.

He did. I carried her through and kissed her before setting her back on her feet. My dad closed the door. We were home.

"This is our house," Mary said, turning to see it from every angle.

"It appears to be," I said.

"Who's hungry?" Mary asked, shaking herself. "Cobb, will you light a fire while I put these sandwiches on plates?"

"We have plates?"

"We have five plates, I'll have you know. They look left over from the 1920s. And at least five glasses. So, really, we can entertain."

She left with the cooler in hand. We heard her moving around in the kitchen. My dad hung his jacket on a peg in the stairway and followed me into the living room. We didn't have much in the way of wood. I had collected a bundle of twigs and small branches from the stream area on our last visit. I had also found some scrap pine down in the basement, the odds and ends of a building project someone had never finished. I built a small tent of wood over a rolled up newspaper and lit it. The flames came up yellow and hungry.

"It should have a good draw," my dad said. "The new fireplaces are built with an enormous firebox, but the old-timers knew that just wasted wood. You want a Franklin design like this one has. It's shallow, but it should draw better that way."

"What did we have at home?" I asked.

"A modified Franklin. It was a little deeper than I liked, but it did okay."

My dad walked to the window and looked up the hill toward the manor house. I put on more wood. The newspaper had given way to burning twigs. The pine started to catch and it popped and cracked.

"You know, I'm not much of a believer in the Bible," my dad said, still checking out the window, "but this house is built according to Biblical instructions. You'll get a southern exposure all year long, and that's the best kind. A lot of people don't give much thought to how a house should be oriented. If you put it so the long axis is east-west, you get a blast of sun in the morning, then another at evening. But not here. You won't even need shades or curtains in here except for privacy."

"Dad says the house is built to Biblical instruction," I told Mary as she came in carrying a rusty-looking cookie tin as a tray. The sandwiches rested on mismatched plates. The bottle of champagne chattered happily against the glasses.

"Well, that's good news," Mary said, putting the tray down on a folding chair Danny Sullivan had left. "That has to count for something, doesn't it?"

"Southern exposure," my dad said.

"Cobb, can you open this champagne, please? Make it shoot up and put a dent in the ceiling or something dramatic. We need to commemorate this day."

"Before we do that, can we step outside to the truck?" my dad said. "I have a housewarming present for you. It will only take a minute."

"I love presents," Mary said. "Let's go."

We didn't bother with jackets. My father went ahead, more animated than I had seen him recently. He pulled out his Leatherman and used the knife blade to cut strands of twine that held a blue tarp in place over the truck bed. Moving quickly, he pushed back the tarp. Mary put her head in her hands when she saw it. Her eyes filled and she glanced at me. The window matched the one in the movie, large and round and expansive.

"When you told me about that window," my dad said, "I put out the word with some of my construction friends. A fellow over in Vermont saw one like it at a salvage shop. I think it came out of a church up in Burlington. Does it look anything like your window?"

Mary nodded. Then she hugged him.

"That's the one," she said when she pushed away. "Or as close as we are likely to get in this lifetime. It's round and it has the same panes, sort of."

"It needs a little touch-up. I'm going to take it to my shop where I can work on it, but I should be able to have it ready by late spring. I thought it might go in the living room, overlooking the brook. Or even up in your bedroom."

"Thanks, Dad," I said. "It's a great gift."

"We're going to freeze out here," my father said. "Let me just cover it up again."

Mary wouldn't let him. She pushed the tarp back farther so she could see every detail of the window.

"Did you watch the movie?" she asked my dad, her hands still moving on the tarp.

"No, but Cobb told me what it looked like. Rock Hudson. I haven't seen a Rock Hudson movie in ages."

"It's big," Mary said, examining the window. "I guess I hadn't fully figured that out. Will it be okay in this house?"

"It will be a wonderful feature for the house," my dad said. "You'll live right next to it. Set up a table or a couch, and you'll stare out every day. The seasons will parade right past it."

Finally Mary let us bundle up the window again. "Champagne," I said, clapping my hands to get them warm. We turned to run into the house, and for just an instant we saw that the interior lights cast a quiet glow on the snow beneath the windows. Snow lined the trees and the window ledges. It clung to the roof and dripped in quiet bows. Far away, up the hill, the last light of afternoon stretched and yawned against the meadow, and night waited to step into the yard.

THE HOUSE BECAME OUR center. Although I had responsibilities at St. Paul's and had to live as a dorm master during the week in my small apartment, I sneaked away as frequently as possible. Mary emptied her apartment and moved into the house bit by bit. She brought her furniture—a double bed, dressers, a few good rocking chairs—but most of it didn't fit the style of the carriage house. In our free time, we haunted secondhand shops, attended furniture auctions, went online to scan Craigslist. *House hungry,* Mary called it. Even old boxes, or dumpy-looking dressers put out on a curb with a *Free* sign, held our interest.

On our forays, we took Francis, the young man whose childhood friend had sent him a suicide letter from the grave.

It did not happen naturally, or easily, but Francis became part of our expeditions. At the beginning, at least, his inclusion was entirely pragmatic. Dean Hallowen had called me into his office to check on Francis's progress, because I served as Francis's advisor. A few teachers had reported troubling behavior. He grunted often and loudly at anything he didn't agree with; he slept frequently in class and yawned when not sleeping; he read about 50 percent of the assignments but became annoyed if challenged on it; he had isolated himself socially, and his mother had called a dozen times trying to get him to see a therapist who might provide him some counseling; he had also, despite his many problems, demonstrated an ability on the piccolo—absurdly small in his hands—that might, if developed, qualify him to play in a major city orchestra.

"He's yours on the weekend," Dean Hallowen had said. "Give him some home life. Take him around. Get him out of the student housing."

It was not an order. It was a request, a kind that private secondary schools made regularly of their instructors.

When I mentioned the idea of bringing him with us to an auction in March, Mary didn't hesitate.

"Of course we should," she said. "It's a perfect idea."

Francis didn't think so. Although I had some rapport with him established by the suicide letter ordeal, he shook his head when I invited him along. He lay in his bunk, his feet up on a volleyball, his eyes half-closed. His wide forehead spilled onto the bridge of his nose, giving him the appearance of a scowl. Some kids, I knew, nicknamed him "Plow" because of his prominent forehead. But he was too big to be saddled permanently with a nickname. His arms and chest stretched his shirt.

"Go where?" he asked, yawning.

"Well, to an auction," I said. "With Mary and me."

"Auction?"

"Old things. It's an old train depot that's been converted. It has architectural leftovers, destruction bits and pieces. If they tear down a church, for example, then they put the windows and the stairs—"

"That is the whitest way to spend a Saturday I ever heard," Francis said. "No offense."

"It can be fun," I said. "Let's get you out of this dorm for a while."

"Why now? Who put you up to this?"

"Mr. Hallowen said you'd been misbehaving in class. I thought maybe you could use a change of pace."

Francis looked at me, his eyes finally open.

"I'll pass," he said.

"What are you going to do instead?"

"You're looking at it," he said.

"Come on, Francis. Think of it as an anthropological adventure. If you hate it, I'll bring you back."

He closed his eyes.

"I've got to throw some things in the truck," I said. "I'll come back for you in a half hour. We're going antiquing, Francis. Shocking but true."

He shook his head.

I grabbed a tape measure, a level, my camera, and a T square. The day had taken a warm turn for late March. The first thaw had drenched the streets with runoff and everything glistened in the increasing sunlight. I cleared off the bench seat in the cab. It felt good to be out, good to be facing spring rather than winter.

When I went back, Francis hadn't changed positions.

"You're killing me," I said.

"Antiquing is not my thing," he said.

"How do you know? Have you ever been?"

He closed his eyes.

"Knock knock," I said.

"Oh come on," he said.

"I'm going to stand here and do knock-knock jokes until you get up."

"This school has rules against hazing."

"Knock knock," I said.

He looked at me.

"Under protest," he said, swinging his feet down.

"You like turkey? Turkey sandwiches?"

He shrugged. He went to the bathroom to wash up. I told him to meet me at the truck.

"WHO'S MARY?" HE ASKED.

We were on U.S. 4 heading toward Durham. The highway had pools of water at the edges and everything appeared hosed down. I kept the windshield on intermittent for the splashes and sprays of water that found the windshield. The heat ran on low. It felt like Saturday.

"My girlfriend. Maybe my wife."

"Maybe your wife?"

"There's a debate about whether we are married or not."

Francis looked at me.

"You're a little different from what I thought, Mr. Cobb."

"So are you," I said. "Why are you being disruptive in class?"

"Who says I am?"

"The grass talks," I said.

"What's that supposed to mean?"

"It means it's the word, the rumor, the buzz."

Francis looked straight ahead.

"The administration says you are yawning and making noise in class and not reading the assignments," I said. "And you are socially isolating yourself. That's the general diagnosis."

"Little hard not to be isolated."

"Because you're black?"

He shrugged.

"Imagine what it would be like if you were a bear," I said. "That's got to be tough."

Francis looked at me. His forehead curled down, then up.

"You're a strange man," Francis said.

"You're smart," I said. "I read your record. You've got a IQ that is out of this world. Probably the highest in the school."

"Hurray for me," he said.

"Not a bad thing to have. It's easier to be smart than dumb. You do better on drivers' tests and in *Jeopardy!* games."

"So I'm smart."

"But you're acting dumb."

"St. Paul's isn't the only school in the world," he said.

"See? You are smart."

He shook his head. He looked out at the side of the road, then looked back at me.

"What I'm saying is, just because I don't like a few of these classes doesn't mean I hate school or anything."

"Fair enough," I said.

"This is a really white place," Francis said. "The school, I mean."

"Yes, it is," I said. "Although we're doing better."

"You mean the push for diversity?"

I nodded.

"We're the raisins in the trail mix."

"How do you know about trail mix?" I asked.

"I was a Boy Scout," he said. "How do you like that?"

"I like it," I said.

"Look," Francis said, "St. Paul's is a pretty place. And the people are connected to the movers and shakers. I get that. You want a big-time life, you go to a big-time school. That's why I'm here."

"You make it sound sort of mercenary. Also, you're not connecting, you say."

He shrugged.

"I'll be all right," he said.

"You still playing the piccolo?"

"Now and then."

"I've heard you're good. I'd love to hear you play sometime."

He pursed his lips and made an indefinite gesture with his neck and shoulders.

"Let me tell you about antiquing," I said to change the subject. "At least the way we do it."

"Buying old crap."

"Sort of," I said. "The trick is to buy interesting old crap. That's the difference."

"For your house?"

"We bought a house together," I said. "Mary has a vision about how it should be decorated."

"What style?"

I looked at him.

"I watched HGTV," he said. "I'm down with houses."

"The house is a carriage house," I said. "Her style is sort of country comfortable. She likes baskets and old quilts. The way I think of it is, whatever a cat would like, so would Mary."

"Got it," Francis said.

"Do we need to keep talking about classes?" I asked.

"No," he said.

"You going to try a little more?"

"No," he said. "Probably not. But I'll think about thinking about it."

"Well, that's settled," I said.

"Appears to be."

"But you're okay? You're not despondent?"

"No," he said. "I'm okay. Just bored a little with school."

We didn't say much after that. Francis found a station he liked on the radio. We listened to music and drove with the windows cracked down an inch, spring hinting at its arrival.

Mary brought her mother from Hanover for the auction and they both fell in love with Francis.

They had already entered the auction by the time we arrived. I spotted Mary's truck in the parking lot. When we pushed through into the musty train depot, Mary found us almost immediately. She wore a red mackinaw, her Mad Bomber hat, and wool trousers tucked into L.L. Bean gum boots. An enormous Franklin potbellied coal stove heated the center of the room, but her breath still fogged as she spoke. The building had no insulation and the doors—some wide enough for bureaus and bed frames—opened and shut constantly.

"We have our eye on a church pew," she whispered to us both, not bothering with an introduction. "It's a crazy old thing. My mom thinks it has *misericords* on it. I told her she was batty, but she won't be talked out of it."

"This is Francis," I said.

"Well, who else would it be?" she said, shaking his hand and turning to him. "I'm Mary. Do you know about misericords?"

He shook his head.

"Well, Mom knows more, but the old English churches had pews up front. Anglicans, I guess, but not always. Anyway, the monks and priests had their seats decorated with figurines and oddities. Carved in, I mean. They had elephants and zebras and sometimes men with arms growing out of their foreheads. Men with tails. You name it."

"I heard about this," Francis said, appearing surprisingly interested. "I read something."

"There you go," Mary said, pulling him away, her hand through his large right arm. "Mom thinks one of these pews has surfaced in good old New Hampshire. There's no talking her out of it."

"How much do they want?" Francis asked.

"There's a minimum bid of three hundred, which is absolute chicken feed if it's the real thing. Of course, it could be some sort of weird knockoff. Who knows? But my mom wants us to bid."

I followed. When Mary pulled Francis next to the church pew—it stood in the back of the room, with a dozen cardboard boxes on its seat—she did not bother introducing him to her mother, Joan, but simply whispered that he knew about misericords. Immediately he was part of the conspiracy, and bent with the two women when they showed him details about the bench. Mary's mom had him hold up several boxes so they could see the seat better.

"If it's real," Joan said, "it's very valuable."

"You all sound as if you're robbing a bank," I said.

"Hello, Cobb," Joan said, stretching her back a little and hugging me. "You're just in time. This is by far the best find I've ever stumbled on at an auction."

"Is it listed in the catalog?" I asked.

She shook her head.

"Did you meet Francis?" I asked.

Francis turned from where he still held the boxes.

"Hello, Francis," she said. "I'm sorry to put you right to work."

Francis put down the boxes.

"Who's hungry?" Mary asked. "They have shepherd's pie for lunch and marshmallow something or other for dessert. Would you like a plate, Francis?"

"Yes, m'am," he said.

"Mom?" Mary asked.

"I'm too excited to eat," Joan said. "But I'd nibble at one of their desserts."

"Such a sweet tooth," Mary said. "Cobb, will you give me a hand?"

The snack bar circled the coal stove so that the women working at the tables would at least stay moderately warm. We ordered three shepherd's pies, four marshmallow pies, and four hot teas. Mary grabbed paper packets of salt and pepper and napkins while I paid and put the plates on a cardboard tray. The shepherd's pie steamed in the cool air of the depot.

"He's such a handsome kid," Mary whispered to me as we collected everything before heading back to join them. "Did you have a nice ride down?"

"We did."

"Did you talk?"

"We did."

"And?" she asked.

"Let's say it's a back-burner issue for him."

"What is?"

"School. The environment. The whole New Hampshire prep-school thing. He's a bit mixed up about it. I don't much blame him."

"We have to get him into the woods," she said. "Show him that."

"Okay," I said. "It couldn't hurt."

"'Go to the woods and leave your troubles behind,'" Mary said. "Didn't Thoreau say something like that?"

"I think that's the Carnival Cruise ad," I said.

"Well, we'll fix him up. I've got a few ideas."

We went back to Joan and Francis. To my astonishment, Francis had stretched out near the bench but not directly under it. He seemed to examine a sideboard, but when I studied him carefully, I realized he used the vantage point to check on the pew bench.

"You put him up to that," I said to Joan.

"Shhhh," she said. "The auction is going to start."

Francis stood and clapped his hands together to clean them. He bent and whispered something to Joan. She put her hand on his back and nodded.

"It's a go," she said as if describing a bank heist.

Francis nodded.

We sat—as much as we could—on a long back window overlooking the former train tracks. We had to juggle our plates on our laps while the auction slowly got under way. The auctioneer—a beaky-looking man with a flannel shirt buttoned all the way to his Adam's apple and a microphone propped in front of his mouth so he looked to be swallowing a fly constantly—welcomed us and explained the ground rules. Joan hurried off and returned with a number. Fifty-seven. From sideways glances, I watched Francis. He looked contented and involved. Apparently he didn't exaggerate when he said he liked houses. He shook his head after the first two items went. "Too much," he whispered to Mary. She agreed.

It took nearly three hours for the bench to come under the gavel. By that time we felt like experts.

"Who will start me at three hundred for this fine old bench?" the auctioneer asked. "Do I have three hundred?"

He did. From a woman wearing a houndstooth jacket on the opposite side of the depot. She had a red scarf tucked into the jacket and calfskin boots that climbed above her ankle. She looked wealthy. Francis mumbled a warning to us all.

"We're bidding against Martha Stewart," he said.

"Oh, good grief," Joan whispered.

"Three hundred, do I have four? We have three hundred to my left."

"Four," Joan said.

Francis nodded.

"And five? We have five on my left."

"I'm out," Joan said. "We don't know if it's genuine."

"Five," Mary said. "We don't know if it isn't, either."

"Now six? And six? Who has six?"

The auctioneer got it from a small man close to the auction lectern. The man wore a mushroom-colored raincoat and carried an enormous golfing umbrella. We could only see the back of his head.

"We're now at seven."

Martha Stewart gave him seven and the umbrella man answered back at eight.

"This is just nasty stuff," Francis said. "You folks play hardball."

"One thousand," Mary said.

That slowed it.

I looked at her. We didn't know everything about each other's finances, but I would have been surprised if she had a thousand dollars ready to toss at the bench as easily as it seemed. We had the expense of the house, the bills, and so on. A second, darker thought entered my mind, and I did my best to push it away. It persisted. Maybe, I thought, she had lost track of what the money represented. But she had followed the numbers accurately, and she simply nodded when Martha Stewart calmly said, "Two thousand."

"So they know," Joan said. "They know about the bench."

"Three thousand," Mary said, at which point Francis jumped off the windowsill and did a little dance of amazement. He snapped his fingers a couple times. It was the most animated I had ever seen him.

I looked at Joan. She had her eyes on Mary.

"Let it go," Joan said. "It's not worth that. At the end of the day, it's just a bench."

"She is cold," Francis said, still enjoying himself. "Stone cold."

"We have three thousand. Do we have four?"

Umbrella man bid four. Martha Stewart pulled out a cell phone and dialed a number quickly. Our group remained in place, watching Mary.

She didn't bid. The auctioneer raised his voice. He understood we had come to the last calculations.

"Going once. The gentleman before me holds the bid at four. Going twice." He tapped his gavel on the lectern.

Martha Stewart snapped her phone closed and stood up to go.

"You scared me to death," Joan said, marveling. "What did you bid? How high was it?"

"Three thousand," Francis said. "Clint Eastwooded it, too."

The auctioneer called the next lot. Mary looked at me and smiled.

"LONG AGO, THE WORLD consisted only of water. Then Raven called the earth to form, and from that earth he created humans. He used sticks and mud and that is why, when we die, we return to sticks and mud and become earth again."

We sat before the fireplace. Francis had toured the house and had given it his approval. Joan had driven home, citing an early shift the following morning. Francis appeared comfortable. He slipped out of his shoes and he leaned back in one of Mary's armchairs, his eyes a little sleepy with the flames. Mary had told him about her interest in ravens and crows. They had also made a date to visit a vernal pool the next morning, where Mary promised to show Francis tadpoles and mud turtles.

"The Inuit tell a story that Raven had a sister," Mary continued. "He refused to let her have male children and killed them as soon as they were born. He worried, you see, that one of the males would challenge him. Then Heron visited in the early dawn and told Raven's sister to swallow a burning stone. Heron promised the stone would impregnate Raven's sister and it did. When this second raven entered the world, he became known as the Lesser Raven, and he is a figure like the Coyote in Native American stories. Divinity is divided into two aspects: the sublime and regal, and the mischievous and resourceful."

"Like Loki," Francis said. "In the Norse myths."

"Exactly," Mary said. "It was the Lesser Raven who stole light for the world. After he had spread meat and fruit all over the earth so that he would always have something to eat, he worried that he would not be able to find his caches of food. So he flew through a hole in the sky and entered a second world, not unlike this one. The daughter of the chief of Heaven came to a stream to drink and the Lesser Raven changed himself into a needle from a cedar tree and slipped quietly into her bucket. When she mistakenly drank him down, he remained inside her and she became pregnant. He was born to her as a little boy. The Father of Heaven found him charming and permitted him to play with a box that contained the light of day. Lesser Raven ran away with the box, changed back into a bird, and flew down through the hole in the sky. The Father of Heaven reached out and managed to seize the box, but in their tugging back and forth the box broke and the sun and moon and stars exploded out. The Lesser Raven had half the light, while the rest remained in the second world with his mother and the Father of Heaven."

"That's a good story," Francis said. "I like stories. So that's the whole night and day thing?"

"That's it," Mary said.

I put on more wood. Now and then the wind hit against the side of the house. The fire burned steadily, gobbling up the sticks and small chips of wood I had scrounged around the property. I had three cords on order from a fellow named Carrol, but he said it depended on the mud and whether he could get his truck into his wood lot. Meanwhile, we scraped by.

"All I can think about," Mary said as the mood changed from storytelling to conversation, "is that bench."

"You think it was real?" Francis said.

"Hard to believe that it was," Mary said. "But I'm a sucker for those kinds of things."

"A fellow found an original Poe manuscript at a yard sale several years back and sold it for one-point-four million dollars," I said. "He gave the seller a hundred grand."

"Should have given him more," Francis said.

"I guess the buyer knew something the seller didn't know," I said.

"I'm with Francis," Mary said. "Share your toys, that's the best motto."

"I don't think the bench was real, now that I think about it," Francis said. "Seems too much of a strange little twist. Things like that don't happen."

"But it did," Mary said.

"We don't know that," Francis said. "We just saw a guy buy an interesting bench at an auction."

"I'm with Francis," I said.

Before bed, we went outside to check the stars. Mary always checked the stars before turning in. She quoted Darwin that 80 percent of the population failed to raise its head above the horizon line once a day. She refused to be in that number. *"Sheep,"* she said, looking down at the ground. So we went out to look at the stars.

On this night they were full and bright and the moon sugared everything with pale light. The hillside above us rose in a quiet lump and more stars rested on its top, some of them bright enough to challenge the moon. Light caught the white fences running down toward us. The temperature had dropped; we could see our breaths easily. A horse neighed somewhere, but we couldn't see it.

"I'm glad you came down today, Francis," Mary said. "I hope you'll come back again soon."

"Thank you, m'am."

"Cobb told me about your friend," Mary said, looking up at the sky. "The one who wrote you a note. I hope you don't mind that he told me."

I looked at Mary. I tried to catch her eye but she wouldn't look at me.

"I'm not sure," Francis said, his voice tight. "I'm surprised to find out he was discussing my business."

"He wasn't discussing it," Mary said. "And it isn't, it never was, business."

"Still," Francis said.

"What your friend did, to write you a letter like that, it wasn't fair. These stars will be gone one day for you. They will be for me, too. The Raven promises me I will turn back to sticks and dirt, and I believe him. But until then I am a human being and that is something to be. I stand on my feet and I look at the stars and I feel the seasons. If you work at it long enough, I promise you that will be enough for you, Francis. This world, every day, it's enough."

She hugged him. His arms stayed at his side. After a three count, he hugged her back. I couldn't be sure if what she had said was fair, or even legal in an academic setting—students' records were confidential—but she had gotten away with it. When they stopped hugging, she hugged me. She took a couple deep breaths and declared the air *mudlicious,* after the e.e. cummings poem. Then we all went inside.

# 12

WE HAD ONLY TWO PAIR OF waders, so I volunteered the next morning to stay in the truck and correct papers while Francis and Mary hiked to the vernal pool. Mary had her own truck, because after the pool Francis and I had to hustle back to school. I took pictures of them as they shoved their legs into the waders. Francis seemed a bit giddy. He had never been in waders, he said, and he couldn't imagine what his homeboys would say if they saw him. I told him I would send the pictures so he could post them on Facebook. He declined the offer.

The sun had failed to burn off the clouds and a light rain fell on the dull leftover snow. Mud season. I turned the engine on to get heat as they waddled off toward the pond. I knew its location. Mary had taken me before, just as she had taken countless students. The pond had no name, but each year salamanders, turtles, and frogs rediscovered the pond and reproduced there, hurrying against the warming season to live out their cycle. It was magic, the best kind, Mary said, and I felt confident watching them disappear that Francis stood to receive a wonderful introduction to the life sciences. Mary in waders was unconquerable, and she knew spring peepers—the first nightly callers—and had written several papers on their oxygen use during their calling on spring nights.

Sitting in the truck, I opened up a folder full of student papers. Student work, of course, is the blessing and bane of most teachers. I knew, however, that if I could concentrate and meet the papers halfway, they would eventually absorb me. The assignment had been to study a colonial building—several existed in Concord, where the school was located—and see if they could discover anything in the vernacular of the buildings that mirrored colonial life. I showed my students slides; we studied farm tools, and bank barns, and cupolas, and post and beam mortise joints, trying in each picture to discover meaning. We talked at length about twentieth-century skyscrapers as emblematic of America's ascendancy. "'We shape our buildings; there after they shape us,'" I said, lifting a quote from Winston Churchill. It was a subject I liked and one the students usually found interesting.

I turned to Penelope Child's work first.

It wasn't quite fair to the other students to read hers first, because I knew, we all knew, that she would write something incredible. She always did. She was *that* student, *that* girl. Tall and willowy, beautiful in a quiet way, she held a 4.0 academic record, had already been accepted to Yale, led the debate team in nationals, danced *The Nutcracker* each year with a visiting New York company, and once, nearly in her spare time, organized a mini-nonprofit to direct our school's used computers to neighboring schools that struggled without the funding we enjoyed at St. Paul's.

Her paper, not surprisingly, surprised me. In clear, measured prose, she wrote about subways. She tied in Hephaestus, the Greek god of the underground, teasing out the meaning of a culture going subsurface, returning to earth, when a competent trolley car system already existed. She also described the construction of the original Penn Station, what it signified, then examined Grand Central Station as a contrasting notion. Her work was brilliant and absorbing. Giving it a grade was pointless. It deserved discussion, thought, perhaps even publication. I wrote a short note in the margin, congratulating her, and asked her to swing by sometime to discuss it. Unlike many students who might blow off a chance to sit down with her teacher, I knew she would make time to visit and I looked forward to it.

I was so involved with the paper—and starting to think about who to read after Penelope—that I didn't see Francis returning with Mary. He held her by the elbow and walked nearly sideways, guiding her carefully. Mary appeared dazed and shaken.

"What happened," I asked, jumping out of the truck.

"She couldn't find the pond," Francis said. "She became a little upset and shaky."

"Mary?" I asked, stepping closer. "Mary, are you okay?"

She nodded.

"Let's get her warm," I said to Francis. "Do you know how to drive a stick?"

"My uncle drove a milk truck," he said, nodding. "He taught me."

"Will you drive her truck then? And follow me. We're going to take her to Concord Hospital. It's not far. You're sure you're okay with the truck?"

"I got it," he said.

"I don't want to go to the hospital," Mary said.

Her voice slurred the tiniest bit.

"Let's just run you down there," I said. "It can't hurt to check you over."

"We know what it is," Mary said.

"Actually, we don't," I said. "It could be any number of things."

"Oh, great," Mary said, smiling. "I have options."

"No options about the hospital. We're going to get you looked at."

I made her sit on the tailgate while I helped her with her waders. Francis stripped out of his. Mary shivered several times.

"I just met you and I am putting you to all this trouble," Mary said to Francis.

"It's no trouble," Francis said.

"You're a fibber, just like Cobb. Okay, my two big strong men, lead me away."

Her voice slurred a mere fraction, so little, in fact, that I dismissed it an instant after recognizing it.

With Francis's help, I put her in the passenger side. She told him to look under the visor of her truck for the keys. He hurried off while I started the engine. I turned the heat high.

"This is how we begin to end, we don't know why, and we don't know when," Mary whispered.

"Shhhh."

"Do you know the poet?"

I shook my head.

"Neither do I."

"You just got turned around."

"Don't," she said. "Please don't do that."

"Okay."

"I'm counting on you not to do that."

"Okay," I said.

"Okay," she said.

MARY WAS NOT AN emergency. The receiving nurse made sure we understood that. But Concord Hospital was not so large that it had dozens of emergencies, so after filling out identification forms, producing an insurance card, and giving a brief rundown of her medical history, a nurse came and led Mary away.

"I'll be back," Mary said, doing a horrible imitation of Arnold Schwarzenegger.

"You better be," I said.

Francis sat in the waiting room, a magazine open on his lap. I sat down beside him.

"Sorry this is happening right now," I said. "With you just meeting her."

"I'm sorry," he said. "Mary's awesome."

"I know," I said. "Listen, I'm going to try to get you back to school. I may be able to catch someone coming through Concord. It's not far. Maybe I'll ask someone to run down and pick you up."

"How would you get Mary's truck back?"

"I don't know yet. Let me make a few calls. Just hold on."

I called Mary's mom to let her know what had happened. She had a thousand questions, but I told her I couldn't answer them. Then I called four people I knew at school, but only one picked up. It was a friend named Jim and he agreed to run down and bring Francis back to school. Then I called Dean Hallowen and explained my situation. I wasn't sure if I would be free to teach the next day. He said not to worry, to take the time I needed. Then I called my father. My father said he would get a ride from his friend Pole, and he would be there inside of an hour.

Then we had hospital time. It's hard to be in a hospital and not feel as if you're living through a bad television show. Nurses in smocks, children's crayon pictures on the walls, squeaky floors, rubber-tired carts, old magazines, antiseptic smells, the sense that the world existed somewhere else, that this was a land of lotus eaters, that the hospital strained all life until it distilled this strange, medicinal elixir that satisfied no one but was somehow necessary. I could not imagine Mary staying long in any hospital.

"She was slurring," Francis said after a while.

"You okay?" I asked.

"Sure," he said. "I had a grandmother and I took care of her."

"I understand," I said.

"I'd be happy to stay with you, if you want me to."

"I appreciate it, Francis, but you should get back to school. There's not much either of us can do."

"Okay," he said.

A few minutes later Jim arrived. He was a short, round, squash player who also taught Italian. He listened to our account of the situation, expressed his good wishes, then told Francis they should roll. I hugged Francis good-bye. He nodded as he pulled away. They pushed through the glass doors and disappeared to the left.

"You can go in," a nurse said.

I hadn't heard her approach. She had bleached hair and a stethoscope around her neck.

"They've just finished some tests and they drew a little blood. She's alert and fine. She'd like to see you."

I followed the nurse. We pushed through two swinging doors, took a left, then pushed through one more door and came to Mary. She wore a hospital johnny and sat on the edge of the examination table. She smiled. She looked beautiful.

"Hello, Mrs. Blanding," I said.

"Why, hello. Fancy meeting you here."

"How do you feel," I asked, kissing her lightly.

"Like a duck in the rain."

"They took tests?"

"Of course they took tests. It's what they do."

"And?"

"And eventually they'll read them and get back to me. They have to read the chicken innards and declare prophecy."

"You're feeling spanky," I said.

"They asked if I might be pregnant," she said, smiling. "I told them I was and that the ultrasound said triplets."

"You're a goof," I said.

"I have a very nice doctor named Sing."

"Chinese?"

"Irish," she said and laughed.

"I'm glad this is fun for you."

"It's not fun, Cobb. It's just the state of the state."

"I hate it," I said.

She grabbed my hands and pulled me close.

"We're going to be strong and proper about this. We both are. You promised me and you promised Freddy."

"I had my fingers crossed."

She looked at me.

"You shouldn't have come to Indonesia," she said. "You knew, didn't you? And you came anyway."

"Are you angry?"

She thought for a moment. She shook her head.

"I couldn't . . . ," I said and failed to finish.

She took me in her arms.

"I want you with me, Cobb," she whispered into my ear. "It's all I've ever wanted from the moment I met you."

I nodded against her. She squeezed me harder.

"You also wanted me to cook for you," I said, trying to lighten things.

She kissed my cheek.

"We start from where we stand," she said. "That was my father's motto. No sense looking back."

"When can you leave?" I asked.

"Doctor Sing will be back in a few minutes. He has a little trouble understanding English, but he's very nice."

"Okay," I said.

"I've been trying to recite 'Annabel Lee.' I committed it to memory when I was ten and I've said it every time I wondered if I was slipping. But I can't remember it now."

"None of it?"

"Just a little."

"It doesn't matter."

"But it does, you see. That's the deal."

"It will come back to you."

"Hard to know," she said. "I was really lost with Francis. I kept turning around and starting off in a new direction. He followed without a question until he started to realize something wasn't right."

"He's a good kid."

"Are you kidding? He's a great kid. Smart and funny and handsome."

"He said you were awesome."

"And he has good taste," she said.

Dr. Sing returned. He was tall and square, with a long mop of hair and a quiet step. He carried a laptop and typed on it as he held it. It reminded me of someone feeding a bird or a small creature that clung to his wrist. He shook my hand, then made a few notations on his laptop. When he typed in whatever he seemed to think was necessary, he turned to Mary.

"How do you feel now?" he asked, sliding the computer onto the countertop near the sink.

"Fine," she said. "Perfect, actually."

"Okay," he said. "There is nothing we can do at this moment."

His English was heavily accented, but it came through.

"Fair enough."

"I've written out a prescription for Valium. To help you with the anxiety."

"Thanks, but I'll pass."

"Well, you can take the prescription and decide later. Do you have any questions for me?"

I expected her to say something funny, but she merely shook her head.

"Okay, then," Dr. Sing said. "Nice to meet you both."

We shook hands all around. Dr. Sing left with his laptop level on his left hand.

"Let's get out of here," I said.

"You want to watch me dress?"

"I'd pay to watch you dress."

She slipped out of her johnny and yanked on her jeans. Then

she buttoned up her flannel shirt. After she slid into her shoes, she checked her look in the mirror.

"How dazzling I look," she said.

"Are you hungry?"

"I'm starving," she said.

"I know a place."

"You always know a place. It's one of things I love about you."

"Food, then home. My dad should be in the lobby. We'll bring him with us."

"That's a plan."

"You scared me," I said, stopping and kissing her.

"I'm afraid this is the way it goes from here on in," she said.

"You don't know that."

"The thing is, I do," she said. "And so do you."

My father had brought Pole along, his lifelong buddy. Pole stood six feet seven and weighed less than a broom closet. He gave me a hug when he saw me and shook Mary's hand. My father, I knew, studied Mary in quick glances. He could no more resist doing that than he could allow a faulty foundation wall to go into one of his building projects. He liked things plumb and I could tell he worried she had lost her level.

"Pole's got to be back," Dad said when I invited them both to lunch. "He's squeezing in this run as it is."

"Afraid so," Pole said.

"We'll drop Mary's truck back at the house, then head home. But I can shake free next week if you need me," my dad said.

"We'll play it by ear," I said.

We walked out with them after giving our co-pay to the cashier. The day had turned fine. The snow had pulled back even farther in the warm light, and everywhere water moved and made shiny veins as it passed. I opened my truck door for Mary and closed it afterward.

Then I walked my dad to Mary's truck while Pole climbed into his Dodge Ram.

"Is she okay?" my dad asked.

I nodded.

"Is this . . . ?" he asked.

"Not sure."

"Not knowing is tough."

"Yes, it is," I agreed.

"I meant what I said. I can help out next week if you need me. Don't be stubborn and think you're inconveniencing me by calling."

"I called you today, didn't I?" I asked.

"Appears you did."

"I'm going to get her something to eat. Thank Pole again for me."

"Oh, he's happy to do it. I'm up six," he said, referring to an elaborate, essentially indecipherable favor system they had been trading for close to fifty years. They bartered time and work like medieval guild members.

"I appreciate it, Dad. I appreciate being able to call you."

"Job description," he said.

He hugged me quickly, then hopped in Mary's truck. Fortunately, Francis had left the keys underneath the visor. The truck started after whining a little. My dad waved and pulled out.

I found Mary crying in the truck.

"I can't remember it," she said. "'Annabel Lee.' I've known it all my life."

"It's okay."

"No, really it's not," she said. "That was one of my checkpoints to see if I was failing."

"You'll remember it after a good night's sleep."

Mary looked out the window. I climbed in and turned on the ignition. Before she could say anything else, her cell phone rang. "Hi, Mom," she said, her voice blooming back to cheerfulness.

"Two hundred thousand people have died of Huntington's since World War II," Mary explained. "If each person who died had two or three people as caretakers and you add that into the equation, then Huntington's has probably touched a million people since the middle part of the last century. It's different from a lot of diseases. Huntington's doubles and slips into the next generation, then the next. It's always fatal. It puts a strain on everyone around the Huntington patient. You can talk about quality of life until you are blue in the face, but the simple fact is that once symptoms present, you're looking at a serious decline. I can't manage the disease. Nobody can. I don't like imagining myself as an invalid, not in control of my functions. I hate that. But I also worry about the people around me. You, for instance. And Mom. Pretty soon you'll both be nursing a stalk of celery. Sorry, that's all I'll be. I won't remember, I won't recognize you. I'm talking frankly now, Cobb. I have no place to hide anymore, no raven tricks."

We sat in a cute diner called The Serengeti. The owner had decorated with an African motif despite the café's location outside of Concord, New Hampshire. They made good coffee and we each had a cup. We also had sandwiches and small salads. Mary picked at hers. Mostly she talked, her voice low.

"I'm not going to stay around for the final act, Cobb. That's always been the deal for us. If you love me, you'll understand that. I'm not going to run and jump off a bridge, but in time, when it's right for both of us, I'll leave. That's all. And it will break my heart, but it's the practical thing to do, the loving thing to do in the end. I'm a biologist. I'm not overly sentimental about death."

"What if I am?"

She smiled wanly.

"You're a softy about everything."

"I'm not arguing," I said.

"I know you're not. Some of this, this talking, is just to remind myself. It's as if I'm at the most perfect party and I don't want to go home, but I have to."

"We have to make a deal, though. We can't keep talking about it. When the time comes, okay. But I can't discuss it matter-of-factly. I can't."

"Okay."

"And one more thing," I said.

"What is it?"

"I want you to marry me."

"We are married."

"By law. In the face of God. Under the Great Raven. Whatever you want to call it. You and me."

"Are you proposing to me?"

"From the minute I met you."

She slipped out of her chair and came and sat on my lap. The few customers in The Serengeti glanced over at us. Mary kissed me and whispered in my ear.

"'This maiden she lived with no other thought, than to love and be loved by me,'" she said, quoting Poe's "Annabel Lee."

"You remembered?"

"Only parts," she said.

"Have you given me an answer yet?"

"Yes," she said.

"Yes, you've given me an answer? Or yes?"

"Yes. Yes to everything about you, Cobb."

"When?" I asked.

"Soon," she said. "Sooner is better."

"Okay, you are my fiancée, Mrs. Blanding. How about the summer solstice? We'll dance around a fire, or something primitive like that. We'll go completely Celtic together."

"Okay," she said.

"I need a ring."

"I want an enormous fake stone. And we will give it to Madrid and his ravens when the time comes."

"A deal," I said.

She kissed me. Then she put her head on my shoulder.

"Take me home," she whispered. And I did.

# 13

On a bright June day my father and Pole arrived with the restored circular window and more tools than two men should own. According to my father, Pole had negotiated for three favors in payment for putting in the window. That put my dad down one, which made Pole both happy and the ostensible foreman on the job. Pole delighted in bossing my dad around.

Their arrival had been preceded by days of painstaking study as to whether we should install the window upstairs—where we would be able to look out from our bed—or in the main living room, where we spent the majority of our time. Mary, usually quick to make up her mind, waffled. As soon as she persuaded herself of one placement, the second location seemed more desirable. We talked a good deal about heat—whether the window, placed so near the fireplace downstairs, would draw cold air into the room. We also spent time in bed, staring at the potential location for the window, trying to imagine being able to see out. When my father mentioned the possibility of finding two windows—one to be put in now, the other later—Mary went nearly faint with worry.

"He's trying to kill me," she said after I had hung up with my dad.

"You can have both eventually," I said.

"What about Madrid? Didn't Madrid have only one earring? I can't have more than one of anything. If you have two of things, if you can always get another, it takes away from the specialness of the first thing. Tell me you understand."

"Absolutely," I said.

"Downstairs," she said. "That's where we spend our time."

"Okay."

"But promise me we'll build a sleeping porch and sleep out under the stars."

"I promise."

"There," she said. "That's settled."

Of course, it wasn't. When Dad and Pole arrived, Mary took them upstairs first, gathered their opinions, then stood with them a long time in the living room. Diplomatically, the men said either place would be lovely. When Mary looked ready to collapse, my father asked a simple question.

"Which one is in the movie?" he asked.

Mary sighed.

"That's it," she said. "Downstairs. They kiss in front of it and Jane Wyman sees a deer outside."

"There's your answer," my father replied.

Decision made. My father said it would take two days, maybe three, to do it right.

The construction and demolition turned our house into a rolling, happy party. Joan arrived on the first day to watch, and Francis, visiting from Philadelphia for a few days to resolve a grading issue at school, swung by in a borrowed van. We burned the construction debris in an outdoor fire pit and a few other friends—people from the University of New Hampshire, two teaching friends of mine—came by in the evening to cook out and visit. On the third day Wally called. She was passing through on her way to the river and she wondered if she could spend the night. She had a ton of gear and a rack of canoes in tow, but she said she had two days to make the drive and she had wanted to see us for some time.

"The Chungamunga girls are gathering," I warned my father and Pole. I worked as tender, clearing junk away, separating out metal and recyclables, then wheelbarrowing the scrap wood to our fire pit.

"Chungamunga girls?" Pole asked, lifting the stonework carefully away from the building. "Sounds like bubblegum."

"They are eternal on the river," I said.

"What river would that be?" Pole asked.

"The Allagash," I said.

"I don't think they do it that way down South," Pole said, which is a saying he usually pronounced when he wasn't sure what else to say.

After the first night of construction, we held a viewing of *All That Heaven Allows* in the backyard. Francis, who had been at the school all day, arrived with a projector and an enormous portable screen. We plugged it in by the fire pit and aimed the beam away from the light. It took us a while to get it right, and we had to wait for full darkness, but by nine o'clock we had a sharp picture and a comfortable seating arrangement. Mary popped popcorn over the fire and we filled individual bowls and passed them around. The mosquitoes relented a little and the stars above us looked smoky through the overcast clouds.

"I've seen this movie," Pole said as it got under way. "I don't remember a thing about it, but I've seen it."

"Now how would you know you've seen it if you can't remember it?" my father asked. "That's illogical."

"It's called a sense memory," Pole said, mostly because he liked teasing my father.

"A nonsense memory is more like it," my father replied.

Mary held my hand. She shushed them both. Little by little, we fell into the film. At the famous window scene I jumped up and paused the DVD. We all examined the window to see how closely it resembled the window we hoped to put in the following morning. Pole tried to estimate the diameter of the film window, but his guesses were undermined by my father's tsking. Finally we agreed that if Rock Hudson put his arms out like the famous da Vinci sketch, and if he spread his legs to forty-five degrees, he might touch the perimeter of the window frame. Francis, however, pointed out that we didn't know what that meant without knowing Rock Hudson's exact height, then Mary threatened to get out her calculator to figure out the circumference.

Instead, we watched the movie.

"Admit it," Mary said when the movie ended, Rock and Jane Wyman firmly committed. "You guys were getting a little dusty at the ending."

"I was tearing up about the window," Pole said.

Dad put more wood on the fire. The night became quiet. The overcast sky muffled everything and it was easy to believe that only the fire existed. After a little while Francis pulled out his piccolo. Although we had become close over the spring semester, I had never heard him play. Something in the mix of emotions, the night, the warm fire, the quiet sky, inspired him.

He started with a few finger exercises. The piccolo seemed shrill and bright, nearly painful to hear, but then his breathing leveled and the music started quietly complementing the night. For a few moments it seemed to follow the movement of the flames. It rose and sank, then dipped some more. I looked at Francis. The flames obscured his face and the darkness covered him, and he seemed old and wise, a creature that appeared out of the forest. In time his fingering became music and he began to play something beautiful and playful. It was Berlioz's "Dance of the Sprites" from the *Damnation of Faust,* though I didn't know it until he informed us afterward. But even without the name for it, I imagined creatures dancing, a festival, though the music was also tinged with sadness. Francis rocked a little at the waist as he played. He also closed his eyes. His whole spirit seemed involved in his playing.

"That was beautiful," Mary said when he finished. "Absolutely beautiful."

"My," my father said.

"I didn't see the instrument at first and I thought you had just started whistling," Pole said. "Damndest whistling I'd ever heard."

"Wonderful," I said.

"Now what's the difference between a flute and a piccolo?" my father asked. "One's smaller, isn't it?"

"The piccolo," Francis said. "The word flute came from an early Latin word, *tibia,* like the shinbone. Flutes were made of bone originally. A piccolo is smaller, about half the size of a flute, and one octave higher. Orchestras don't always use piccolos. They are so bright they can be heard over all of the other instruments combined. Anyway, that's my piccolo speech."

"What was that piece you played?" Mary asked.

Francis told us.

"Like Pan," Mary said.

"Yes," Francis said. "Something like that."

We turned in after that. In bed, Mary and I made love fiercely and quietly. Afterward, we stayed together, her body clutched around mine, our hands intertwined. "I love this day," she whispered into my neck. The windows sent in a spring breeze; the scent of late snow tucked into the glaze of fresh earth and things growing.

WALLY ARRIVED AT SUNRISE, a box of coffee from Dunkin' Donuts and a dozen mixed doughnuts on her lap. She wore jeans, a pair of lavender crocs, and fleece that said *Chunga* across the front, and *Munga* on the back. She drove a Ford F-350 with a canoe rack bursting with boats attached behind the truck. My father and Pole had already set to work on the window, clearing the last of the debris before they would frame in the glass. Wally didn't bother to knock—for fear she would wake us—but sat at a picnic table and talked to the guys. She gave them coffee and doughnuts and they were fast friends by the time Mary and I rose from bed.

"Wally," Mary said, hugging her. "I've missed you. Why didn't you yell up and wake us?"

"The young need sleep," Wally said.

"We're not so young," I said. "Just sleepy."

I hugged Wally, too. She made Mary and I stand side by side.

"Well, you two look fit as calves," Wally said. "And the house is beautiful."

"Do you like the window?" Mary asked, pointing to where the window stood against a small maple.

"I took a peek already," Wally said, standing and walking around it. "Lovely."

She inspected it again, then poured us coffee. We sat at the picnic table. The sun had cleared the hilltop and begun to dig into the damp soil. The weather report called for temperatures in the sixties. A spring day. Pole and my father continued working. They refused any offer of help. They had reached the point of final measuring and ignored us for the most part.

"This seems early to be going to the river," I said when we had settled with doughnuts. "Don't you usually go in September?"

"Oh, the kids aren't coming yet. The river would be too cold at this point. Too many bugs. I'm just delivering gear. And we have a few tricks we want to arrange. The usual stuff, but maybe with a few new twists. We've got a new donor who had agreed to underwrite a performance of our choosing. You can't breathe a word of it, but we may be able to bring in a troupe of dancers with music. We're thinking of some sort of nymphal dance, if *nymphal* is a word. You know, the kids finish their day, then they hear music off in the distance. And voilà. Under the stars, a little pagan dance."

"You should have been a theater producer," Mary said.

"I try."

"We have a piccolo player staying with us if you need one," I told her.

"Is that Francis?" she asked. "Mary told me about him."

"Yes."

"Well, I may call on him," Wally said. "By the way, I have a message for you from John and Annie. You know them, of course."

"They ran the fishing camp," Mary said, "and they fed us a delicious dinner. How are they?"

"They came up with a lease-to-buy arrangement on the fishing camp. They wanted to go north, up to Labrador, but after staying for the winter out on the lake, they fell in love with the place. I talked to them about storing some canoes there, and it slowly dawned on both of us that we knew you. So they say hello. They want you to come and visit this summer."

"Please say hello to them," I said. "They took us in one rainy night."

"They're very sweet," said Wally. "Very interested in the Chungamunga program. They've offered to provide a meal one night. I guess Annie is quite a cook. People in the area rave about her food."

"It makes me happy to hear they are making a go of it," Mary said.

We talked a little more. In time Francis came down, his face heavy from sleep. He shook hands with Wally and dug into the doughnuts. Pole and my father took a break, too, and told us when we finished we could all help setting the window into place. The hole was as ready as it would ever be, they said.

The window, when we lifted it, was surprisingly heavy. Wally and Francis took one side, and Mary and I carried the other. Dad and Pole stood inside the house with a variety of shims ready to use. We waddled over carefully, carrying the window vertically. My father murmured, "there we go, there we go, steady as she goes," and we put the bottom edge in first. Little by little, with some back and forth from Pole and my dad, we walked the window higher, gradually fitting it into place. It didn't work at first. We had to back the window out, then gradually fit it in without tilting. On the second try it went in snugly, fitting so perfectly that Pole let out a whistle.

"Almost like we knew what we were doing," Pole said.

"Good enough for government work," my father answered.

I could tell the fit pleased them. Mary grabbed my hand and made me close my eyes, then she led me away, nearly to the brook. When she had me properly lined up, she spun me around and told me to look. The window looked beautiful and somehow fit the style and vernacular of the building.

"You're a genius," I said. "Seriously, honey, it's perfect."

"It's beautiful. Francis, Wally, what do you think?"

Francis and Wally walked out to join us. Francis had a powdered doughnut in his right hand, half of it already gone.

"Sensational," Wally said, and Francis agreed.

"You don't think birds will fly into it, do you?" Mary asked.

"No, it should be fine," Wally said.

"Let's look from the inside," Mary said. "Oh, it's perfect. Just perfect. I worried so much about it. What a relief."

Pole and my father had shimmed it into place so that the window stood on its own by the time we made it inside. Mary hugged them both. Then she made everyone stand back so she could take it in. She stood midway in the room, stared at the fireplace, then quickly turned to see the window. She did it four times. I knew the window worked. It brought light into the room, but it did not overload the room as a French door might have done. If anything, it made the room more cozy, more pleasant to be in because the outdoors lay just beyond the window.

"Stand over there," Wally said to us both, drawing a camera out of her fleece.

"I want the men in with us," Mary said.

"First you two," she said. "Just a couple."

"Come on, Rock," Mary said.

We stood in front of the window. Francis directed us, calling out the poses Rock Hudson and Jane Wyman had used in the movie. We kissed. Wally snapped a half dozen pictures. Mary filled my arms.

# 14

"I WANT TO MARRY YOU TODAY," MARY said.

It was early the next morning, the first light just warming in the east, but she nuzzled into me and kissed my neck. The rest of the house was silent, though I knew we had people sleeping everywhere.

"Today?" I asked, still half-asleep.

"Yes. Everyone I love is here. I have a place we can go. Wally is a justice of the peace. It's perfect. We can get the licenses signed afterward."

"What about a dress and flowers and all of that?"

"Are you trying to back out?" she asked, still kissing me.

"Not for a second."

"I don't care about dresses. And where we're going . . . it's way better than flowers."

"Your mother's not here," I said.

"She has off today. I already thought of it. I'll call her as soon as it's light. We can call Freddy on the cell phone and have him attend that way."

I pushed her slightly away so I could see her eyes.

"You're serious," I said, a little surprised.

"I want to be your wife. I want you to be my husband. We

already have people gathered here. We can be married by noon or a little after."

"Yes," I said. "Let's do it."

"No invitations, no food worries, no corny band. Just our friends on a summer's day."

"And you have a place?"

"You'll see. It's magical. And I already have wedding favors. I have enough for everyone."

"Honeymoon?"

"I hate the idea of a honeymoon. I'll go anywhere with you, whenever you want. We don't need a honeymoon."

I pulled her closer. She twined around me, her leg over mine, her head under my chin.

"One day we woke up and married," she whispered. "It's like a line from a fairy tale."

"And lived happily ever after."

"And lived happily ever after," she repeated.

"I've always wondered if it shouldn't be, *they lived ever after, happily.*"

"A question of emphasis, I think."

"What am I going to wear?" I asked, teasing her. "I have to look fab enough to marry you."

"Your good khaki shorts and your best T-shirt. Sneakers."

"We'll match," I said. "Are you sure we won't look like a hippie wedding?"

"It *is* a hippie wedding," she said, and I felt her smile against my neck. "Let's have a hippie wedding. I have a tie-dye sundress somewhere. We will be earth children."

"Let's go watch the sun come through the window," I said. "Let's wake people up."

"Our wedding day," she said and scrambled out of bed.

We sneaked outside before we woke anyone. Mary had purchased cricket cages as wedding favors. They were small cylinders, made of coarse screen, with a tiny hatch that opened with a hook and eye. In another lifetime they might have been miniature cages for a set of bingo balls. She had purchased them through an entomologist at the university, a colleague who did her fieldwork on beetle and grass larvae. Mary led me outside to the creek that ran beside our property. In the near darkness, with the sun gaining strength every moment, we captured a dozen crickets and carefully slid them into the cages. We placed twigs and grass inside, especially grass for food, in all the cages. Watching her, I realized I had fallen in love with a woman so exceptional, so rare, that it frightened me to think that I might have missed her. Seeing her bend to the grass, her feet bare, her hands cupped and gentle, her joy at being awake and alive at the first roll of light on a summer morning, filled me with profound happiness.

"I'm truly in love with you," I said to her softly. "I think I just realized how much in love I am."

She stopped from her collecting and stared at me. I stood only a few steps away.

"And I with you," she said.

"Today we marry," I said. "I'd marry you every day from this point forward."

"You are a mush," she said.

"I can't help it when I'm near you."

"This is Yeti love," she said. "You're my romantic Sasquatch."

"You're a goof," I said.

She stood and climbed me. I have no other words for it. Her body wrapped around me and she left the ground, clinging to me. We kissed. I kissed her as if something threatened to slip away from us, as if by kissing her ever deeper I could save us both. She felt the same way, or seemed to, because she kissed me through to my backbone.

"Who was the Irishman who couldn't let his foot touch the ground?" she whispered, kissing me. "The one who left his love and rode across the sea on a white horse? We read about him in Indonesia in that funny restaurant."

"I'm not sure," I said. "It started with an *O*."

"If I touch my foot to the ground, will I turn to salt?" she said.

"No," I said. "I promise you won't."

We kept kissing. Over and over and over, each time newer and more familiar.

"And I won't lose you?" she asked.

"Not for a day."

"A day is too long," she said.

And then the sun finally cleared the hillside and shot a long, sharp ray of light down through the meadow. Mary lowered herself off me and grabbed the cricket cages. She held them against her chest.

"Won't they be excited?" she asked, and her joy at giving such a small token overwhelmed her. I thought of the others, how they would love the gifts because they came from Mary and how they would see the gifts reflected her nature, her entire being.

"Yes," I said. "More than you can know."

Mary wore a wreath of wildflowers in her hair. She wore a pale blue shift, a beautiful dress that followed her form past her knees. She wore hiking boots below the dress, which added a comical touch that made the day more festive. She had pulled her hair behind her and someone—her mother or Wally—had twined it into a French braid. She carried a bouquet of sedges and more wildflowers. When she looked at me, the flowers trembled gently in her hands. Our eyes met every few seconds.

"Is everyone ready?" she called to our small company.

It was still early. Birdsong filled the trees and morning air. At Mary's direction, we had parked on a back road next to a small, inconsequential spot of land somewhere between Newmarket and Portsmouth. The land appeared swampy, a cast-off wedge of gnarled trees and cattails that no developer had bothered to touch. In the early morning light, the patch of woods looked incredibly green.

Nevertheless, it was a piece of land that one might have passed a thousand times without noticing. Everyone—my father, Pole, Francis, Joan, and Wally—wore expressions that revealed their confusion about this particular spot. They also wore sneakers or boots, because Mary had told us all to dress for a short hike.

"I have to have your word," Mary said when we collected around her, all of us absurdly holding the cricket cages, "that you will tell no one the location of this wood. I know I can trust all of you, but I want to be sure you never let it slip what went on here today."

"This is sounding mysterious," Wally said, laughing.

"It is mysterious," Mary said and wiggled her eyebrows.

"Oh, Mary," Joan said, shaking her head. "What do you have up your sleeve? Isn't a surprise wedding enough for one day?"

"Follow me," she said.

We did. It felt funny to be out so early in the morning heading into a small wetland. If I thought of a wedding outdoors, I suppose I thought of a sweeping hillside or a beach. But instead I had to duck under several wiry maples with bands of Virginia creeper climbing their trunks. Francis, ducking along with me, called out something about Shrek and we all laughed. He had put his finger on it. It felt exactly as though we headed into a make-believe forest, an animated drawing of a swamp. We trusted Mary, of course, but the incongruity between a wedding and this particular patch of woodland seemed too wide to reconcile. A narrow footpath, arching to the north through the densest portion of the lot, seemed the only thing that offered proof anyone else had ever come this way.

We walked for fifteen minutes, all of us keeping our cricket cages horizontal in our hands. Pole, the tallest of us, had the most difficulty on the cluttered path. He became a source of good humor and he played along, happy to divert us. Francis went on about the donkey in *Shrek,* which one of us filled the bill, and Mary threatened to tell knock-knock jokes to pass the time. But before any of the conversations became rooted, she turned around and faced me.

"We're here," she said and kissed me, laughing as we broke apart.

She had never looked lovelier.

"Where are we, sweetheart?" Joan asked.

It was a good question. For the tiniest fraction of a second, I thought of her trip to the vernal pool with Francis. But she looked confident and happy. The place we had stopped did not seem markedly different from the area we had traversed on the way into the wood. But Mary smiled. She waited until we had all collected around her and she waved us closer until we stood in a small huddle, a football team awaiting a play call.

"This is New Hampshire's great secret," she said softly. "You are in the presence of a king of the forest."

She walked to a dark, gnarled tree on her left and put her hands on it. I had noticed the tree, its weepy beard, its rotted branches, but I hadn't fully examined it. When she turned back to us, tears filled her eyes.

"This is a black gum tree," she said, smiling at us even as her eyes remained filled with tears. "It is the oldest hardwood tree on earth. There are redwoods and sequoias that are older, but for hardwood, for maple and oak and beech, this is the oldest tree remaining. Nothing surpasses it. It was because of the wet, swampy land around it that it survived the initial timber cut of the early settlers. The Nature Conservancy owns this land and the secret of this tree is as closely guarded as any secret in the biological sciences. I want to marry my husband with this tree as a witness."

"Wait a second," Pole said. "I don't get this."

"They did a core sample," Mary said, "and the results bowled them over. This tree was growing when Joan of Arc was burned, and when we walked on the moon. It saw the Indians leave the woods and it has hosted a thousand thousand bird nests."

Pole pursed his lips. Francis smiled. My father shook his head and laughed softly.

"How do you want to arrange this?" Wally asked, practical as always.

"I want to be touching the tree when we say our vows," Mary said. "Mom, can you call Freddy?"

"Of course, honey," she answered.

We waited. In a surprisingly short span of time, Joan had Freddy on the line. She said hello, explained what was going on—she said she had already called to alert him to stand by—then handed the phone to Mary.

"How are the turtles?" Mary asked.

Then she didn't say anything for a while. When she handed the phone to me, her eyes were wet.

"He wants to talk to you," she said. "My husband-to-be."

Freddy's voice sounded far away, and misty with static, but his voice was unmistakable. He said it was getting dark there, nearly twelve hours ahead of us, and that the sea had become calm and beautiful.

"I know that you are aware of how precious Mary is," he said, "and that we love her. I know you love her, too, Cobb. It's not my place to give a blessing and I don't believe in any of that anyway, but I want you to know that I consider you my brother and that I invite you into this family with all the love I can."

"Thank you, Freddy."

"Now get married! Give the phone to Mom and let me listen in."

I did. I thought perhaps Francis should play his piccolo, but then a wind passed through the trees. It silenced the birds. Light filtered down and flecked the trillium and trout lily that poked shyly from the sides of the path. And the crickets inside our cages, detecting a change of light, began slowly to chirp.

"Are you ready?" Wally asked, taking a small book from her backpack. "Everyone step around, please. Cobb, step closer to the tree."

I put my hand on the tree. Mary stepped beside me and also put her hand on the tree. The tree connected us.

"We've come to this small wood on this beautiful summer morning to join Mary and Cobb in matrimony," Wally said, her glasses glinting a little in the light. "It's fitting that this tree stands beside us in witness, because its life force is a secret to most of the world. Your love, Mary and Cobb, must grow as this tree has grown. It must grow away from public attention, from the busy-ness and clamor of the world. And your love must add rings of years and friendship and joy. This tree is a simple thing and in its simplicity an inspiration. It has drawn life from soil and water and sunlight, but it has also weathered the storms of centuries and the snows of our harsh New Hampshire winters. It has taken the most elementary forces of nature and transformed them into aged beauty. In her famous poem about love from the *Sonnets from the Portuguese,* Elizabeth Barrett Browning asks, 'How do I love thee? Let me count the ways.' Most of us know that line and many of us mistake it for Shakespeare, but although those lines are famous, the next lines have more meaning to married couples. She says she loves him to the depth and breadth and height her soul can reach, which is lovely language and worthy in its own right. But then she adds a line or two aimed specifically that couples of any age would do well to contemplate, a line that I love above all the others in the poem. She says, 'I love thee to the level of every day's most quiet need, by sun and candle-light.' Love, in other words, is built not only of the large and sweeping emotions each of us seeks, but, more important, to the level of every day's most quiet need."

Wally paused. I took Mary's hand. She looked at me. Wally smiled at us both.

"I know Mary, and I know the joy she finds in Cobb. One glance at Cobb tells you the love he has for Mary. Remember the love of every day's most quiet need. Love by sun and candle-light. Be kind. Stand for each other. Grow like this tree.

"And now by the power vested in me by the State of New Hampshire, and in honor and memory of those who are eternal on the water, I pronounce you man and woman, partners, equals, lovers, and keepers of the other's wishes."

I started to move, but Mary held my hand and kept me in place. Wally lifted her voice and began to chant the same verse the girls had used to marry us on the river. I had thought it was a childish rhyme at the time, but in the woods bedside the grand old tree, beside the memory of the Chungamunga girls, their quiet dignity, I heard the words again. Mary spoke with her and I realized that our wedding on the river had been blessed by the girls in a way that counted for everything with Mary.

*To the wedding one, to the twoing-two*
*To the side by side, and the who loves who*
*To the family around you, and all in the room*
*To love and memory, to the bride and groom.*

*Remember us, remembering you*
*Remember time, remember new*
*Remember now, remember then*
*Remember how, remember when.*

Then laughter. Then tears. Then joy.

WITH THE SCRAPS FROM the window work and a few additional lumber purchases, Mary and I built a sleeping platform in the days after our wedding. We built it at the far end of our land, close to the brook so we could have the water's chatter and coolness in summer. In the winter, we calculated, we would see the stars flash out of the hills, and the sun, rising in the east, would find us slowly. Mary had specific rules about when we slept outside. Clear weather, always. No fighting, no bickering, no submerged anger allowed in the sleeping area. No phones. No electrical devices. No bug dope.

"This is for sleeping and stargazing," Mary said on our last day of construction, her hair tied back and a hammer in her hand. "No electrical junk. The modern world ends when we step onto this platform."

"How about in the winter? Are we going to sleep out here all winter?"

"We'll cross that bridge when we come to it," she said. "I've got plans."

She pounded a nail into one of the crosspieces. Then she looked past me to the front yard.

"Mail's here," she said.

The Newmarket mail Jeep crept by, the driver waving as she drove on the wrong side of the vehicle.

"Do you ever think it's weird that our post lady has to drive with one hand and lean across the Jeep as she goes along?" I asked.

I had two nails in my mouth.

"I think it shows talent and perseverance," she said.

Then she dropped the hammer and went off to get the mail. A minute later I heard her whoop. She came around the house, smiling at something.

"We're going to Yellowstone," she said, her voice excited, an open letter in her hand. "All expenses paid. A honeymoon."

"I thought you didn't believe in honeymoons."

"When they're paid for by someone else I do."

I took the nails out of my mouth.

"What are you talking about?" I asked.

"Elks!" she laughed.

"I'll need more than that," I said.

"They're doing an elk survey and looking at the effects of wolf predation. Environmental impact," she said, "and when you have elks and wolves, you have crows. And who are you going to call to assess the impact on corvids?"

"Mary Fury, who else?"

"You in?" she asked.

"When?"

"Ten days from now. Come on. We're teachers; it's summer break."

"Yellowstone?"

"The U.S. Forest Service is behind it. They'll put us up, feed us, and give us a per diem. I've done one of these studies before. It's not heavy lifting, but it's fun. Good people working together. And we might see wolves."

"The blessed trinity of wolves, men, and crows."

"You're learning," she said. "And elk."

"I'll make a couple calls, but I don't see why not. How long have you known about this?"

"I heard something on the grapevine and let people know I might be interested, but that's all. Nothing solid before now. We don't have to take it, but it's exciting."

"You're not that subtle," I said. "Sorry. You lobbied for it, I bet."

"I did a little, but I didn't know it would happen. Crows and gut-piles," Mary said. "Can it get any better?"

"Do they really call them gutpiles?"

"Gooey green gobs of it," she said and laughed. "Road trip! We're going on a freaking road trip."

"You're crazy," I said.

"Knock knock," she said.

"I refuse."

"Come on, please. Come on, Cobb. It's a perfect knock-knock moment."

"There is no such thing."

"Yes there is, and this is it."

I looked at her.

"Who's there?" I asked.

"Wendy."

"Wendy who?"

"Wendy wind blows, the cradle will rock."

"I share a house with someone who tells knock-knock jokes," I said.

"That's your fate. One more?"

"No," I said. "Mercy."

"Gorilla," she said.

"Gorilla who?"

"Gorilla a cheese sandwich and I'll be right over."

"No knock-knock jokes on the road trip. You have to promise."

She looked at me. She didn't promise.

We left July 1 at seven in the morning on a beautiful Tuesday. I purchased a cap for my truck from Otter Caps and Towing and we outfitted the truck bed with an air mattress, a camp stove, sleeping bags, a down comforter, and four large, fluffy pillows. We strapped the kayaks to the roof, tied them to the front and rear bumpers, then piled our backpacks on top of the mattress. Mary had climbed in the night before and tried out various scenarios. She finally decided we should sleep with our heads at the rear of the truck so that we could see the stars.

Before we left, she insisted we cut a tiny piece of our hair and bury it in front of the house.

"You're not serious," I said.

"It will help us find our way home."

"Did you do that when you went to the Allagash?"

"Yes, of course."

"It's a little strange, Mary."

"It works. It's ancient. Humor me."

So we did. In the dawn light we buried two locks of our hair, braided, beside the large window my father and Pole had installed.

"There," Mary said, straightening. "Our stars are fixed."

"Someone told me they invented compasses recently. Even GPS devices."

"Older," she said pointing at the divot of soil we had scraped up. "Better."

I drove the first leg. Mary made a nest for herself in the passenger's side. She had brought along the field notes to study. She read them as we passed out of New Hampshire and into Vermont, her voice taking pleasure in the description of elk gutpiles, wolves pulling down ruminants, crows flocking in aspens.

"It's fascinating," Mary said several times. "This is an initial report from the U.S. Forest Service examining the effects of wolf reintroduction to Yellowstone. Controversial as anything. Ranchers hate wolves, though mostly they get the science wrong. Environmentalists love them but they romanticize them. That's the nut of it. Wolves were reintroduced to their ancestral range in Yellowstone. Enormous expense. The Forest Service held more public testimony sessions on this issue than any other issue in the history of our country. So when they reintroduced the wolf packs, they didn't know exactly what would happen. The wolves did fine. They broke off into about half a dozen packs. They war with each other and make life a living hell for the coyotes. But when you introduce an apex predator, what happens to those below?"

"The crows," I said.

"Ravens mostly," Mary said. "This is an old triangle. So now with a superabundance of gutpiles, what happens to the corvid populations? Do they go wild and reach unsustainable levels? Remain stable? And if the corvids become too numerous, what impact does that have on rodent life, songbirds, you name it."

"So what do you do?"

"Count. Extrapolate. Take a survey as best I can. Have you ever been to Yellowstone?"

I shook my head.

"Me neither. But it's our oldest national park. It is America's backyard, in some sense. You can do things in some parks, just regular fieldwork, but when you start messing with Yellowstone, everyone takes notice. We have to be on our toes."

"You do," I said, correcting her. "I'm a lazy tourist."

She ignored me. Her eyes stayed down on the report, her voice excited.

"One of the places we might visit is way down off Yellowstone Lake. Tons of grizzlies in there. I guess it's gone back about a hundred years in the backcountry. Returned to its original state. Grizzlies, wolves, elks, bison. We're going to do some time travel."

"Do grizzlies come to dance by the firelight?"

"Heck no. Grizzlies don't mess around. They wouldn't smell of honey. They'd smell of gutpiles."

"Makes sense," I said.

"Are you sick of being dragged around to look at crows and turtles?" she asked.

I had to look at her to see if she was serious.

"Not yet," I said.

"I love this kind of work," she said, her eyes bright. "And going with you makes it better."

I took her hand.

"Yellowstone," I said. "I've always wanted to go."

"Indonesia and Yellowstone in the same year," she said. "That might qualify us as intrepid."

"And the Allagash."

"Last year," she said. "Technically."

"But within a year."

She nodded.

"And a house," I said.

"It makes me think that there could be another year like it," she said, closing the report. "I mean, we might be right on the verge of a wonderful year, but we wouldn't know it right now. The most fantastic thing in the world could be just around the bend, but you sit and look at this one small corner and you think that's the end of it. I didn't know when I went to give a talk to the river girls that I was going to meet you."

"In other words," I said, "you could be ready to meet another guy soon?"

She raised up onto her knees and kissed me. She kissed me a dozen times on my neck and ear until I had to scrunch my shoulder away to keep my eyes on the road.

"No other guys," she said, pulling back.

"That's a deal."

She sat back on her side.

"Tell me about your mom," she said, surprising me. "You don't talk about her."

"I never knew her very well."

"She died in a car accident?"

I nodded.

"How?" she asked.

"A teenager went through a stop sign. No drinking or anything sordid on either side. Just an accident. The teenager was an average sort of boy. Red-haired. He was a second string forward on the high school basketball team. You want to have a villain, at least I did, but the kid didn't fit that bill. He had a big Labrador retriever with him in the front seat and the police and insurance company thought maybe that distracted him. Roscoe, the dog was named. Funny I remember that name, but not much more about the boy."

"Was the dog hurt?"

"No. Just my mom, really. The nose of the boy's car went right into the driver's side. Pretty quick, my dad always said. But he might just say that to make me feel better. To make himself feel better, too."

"Do you know what she was like?"

"I remember her. She was kind, very even-keeled, and she had a throaty sort of voice. A little froggy. I asked my dad about it later and he confirmed she did. Polyps or something. She liked honeyed tea, so maybe she was a bear."

"What else about her?"

I looked at her.

"Is this really interesting to you?" I asked.

She nodded. Her complete attention rested on me.

"She went to Mount Holyoke," I said after a second, my eyes on the road. "She liked photography. People used to ask her to take photos at weddings and reunions. Family gatherings. She liked black-and-white photographs. She collected photos from yard sales and flea markets. Sometimes we'd lay them out on the kitchen table and we'd try to construct a story about the people in the photo. Who was right out of camera range? What had they been doing? She liked that. She liked stories and the quirky things that happened to people."

"Did your folks have a good marriage?"

"Seemed to. Dad never remarried. He never really dated again except maybe right at the beginning when everyone sort of pushed him to get back into it. You know. Setups and blind dates. He eventually learned simply to say no. We're one-women men, we Cobbs."

"You better be," she said. "You said your dad lives in a trailer? You've told me, but I've never quite understood it."

"No, not really. I grew up in a conventional house. It was kind of boring, actually. The house, I mean. When I went off to college my dad sat me down and asked if I had any objection to his selling the house. I said no. So a little while later he took the equity from our house and bought twenty acres of land near White Mountain National Forest. Then he got Pole to help him set up cargo containers. Do you know the kind? When you see a big truck go by with a container on the back, that's what he bought. He had read some crazy article in *Mother Earth News* about recycling products, so he did this sort of hippie, back to the earth thing and built a compound of containers. He stacked them in interesting ways, using the edge of one as an overhang for a porch, another for a patio . . . you'd have to see it. He cut holes into the sides for windows, built lawns and gardens on some of the roofs. The containers are all insulated, so he can heat the place for next to nothing. And he has all the other amenities. So he doesn't have to work, really, except to pay off the taxes. He used to be a mortgage broker for Northway Bank. But he doesn't work anymore. Not in a regular job. The taxes don't amount to much because he tells the town officials the containers don't have a foundation and they are bob houses for ice fishing."

"He's my new hero," Mary said, smiling. "I have to see this place."

"You will. The opportunity just hasn't presented itself."

"Soon," she said. "When we get back. Promise me."

"I promise. Anyway, the reason I mentioned his house is that it seemed to take up his interest these last years. It almost reminds me of the Swiss Family Robinson . . . like he was marooned on a strange parcel of land in New Hampshire and this is how he coped. It's really quite beautiful the way he integrated it into the land. It occupies him. He's almost inventing a new way to live for himself."

"I like your dad," she said. "I admire that kind of self-reliance."

"Most people do," I said.

"And his friend Pole helps him?"

"Pole's an electrician and still lives in his family home. Sort of arrested development, in a way, but maybe a wise man, too. Hard to say. He takes a dozen jobs a year, when he needs money. Expert electrician, so he's always in demand. But he doesn't want to be busy constantly. They are sort of interesting men."

"Thoreauvian."

"Nice word."

"But they are. That's why you like Thoreau so much."

"Maybe so," I said, trying to frame things as I spoke. "It's true I never saw the point of working at a job simply to get money to buy time somewhere down the road when you're seventy-five. Seemed like a lousy plan. Imagine if someone came to you today and said, look, work the rest of your life, two weeks off a year, and when you've worked fifty years and you have marginal health, then we'll give you some time off . . . but many of your friends will be dead and the things you wanted to do years ago, you lack the stamina for them."

"You're an old hippie, Jonathan Cobb!"

"In a way, I guess. Teaching is a nice blend of work and freedom. That's what I think, anyway."

"Do you miss your mom? I mean, of course you do . . . but are you conscious of her absence, I guess is what I'm asking."

"Hard to say. She was gone quickly and it's difficult to know what I remember and what I simply make up about her. My dad used to worry that I didn't have a woman's influence in my life. He was always asking the guidance counselors if I seemed well-adjusted. And I could tell from time to time he worried that he should be dating someone just to have a maternal influence in my life. But eventually we sorted it all out. I don't seem horribly maladjusted, do I?"

She shook her head.

"Just around the edges," she said.

"I looked up the redheaded kid not long ago. The strange power of Google. He was on a high school reunion site that anyone could join for free. James Flanders. Not even an interesting name, really. He went to Lafayette College in Easton, Pennsylvania. He's a financial planner. He likes tennis and juggling. He listens to reggae and rap. Can you imagine? I looked at his picture for a while, but I didn't have any great revelation or insight. Just a guy."

"He's probably a little haunted," Mary said.

"I hope not. I hope he's fine. It was an accident."

She leaned up on her knees and put her lips next to my ear.

"Pull over," she whispered.

I glanced at her.

"Now," she said, her voice melting me. "Right this second."

"On the interstate?"

"First rest stop," she said and kept kissing my neck.

"WE NEED COWBOY HATS," she said in South Dakota.

It was late. The stars came slowly out of the western sky. The road ran ahead of us as far as our headlights. She had country-western on the radio.

"You're a New Hampshire girl," I said.

"Without a cowboy hat," she said. "That's my point."

She rolled down the windows. Wind blasted in and she cranked up the radio.

"South Dakota," she said, rapping a little beat on the steering wheel.

"Are you the type to get an accent wherever you go?"

"Absolutely," she said.

She stuck her head out the window and made a coyote howl.

"If you could see one thing right now," she said. "One magical thing, what would it be?"

"You naked."

"Good answer," she said, nodding, "but I am looking for something more soulful."

"A white crow on a black night," I said.

"Now we're getting somewhere."

"You?" I asked.

"I would like Godzilla to be off in the distance. You know, far enough away so he couldn't get you, but you could see him and you would be really glad to be in a fast car."

"Would he be killing other people? Because that goes under the heading of disturbing."

"No, he'd just be Godzilla-ing around. Making noise and maybe honking out fire."

"You're very strange, Mary," I said.

"Imagine him running across the plains trying to catch you, but he wasn't quite fast enough. But for a second you thought maybe he was. That's why *Jurassic Park* is my favorite movie."

"I thought *All That Heaven Allows* is your favorite movie?"

"Of a type," she said, still tapping on the steering wheel.

"You can't have favorite types. A favorite means the boss of all the others."

"I have to have a movie boss?"

"One favorite is what I'm saying."

"That's so boy of you. All that hierarchy and marking behavior."

"A virus comes from outer space and threatens to destroy all movies everywhere, but you are allowed to save one. Would it be *Jurassic Park* or *All That Heaven Allows*?"

*"Star Wars,"* she said.

"I'm going to sleep," I said. "You don't play fair."

"We still need cowboy hats," she said. "Black ones. Bad guy ones."

WE SLEPT ON A blue tarp under an enormous July sky in South Dakota. We had pulled off the interstate and found a back road that took us to another back road and another back road until we finally parked near an abandoned corral on a slanted piece of land. We shined our headlamps around, looking for horses, but we didn't find any. As late as it was, Mary insisted we pull out the air mattress and make ourselves comfortable. In ten minutes we had an excellent bed with a view to the west. The slight incline tilted us up and made it easy to watch the stars tucking down over the horizon. The land smelled different from the land in Maine or New Hampshire. It smelled of sage and dry dirt and a wind that seemed to travel farther to reach us than the winds did in the east.

I felt tired and road weary. The landscape continued to move toward me as if we remained in the truck. In time, though, the sky tugged my vision up and the warmth of Mary beside me, tucked close, settled me. We watched for shooting stars for a while, but my eyes kept closing. Mary whispered when she saw one. "There," she said. "Another." She didn't make wishes on the stars. She simply watched them burn and disappear in the atmosphere.

"You never asked about Freddy," she said at one point, her head on my shoulder. "Whether he has Huntington's."

I came fully awake slowly. I wasn't entirely sure what she had said.

"About Freddy?" I asked, still cloudy.

"If he has Huntington's. If he presented symptoms."

"Has he?"

She shook her head no.

"Has he been tested?" I asked.

She nodded yes.

"Why did he decide to be tested?"

"He wanted to know," she said. "It would have driven him nuts not to know."

"What was his reasoning?"

I felt her shrug against me.

"Knowledge is power," she said. "That kind of thing. Once I know for certain one way or the other, then I can plan accordingly. We're different that way. I'm orderly on the outside, and a bit freer on the inside. Freddy is outwardly a free spirit, but he's a tiny bit fussy. He had to know. I didn't need to know, I guess."

"I like your way," I said.

A long time passed before she said the next thing.

"Did you go to the prom?" she asked.

"Yes. Did you?"

"With Gil Rollins. He was a science geek like me. He wore a tie with a Bunsen burner print on it. It was kind of an inside joke thing."

"No tuxedo?" I asked.

"Not in our neck of New Hampshire. Did you wear a tux?"

"Sure. Teenage James Bond."

"I bet you were dreamy. Who did you go with?"

"Polly Peterson."

"Sounds like a poodle."

"We rented a U-Haul, a bunch of us, and we decorated it with furniture. We had a little moving living room. We thought we were the coolest ever."

"That is kind of cool. What did Polly wear?"

"I don't remember. Something yellow. She did a fake tan that backfired so she looked a little orange. The yellow didn't help."

"Poor thing. She must have been crazy about you."

"Not really. She drank two vodka nips in the girls' bathroom and felt sick the rest of the night."

"Gil Rollins smoked a cigar. His uncle had given him a bunch or something. He and his geeky friends smoked these horrible cigars out behind the gym."

"You were really a geek?" I asked.

"A science geek," she said. "There's a difference. My mind was geekish, but my body was pure dodgeball."

"I have to sleep now," I said.

"What can we have for breakfast?"

"Flapjacks," I said, knowing that's what she wanted me to say. She liked to fall asleep thinking of breakfast.

"And?"

"And butter and maple syrup and we'll eat it with our sleeves rolled up and we won't set down our knife or fork once."

"And?"

"Scalding coffee."

"And?"

She pulled her body closer.

"There," she whispered before I could continue, her head nodding to point out a shooting star. "Right above us."

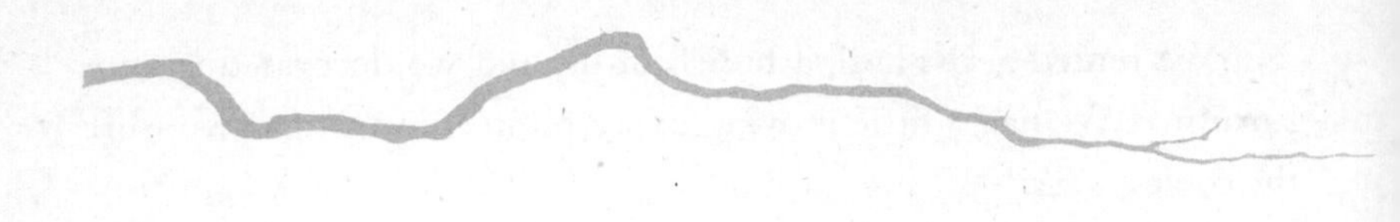

# 15

*You Are In Grizzly Country.*

That's what several signs told us as we followed Wyoming Route 212 across a mountain pass still mushy with summer melt, then through Cooke City and finally into the park. It was three o'clock and cloudy. Mary held a map of Yellowstone on her lap and guided me. From what she could ascertain, we needed to go to the southern portion of the park, at the tail end of Yellowstone Lake. One of the wolf packs—the Druid Peak Pack—had actually staked a claim near to where we entered the park. Mary nodded when she saw the landscape and read the geographical details to me as we drove. Yellowstone, she said, is the product of an enormous, and ancient, volcanic eruption. The caldera—the remaining empty cupcake wrapper, slightly collapsed and still bubbling with sulfur—constituted the rest of the park. She stopped only when we saw our first bison herd. They had collected on a wide plain, and ferns of fog from sulfur pots obscured their outlines. On such an overcast day, they appeared mythic, bison out of a cheesy western, or from a *National Geographic* documentary. But as we drove closer we made out the silhouettes of the animals, and in time we picked out individuals. Their sable manes shone with dust and winter debris and many of their pelts had shed down to summer tolerances.

"Now we're talking," Mary said, still glancing back and forth from the map to the landscape. "Did you know bison kill more tourists every year than bears do? It says it right here."

"But bison don't eat you afterward."

"Fair enough."

"So wolves get bison, bison become gutpiles, and crows win again."

"Crows always win," Mary said.

"And the bison manure the plains and keep everything aerated and open. The big circle."

"You're going *Lion King* on me. All Circle of Life."

"It's hard not to," I said.

I pulled the truck onto a turnout. Mary opened the glove compartment and handed me a pair of binoculars. She had another for herself. Both were small but powerful. We climbed out and went to the front of the truck and sat and watched the bison. They rolled in a mud bowl. A few had turned cinnamon colored.

"The richness of the ungulates on the Yellowstone caldera are surpassed only by the grazing animals on the Serengeti in Africa," Mary said, the glasses to her eyes.

"You are such a little plagiarist," I said. "Where did you read that?"

"I just read it on the map."

"But that's why we people wanted wolves here," I said. "Right? Hoof and claw."

"Balance."

I had to look closely at Mary's glasses to realize she had forgotten the bison and was busily scanning the trees for crows or ravens. I nearly said something when I noticed a single muscle along her jawline contracting and moving. The muscle moved disproportionately to what we were doing. It ran like a bright twine through the left side of her face and into her scalp. If Mary noticed it, she made no telltale adjustment.

"You okay?" I asked, hoping to get her to turn her face to mine.

She nodded.

The flashing muscle subsided. *Maybe,* I told myself, *just a fluky muscle contraction to accommodate the binoculars.* I continued watching her, though. The muscle did not move again. The line of her sight remained high in the trees, the aspens empty but waiting for crows.

"YOU WANT TO MEET some wolves?" Jidad Billups asked.

Jidad Billups was a bulky black man with a buzz cut, a crisp khaki uniform, and a large green patch over his right breast. He was probably forty and had a great smile that crinkled his eyes. His arms, when he reached to shake our hands, ran tight with muscle. It took me a moment to realize what I had first perceived as bulk was, on second look, a bodybuilder's knotted frame. His neck fanned out against his collar with a cobra flair of muscle. He filled up the room of his gray office, a cinder-block box that seemed an afterthought to the larger compound in which it was located.

*Wolf Management,* read the sign on the offices. *West Thumb, Yellowstone.*

"Where?" Mary asked.

"We have a holding pen," Jidad Billups said, inviting us to sit. "We used it originally for the first pairs we brought here, but now it serves as a kind of hospital way station. We've got some pups in there now. Some jerk killed the mother outside of the parklands. He said he thought he shot a wild German shepherd, not a wolf. Anyway, that's what he claimed to cover himself. We found the pups denned on a south-facing moraine, up near the northeast boundary of the park. We lost three of them, but three survived. They have their run of the place, but they don't go far."

"I'd love to see them," I said.

"Let me just close up shop," Jidad said, shuffling a few papers and shutting down his computer. "I'm done for the day. We can get you situated and show you the wolves."

Five minutes later we followed him outside. He walked us first to a bunk room, used, he said, for biologists and staff passing through. No one else was in the room now, he informed us, but that wasn't to say people wouldn't show up. The room, at a glance, didn't promise much except a roof and a cot for a bed. The showers, Jidad showed us, were in a locker room used by everyday staff.

"Can we pitch a tent anywhere?" I asked. "Or sleep in our truck?"

"Out back," Jidad said. "A lot of people prefer it to sleeping in the bunk room. Can't say I blame you."

Then he took us to see the wolves.

We climbed into Jidad's green pickup and drove two miles to a fenced lot set among beautiful ponderosa pines. The overcast day had turned darker. A drizzle flicked wet drops against the windshield, only enough to make Jidad switch his wipers on to intermittent. At the entrance Jidad climbed out and opened a padlock, climbed in, drove through, then locked the pen behind us.

"Security," Jidad said. "These wolves are a flashpoint for political talk on both sides. That's why we need someone to survey the crows and ravens. Environmental impact assessment. People skim the report and then start arguing the same points over and over, no more informed than before. It's frustrating."

"How long will you keep the pups?" I asked.

He shrugged.

"Depends on how they grow and on their sex," he said, parking the truck near another wire pen. "Young males often have to fight their way into a pack, but they can get killed easily, too. Females should probably be accepted as a submissive pack member. We put out the word that we have three good-looking pups. We might have to give them away, transfer them up to Canada or Minnesota. Wolf people work together. And it's good to mix up the DNA."

"What do you feed them?" Mary asked.

"Roadkill, mostly. Dead deer, elk, whatever we have. They're off milk now. They were probably born late winter, maybe March or February. The mothers regurgitate back to them, but that's not easily replicated. We try to keep human contact to a minimum. We don't want them to grow dependent."

We climbed out. A ten-foot-high fence, with razor wire on top, ran out of sight to the left. A sign informed us that we had entered secure federal lands and we risked fines, imprisonment, or both if we ignored this warning. Nothing indicated the presence of wolves, perhaps because to put up signs invited curiosity and troublemakers. Jidad did a small stretching exercise to loosen his neck. Then he raised his hand and pointed.

"Right there," he whispered.

It took me a moment to see them.

My first thought on seeing the wolves—three youngsters, all gray, all beautifully trim—was that I had never imagined a wolf properly. It was an odd thought, but it made sense to me. A wolf is not the wolf of your dreams, I realized. They looked much more canine, for one thing, and more wild in the same breath. Their wariness, their quick glances, their desire to see but not to be seen, thrilled me a way a dog could never do. They lay with their paws in front, all studying us, all poised to react. Now and then the soft light caught their eyes and I saw the crepuscular sheen, the reflection that is the mythic quality of a wolf.

"They just ate, looks like," Jidad said. "They're full and sleepy."

"Which are the males?" I asked.

"The two on the left. The one on the right is a female. Females don't get as big as males, but she's good-sized."

"Did you name them?" Mary asked.

"Officially? They have numbers. A flesh plug of their ear is on record in Casper. DNA, blood, and so on. They are better documented than we are."

"And unofficially?"

"The girl is Wheezie. The boys are Spud and Thomas. Thomas is the one on the far left. He was the last one to come out of the den. A guy named Thomas reached in and just found him with the tips of his fingers. We were ready to go and would have missed him."

"They look different from what I thought," I admitted.

"People think wolves look like big Malamute dogs. Some do, a little. But most wolves are long and thin. They can be gray or black or just about any color. They get beat up bringing down elk. It's hard work. Always a couple injured wolves in any pack, but they are resilient. They're thriving in the park and out of it."

"Are the herd numbers remaining solid?" Mary asked.

"They're healthy and stable," Jidad said, nodding. "The wolves do what they're supposed to do. They cull the weakest. We used to have some winter kills, you know, stragglers who appeared to be suffering. The wolves take care of that."

"Do you have binoculars?" Mary asked Jidad. "We left ours in our truck."

"Sure," he said. "Just a second."

He went to his truck and pulled out a powerful pair of binoculars. He handed them to Mary. She looked for a long time at the wolves. Then she handed them to me.

"How long were they gone from the park?" Mary asked.

"A hundred years or so."

"It's not a wilderness without wolves," she said.

"Never seemed that way to me, either," Jidad said.

Afterward, he drove us back and dropped us at the office.

"The bunk rooms and the showers are open all night," he said. "I'll be back at eight tomorrow morning. Mary, we can go over the reports and previous surveys. Should take us a couple hours. After that, we can do some fieldwork. If you'll sign a waiver, Cobb, you're welcome to join us."

"Absolutely," I said.

"Okay, then good night. We've had a juvenile grizzly around here lately, so keep your food out of your tent. You might prefer to sleep in your truck or in the bunk room. Up to you, of course."

We said good-bye. When Jidad pulled out, Mary turned to me.

"I had to wait 12,919 days to see a wolf. But now I have."

"You've been counting? You hadn't mentioned it in a while."

"And I saw bison today. This was a good day."

"Any way to make it better?" I asked.

She looked at me. She nodded.

It was late, nearly midnight, when my cell phone rang. I came awake instantly, but for a moment I forgot where I was. We had decided to sleep in the truck. The drizzling rain and the potential presence of a grizzly had simplified the decision. Mary woke at the ring of the phone, too. She switched on an electric lantern. I wrestled through my jacket and sweaters, searching for the phone. I found it on the fifth ring. I flicked it open, my heart going fast.

"Yes?" I said.

"Cobb? I'm terribly sorry to call you so late. This is Dean Hallowen. I must have scared you to death."

"Hello, Dean," I said, trying to shake the cobwebs out. "Is everything okay?"

"I'm afraid not. We have a situation with Francis Loftus that's developing right now. You're our best contact for the young man."

"Francis," I whispered to Mary.

She poured me a glass of water from our traveling jug. She held it out to me.

"He's having a rough time of it," Dean Hallowen said. "Do you remember the incident with his friend? The one who committed suicide?"

"Yes, of course."

"Another friend of his committed suicide a few days ago. The young man cited the first letter in his letter. So that's two boys who have committed suicide from this pact they drew up. This one did something called death by cop. Do you know about that term?"

"Not really," I said.

"Well," Dean Hallowen said, his voice sounding tired, "I'm not sure I understand it entirely either, but it's taking steps to get the police to kill you. You approach them with a gun, or put yourself in a position where the police will have to use deadly force. This young man—his name was Robert, by the way, Robert French—he held up a liquor store with a toy gun. Apparently the video in the store is painful to watch. The boy is distraught and hardly even bothers to take the money. He delayed longer than he needed to, talked to the Korean store owner, and by the time he stepped out of the store, the cops had arrived. He waved his gun at them and they shot him down."

"Horrible," I said.

"Francis's mother is completely terrified. She doesn't want to allow Francis to attend the funeral, because she says it will reinforce the whole suicide-pact notion. Apparently Francis and one other boy are the only remaining members of this group. Francis is the only one who has a chance to get out, realistically."

"What can I do to help?" I asked.

"Maybe nothing," Dean Hallowen said. "I have his number. It's a cell phone. The mother seems to think you have had a good influence on him. He likes you, at any rate. He enjoyed spending time with you. She wondered if you might be able to call him, just talk to him now and then. The funeral is tomorrow. Francis is understandably pulled in a number of directions right now. You'll have to feel your way. And naturally, I have no right to ask you to do this. Even his mother, Ida, her name is, even Ida said she understands this is way above and beyond any expectation for a teacher. But there is no man in any of these boys' lives. No one dependable. So that's what she's hoping you might provide."

"I'll call him," I said.

"I knew you would," Dean Hallowen said. "But only insofar as you feel comfortable. It puts the school in a little bit of an uncomfortable spot. You're not a psychologist. You should try to function as a friend or a teacher. We don't want to open up questions of liability."

"I understand."

"What Francis needs, his mother thinks, is to be reminded there is life beyond Philadelphia, beyond this hideous suicide pact. She seems to think you could do that."

"I'll call him as soon as we hang up."

Neither one of us said anything for a moment.

"Are you in Yellowstone?" Dean Hallowen asked.

"Yes, as a matter of fact. We arrived today."

"Well, this is a mitzvah I'm asking of you. It's a good act. See what you can do. And will you give me a call back? Tomorrow morning will be fine unless something critical comes up. I'll leave it to your discretion."

I kept him on until I could copy down the various phone numbers. Mary held the light so I could see what I wrote. After I said good-bye to Dean Hallowen, I punched the numbers into my phone while I filled in Mary.

"Oh, Francis," she said when I finished. "The poor kid. What a horrible loss of potential."

"Give me a few things to say. What should I concentrate on?"

Mary thought a moment.

"You'll know what to say," she said. "You're Jonathan Cobb, and this is your gift. I've never met anyone who knew more what to say at the correct moment. I'm going to leave you alone and run to the bathroom. Give Francis my love. Tell him he is my mom's antiquing buddy."

I nodded. Mary kissed me, then she slipped out of the truck. I took a deep breath and waited for Francis's number to go through.

"SO MY MOTHER GOT to you, too," Francis said, his voice loud, some kind of music playing in the background. "She's pulling out all the big guns."

"Hello, Francis. This is Jonathan Cobb."

"I know who it is," he said. "This is that concerned white teacher who is calling to tell me life is good if I give it a chance."

"You okay?" I asked. "You sound a little cynical."

"Is that supposed to be a joke?"

"Supposed to be."

He didn't say anything. Neither did I.

"It's late," he said.

"I saw bison today. And wolves," I said. "They were something else."

"Where are you?"

"In Yellowstone with Mary. Remember? She's out here doing research on crows."

"How I spent my summer vacation."

"It's pretty out here. It smells different."

"Different from what?"

"From the east, I guess."

Again, a silence.

"Listen, my mother doesn't get what's going on," Francis said. "She's got these upwardly mobile fixations."

"That doesn't sound like a bad thing."

"It's not, necessarily. But it's not realistic."

"Why not?"

"You really want to do this? Come on, Mr. Cobb, you're smarter than that."

"You need to see a wolf," I said. "A wolf isn't anything like what you think it is. You go through your entire life, and you think you know what a wolf must be like, but it turns out you're only about fifty percent right. You've been living with this huge misperception of what a wolf is, and you've been leading your life thinking you have properly understood a wolf. But when you see a wolf, then you know."

"And that's a big metaphor for . . . ?"

"Oh, hell, Francis, I don't know. It's a metaphor for saying you are young, your friends were young, and what they thought they knew about wolves might have only been half right. You need to see a wolf up close. Some things you think right now, they're a distorted image of what you think you know. Maybe what you think you know about the wolf isn't entirely accurate."

"I don't think about wolves," he said.

We fell silent again.

"Can I give you my number?" I asked him. "If you want to talk, call me. I'm going to call you a couple times. Just to talk and to tell you what I'm seeing."

Mary slipped back into the truck. She climbed under our down comforter. The drizzle had stopped and the night had grown chilly.

"You can call if you want," Francis said. "But you sound like you're on some *National Geographic* kind of thing."

"Sort of," I said. "Mary says hello. She says her mother wants to go antiquing with you."

"I know. I'm the much-loved inner city child."

"Come on, Francis, give us a break."

He didn't say anything to that. I gave him my number. I couldn't tell if he wrote it down. It was probably on his cell phone anyway.

"Your mother has your best interests at heart," I said. "Somewhere deep down you know that."

He murmured something. The music turned up in the background. A loud crunch like a car door closing hard snapped through the phone. Then the phone went dead and Francis wasn't on the line anymore.

"Is he okay?" Mary asked.

"Not really."

"Do you want to call Dean Hallowen back?"

"It can wait until morning," I said. "Nothing anyone can do for the moment."

"Will Francis go to the funeral?"

"We didn't get into the details," I said. "I felt like I was pushing too hard to begin with."

"I can't believe it's the same young man who came and went to that auction with us. Or played the piccolo by the fire that time and came to our wedding. He's our friend."

"Different places, different demands. He's a brilliant kid stuck in a horrible environment. His mother is on his side and she may save him, but young men that age are drawn to their peer group. It's important to be a man, to save face. Hanging around a prep school in New Hampshire doesn't exactly earn him any street cred."

"Did you just say street cred?" Mary said, a smile cracking her face.

"I did. It hurt coming out."

"So what will happen?"

"Who knows? I'll call him a lot. I'll call him every day. And I'll hope that he can see the choices clearly. A part of him knows what he should do, what the better choice is. But he's blinded to it right now. Or he's confused about it. He is that bright young man who visited us. And I believe he liked us. He had wonderful impulses, wonderful sensibilities. But he's experiencing a sort of situational morality. Culture imperatives."

"Let's get him out of there," Mary said. "Tell him to come up to our house for a while."

"That was my next move, but I wanted to ask you first."

"Always," she said. "Anything like that for a student."

"That goes for both of us."

"But especially for Francis," she said.

"I don't want to rush in and act as if we know best. Drag the Native Americans out of their homes and stick them in Christian schools."

"No one knows best. But we know that suicide pact has drawn two kids into it. Sounds pretty desperate to me."

We stopped talking for a while. She slid next to me.

"Did the grizzly bear try to get you when you were out there?" I asked.

"No," she said. "but I'm pretty sure Chungamunga girls can't be bothered by grizzlies."

"Does the power of Chungamunga girls reach all the way out here?"

"And beyond," she said.

She yawned and pushed her body against mine. The moon threw light somewhere and the light got pushed and pulled by the trees moving in a quiet wind. I held Mary close and thought about Francis, about Philadelphia, about city streets. I thought about Francis's friend, the first boy to kill himself, who lived in an apartment with part of the roof missing. In a box, on a street, with the rain flashing by, the chair, or couch, or simple milk crate tucked back to keep the weather off it. Kids sitting and watching TV, maybe, the streets like so many rivers outside, the line between inside and outside, between acceptable and unacceptable, blurred beyond any conventional meaning. Ulysses strapped to the mast with the sirens calling, their song irresistible to a boy on the edge of manhood.

"We've got a grizzly on an elk carcass," Jidad said first thing in the morning. "Not far from here. People are lined up to take photos, so a portion of our staff will be diverted there. But you might want to check it for crows."

He offered us coffee out of a Farberware percolator. The coffee tasted excellent, especially against the chill of the morning air.

He waved us to seats, then reached down and began pulling out enormous binders of papers from a drawer. He stacked them on the left side of his desk. It became almost comical to watch the reports mount.

"We have everything here," he said. "Surveys on grasses, on trees, on insect distribution, you name it. We have songbirds, but we don't have corvids. Of course, soon after a report is filed, it's obsolete or dated. That's the nature of the game here. Frankly, I could probably have you back every year for the next decade."

"It's a deal," Mary said.

"Be careful what you wish for," Jidad said, smiling. "But I'm showing you these reports to let you know the kind of interest that swirls around this project. Do your best. Someone somewhere will use it for or against wolves or against any other political goal they might have. Make it as factual as possible. You'll probably go home to write it up?"

Mary nodded.

"How many days will you need to gather data?" Jidad said.

"To survey the entire park?" Mary asked, her eyes going a little wide.

"Probably one section of the park. You can extrapolate. Everything in this biz is a snapshot, as you know. Things change constantly. But we're hoping you can provide a baseline. I understand it's a fairly impossible task. Can you count nests?"

"Might be the way to do it," she said, "but the young have probably fledged already. I don't know. You can do a distribution study, over, say, a ten-kilometer by ten-kilometer square. You monitor the population over a span of years. That would be my recommendation. Pick an area where you know there is wolf activity, then set us up there. We'll count what we can."

"Physically count?" Jidad asked.

Mary nodded.

"Not very high-tech, but it works," she said. "Do it for ten years running and you may be able to draw some conclusions about the health of the corvid population. Did they do any studies on corvids before the wolves were introduced?"

Jidad waved at the reports. He raised his eyebrows to say he couldn't possibly know for certain.

"Let me go through the reports this morning; then we can set up in a proper location this afternoon, if that's okay. How does that sound?"

"I'm afraid I'll have to leave you with the reports. I have to go out and check on this grizzly. Would you like to come along, Cobb?" Jidad asked.

"Oh, so I stay and do homework while you two go off to see a grizzly?" Mary asked.

"Isn't it wonderful the way it worked out like that?" I asked. "We're both occupied."

"Go ahead," she said. "Can I set up in the conference room back here? That way I can spread out."

We helped her carry the reports back to a wide cafeteria table in a dull office topped by frosted windows. She started reading them almost before we got them on the table. She asked Jidad for a quick tutorial on the coffeepot, then sent us on our way.

"I feel a little like a kid getting out of school," Jidad said as we climbed in his truck.

"She'll devour those reports," I reassured him. "She loves this stuff."

"Well, she came highly recommended. Anyone I asked about corvids pointed to her."

"She'll figure it out one way or the other," I said.

THE MORNING SUN HAD barely cleared the mountains fully by the time Jidad and I reached the elk carcass near Yellowstone Lake. At first I didn't see the grizzly. The kill sat well off the road near a stream, and the bear, brown and peppered with white, reclined next to the dead elk. The bear had obviously eaten a good deal of it. The elk hardly resembled an animal any longer. Its skin had been pulled back and its white ribs showed pale and yellow in the morning light. The bear did not move, but whenever a breeze passed, its fur rippled.

Traffic had lined up along the road. Jidad sat a moment with me, handed me the binoculars we had used the evening before to look at the wolves, and hopped out of his truck. He walked over to a female officer who stood with a group of sightseers. The officer appeared young and a little nervous. A number of people had tripods out and expensive cameras mounted to snap pictures of the bear. Jidad spoke with the young female officer, checked up and down the line with people who had stopped, then came back to the truck. We sat inside.

"Consensus is, the bear made the kill last night," Jidad said, climbing in. "It wasn't here yesterday anyway. Might have surprised it, might have ambushed it. Of course, the bear might have chased off some wolves and claimed the carcass, but that could have gone the other way around, too. Sometimes the wolves chase off the bear."

"Is the bear right on it?" I asked, trying to see through the binoculars. "It's hard to get these in focus."

"They're good, but we have a telescope coming. People want to see the bear and we want them to see it. Best kind of publicity to lock down public interest. No one who sees this bear today will forget it in their lifetime. Do you know the first time I came to Yellowstone I watched a bison herd ford the Yellowstone River. Magnificent sight. But a calf started to get swept downstream and the mother had already made it across. She snorted and made an enormous fuss, but the calf got farther and farther away. Horrible, really. Then at what seemed the last minute, the calf got its footing. It surged forward, got swept down farther again, then regained its feet. The entire episode seemed to take hours. But it finally made it across and everyone watching clapped. Some had been crying. I'll never forget it, and I'm a biologist."

"People see the animals and the next time they have to vote on a referendum about an animal's status on federal lands, they remember. Is that what you're saying?"

"Something like that," Jidad said. "And the kids get a vivid impression that stays with them. At least that's what we're aiming at."

"Are the wolves safe here? Politically, I mean?"

"You can't undo them. No one's taking them away now. Have you ever heard a wolf howl at night?"

I shook my head.

"Coyotes do a kind of bark and howl mixed. Sounds like a woman on a bad drunk crying. But a wolf, there's no mistaking it. You hear it and the hackles go up on your neck, I promise. Then it gets into you. It's all sorts of lonely, which is ironic because ultimately wolves call to reconnoiter and connect with each other. You know, you risk cliché whenever you talk about it, but wolves are the sound of the wilderness. In North America, anyway. We take people out on night trips to hear them."

Another ranger pulled up beside us.

"Here comes the telescope," Jidad said.

We climbed out. Jidad introduced me to a ranger named Carol, a blond woman, about forty, who went to the back of her truck and pulled out a tripod and a black box. We helped her set up the tripod, then she removed the telescope from the black box and perched it on the stand. More cars slowed down, complicating traffic. A huge Winnebago sputtered by and the driver, a man in a cowboy hat with a bright red nose, asked what we were looking at.

"Bear," Carol said, bending over the telescope to get it properly focused.

*"Bear,"* the man repeated to someone on the passenger side.

"Grizzly or black?" the cowboy hat asked, as if one might not be worth seeing.

"Grizzly," Carol answered.

That's how it went for most of the morning. At one point the bear stood and began slowly sauntering toward the road. Jidad walked calmly down the line of photographers and announced, as if they hadn't seen it for themselves, that the bear was up and moving. People murmured. Jidad said in a louder voice that if the bear moved beyond the small bluff—a tiny hill that rose about halfway to the kill site—then we must return to our vehicles. *For the bear's safety,* he said.

"Some guy thinking he's going to get the shot of a lifetime will try to stay," Carol said to me.

She had spent the morning bringing people to the telescope and letting them see the bear up close. Each person who saw the bear became an expert for the next person, explaining what the newcomer would see when she or he put an eye to the viewfinder.

Fortunately, the bear went back to the carcass. It drank for a long time in the stream, which made the cameras click. Then it sat for a while like a dog on a kitchen floor and watched the line of people. I popped my eye on the telescope again. I had seen the bear several times during the morning, but it had never been sitting up and open. As I peered through the lens, the bear sat in perfect focus. I tried to remember what I was seeing, tried to remember individual parts of the animal so that I could detail it later. Its claws, more than any other feature, fascinated me. They looked long and orange, as thick as bananas. The word went up and down the line that with the better view afforded by the sitting position, the grizzly was confirmed to be a male.

I stepped away from the telescope to let a teenage boy take a look when Jidad moved up beside me.

"Cobb," he said quietly, his eyes still on the grizzly, "I just had a strange radio report from back at the office. Mary was found disoriented . . . the report is unclear, but apparently she had trouble articulating why she was there, and she seemed panicked over it."

"Just now?" I asked.

"In the last half hour or so."

"Let's go," I said.

My stomach felt hollow and scared as I climbed in next to Jidad. To make matters worse, traffic had come to a standstill and it took us an absurd amount of time to push our way through. Jidad filled me in on what little he knew. She had been sitting outside the bunk room, not clear about where she was. Someone had asked her a question or two, and she had been incapable of answering them. The person called the park medical team and it came to make an assessment. They had radioed Jidad because she had been found near the Wolf Management offices, and they couldn't quite make out the woman's explanation. The woman seemed agitated, the report stated.

"She has a condition," I said, saying it aloud for the first time.

"I'm sorry," he said.

"It will pass. We're kind of new to it."

Jidad nodded.

We didn't say anything else for the remainder of the ride.

# 16

AN EMT NAMED BLANCHE SAT NEXT to Mary in the small conference room where we had left her. Blanche didn't stand when I entered, but simply stretched out her hand to shake mine. I knelt in front of Mary, who leaned forward and put her head on my shoulder. Blanche caught my eye.

"Here he is," Blanche said. "I'm Blanche. I've been keeping Mary company here. You must be Cobb."

"Thank you," I said, holding Mary and nodding. "We'll be okay now."

"It might be a good idea to bring her in for observation. Just to check things out."

"We know what this is," I said.

Mary nodded against my shoulder.

"I gave her a mild sedative," Blanche said. "Nothing too strong. I thought it might calm her."

"Thank you."

"She's probably a little tired and overwrought right now. Are you camping?"

I nodded.

"Well, just stay with her," Blanche said. "For the time being anyway, stay close to her."

"I will," I said.

Blanche stood. She was a short brunette. Her EMT vest bunched around her waist.

"Nice spending some time with you, Mary," Blanche said.

"Thank you," Mary said, her voice far away and drained.

Blanche touched Mary's shoulder and went outside.

"How was the bear?" Mary asked against my shoulder.

"Beautiful. How are you is the question."

"We know how I am, Cobb."

She sat up and took her head off my shoulder.

We looked for a long time into each other's eyes.

"Until," I said and I kept my eyes on hers. Her eyes filled with water and she put her head back on my shoulder.

THE NEXT DAY JIDAD showed us a prime ten-kilometer by ten-kilometer plot in the park, a terrain in dispute by the Druid Peak Pack and the Slough Creek Pack. The section consisted of a wide plain leading to a dark, brooding mountain called, logically enough, Druid Peak. Food was abundant. Bison grazed along the rivers and elk ranged farther into the high country. The packs had once been united, Jidad theorized, but the Slough Creek Pack had splintered off, collected a few transient wolves, and had grown to rival the original pack. The same thing occurred, he said, in the Swan Lake Pack, with a group of young males splintering off and re-forming as a new entity.

He had some concerns about Mary, who had returned to normal and had eaten an enormous breakfast, but we explained the situation and finally persuaded him that she was fit for the assignment. He made us promise to notify him if we encountered any problems, and he extracted from me, furthermore, a promise that I would not let Mary out of my sight.

"No problem," I said on the day he led us to the Slough Creek Campground, where we intended to set up our base.

"Not the place to become disoriented," he said.

"I understand."

"Sorry about all this," he said. "I didn't know."

"It's fine. She's looking forward to this. She'll do a great job on the report. She's fanatical about corvids. The rest, that's down the road."

He left us at noon. We set up camp beside Slough Creek. It was a primitive campsite with a hand pump for water, and a basic latrine. A dozen other visitors—some in tents, some in campers—took up places around the small looped road that led into the campground. A number of the campers had wolf decals on their sides or backs, which indicated, as Jidad had mentioned, their commitment to the wolf restoration project. Because it was midday, most of the campers were out exploring. We had the campground to ourselves.

"I have to call Francis before we go out," I said. "I think I can get reception here."

"I'll get the gear together," Mary said.

I dialed Francis's number. It rang for a while. When voice mail picked up, I told him where we were, what we were doing, and to call back. I said I wasn't sure about reception, but that I'd call again later. I had missed the day before.

"Not there?" Mary asked, shoving a water bottle in her backpack sleeve.

"Or screening calls," I said. "How are you feeling?"

"Fine, Cobb. We need to make a little rule that you can't ask me that more than thirty times a day."

She looked up. She smiled a little. Then she hugged me.

"Sorry," she said. "That was just a little bitchy."

"It's okay."

"Look," she said, "we've been over this. I don't know how this will progress and neither do you. For now, I guess I'm winding down on my driving career. Otherwise, I intend to go forward. Just forward."

"Got it."

"Pedal down," she said. "Live it all."

"You stole that line from Freddy."

She kissed me.

"Don't be angry," she said. "Or hurt. Especially not hurt. Think of me as Jekyll and Hyde. This is uncharted territory for both of us."

I nodded.

"You ready?"

"Counting Crows," I said. "We're like a rock band."

"You know they put out a song called 'Murder of One'?" Mary asked, swinging her pack onto her back. "They used the old Scottish rhyme about crows. Have I told you that one?"

"No, I don't think so," I said, hoisting my own pack. "How does it go?"

"Well, in Scotland and the UK they usually say it about magpies. And different rhymes come with it, depending on who is telling it. But it usually goes, 'one is for sadness, two for mirth, three for marriage, four for birth, five for laughing, six for crying, seven for sickness, eight for dying, nine for silver, ten for gold, eleven for a secret that will never be told.'"

"You hadn't told me," I said.

"It's my favorite of all the rhymes and stories about crows. We are two for mirth, Cobb."

I kissed her. I told her I loved her as I pulled away.

"Burning daylight," she said afterward, and we headed off.

YOU CAN COUNT BIRDS along a line. You can count them in a circle. You can count them by pairs, by half pairs (they are on the edge of a plot), by hearing any attendant-calling behavior, by simple observation, by spot mapping, by variable distance line transect (never understood it), by a fixed radius point count, or by a no fixed point count.

Mary used them all. Or she used them all at once. I walked behind her and took notes for most of the afternoon. Whatever she said to write down, I wrote down. We surveyed the area to the north and east of Slough Creek. We talked loudly to alert bears to our approach, but otherwise we stayed on task. Whatever confusion, or disorientation, had clouded Mary the day before had now been replaced by absolute concentration. She barely stopped for water. She spotted crows everywhere. Often she found them in trees, tucked back against green pines, their bodies submerged in deep shadow. Other times, when a bird cawed and flew overhead, she told me not to count because she had already noted it.

"You recognize individual birds?" I asked at one point.

We stood on a rise looking across the plains to the south.

"Sure," she said. "When you look at enough crows, you recognize individuals."

"You know that sounds a little out there, right?"

She pursed her lips and shrugged.

"It's what I do," she said. "A count is an approximation. We'll have to visit this spot eight or nine times to get a spread. By the end of it, you'll see. You'll recognize individuals, too."

"Is Madrid anywhere around here?"

"Madrid is in Corvid Heaven. But these birds are bigger than the ones we see around our house. Have you noticed?"

"They look bigger. Blacker, too, somehow."

"The population seems solid," she said, turning so I could dig out a water bottle. "I mean, land like this, who can say? What's the correct density? Or you can look at it as a relative abundance, presence-absence data. We'll know more by the end of the week."

"A week?"

"At least," she said.

By evening we found an overlook that provided a panoramic view of the territory. In the distance, in the shadow cast by the mountain behind us, bison grazed like brown iron filings on a yellow board. Slough Creek broadened and curled into the distance. Under a large ponderosa pine, I sat on a rock and pulled out the water bottle again and some peanut butter and crackers. A Richardson's ground squirrel poked its head up from a mound fifty feet away. A few more popped up behind him.

"Hold on a second," Mary said, sitting beside me.

She grabbed her backpack and swung it up onto her lap. Then she dug around for a second and finally withdrew her arm.

"I've been waiting for the right time to give this to you," she said.

"Give what?"

"This," she said and turned her hand up so I could see what she had been hiding.

It was an everything-knife.

"That's not yours, is it?" I asked.

"No. I found it a month ago and I've been waiting to give it to you. I can't imagine any better setting."

I took it. It resembled Mary's but seemed wider and heavier.

"Where did you find it?" I asked, turning it over and examining it.

"A yard sale. It was under some Scouting stuff. Always check the Scouting stuff, I say."

"Male or female, do you think?"

"I think your knife may be royalty, Cobb. I think it may be a lost everything-knife king."

"I'm honored," I said.

"Remember, it may decide to leave you. Don't fight against it and don't blame yourself if it happens. The knife may be on a journey of its own."

"Fair enough. And thank you."

I opened the large blade and fixed us each a peanut butter cracker. I gave Mary hers. She ate it in two bites and asked for more. We both kept our eyes on the vista. Every change in light altered every element of the plain. The Richardson's ground squirrels watched us intently.

"'A man and a woman are one,'" Mary said, her eyes ranging far away, her voice in the cadence of a poem. "'A man and a woman and a blackbird are one.'"

"What's it from?" I asked, buttering more crackers.

"Wallace Stevens, 'Thirteen Ways of Looking at a Blackbird.' Do you know it?"

"I've read it," I said.

The phone rang.

It was such an odd sound given our surroundings that neither of us knew quite what to do. We listened to the second ring and I recognized it as mine. I shook my head to indicate that I didn't want to answer it, but Mary dug in my backpack and picked up the phone. She flicked it open.

"Hi, Francis," she said, smiling at me.

She listened. Her face clouded over a little. I reached for the phone, but she held up a finger. I tossed a cracker in the direction of the Richardson's squirrels. They ducked down in their holes.

Then we heard the first wolf. It came off to our left, deep in the shadows of Druid Peak, and it rose and soared and became painful to hear. Moments later, before the first howl had quite died, a second howl joined it. This one braided around the first, and they soared higher, coming from all around us, echoes bouncing the sounds in unexpected ways. "Wait, wait, wait," Mary whispered into the phone. "Wolves, Francis, wolves."

She held up the phone. At the same time other wolves joined the first two, and we heard, for the first time, the full-throated quiver of the pack. It haunted everything it touched, sanctified it. It rolled down the mountains and onto the plains and the bison heard it, the ground squirrels heard it, the crows nesting in the trees heard it. Mary began to tear.

*We are alive,* the wolves said. *And the world is beautiful.*

On our last night in Yellowstone, Jidad showed us on a map a small island near the northeast corner of Yellowstone Lake and offered to run us up to the launch site and pick us up the next morning. He issued us a backcountry camping permit, asked us not to make a fire, and told us he had it on good authority that the weather promised to be spectacular.

"Full moon night," he said. "Hunter's Moon, I think, or Strawberry Moon, I forget. You might even get a look at the northern lights, but I doubt it with the moon promising to be so bright."

"A July moon," Mary said. "Summer moon."

"It's going to be one of those nights," he said. "No bugs to speak of out on that island. It's one of my favorite places."

"Does the island have a name?"

Jidad shrugged.

"Too small," he said. "It's just a little speck. But it's located right near where a creek comes in and the fishing is pretty great there. Mostly whitefish. I can lend you a fly rod if you like."

"Good to smell like fish when grizzlies are around," I said. "No thanks."

"Grizzlies will leave you alone out there. They don't have any reason to swim around in the lake."

It took a while to pull our stuff together, but by early evening we launched. Jidad pushed us off and pointed us in the right direction. The kayaks dipped under his hands, then settled.

"Go north for a mile, then start looking to the east. On your right, in other words. Be careful not to miss it because there isn't any decent spot to camp beyond the island. You'll find it; don't worry."

"This is our honeymoon," Mary told him, grinning at me. "This single night."

Jidad smiled. He promised to be back in the morning to retrieve us. Meanwhile, the water had turned calm while we loaded our kayaks. Every paddle stroke put a small dent in the surface, but otherwise the water remained flat and filled with reflections of the trees along the shore. Clouds moved in the reflection, too. A few fish rose and sipped at flies. A frog, a bullfrog with a voice like the hood of a car opening, called from a weedy area near the bank.

"Some writer called this the hour of the pearl," I said. "John Steinbeck, maybe."

"This quiet?" she asked.

"Most evenings. My dad used to fish and he said every evening you could count on the wind stopping. He doesn't fish anymore, but he still calls this the hour of the pearl."

"I like your dad."

"So do I," I said.

"You'd be a good dad," she said, looking at me across the boats. "A great dad, actually."

"You think so, do you?"

"You're calm. A dad needs to be calm. Women are the wind and men are the sails. Someone said that, too."

"John Steinbeck."

"From now on," Mary said, "whenever we quote anything, we always attribute it to John Steinbeck. Is that a deal?"

"Yes."

"And the other person has to agree wholeheartedly."

"Absolutely."

Mary liked that little secret, I could tell. We paddled. Pretty soon I saw the island. It was slightly deceiving because it blended with the land behind it. But as we neared it the outline became more recognizable. We landed on the southern end and yanked our kayaks up on shore. The evening remained calm. Calling the land on which we stood an island might have been an overstatement. It was an islandette. It may have been twenty yards across at the center.

"What's the difference between an island and a prison?" Mary asked, stretching her back and looking at our site for the night.

"I don't know."

"Nothing," she said and laughed.

"Did John Steinbeck say that?"

"As a matter of fact, he did."

We set up camp. We didn't bother with the tent. Mary spread out the blue tarp, then we put our air mattress down and our sleeping bags. It made a nice bed. I dug out cheese and crackers and a bottle of wine. I opened the wine and poured two drinks into plastic cups.

"How come the honeymoon keeps following us around?" I asked her, toasting. "I'm not complaining, but I thought you didn't like honeymoons."

"I like honeymoons to be expandable," she said. "I don't like that they're only supposed to happen once."

"So you could have a dozen honeymoons."

"Or a thousand," she said. "John Steinbeck said that, I think."

"That didn't work just then," I said and she frowned. "That was an overuse of the Steinbeckian attribution."

"Says John Steinbeck," she said.

"Exactly," I said.

The sun went down quickly, but the night remained warm. We had nothing to cook, no fire to tend. We sat on our bed and watched the light fade from the lake. The moon came up shortly afterward, rising from the southeast. The glow of the moon looked almost like the lights of a distant city.

"I want to visit your father's house when we get back," she said. "Can we do that?"

"Sure."

"And I want to figure out a way to iChat with Freddy. I miss him. We can figure that out, right?"

"Of course."

"I want to rig it up for Mom, too. She also misses him. She needs to go out and see him. She'd be very proud of him."

I nodded.

A little while later she turned away from the moon and looked at me. She leaned over and kissed me softly on the lips. Then she looked back at the moon.

She said, "I'm not afraid, you know, Cobb. You don't have to worry about that. I don't know why I'm not, but I'm not. I've been afraid of not living fully from time to time, but maybe meeting you, having my friends around, has made it seem okay. When the time comes, it will be okay. I don't know how I know that, but I do."

"Shhh," I whispered.

"No, sweetheart, I don't want to hide from it. I don't want it to be a dirty little secret. I'm dying. We're all dying, but I'm probably going first. We don't fear birth, so why do we fear death so much? No one knows where we were before we came into the world. After we leave the world, we'll be okay, too. I've just taught myself that these last few weeks."

"Okay," I said. "No dirty little secret. I know what you mean."

"I hope you do. I couldn't stand it if we had to pussyfoot around it."

"Pussyfoot is a good word."

"This is our honeymoon night. We have to make love soon."

Before we did, though, we saw a moose swimming in the lake. It swam across the moonlight a hundred yards away, bisecting the light, its antlers not yet fully formed. It swam as a dog swims, with its neck cranked forward, its shoulders shrugging at the milling of its hooves. We stood and walked to the edge of the island so we could see better. The moose soon left the moonlight and quickly became a dark form slicing a wake out of the stillness. At the end of his trip we had to follow his progress by sound. He clattered over the shoreline rocks, shook water from his heavy skin, and crashed his way into the pine breaks.

"Moose are good omens," Mary said.

"I saw one before I met you," I said. "A Maine moose."

"What if the moose had turned and gone right into the light? Do you think he would have sprouted wings and flown away?"

"Probably," I said.

"Come to bed," she said. "It's our honeymoon night, you know."

We climbed into the sleeping bags and shivered until we warmed them. Then we made love with the stars pulling through the light of the moon. We did not hear a wolf, but the sound of the water lapping on stone rinsed everything away until there was only Mary and the warmth and the kisses we could not save or squander, or lose or refrain from giving.

# AN EGG OF AIR

# 17

TIME PASSING. A TRIANGLE LIFE OF work, love, family. Mary in everything. A trip to Mount Desert Island, Maine. Another to the Idaho panhandle, a hike up the St. Joe River. A trip into the Wind River, Wyoming, to Double L Reservoir, where we found grizzly prints outside our tent one morning. My dad's house, funny and strange with its cast-off industrial containers, but beautiful, too, as it merged into the mountain. Pole and my father. The Chungamunga girls, always present, always forming and disbanding, then re-forming again. Students, Francis, the autumnal rite of convocation, the calling of students to study, the rejoining of academic life, the long immersion into books and history and science. Firelight. Wood snapping against the andirons, snow bitter and sharp and crawling at the windows. Apples in the fall, the taste of sunlight turned to sugar. Summer days of bees drifting, and the garden filling, and a spring bank of nodding lilacs blue-purple sending its flavors out in winds still cold from the mountains. Crows mixed in it. A modest book on Thoreau's Maine trips. Three corvid surveys in Yellowstone, Jidad coming east to visit, good Scotch whisky, kayaks on clear New Hampshire lakes. Joan with a lumpectomy. Freddy's Lamb nearly dead from a staph infection complication after a minor surgery. Life passing.

Our lives entwined, in tempo, only occasionally missing a beat because of a seizure, a lapse. But together we were strong, happy.

The great window and the slanting afternoon light, geraniums, cupboards opening and closing, soup and the clank of spoons against cookware. Friends visiting, an annual trip to see Annie and John, their hair the tiniest bit gray, the fishing camp a success.

Then an ice-skating party, Mary, one year, skating with a chair in front of her as weakness claimed her. Our bed outside, the stars turning, the earth underneath us warming and cooling, the morning frost dense and beautiful on our bedclothes. And Mary. And Mary again. Time passing and closing on us, changing us, pulling us closer and closer. The small cadences of disease. The small claims made by the inevitable ending.

And then remission, a quiet period, a deep chair with a good reading light, birch wood, old movies, a game of hide and seek, a horse eating the meadow grass down, morning mist rising from his back like smoke.

John Steinbeck said it. Knock knock. Knock wood. My arms around her. My lips on hers. At night we held hands and woke in knots around each other.

Popcorn late at night, the fizz of soda, salt and butter, a game of Monopoly played on a day when the lights went off and would not come on for three days. The sound of dice on a game board. Minus forty-two degrees one January.

A New Year's Eve party dressed as clocks. Halloween as a werewolf and a crow, of course. Quote the raven, nevermore.

My career building, a dean of students, the quiet walks on Pillsbury grounds, the woods and Turkey Pond, the spring sculling races. Students again, more names and dreams, lives passing through ours. Mary with an award for scholarship, a donation of her prize to Freddy's Indonesian turtles.

Cutting Christmas trees from the White Mountain National Forest, the snore of a dull bow saw, the *Tim-ber!* she predictably called, the furrow the pine made through the snow on the march back to the house. Cold noses. Cold toes. Kissing Mary underneath the mistletoe, having mistletoe only to kiss and surprise her.

Summer thunderstorms, the dash around the house to slam the windows down, the late creep around the house to reopen them to the clammy heat. Snippets of poems. It was many and many a year ago, in a kingdom by the sea. The black gum older.

News of young Myrtle's death coming on a cold February, a call from Wally, my heart breaking.

Madrid searching the great north woods for a diamond earring, his eye sharp and turned sideways. Nothing in the world moving except Madrid and the snow around him deep and peaceful.

I DROVE MARY TO the University of New Hampshire the day she retired. Eight years had passed since our first trip to Yellowstone. She had been sick a good deal and she no longer felt capable of lecturing for an entire year. A few months before, the dean of life sciences at the University spoke to her about recording a series of lectures on crows for the department. The dean set her up in a recording studio and she spoke straightforwardly into a camera. She was a scientist, in the end, and she spoke at length about corvid behavior, morphology, everything you could want to know about crows or ravens or magpies. I wasn't able to judge the result accurately because I lacked the scientific background, but her colleagues in the biology department felt the series was exceptional. They still use it.

She became friends with the young student who served as an engineer for the project. He was a young man, a long-boarder, studs through his nose, the whole bit, but who knew the equipment cold. He called himself Tommy X. On a whim I suggested he record a series of Mary telling crow stories. She balked at first. But he encouraged her and he donated his time and she recorded three hours of crow stories. This was before she found she could no longer rely on her memory. It is the most charming piece of storytelling you could imagine. She ends it, in a little outtake with Tommy offscreen, telling rapid fire knock-knock jokes. The anthropology department found out about it and asked to use it. They show it in tandem with Joseph Campbell's discussion of myth.

A college campus is a sweet, poignant place in May. People are leaving, or commencing a new stage of endeavor, while others stay and carry on traditions and the long conversation of academic life. Few places mix together the young and the old as well as colleges do, and around the University of New Hampshire campus a sense of anticipation, tinged with nostalgia, felt solid and real. The vernal witch hazel near the Life Sciences building had bloomed; so had the crab apple trees and the forsythia. It was spring; it was also the time for looking back.

The day of her retirement came up rainy and quiet. Mary was the only member of the Life Sciences Department retiring that year. Near two o'clock we arrived and parked near the Life Sciences building, using a handicap spot that Mary hated but had come to accept. Mary did not have a wheelchair yet, but she leaned heavily on my arm as we went inside. I'm not sure what she expected, or what I expected either. Usually these kinds of events, formal and dull, revolve around bad punch, small stale sandwiches, and numerous obligatory handshakes from colleagues. Afternoon things with everyone ready to leave as soon as it has concluded. Mary felt it would provide a sense of closure to attend. Otherwise she avoided social gatherings such as these that brought attention to her.

When we approached the lecture hall on the main floor—it was scheduled in the smaller classroom next to it—we heard a commotion. We tried to guess what had been scheduled against the retirement party. It was too late in the year for classes. Exams had already concluded. We turned into the designated room and felt a bit disoriented, because the room appeared empty. I saw no signs of any celebration—no cake, no food, no balloons.

"Did we miss a memo?" Mary asked, her arm on my forearm. She looked bemused.

"I don't think so," I said.

"Strange," she said, looking around. "Do we have the correct time?"

"Two o'clock," I said. "That's what the invitation said."

I had a moment's panic where I thought I had gotten it wrong, but I couldn't fully indulge it before a colleague, Sylvia Peters, stepped into the room. She was a tall, handsome woman, with a long carriage and a wide step.

"We're over here!" Sylvia said, her voice light and happy. "Someone said they saw you creep in here."

"Creep is the word," Mary said.

"We're next door," Sylvia said again.

We followed Sylvia.

The doors opened. Someone let out a loud shout. Someone else yelled, "Bravo!"

The entire room came to its feet. Mary grabbed my forearm as the room broke into loud, raucous cheering. A hundred, two hundred faces turned to see Mary, all of them standing, all of them applauding. I knew many of them. Francis was there, and Mary's mother, my father and Pole, and Wally, and John and Annie, our friends from Maine, and a dozen other colleagues I immediately recognized. But the room held students—young people, some not so young any longer, all of them on their feet, clapping, cheering. A person in a crow suit, absurd and black, flew up the aisle of the lecture hall. Mary smiled. And that made the crowd cheer more wildly. Then an instant arrived when, in the usual run of things, the clapping should have stopped, but it continued. It rose and filled the hall, and people began calling to her, "Mary, Mary, professor, my professor."

"Speech, speech," people yelled.

Others rushed up and took her hands.

Mary shook her head, but they continued to yell and began to pound their feet. Mary nodded and that began them again. She walked down the center aisle, her hand on my arm, the crow flapping idiotically in front of us. Mary turned. She smiled. Her body moved a little without her control, but I felt her draw herself up. Little by little the room quieted.

"That," she said when the crowd had been silent a moment, "is the ugliest crow I ever saw."

People whooped. I saw the old glint come into her eyes. She smiled. Photo flashes came from every direction.

"Thank you," she said when the crowd quieted enough and sat down. "Thank you for being here."

She paused. I knew she had difficulty controlling her body motions and her breathing. She looked out at the array of people, smiling at many, nodding her head in recognition at others. Slowly, she gathered herself.

"Teaching," she said and the room became silent to hear her weak voice, "is my third love. My first love is my husband, Jonathan Cobb. He has been my friend, my companion, and, as the poet W. H. Auden says, my east, my west, my Sunday rest. He is part of my family, and my family is the source of whatever strength I have had . . . my mother, Joan Fury, my brother, Freddy, a fine biologist in his own right, and my two fathers, Jonathan's father and my own father, dead these many years from the same disease that will take me."

She paused again. I knew the effort she made to keep from showing the extent of her frailty. People watched intently, I knew, to see what had become of the Mary they loved. Their faces shone with the pleasure of seeing her.

"Crows are my second love," she continued, her voice wavering. "Who knows why we choose to study the things we do? How could I have known as a young girl that my life's work would be all around me, would be these bright, inquisitive creatures, that I would delight in them and find them everywhere, ready to challenge and entertain me? It is an old saying that we should work at what we love, but I loved crows and ravens long before I possessed any clear notion of work. On the whole, I have not worked a day in my life, because the crows and ravens, learning about them, learning from them, has been a daily joy. I wish every person in this room the pleasure of finding what interests them. It is the best and most valuable wish one person can have for another."

She seemed almost to conclude at that moment, but no one moved. I stood ready to step forward and support her. She looked at the crowd, scanning it quietly. She nodded her head as if understanding something of what her life had meant.

She started to speak again, stopped, then found her voice once more.

"I shouldn't talk much longer," she said, "but I want to say about teaching that it was my third love, but that does not diminish it, I hope. We cast ourselves into the future when we teach. Today, standing before you, I hear the voices of my teachers, my beloved professors, who sought to understand the world, who told me to be observant, who said with conviction that my interior life, the life of learning and study, is as important, and much more so, than all the getting and spending that occupies too much of our lives. If my teaching has touched you, I am rewarded. If I have nudged your boat a tiny bit on the stream we all follow, then I am satisfied. Perhaps my crows will remind you some day of our time together, of the learning we asked of one another, of our joining together to forward what we know of the natural world, so that we can be good shepherds of this lovely earth."

Absolute silence. Tears filled her eyes. Many of the people in the room bowed their heads, then looked up quickly to make sure they did not miss a word.

"I want to say two final things. The first is good-bye. I am going before you on an adventure, an adventure we all must undertake, and I meet it without dread. If you are a biologist, as many in this room certainly are, then we understand a moment is allotted to each of us, to all creatures, and that the death of one organism often brings profit to another. I would not be much of a student of the natural world if I grew tremulous as my own time approached. It would not be fair. We cannot know what is ahead of us, but I have faith that the best preparation for whatever we will meet in the future, if anything at all, is by all means a well-lived life. You, the people gathered in this room, have shared your lives with me and for that I want to say thank you."

She looked around the room and smiled. Many people smiled back, their hands at their cheeks to wipe them of tears.

Mary whispered the last part.

"'When the blackbird flew out of sight, it marked the edge of one of many circles,' the poet Wallace Stevens said. He also said, 'But I know, too, that the blackbird is involved in what I know.'"

She stopped. A long moment passed before anyone clapped. Then cheers. Then clapping and tears.

WE SAW THE REDWOODS in her last year. It happened by chance. I was invited to speak at a convention for independent schools in San Francisco. I had intended to go by myself—not sure of Mary's strength—but she surprised me by saying one night that she had never seen the sequoias and had always meant to. She said if the black gum was five hundred and fifty years old, the sequoias could be double that, even four times that, living two or three thousand years or more in California.

When Wally caught wind of our plans, she offered a Jeep Wrangler convertible.

"I always use it when I go to the West Coast," she said over the phone a day or two before our departure. "A company perk. It was given by a wealthy patron to the Chungamunga Foundation for West Coast trips. You'll be a happening West Coast couple. You'll be like movie stars."

She wouldn't listen to my protests. She said the car sat idle most of the year and that I would be doing her a favor to take it, get the oil changed, check the tires, and so on. A day later a FedEx package came containing the keys. She included a note with directions to the parking garage that housed the Jeep. Mary teased me that I would need a whole new music makeover for the Jeep. I had to dispense with the old swing music I habitually played and come up with new wave, indie rock.

The flight west tired her. She recovered in the hotel room at the Hyatt while I attended the conference. The next morning she came to breakfast and met a few of my colleagues and delegates from other schools around the country, but she retreated to our room again quickly afterward, the effort of making small talk too exhausting. Instead she watched a few hours of television, and reported her observations when we had a drink that night in the hotel bar.

"I had no idea what television had become," she said, sitting in a banquette, her old enthusiasm creeping out as she sipped a glass of red wine. "I feel as though I've been to a different country. I do. Did you know about it?"

"Know about what, exactly?"

"Oh, about television. Everyone says it's a wasteland, but I could watch it every minute of every day! All those reality shows? The West Coast Orange County Dracula Mothers, or whatever it's called? It's fascinating."

"They're playing for the cameras, aren't they?"

"Even if they are, so what? They have to know what to play. I wouldn't have a clue. I don't even know the designers they're talking about, but now I want one of everything."

"You've always been a designer diva. You're kind of a runway model for L.L. Bean."

"I'm going to be a true diva from now on. And there was this guy, this survivor guy, who jumped out of a plane into a swamp and the rest of the show you had to follow him as he made his way to civilization on a homemade raft. Forget the Allagash. Next time we go boating we're jumping into the Everglades. I'm telling you, Cobb, television was a revelation. I want a satellite and two thousand channels."

She was enjoying herself. I could tell she felt good. I also knew she was trying to jolly me up after the disappointing fatigue she had experienced after the flight. Above all, she didn't want to distract from the pleasure of the conference for me. But by the time I had finished my drink, she had begun to fold. She tried very hard to resist, but her chorea began to assert itself. It grew worse, I knew, when she was tired.

"You're such a party pooper," she said when I paid for our drinks and stood to help her out of the banquette.

"I am taking you clubbing," I said. "We just have to run upstairs to change."

"In that case," she said and she held out her hand for me.

In the same motion, she fell. It happened so quickly I couldn't catch her. She fell forward, knocking the silverware from one corner of the table. My Scotch glass slid toward her, then shot backward when her falling weight bounced free of the table. Two ice cubes skidded in a lazy circle on the surface. I saw all that motion while also watching Mary fall in sections, her pelvis trapped a little by the banquette seat, her arms going out to break her landing. I heard her cough as the leg of the table caught her ribs, and I helplessly held out my hands, appearing ridiculously like an umpire signaling a runner safe long after the action had occurred.

When I knelt beside her, she covered her face with her hands.

"I'm okay," she whispered. "Just give me a second."

"I'm sorry, sweetheart, I should have caught you."

"I fell," she said. "That's all."

"Can I help you up?"

She nodded. She put her hand in mine.

Before I could lift her, a few people gathered around and began wondering aloud if she shouldn't be allowed to stay where she was. The bartender, a plump man of about sixty with mutton-chop sideburns, came and slapped a towel over his shoulder. He looked concerned and slightly guilty, as if his chief worry was whether he had overserved a customer. He bent over my shoulder. He smelled of bourbon and lemons.

"She's just a little light-headed," I explained to the group in general. "She's okay."

"We have a hotel nurse on call," the bartender said. "Wouldn't take a minute."

"We've had this experience before," I said. "We'll be okay in a moment."

"Now you're embarrassing me," Mary said to the bartender. "Be a gentleman and help me up and I'll be on my way."

The bartender took her other arm. We lifted her onto her feet. She weighed very little. A woman I vaguely recognized as a fellow delegate handed Mary a glass of water. Mary took a good swallow. We backed her temporarily onto a chair.

"We're going out clubbing," Mary said to the group and that got a small, nervous laugh out of them. "I'm an excellent dancer."

"How are you feeling, Mrs. Blanding?" I asked.

"Have I lost an earring?" she asked, playing along and checking her ears.

"No," I said. "I don't think so."

We took our time going upstairs afterward. The elevator carried us to the twelfth floor. She kept her hand on the wall as we made our way slowly down the hallway. I went ahead slightly and had the door open for her by the time she arrived. She went in and sat down on the edge of the bed.

"Well," she said, her voice weary, "that was novel. You don't often get to stumble and fall in a bar. It wasn't bad, really, once I accepted the fact of it."

"You know," I said, bringing her more water from the fridge, "people do fall. Even people without any illnesses."

"It's a first for me, Sir Galahad."

"Still."

"You should go out and enjoy the city. San Francisco is wonderful, from all accounts."

"I'm where I want to be," I said. "Besides, I want to meet this survivor guy. You sound a little too impressed with him."

"He's cute, I warn you," she said, her chin sagging a little toward her chest. "And he wears a machete in a sling over his back. You have to go for a guy like that."

"Fair enough."

I helped her undress. By the time I slipped her under the covers and pulled them up to her chin, she could no longer keep her eyes open. I kissed her lightly. But before I could pull away she put her arms around my neck and pulled me more deeply into the kiss.

"We're going to see the redwoods tomorrow," she said when we broke apart. "Promise me."

"I promise."

"I'm better with trees than bar stools."

I nodded. She reached to the nightstand and handed me the remote.

"Check your competition," she said. "I have to sleep. Don't blame me if you fall a little for the survivor guy."

I TOOK THE LAST photograph of Mary the following afternoon. After quizzing me on the ride north about the difference between sequoias and redwoods (sequoias achieve greater mass and are probably older; coastal redwoods are the tallest trees in the world and part of the same classification, I think), the sun glorious through the topless Jeep, she stood beside one of the redwoods and smiled. It did not strike me as a particularly good shot. In fact, it seemed somewhat corny, the obligatory touristy shot of a person beside the magnificent trees. She raised her hand and waved. It was only later, when I realized we took no more photos of her, that I understood it was a wave of good-bye. With the trees surrounding her, the gloaming half-light of sunshine penetrating the ancient grove, she said farewell.

She also took her last photo of me. In her inimitable style, she forced me to lie on my back with my feet on the trunk of one of the trees. It was a pose, she said, she had seen on a postcard a million years before. Once she had me in position, she slowly knelt on the ground, then put her head sideways against the earth. Instead of running vertically, the tree now ran horizontally in her lens, giving the impression that I walked up the trunk by magic. She clicked three photos like that, then was so pleased with her composition that she made me perform a series of idiotic tricks. I stood on one finger against the tree. I stood on my head. I pretended to walk on my hands and wave while I did it. Mary rested on the ground, the camera squeezed to her eye, and laughed hard. It was an old Mary laugh, one that I hadn't heard in some time.

When she lowered the camera at last, we lay ten feet apart, the trees towering miles and miles above us. She faced me and I faced her. We might have been in our own bed, on two pillows side by side, so perfectly did our eyes meet. She nodded. I nodded in return. We didn't speak. The wind passed quietly through the trees.

LATE SUMMER ASTERS. THE stars nearer, somehow. Meteors grinding in small splashes in the eastern sky. A trip to the Maine ocean, the great rocky shoreline a saw of land chafing the incoming tides. Cookie dough batter in a yellow bowl. The woodpile taking on the last of summer's light. The meadow becoming dull and quiet, the heads of the grasses bending and turning back to earth. The brook finding stones and running past them. Late at night, geese calling and traversing the moon, the globe spinning, the geese suspended above, arrows pointing south.

"It's time, Jonathan Cobb," Mary said a few months later.

It was a long autumn afternoon. She sat on a chaise in our garden. I had covered her legs with a blanket while I fiddled with day lilies. I had divided a half dozen and replanted them around the yard. Mary drifted in and out, sometimes watching me, mostly dozing. I thought she was asleep and the sound of her voice, steady and sure, surprised me.

"You want to go inside?" I asked, still fussing with a reluctant day lily. I stood on the spade and tried to slice through the root ball.

"No, it's time," she repeated.

I tried to turn and face her but I couldn't. I held the spade against my gut. I knew immediately what she meant. I had trouble breathing.

"Come here," she said softly.

I couldn't.

"Oh, Cobb," she said. "If I could spare you this, I would."

A bird fluttered through my stomach and my eyes filled. I couldn't help it. I bent over the spade and held it tight against me. I stared at the day lily, its core nearly halved by my spade.

"Oh, come here, *shhh, shhh, shhh,* come here."

I couldn't move.

"It's all right, darling. Come here. Come next to me."

I went and sat on the chaise and put my head in my hands. I leaned the spade against my shoulder as if getting back to work might be a possibility.

"Cobb, don't cry. Come here, sweetheart. Stay next to me."

I tilted on my side, facing away from her. The shovel slid down to the ground. I didn't want her to see me crying. I didn't know where to rest my eyes.

She put her arm over my side and held me.

"It's time," she whispered in my ear. "Trust me, sweetheart. It's time to go. Let me go, please. You are the only one I would stay for, so you must let me go."

I nodded. I couldn't speak.

We stayed like that until our breathing matched.

"We always knew this day would come," she said, kissing me. "It's here now. It's okay. Don't resist it. I feel good about it. You will let me go and that's what needs to happen now."

I nodded. The bushes beside the stream had turned brown and red and yellow. I heard a squirrel chatter from a branch above us.

"Could we sleep out tonight?" she asked after a little while. "We'll put a hundred blankets on and I promise I won't be cold."

"Yes," I said.

My eyes filled again.

"Here's what I want to say to you," she whispered close to my ear. "This is what I need to say. You go on, Cobb. Honor me by going on. Pedal down, live it all. Promise me?"

I nodded again.

"I will not haunt you. Don't make me into a ghost. When you let me go at last, don't regret anything. You have a long life ahead of you. You have friends and work. You have our beautiful home here, which I love and which should not become a stuffy, ridiculous mausoleum. We haven't talked about this, Cobb. We've avoided it. It's not an easy thing, but I'm asking you to put more into going forward than into looking back. Do you promise me that?"

"Yes," I said, my voice choked.

"Time will fix it," she said. "You don't believe that right now, but it will. I promise you it will. Believe in that time. Trust it."

I nodded.

"Okay," she said. "We're sleeping out tonight. I can tell as many knock-knock jokes as I like."

We didn't speak for a long time. She slept a little. I looked out at the trees, which had started to turn in the late sunlight. The brook ran past the house, slow now in autumn. Winter felt not so far away.

Later, I made a bed for us on our outside platform. We had refrained from sleeping out too much due to her health, but I tucked her in under a dozen blankets and climbed in beside her. A cold, crisp night fell out of the trees above us. The stars burned with bright energy. I held her in my arms and she put her head on my shoulder. For a while I felt her movement, the quakes and trembles that accompanied her illness. They slowed eventually. She put her lips against my cheek and kissed me.

"Do you remember we slept out like this the first night we met?" she asked.

"Yes," I said. "It was a night a lot like this one."

"Bright stars and you were on your way to follow Thoreau."

I nodded.

"Did you think I was a complete hussy letting you sleep next to me after just meeting?"

"Yes," I said. "Absolutely."

She elbowed me lightly.

"You were such a gentleman. You've always been a gentleman."

"I groped you during the night."

She kissed my cheek again.

"I wish you had," she said. "I knew the first minute I met you. I knew we belonged together."

"I did, too."

"Life is so funny," she said after a minute. "So strange, really. It happens all around you and you can only see this little frame, this moment, and then it goes on. And you never know who is going to star in your life movie. It's always a surprise."

"Are you warm enough, Mary?"

She nodded.

"What glorious stars tonight," she said.

"It smells like winter."

"I'm going to have to sleep. I hate having to sleep when I don't want to. It's like I am sucked down a drain and I begin spinning and it's no good to resist."

"Sleep," I said. "The stars will be here when you wake."

"And you," she said.

"Yes," I said. "And me."

We did not approach the river from the headwaters. Mary could not have boated across three lakes, then run the Chase Rapids. We arrived in a patch of glorious weather, Indian summer, that brief, quiet interlude before winter finally takes hold. All the way up, we kept the heat on in my truck—not the same truck as years before, but another Toyota pickup truck, green like the first—and the windows rolled down. Mary had not been into the woods, the true woods, in a year or more. She breathed deeply and let the air surround her.

She was not sad. Looking over at her, she appeared younger than ever, relieved, I felt, to be concluding something hard and troublesome. She had been ill. And her mental state, while still largely intact, had been tenuous at best. Huntington's is a thief. It steals the personality of its hosts. Mary had resisted it as strongly as possible, but in the end the disease wins every time.

We held hands a large part of the way.

With the aid of a GPS system, we found our rendezvous point near American Realty Road, a dirt track that cuts into the Allagash near Squirrel Mountain. Obviously, we required a road. We camped at Sandy Point, a spot recommended by Annie and John. They had towed an Airstream camper to the site, a beautiful little ten-foot trailer that had been donated by the Chungamunga Foundation. We did not want Mary sleeping on the ground, naturally. The trailer sat parallel to the water, and Mary, from her bed, could look out and see the river spinning by, the leaves flowing northward on the surface. The sound of water filled every moment.

John and Annie arrived first. They had set things up, of course, but they had responsibilities at the fishing camp and had to shuttle back and forth until they could finally get away. They brought a truckload of food and firewood and tents. When they climbed out of the truck, I understood time had passed. Though they remained young, they were not the starry-eyed couple Mary and I had met eight years before. Their business had gone well by all accounts. They had a reputation for quality service, and for fine fishing, that extended far south into the Boston area. We had seen them many times over the eight years we had known them. We would not have considered visiting the river without them.

We hugged. Annie kissed me, lightly touched my check with the back of her fingers, then went inside with Mary while John and I set up the camp.

"How are you doing with this?" John asked at one point, a tent pole in his hand. "Are you okay? I know, it's kind of crazy to ask under the circumstances."

"I'm all right," I said. "I think I'll be okay."

"We think of you both so often," John said. "You were our first guests."

"We've always counted on your friendship. It's meant a great deal to Mary, and to me."

"If at the end of this . . . ," John said and faltered. "If at the end of this you need to get away, please come to us. You can stay in one of the cabins as long as you like. Annie wanted to make sure you knew that."

"Thank you," I said. "I may take you up on it."

"I mean it. We both mean it."

It took us an hour to erect the tents and rake out the fire pit. The sun had grown weaker and we decided not to wait for darkness to get a fire going. Annie called to us and said that Mary wanted to come out. We carried her out carefully and put her in a chair near the edge of the fire pit. She wore her Mad Bomber hat, the one from so many years before. Annie draped a blanket over her shoulders. I could tell—although perhaps the others couldn't see it—that Mary had mustered her remaining strength to engage us.

"I must look like an old lady," Mary said. "Grandma Moses."

"You look beautiful," I said and kissed her.

We had barely got the fire started when we heard a truck coming along Realty Road. It stopped and started as if lost, and then finally gunned forward. A minute later the truck lights pushed into our camp area and a large Ford 250 bounced across a final pothole and came to a stop beside the Airstream. Someone inside whooped. The lights blinked and the horn squawked.

Freddy jumped out.

He looked magnificent. Large and tan, his coat flapping around him, a crazy wool cap sunk like an Inca headdress on his skull, he stood for a moment beside the truck as if astonished at the wonder of being here, in Maine, beside the Allagash. His breath bloomed in a small white cloud as he adjusted his coat. He smiled. Our eyes met for the briefest instant, and I nodded quietly that she was here, Mary, his sister.

Suddenly the great energy that had brought him, the happy, capable man I knew from Indonesia, shrank away. He appeared to understand finally what he had traveled to witness. Ignoring us all, he crossed to Mary and fell on his knees in front of her. He put his head on her lap and he wept.

"Oh, Freddy," she said in her quietest voice, "you big softie."

She slid his hat off and combed his hair with her fingers. She did not for a moment appear embarrassed. After a little while she pulled him into her arms and whispered something in his ear. He choked a small laugh; then the laugh grew and he leaned back on his knees, his eyes still tearing.

"I'd forgotten how damn cold it is here," Freddy said, wiping his eyes with his hat. "You people are nuts living in this climate."

"You used to love this time of year," Mary reminded him. "You said autumn made you sprout antlers, if I remember correctly."

"My blood was much thicker then. I nearly hit five moose on the way into this nutty place. What crazy, absurd animals they are! If I hadn't had the GPS coordinates, I would have ended up in Canada. Oh, Mary, only you would drag us all out here."

"Sorry to inconvenience you," she said and laughed.

He took her hands. He kissed her cheek.

"That's from Lamb," he said. "She sends her love. And the little boy who you saved that night, he's a teenager now. I saw him before I climbed on the jet boat to go to Bali. He's a big drug boy now. A dealer, I guess. But when I told him I was coming to see you, he stopped his usual crap and said he salutes you. That was his word. So, you are saluted officially."

Freddy rocked back on his knees and climbed to his feet. He looked around him. Again he hardly seemed to believe he stood in the Maine woods in October. He took a few breaths, straightened his shoulders, then hugged me. We hugged a long time. Then I introduced him to Annie and John. He hugged them, too. When he finally broke his last hug, he turned on me.

"For the love of God, Cobb," he said, "could someone give me a drink?"

I took drink orders. Mary asked for a small glass of wine. I ducked into the Airstream and played bartender. John and Annie had provisioned it well.

"What time is Mom getting here?" Mary asked Freddy when I came out.

"Tomorrow morning," he said. "Bright and early. She didn't want to arrive in the middle of the night. She figured she'd get lost. She's spending the night in Bangor."

"Mom in the north woods," Mary said. "That's a sight."

"Your mom is a nurse, isn't she?" Annie asked.

"A nurse's nurse," Freddy said. "She sleeps in a starched cap."

"She does not," Mary said. "She's softened in her old age."

"Let's have a toast," I said. "Someone say something brilliant."

"That leaves me out," Freddy said.

"I'll say something," Mary said.

She thought a moment. She looked out at the river.

"To the crows that fly and the winds that blow, to the leaves that fall on all below, to summer pasture, winter field, to snow and rain, to the ship's straight keel," she said.

We raised our glasses.

"I have no idea what you just said," Freddy said, "but it sounded quite mythic."

"Who's hungry?" Annie asked after taking a sip of her wine. "I'm going to get some things started. Mary, are you comfortable?"

"I'm fine," she said.

She did not look fine. She appeared tired and worn, but I knew she would not show it in front of Freddy if she could possibly avoid doing so. I built the fire higher, trying to keep her warm.

Then for a little while she went away.

That was the name we gave to her dementia. *Going away.* Freddy raised his eyebrows. I nodded. Annie put more covers over Mary's shoulders. The sun began to set.

On the campsite picnic table Annie served beef stew, homemade dinner rolls, a cucumber salad. John served wine. He told us that when he took over the lodge he had also taken over the wine cellar. People, he said, would no longer stand for a lousy bottle of wine with poorly prepared food. He claimed he was the foremost wine critic on Chamberlain Lake, Maine, population fifty-three.

"It's excellent wine," Freddy said, polishing off half a glass. "Thank you for bringing it. That's one thing I miss in Indonesia. We get wine, but it doesn't feel the same to drink wine when it's warm."

"Is this the first meal we had together?" I asked Annie, tasting the stew, which was delicious. "Was it beef stew?"

"Onion soup," Mary said. "And corn bread."

She had come back to us a while before.

"You remember?" Annie asked. "That's remarkable."

"Some things I remember so clearly it feels positively haunted," Mary said. "Other things slip by."

While we ate, Freddy filled us in on his turtle project and life on Gili Trawangan. John and Annie were fascinated. Freddy had received two more grants. He had expanded to the other two islands, Gili Meno and Gili Air, and had taken on a consultancy on Lombok. He now employed fifteen Indonesians, several of whom showed talent with both the turtles and the necessary fund-raising. The University of Rhode Island's marine biology department had adopted him, and now they sent two or three interns each semester along with adequate funding to increase his program. A Dutch conservation group, relying on Holland's colonial ties, had given them an unlimited account on scuba gear. Nothing about his operation went unfunded or undersupported. He was, he said, the Jacques Cousteau of turtles, or at least as well-established as he needed to be. He had ridden the push toward green causes adroitly, and what had been his private passion had caught the public imagination.

"That's wonderful," Annie said when he finished. "And the turtles are flourishing?"

"They've made a strong comeback," Freddy said, drinking his wine. "As long as we protect the reefs, the turtles should be fine."

"Turtle Freddy," Mary said, obviously amused. "You know, he's doing the same thing he always did. He's playing around with animals."

"It's a family curse," he said. "You did likewise. We were both horribly tainted by Dr. Dolittle. Do you remember, Mary? We used to wish we could talk to the animals. We used to see if we could communicate with the neighborhood dogs by barking certain ways. We were nutty little kids."

"But my interest was more theoretical. You've kept your hands involved."

"Oh, I don't know about that. I remember one year you tried to climb up a cliff to a raven's nest you discovered. You wanted to steal a chick, and every night we had these lengthy arguments about the morality of it. You were so divided it was nearly comical. Finally Mom found out how high you had to climb to get to the nest—and of course the bird would have been flapping and dive bombing you while you dangled from a fingerhold—and she forbade it. 'I forbid it,' she said. I think it was the only thing Mom ever forbade, if that's the word. Pretty funny."

The temperature dropped after we finished eating. The river seemed to push cold air along its surface. An owl began calling to the north. We moved closer to the fire. Mary dozed. A few stars began to flicker. Leaves now and then fell from the trees and drifted down in the slightest wind.

Annie began clearing the dishes and putting them to one side. I carried them to the river's edge and washed them in the sand first, then rinsed them. Freddy and John decided we needed more wine. They began pouring a nice bottle of merlot when suddenly, far off in the distance, we heard a shrill piping sound. I stood. I put the dishes down. I moved closer to Mary and put my hand gently on her shoulder. She came awake. I wasn't sure if she recognized me and I bent down to check. She nodded—our sign—and tried to straighten in her chair.

The high, beautiful sound of the piccolo came again.

"Oh my," she said and smiled.

With the water passing, the wind stirring, the sound of the piccolo drifted from place to place. Or maybe, I concluded, Francis moved deliberately through the woods. For a moment he seemed nearly on top of the water, then the sound bent and changed and the piccolo ranged behind us. Mary turned in her chair, but she could not move her neck and shoulders very well. Suddenly the music came closer. A branch snapped. I looked at Freddy and Annie and John. They moved their eyes back and forth between Mary and the sound of the piccolo.

Then, as mysteriously as it had begun, the music ceased. The wind covered any trace of it. Mary nodded as if this, too, made sense to her. She smiled.

In that moment a bear stepped out of the woods and slowly approached the fire.

It walked on its hind legs and it hesitated, obviously afraid to come forward. Mary put her hand to her eyes and began to cry quietly. In pantomime, the bear stood in the dimness, apparently torn about whether to join the human fire or to remain in the woods. The costume might have been ridiculous under other circumstances, but in the Maine woods in October, with the wind pushing its fur, the darkness surrounding it, the bear seemed entirely lifelike.

"I smell honey," Mary said, her voice tight with emotion."Does anyone else?"

"I do," I said.

"It must be difficult to be a bear," Mary said. "But he should know he is welcome at the fire on such a chilly night."

"Should I invite him in?" I asked.

"A bear needs to make up its own mind," Mary said. "That's always been the way."

The bear—Francis—played his part with grace. He did not overact. At one point he disappeared back into the woods, and we thought he had gone for good. But he reappeared from a different angle and stood motionless near the darkest ring of forest. By blinking, one could conjure him out of the woods, or let him vanish. He stood quietly for the count of fifty. Then, almost without discernible movement, he became part of the woods again.

"How lovely," Mary said, "to be visited by a bear."

"Didn't you dance with a bear once at your cousin Maurice's wedding?" I asked.

"I did," she said. "And he was a gentleman."

"Are they always so shy?" I asked.

"A bear has a friendly nature, but it finds its shape somewhat embarrassing. They're often self-conscious, though of course they shouldn't be."

"Mary," Freddy said, "you were born a hundred years too late."

"Two hundred years," she said. "Maybe more."

After we had put Mary to bed—she was exhausted—Francis arrived with my father. They drove in my father's truck. I knew they had planned to come up together. Francis worked in a Boston architectural publishing house and he had taken the bus to Concord to meet my father. Francis looked strong and steady. My father, a month before, had turned sixty-seven.

After introductions, Annie reheated a little stew on the fire; John poured wine. I whispered to Francis that his bear imitation had been wonderful.

"What imitation?" he asked, obviously enjoying his part. I wondered how he had connected with my father for the ride into camp, but I didn't ask. They had their own ways of arranging things.

"Okay," I said.

"Did you see a bear?" he asked.

"It seems I did."

"Don't pull the leg of a city boy," he said.

Annie and John turned in not long afterward. Freddy, citing jet lag, soon followed. It was difficult to resist bed. The night had turned white and cold. It smelled of snow. I sat with my father and Francis as they finished their stew and their wine. We stirred the fire but did not add more wood. I knew my father would bank the ashes so that they could be easily brought back to life in the morning. He loved fires and often burned one in his fireplace even during the summer.

"I've thought things over," my father said eventually, "and I talked it over with Francis. I'd like to stay if you'll let me. At the end, I mean."

"Thank you, Dad, but no."

"Hear me out," he said. "It will be easier to manage with two people. And if there are any legal questions afterward . . ."

"Thank you, but no. I've thought this through every way possible. If there are any legal ramifications, well, they should be mine. I gave my word long ago to Mary."

"But two of us could testify on each other's behalf. It might be more persuasive."

"Your dad may be right, Cobb," Francis said, poking the fire with a stick. "It may look a little suspicious otherwise."

"If anyone really wants to pursue it, she or he can probably put together a solid case against me. I appreciate it, Dad, I really do. But I think this is something I'm going to have to do on my own. I'm not looking forward to it, but I'm not afraid of it, either. It's hard to explain. She's going to rest. That's how I think of it. This disease, these years, have exhausted her. She's ready. She's unafraid. Pretty soon she won't know morning from night. It's time."

"All I'm saying . . ." my father said, but I put my hand on his.

He nodded.

"You know," Francis said, "if we don't clean these dishes, we may actually have a bear visit us."

So we did a little work straightening the campsite. Then for a while we stood at the river's edge and watched it spool past, its black surface carrying a thousand leaf boats. The moon rose slowly across the river. Its yellow light fell muted and warm on the river and it was not pushed away, but lingered in a hazy path connecting one shore to the other.

AT FIRST LIGHT, MARY's mom arrived. She wore a heavy mackinaw and a pair of jeans. She tapped lightly on the door of the Airstream, then pushed through. Mary did not wake. Joan slipped out of her wool hat. "Coffee," she whispered. A moment of confusion passed where I thought she wanted coffee. Instead, she had brought it and put it on the picnic table outside. She pointed to the outdoors, then slowly backed out of the trailer.

I slipped out of bed and dressed quietly. Joan had a cup of coffee ready for me by the time I stepped outside.

"I couldn't sleep," Joan whispered. "I left the hotel at four, I think."

"I know," I said. "I figured it would go like that."

"Our last day," she said.

I put my arms around her. She put her face in my chest. We stayed like that for a moment.

"Is Freddy here?" she asked, when she pushed away.

"He made it last night."

"I'm glad. He's probably beat."

"He was pretty tired, but he's all Freddy."

"How is she doing?"

"She goes in and out. She's trying hard to stay with us."

"She would, wouldn't she?"

"She's seems confident, Joan. She's ready."

"I know she is," Joan said. "I only wish I were."

Annie woke next. She hugged Joan. She clapped at the sight of the Dunkin' Donut coffee, which she rarely enjoyed in her life on Chamberlain Lake. I mushed the ashes around in the fire pit, added a couple pieces of birch bark, and had a flame going in no time. We stood next to the fire and drank our coffee. The last day. The flames built until we had to move back from the heat. White mist rolled down the river.

"When I was a little girl," Joan said, "my family lived next to a river. In October the river would be warmer than the air, I think that's right, and so each morning we would see a large plume of mist over the riverbed. My father told me that it wasn't the river at all, but the winter train that arrived with the cold stored in long cars. He claimed all the snow for the winter came on the train and I believed him. It looked like a train with its big curl of white smoke."

"That's a lovely image," Annie said.

"My father liked telling stories like that," Joan said. "I think it's where Mary got her imagination. She certainly didn't get it from me."

One by one the others woke. Francis first, then my father, then Freddy and John. Freddy and Joan hugged. Although Joan had traveled to Indonesia once in the past eight years, they had not seen each other in a long time. Freddy kept his arm around Joan's shoulders as they drank coffee. Annie and Francis began frying bacon. The smell carried through the woods.

"Unless I'm mistaken," John said when he returned from collecting some wood, "we had a bear visit us last night."

Francis looked up.

"It looks like tracks down by the river," John said. "A good-sized bear."

"Are you serious?" Joan asked.

John nodded.

"Well, that's a lucky thing," Freddy said.

"They're fat and sleepy at this time of year," John said. "He probably wanted to climb in one of the tents and take a nap."

"Do you hunt them?" Joan asked John.

"Sometimes. But the meat is a bit greasy for my taste. I like seeing them roaming around. It always makes me think the woods are still wild when I see one."

Joan excused herself to go look in on Mary. Annie went with her after assuring herself that Francis could cook breakfast. Freddy pitched in. My dad became the fire stoker. I laid out dishes on the picnic table. The sun continued to push through the morning mist.

After a half hour, Joan and Annie called for Freddy and Francis to help Mary out. They placed her in a chair at the head of the table. I kissed her. She looked happy and hopeful, her Mad Bomber hat pulled down close around her ears. She said she loved the smell of bacon in the woods. When John told her that he had seen a bear track, she nodded and said, "Of course you did."

We had an excellent breakfast—bacon, eggs, toast, English muffins, fresh raspberry jam, thick wedges of butter, a cinnamon Danish, and more coffee. We were still at the table when we spotted the first canoe.

For a moment it made no sense to me. I had forgotten, somehow, that the river could be populated by other people. Then the first canoe was joined by a second, then a third. We stood. Mary leaned forward, her face curious and weary. An instant later she began to nod her head and she tried to stand. Her weakness kept her seated, but she rocked forward, her hands grasped together near her chin. Her eyes filled.

The Chungamunga girls had arrived.

They drifted slowly toward us. Somewhere upriver above us, they had released hundreds and hundreds of small tin dishes holding candles. The candles, glowing softly in the mist, drifted in and around the canoes, turning them all into a radiant cloud. The first few boats we had seen turned out to be only the beginning. More canoes came. The canoes, I realized, were not piloted only by young girls. They were Chungamunga girls of all ages. A number had difficulty holding a paddle; some appeared badly constricted by disease or infirmity. I counted thirty boats, but I could not begin to estimate how many candles drifted past. One by one they came slowly by and as each passed a spokesman from the canoe chanted, "We are the Chungamunga girls, eternal on this river."

Mary answered, "I am a Chungamunga girl, eternal on this river."

Wally arrived in the last canoe.

Mary, for the first time since I had known her, wept openly.

# 18

I TOOK A NAP NEXT TO MARY in the afternoon. She had begun to let go and her body hardly stirred when I woke and slipped outside. My father had the campfire going strong. He and Francis had been working all day and had collected heaps of wood, far more than we could ever use, but it is a custom in Maine to leave the woodpile higher than you found it. Besides, it kept them occupied. They looked drawn and tired when I stepped near the fire. They had made coffee and poured me some. It smelled good in the chilly afternoon air.

"How is she?" Francis asked. "Did she rest all right?"

"She's tired. She's begun to let go, I think."

My father stirred the fire.

"How are you doing, anyway?" I asked Francis, sitting beside him. "I haven't had a chance to ask. The job okay?"

"I like it. And I'm playing some music. I'm sitting in on a few gigs with bands. There's a jazz quartet that plays down in Southie that sort of likes my sound. So that's been fun."

"Think you'll stay with the publishing firm?"

He nodded.

"I like learning about cities," Francis said. "Not sure why. I like learning how they fit together. I like looking under the streets, especially. Isn't that strange? How would someone have an interest in that? But I do. I love books about infrastructure."

"Sounds interesting to me," my father said. "Why not?"

Before Francis could answer, Freddy popped out of his tent. He wore nothing but boxers. He bowed to us all, made a silly face, then sprinted toward the river. He stripped out of his shorts and continued into the water, running until he was deep enough to dive forward. His splash was the loudest thing for miles until his body came back up out of the water and he shrieked.

"Good Lord!" he yelled.

"You could not pay me enough to get me in the water," Francis said.

Freddy charged back out. He stopped to pick up his shorts. He slipped them on, then began doing jumping jacks. He did them for a while. Then he trotted back up, bowed again to us, and ducked back into his tent. He returned a few minutes later dressed in jeans and a sweater under a large parka.

"People in Indonesia," he said, coming to the fire and begging a cup of coffee, "have never known a moment's cold like that. Their entire lives go by, and they never experience it."

"And even some people in Maine," my father said with his dry humor, "can look at a river this time of year and figure it's pretty cold."

"I needed a wash," Freddy said and shrugged. "I needed to shake myself. This is a day I want to remember."

John and Annie returned from a long walk. They had been scouting a few wood-duck nests the Fish and Game Department had hung farther downstream. Francis put more coffee on the fire. Joan had slept inside the camper with us, but she emerged with a stethoscope in the pocket of her mackinaw. At a look from us, she shook her head.

"She's very weak," Joan said.

"She's letting go," I said. "Is she awake?"

"Not yet," she said. "Not fully. I'm going to duck back inside in a second and get her ready to come out."

"I'll help," Annie said.

Joan nodded. When the new coffee finished perking, Francis poured her a cup. John dug out some leftover breakfast food from the cooler in his truck: muffins, cold cereal, milk, and juice. He set it out on the table. We picked. I had a muffin and a glass of orange juice. A breeze came up and pushed things around on the table. We weighted plates and bread bags down with rocks.

"I need a couple strong men," Joan called from the camper a little later. "Mary would like to come out and join us."

Freddy and I went to the camper. Joan and Annie had dressed Mary in a mackinaw, a scarf, her bomber hat, and jeans. Mary looked pale but beautiful. She kissed me when she put her arm around my neck. She kissed Freddy when he took her other side.

We placed her near the fire. The others made room.

"Are you hungry?" John asked. "Can I fix you a plate?"

"I would like one bite of everything," she said with difficulty.

The chorea made her body jerk involuntarily. She ate slowly, with Joan helping, but she seemed to savor the taste of everything. We told her about Freddy running into the river; we told her about the wood Francis and my father collected, and about the temperature seeming to drop. We spoke, she knew, to keep her with us and the topics were mundane and stretched far out of proportion. When she finished eating, she smiled at us all. Her mouth pulled a little from the muscles flexing around it. She looked at each of us in turn.

"Now it's time," she said quietly. "It's time for us to say good-bye. I love you all, but time has no remedy for this. We all know what we're doing here, and there's no sense in delaying it until it becomes something maudlin and horrible. Besides, I'm looking forward to spending a few hours with my husband. This is where we met."

Her mother reached over and hugged her. One by one the others hugged her, too. The fire sent up smoke and sometimes the wind caught the smoke and sent it toward the river. Mary held them close to her, each person having a private moment with her. Later I learned she whispered that she loved them and that their lives had enriched her life. She told them she loved the beauty of this earth. She wished them happiness. And from all of them, she extracted a promise to keep me in their thoughts, to help me in the months to come. "My husband," she told everyone, "is the heart I leave behind."

# 19

*We spent the last night alone, I said.*

*Just you and Mary? Sarah asked.*

*On a blue tarp under the stars, just as we began. We talked and I held her to keep her warm. She drifted in and out.*

*The others left?*

*Yes. They said good-bye and left. It was difficult. It was heart-wrenching.*

*Sarah nodded. The sun had thrown a thin ray of light across the river. Two mergansers took advantage of the first light and flew up the river, their wingtips occasionally striking the surface. The moon had gone. Our fire had almost died. I thought of the line from* Romeo and Juliet *when they wake and realize he must go or be found by the Capulets and killed. Night's candles are burnt out, Romeo tells his love.*

*Can you tell me the rest? Sarah asked. Is it too painful?*

*I stretched my legs. The fire had become hazy and mild with the sun-light increasing. I closed my eyes to remember it clearly.*

*We woke early the day before yesterday. I fought hard to keep her warm, but she was so weak the cold penetrated her body. I had several pills. I won't say where they came from or what they contained. At first light, I packed the kayaks. I packed as if we intended to go forward for a day of travel. John and Annie had removed all the equipment, the camper, everything. It had to look correct. That had all been worked out ahead of time.*

*You must have been devastated.*

*You would think so, wouldn't you? But I wasn't. I loved her too much to betray her at the end. I could remove this terrible weight from her body and that is no small gift. I was glad to do it. I was honored to be the last person she saw.*

*What happened then? Sarah asked, her eyes filling.*

*I lifted her and placed her carefully in the kayak. I tried to make her as comfortable as possible. We had arranged that it would sink slowly. That was merely a precaution. The pills did the work.*

*You drifted with her?*

*I nodded.*

*For several miles. I kept her boat next to mine. Water gradually began to fill her cockpit. The boat went lower in the water. But I knew she had passed away before the kayak sunk. I saw her hand trailing aimlessly in the water. Leaves began to catch in her fingers.*

*Sarah began to cry.*

*And you let her go? Sarah asked, her voice breaking. How could you finally let her go?*

*Because Mary had taught me life is for the living. It's a cliché, I know, but what else can we do? We go on. It's what she wanted. I told her I loved her, but she knew that already. I told her she was eternal on the river. And I thanked her for the joy she had given me. At a bend in the river, I let my hand slip off her boat. But I couldn't. I paddled after her and grabbed the boat again and I drifted beside her for a little longer. Then I took a deep breath and I let the boat slip away. . . .*

*How could you . . . ?*

*Mary had already gone. I had felt it in the middle of the night. She had closed down. So I made myself let the boat go and I watched it drift.*

*It did not turn and I was glad for that. Two crows passed over the river as she drifted away. Remarkable. Two for mirth, she would have said.*

*And what did you do?*

*I camped beside the river one more night. It was hard to think of her alone. It was a long night. I read Thoreau. He wrote about camping and hearing a tree fall in the forest. A big, solid tree, that brought a dozen smaller trees with it. And he talked about the sound a wood thrush makes, almost like Francis's piccolo. The bird is called* Adelungquamooktu *in the Algonquin. I've always loved the wood thrush more than any other bird. I read most of the night. This morning, well, yesterday, now, I came downstream and found the rangers here. I played my part. I didn't know precisely what I would find, but I imagined it would be something like this.*

*Sarah nodded.*

*Sound began to intrude. We heard a door open and close behind us. A radio squawked somewhere. A man called to another in a light, hearty way. Morning had come.*

*Your story is safe with me, Sarah said and wiped her eyes. I want you to know that. I would never . . .*

*Thank you. I had to tell it to someone, I suppose. Mary insisted on writing a letter and leaving it in a safe deposit box. It explains everything in the event that someone challenged me.*

*What will you do now?*

*I hardly know.*

*Will you keep the carriage house?*

*Yes. With the window. At least for now. Maybe later it will be too filled with her and I'll have to let that go, too.*

*Will you go to Annie and John's cabin?*

*Maybe at some point. After I attend to Mary, I have to get back to school. I am a teacher, when all is said and done. I have students who count on me.*

*Are the others waiting for you? The rest of your family?*

*Yes. Everyone but Mary.*

*We stood. The sun cleared the trees. On an impulse, Sarah hugged me. I hugged her back. Out of our movement, a crow lifted off a high pine and the glint of the sun, for an instant, resembled a flash of diamond in its beak.*

# ACKNOWLEDGMENTS

IT IS MY HOPE THAT THIS book presents accurately, and with compassion, the effects of Huntington's Disease on one of its main characters. It is presumptuous to write about any disease one has not personally experienced, and I apologize sincerely if I have gotten any of the details wrong. I am indebted to Fred Taubman at the Huntington's Disease Society of America who helped me find an early reader for this manuscript. I hope that the vitality and joy that Mary brought to her life in these pages is a testament to the courage of many Huntington's patients.

Many thanks to Kathy Sagan, my editor at Gallery Books, whose excellent suggestions made this a better book than it might have been without her help. And to Andrea Cirillo and Christina Hogrebe, my agents at the Jane Rotrosen Agency, thanks beyond counting. You two are aces.

Finally, thanks to my wife, Wendy, who is always my first reader and always the first to pour me a Scotch on winter afternoons.

Reading Group Guide

# Eternal on the Water

*By Joseph Monninger*

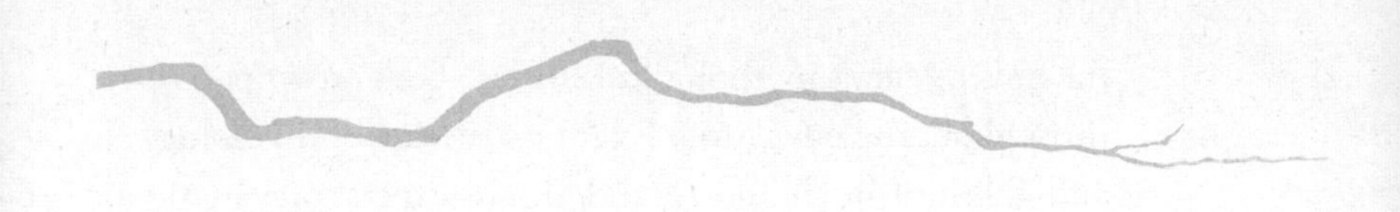

## Introduction

When Jonathan Cobb takes a sabbatical from teaching to go out and experience nature as Thoreau did in the mid-nineteenth century, he does not expect to meet the love of his life, any more than Mary expects to meet him. But from their first camp side meeting, they know they are soul mates. Set against the sweeping natural backdrops of Maine's rugged backcountry, the exotic islands of Indonesia, Yellowstone National Park, and rural New England, nature plays a key role in their romance. But their story is tragic as well as inspiring as their perfect love falls beneath the shadow of her impending fatal illness, and he must help her make an important and difficult decision.

## Discussion Points

1. Cobb has taken a sabbatical from teaching to learn from nature. Specifically, he wants to kayak down the Allagash, along Thoreau's path. How do you think Cobb's trip into the unknown alludes to or is a metaphor for other aspects of his life?
2. Early in the book, before Cobb meets Mary, a moose blocks his way in the road. Then, a female moose crosses, and the male trots after her. How does this foreshadow his meeting Mary? What other appearances do moose make in the novel, and what do you think these appearances signify?
3. During their first meeting, Mary asks Cobb if he's a bear. The mythology of bears turning into humans to steal dances and charm people is a recurring one throughout

the novel. Mary's mythological stories about crows pop up throughout the novel, too. Examine the use of mythology and folklore in the story and discuss their role in the novel.

4. Cobb's fondness for Thoreau is illustrated in his love for nature and his desire to live life simply. Even when they are spellbound in their first romantic days together, Mary respects Cobb's desire to follow in Thoreau's footsteps and gives him some time to be alone on Pillsbury Island where Thoreau camped, and he agrees even as he wants to be with her. What does this say about his dedication to Thoreau's way of life? What draws him to it so strongly? What does it say about Mary's respect for others?
5. Cobb describes his motto as *hurry gradually*. What do you think he means? Do you think he and Mary managed to live by this motto? Why or why not?
6. We know from the very first pages of the novel that Mary has died on the river. What effect did knowing the ending have on your reading experience as you traveled back in time to read about Cobb and Mary's budding relationship? Might you have felt differently had you not known what was coming? Why or why not?
7. The novel features many references to circles throughout. For example, Mary eats her sandwiches in circles, Cobb describes himself as a circular kisser, and birds circle around carcasses. Identify the ways in which circles appear in or influence the story and discuss their significance.
8. Francis is a secondary character who has an emotional impact on Cobb and Mary, just as they do on him. How did you feel about the way Cobb and Mary took Francis under their wings during his difficult times? How would you have reacted if Francis was a student or protégé of yours?

9. The Chungamunga Girls play an important part in Mary's life. What do you think was their main function in the novel? How does their motto, *we are Chungamunga girls, we are eternal on this water,* have an added poignancy for Mary?
10. Freddy, Mary's brother, says that "the real world is always somewhere else" (page 187). What do you think he means by this? Compare and contrast his love for sea turtles with Mary's love of crows. How else are the siblings similar or different?
11. Why do you think the author decided to make reference to Edgar Allan Poe's poem, "Annabelle Lee"? How is the love described in the poem similar to that of Cobb and Mary?
12. Mary does not want to know her test results because, if she tests positive, she does not want to live in fear of the disease and its inevitable conclusion. But Cobb encourages her to find out so she'll know how to plan. How do you feel about this aspect of the story? What does it tell you about these characters? If you were in Mary's position, would you want to know whether you had a terminal illness?
13. Cobb wants what is best for Mary, but he finds it painful to go along with her decision to end her life on her terms—in dignity, before the effects of her disease totally take over. How do you feel about her desire to end her own life doing something she loves? Did you find her decision believable given what you learn of her throughout the novel? Why or why not?
14. This novel delves into the full meaning of love. Was there a scene or a moment that seemed to sum it all up for you? Do you think love can be defined in a moment, or is it the compilation of many moments? Did you find the

evolution of Cobb and Mary's love realistic? Why or why not?

15. Why do you think the author chose the title, *Eternal on the Water*? Discuss the significance of the river to Mary's story in particular.

## Enhance Your Bookclub

1. Cobb likes to live life simply, like Thoreau. Later we learn that Mary does, too, and so does her brother, Freddy, and Cobb's father. Make your own experience living the simple life by turning off and pledging not to use electronics for a weekend, go for a hike in the woods, or plan a camping visit to a state park. If you live near water, try a canoe or kayak ride. Get out into nature, and feel free to take along a good book.
2. This novel implies that you should live life to the fullest, every day. Or, as Mary's mother says, say yes to the good things in life and grab them! What are some things you have been wanting to do, but have been putting off? Identify one or two things that would help you to live your life to the fullest and do them!
3. The Chungamunga girls play a large part in Mary's life. What are some clubs or organizations you can think of that are similar? Girl Scouts? Nature clubs? Consider introducing a young adult novel, such as Joseph Monninger's *Hippie Chick,* to a group of young girls. Encourage them to form their own book club and to discuss the books they read. You will have a lasting effect on the girls just as the Chungamunga girls did on Mary.
4. The idea of coincidences—that two people have to be in the right place at the right time in order to meet, and the odds are against it—plays an important role in this novel.

Can you think of important events in your own life that seemed to come coincidentally? Think about the life-altering coincidences in your life, and all of the variables that had to be in place to make them happen, and share with your book club at your next meeting.

## Author Q&A

1. **This novel is infused with an appreciation for nature. Do you find it easy to use nature to tell a story? Do nature metaphors and settings come, well, naturally?**

I hope so. I live in a beautiful part of the world—western New Hampshire along the Baker River—and my family and I spend a lot of time outdoors. A brook runs past our bedroom and our house opens onto a meadow. We have grown accustomed to seeing the seasons change and we mark time by the way light moves across the field and into our house. We ran sled dogs for many years and raised chickens. It would be nearly impossible at this point in my life to write a "city" novel. Nature is all mixed up in my day to day life. So, yes, nature metaphors come naturally, no pun intended.

2. **Although Cobb and Mary are central, there are scenes that involve a dozen or more characters, and we feel as though we know all of them personally. Do you find it easy to make so many characters come alive with their own personalities and speech patterns, or is that a challenge?**

Well, it's always a challenge, of course. Someone once said plot is character. If you think about it, we like seeing characters in interesting situations. Simple plot is boring, although it serves as a motor for narrative. It provides us with *and then, and then what happened, and then, and then, and then.* If plot were enough, then the

Freddy Krueger movies would be worth rewatching (or watching once!) but the series of startling events becomes silly because we don't care about the characters. I try to make sure I know who my characters are before I let them get swept away by potential plots.

**3. Cobb and Mary both seem to want to live life simply, following in the footsteps of Thoreau. Is that quality a reflection of you as an author? What effect did you hope this thematic choice would have on readers?**

I actually believe in simplicity as a way of life. My wife and I are considering moving into a yurt! I know it sounds a little crazy, but the world, as Wordsworth warned, can be too much with us. How much time do we spend doing things we care nothing about? Living simply, wanting less, asking for little. . . . It is a way to free ourselves, I think.

**4. Bears often pop up in the scenes of this book even when they're not really there. Is this bit of folklore (that bears can turn into people to steal dances and charm humans) something invented by you, or is it something you discovered?**

It's partially invented and partially a long standing bit of folklore. Bears are extremely human, even down to their footprints. But I am also a fly fisherman, so I have fished beside brown bears in Alaska and was once charged by a black bear. I love bears. In our town in New Hampshire, there is a story about a girl who was supposedly sheltered by a bear for a day or two. Many cultures have similar stories. Plus, bears have a comical side. How can you fail to like a creature with a wide bottom who loves more and more honey?

5. **In your writing, you display an intimate knowledge of kayaking, camping, and other outdoor activities and sights—all part of what makes Cobb and Mary's experiences so believable. Do you try to go out and experience the things you know you'll be writing about? Or do experiences you've already had in your life help feed your writing?**

Well, as I mentioned, I spend a good deal of time outside. I kayaked the Allagash River by myself some years ago. It's a spectacular experience. It runs ninety miles northward through a pristine part of Maine. My wife and I have kayaked the St. Croix River in Maine and, of course, we live on a river. When our son was ten we bought him his first kayak. I've been a New Hampshire fishing guide and I've travelled around quite a bit in the west fishing and hiking. And I love Yellowstone. When I travelled to Indonesia and visited those islands, I was interested in seeing green turtles. It was only afterward that I invented Freddy and a turtle nursery. I am aware of the need to keep trying new things. As a writer, you never know how the piece will fit into the puzzle, but you do know you need to keep pawing through the pieces.

6. **It's obvious through this book, and others you have written, that nature influences your writing. When you set out to write a book, do you go out into nature and visit the places you will write about? How does nature inspire you?**

That's a tough question to answer, but maybe it will help to know I don't take pictures. I've never liked the moment of seeing something beautiful—a sunset, a moose, an elephant—and then raising a camera and trying to capture it for some future moment. That's always struck me as strange. Experience the moment now, I say. If the moment is important enough, you'll have an internal album of pictures from which to draw. That's what I hope inspires my work.

7. **Although nature is prominent in the novel, you also make steady reference to new technologies, such as MySpace, Facebook, cell phones, even a scene of these two "old-fashioned" nature-lovers watching a classic film on a laptop in bed. Was it important for you to show how nature and technology can coexist?**

A good life these days seems to require a blend. I like movies and I like computers and I also like getting away from them. I don't own a cell phone, for instance. I'm probably the last human alive not to own one. I do it deliberately. I have phones . . . I just don't want to be on call at all times. Sometimes it's inconvenient not to have one, but I often hear friends grouse about having to answer their phones all the time. Long ago I visited Mark Twain's house in Hartford, Connecticut. It's a great museum, by the way. But he insisted that the new technology in the house—a telephone—be tucked away in a wooden booth. Just because technology is available does not mean we need to employ it.

8. **You have written literary fiction, young adult novels, memoir, and nonfiction. Do you have a favorite genre? How do you choose which kind of story you will write next, or does the genre choice depend on the message or story you have to share?**

Oh, I like stories. I like narrative. I can feel when a story starts churning around in me. I hear most of what I write unlike some people who see their stories. But as a reader I read all sorts of things. So, as a writer, I like to try different things. I love young adult books because the readers—kids—are so honest in their reactions. Also, kids read with a wonderful concentration and joy. But the writing exercise is pretty much the same in all books I attempt.

**9. As a seasoned and successful author, can you briefly describe your writing process? Are you more of a "write every day" or a "write when inspiration hits" sort of author?**

Long ago I read a biography of Jack London written by Irving Stone. It was called *Sailor on Horseback*. In the book, London claimed to write a thousand words a day. I adopted that as my practice. My son had a play fort out in the backyard and when he turned fourteen or so he lost interest in it. I've taken it over. It has a standing desk, a chair, and a woodstove. . . . And nothing else. It's very quiet and it has a beautiful view. I write in the early morning and afternoon. I try to write every day. "Nulla dies sine linea." (Not a day without a line.)

**10. Can you share some of the authors, writers, or role models who have helped to shape your writing?**

I love many, many writers, but I don't dare mention them by name for fear of leaving someone out. I always have a book on hand. I love the feeling, when you close a book, that you have read something truthful and genuine. Hate what's false; demand what's true. I love the writers who don't cheat. And that cheating can take place even in the most so-called serious novels. But I also have to say that I am a teacher, and teaching keeps me honest. Students have a ready-made lie detector. I'm always amazed that they sense falseness in bad novels and detect worthiness in genuine novels. Deep down, of course, it all comes back to the Hardy Boys. If I can give someone the pleasure I felt reading the Hardy boys, that's probably accomplishment enough.

**11.** ***Eternal on the Water*** **delves deep into the meaning of love, illness, and death. Was it difficult to write about the nature of Mary's illness and death, yet still keep it a light, tender love story? What inspired you to write this novel?**

Mary's character made this novel a pleasure to write. I like her. I like Cobb, too, but I really like Mary. I happen to have a lifelong friend who is a biologist at the University of Connecticut. Biologists are different. I've been to parties with him and other biologists where they cook up roadkill. They simply see the world slightly different, perhaps more on a cellular level. So Mary is trapped, sort of, by her knowledge of science and her love for Cobb. But as they say, we are all mortally ill. Mary simply knows she has a shorter time on earth, which provides some of the pressure to make the story move forward. Every story about death is personal.

**12. The reader knows from the opening pages what has happened to Mary and how it happened—including Cobb's part in it. Why did you decide to start with the end?**

The why of something is often more interesting than the how. Or at least it usually is. If I use a headline and say, "a local gamekeeper was swallowed by his own snake today in such and such a place," you are going to read to find how why and how. The story itself is already over. You know the ending. So in this novel I wanted the reader to wonder what in the world happened and be curious. It's up to other people to decide if it worked.

**13. When Mary mentions late in the novel that seeing a moose is a good omen, it brings back the previous scenes—Cobb seeing a male moose chase after a female prior to his meeting Mary, and later, seeing the dead elk. Was that the sort of thing that you had planned,**

**or was it something you went back to fold in during revisions?**

That just fell in! In fact, I didn't even think of it until I was asked this question. Thanks for pointing it out. The first moose that Cobb sees shakes him out of his nervousness about running the river. I always like the Robert Frost poem about the way a bird shook snow off a barn door "saved some part of a day he rued." I know what he means, I think. Nature is restorative.

**14. This novel spans the globe, with sections set in Maine, Indonesia, Yellowstone, and New Hampshire. Have you spent time in all of these places? What kind of research did you have to do in order to use these settings?**

Yes, I have been to those places. I have been to Maine and Yellowstone many times. My son lived for a student year abroad in Indonesia and my wife and I visited him there. It's a wonderful country. We may go back there for an extended stay next time. I've always been a traveler, though. I hitchhiked across country three times while I was in college and went right out of college into the Peace Corps. I spent time in West Africa and led student groups all over the world. So, yes, I love to travel. Research? It's just living.